KU-300-419

HARPERS HEROES

HARPERS EMPORIUM BOOK 4

ROSIE CLARKE

Boldwood

First published in Great Britain in 2020 by Boldwood Books Ltd.

This paperback edition first published in 2021.

1

Copyright © Rosie Clarke, 2020

Cover Design by The Brewster Project

Cover Photography: Colin Thomas

The moral right of Rosie Clarke to be identified as the author of this work has been asserted in accordance with the Copyright, Designs and Patents Act 1988.

All rights reserved. No part of this book may be reproduced in any form or by any electronic or mechanical means, including information storage and retrieval systems, without written permission from the author, except for the use of brief quotations in a book review.

This book is a work of fiction and, except in the case of historical fact, any resemblance to actual persons, living or dead, is purely coincidental.

Every effort has been made to obtain the necessary permissions with reference to copyright material, both illustrative and quoted. We apologise for any omissions in this respect and will be pleased to make the appropriate acknowledgements in any future edition.

A CIP catalogue record for this book is available from the British Library.

Paperback ISBN: 978-1-80048-162-6

Ebook ISBN: 978-1-83889-132-9

Kindle ISBN: 978-1-83889-131-2

Audio CD ISBN: 978-1-83889-241-8

Digital audio download ISBN: 978-1-83889-129-9

Large Print ISBN: 978-1-83889-812-0

Boldwood Books Ltd.

23 Bowerdean Street, London, SW6 3TN

www.boldwoodbooks.com

MIX
Paper from
responsible sources
FSC® C020471

1

It was now the beginning of February 1915 and the war with Germany had gradually crept closer to Great Britain's shores. That morning, Sally Harper stood in the doorway of the bedroom of their London apartment and caught her breath as she watched her husband, Ben, packing his suitcase. She felt the now familiar sense of unease that his absences always aroused in her, though she couldn't have said why. Thus far, Ben had only been called upon to help with the logistics of keeping an army on the move. He was, of course, an American citizen and his country not yet at war with Germany. However, he felt that he owed some service to the country he lived and worked in and had joined the British Army.

Sally had feared he would be sent off to fight. Thousands of other women had husbands, brothers and sons fighting and dying in the trenches of Belgium and France, in the air, and on the high seas – and the casualties were mounting. So many men were being injured and killed that it brought tears to her eyes. Sally forced herself to read the reports in the newspapers every day, even though they made harrowing reading, but she felt it was her duty to know what those brave men out there were enduring to keep the women and children of Britain safe. These were terrible times and everyone had to do what they could.

Now, picking up a pile of freshly ironed shirts, Sally moved them to within Ben's reach and received a smile of acknowledgement. Her heart caught in her breast, because she hated it when he went away on one of his trips for the War Office, even though she knew she was lucky he hadn't been sent to fight overseas.

At first, the war had seemed a long way off, but in December 1914, Sally had been shocked when German warships had shelled the seaside towns of Scarborough, Whitby and Hartlepool, killing more than a hundred civilians and injuring many others. To think that British people had been fired on and died while going about their daily lives was shocking. However, the following January the papers had been filled with the triumphant news that the British Navy had prevented another such attack by sinking the most powerful of the enemy's battle cruisers, SMS *Blucher*. Yet even this success could not prevent death from the air as the devilish Zeppelins bombed the British towns of Great Yarmouth and King's Lynn. The Allies had celebrated when Paris had been saved the previous October and the German advance bogged down in the trenches, but now it seemed they'd turned their attention to subduing the British people with their frightening attacks from the sea and the air.

Putting on a brave smile, Sally looked at her husband. 'Everything all right, darling?'

'Yes, of course.' Ben stopped his packing and moved towards her, taking her into his arms to kiss her briefly. 'I'm sorry this trip was such short notice, but it all came up out of the blue...'

Sally nodded, accepting his words without argument. She knew better than to ask what had come up, because she was aware that her husband's work was often confidential and he'd signed the official Secrets Act, which meant he couldn't tell even her.

Ben returned to his packing without further comment and she continued to watch in silence, her sense of dread deepening. Storm clouds had gathered over her world and seemed to spread across the whole world as Germany had now declared all ships trying to reach Britain with supplies were fair game and could be sunk. In America, the shipping companies were up in arms, and the British Government had immediately retaliated by ordering the Royal Navy to seize cargoes of grain and flour on their way to Germany, as contraband.

That didn't help Sally much, because she'd been accustomed to ordering goods for Harpers' Emporium from all over the world and now there were all kinds of restrictions on what could be imported or exported. So many raw materials were running short and luxuries were low on the Government's list of priorities. Food and ammunition were top of the country's list, naturally – but she felt frustrated by the limitations it placed on her buying power for the store.

Everyone had expected it to be a short war, over by Christmas; the newspaper headlines had shouted that the Allied forces would win in a few months, but the might of the German forces was proving harder to hold back than anyone had guessed. Yes, there had been victories for Britain and her friends, but there were reverses too and at the moment the Allies were fighting in practically all corners of the world.

And now the war was taking Ben away from her. She cried out in silent protest, no words leaving her lips, though they burned in her mind, *Why must you go? Why? We've been married less than two years and our daughter is only just over eight months old...* Of course, she couldn't say the things she wanted to say. Every woman wanted to say them when her husband went off to fight, and Sally was lucky; Ben wasn't going off to the Front – at least, Sally didn't think so, but he might tour military installations and they could be attacked from the air as the Zeppelins had demonstrated in those seaside towns.

'Will you be away long?' Sally asked when the silence and her thoughts had become unbearable. 'Shall I be able to contact you?'

Ben turned to look at her, and then, as if sensing her distress, he came to her once more and put his arms around her waist, looking into her eyes with love and understanding.

'I'm not quite sure where I'll be,' he said. 'I've been told I may be sent here, there and everywhere. We've hit some problems with medical supplies out there in France and Belgium and we have to work out the best way to get what is needed to the right areas. We've been losing a lot of convoys...'

'Yes, I know,' Sally said, swallowing hard as she fought to keep her tears inside. 'I know I'm being stupid, Ben, but I worry and miss you when you're away – and Jenny notices now. You might think she isn't old enough to understand, but she looks for you and cries when you don't come to her...'

Ben nodded, showing he understood. Their beloved daughter was not quite nine months old, but she did seem very aware of him and sometimes when she cried, Ben was the only one that could comfort her. Perhaps it was because he'd picked her up so often when she was first born, walking with her and singing to her.

'I know, love,' he said now and kissed Sally. 'I hate leaving you both – but you know my reasons. We live here and earn our living from the British people and I couldn't look them in the eye if I sat out the war in safety while their men are dying in their thousands...'

'I know – and I'm proud of you, Ben. You didn't have to volunteer.' It was true. Sally was very proud of all he was doing; she just lived in dread of what might happen when he was away from her.

Ben was an American and as his country was not yet at war with Germany; he could have sat it out, as he'd said, but his pride and his conscience wouldn't allow him to do it. So, he'd joined the British Army as a foreign national and at the moment he was being used for special assignments, helping with the tricky business of keeping the country going with food, armaments and medical supplies. A job so important that they'd made him Captain Harper without all the months of training normally expected. It was, she supposed, an honorary title, but it gave him the respect of people who saw his uniform and meant an end to the white feathers well-meaning but ignorant women were giving to all the men not in uniform; they symbolised cowardice and that had irritated Ben so much, but they had stopped now he was wearing the uniform of an Army captain.

'Thank you for being so understanding,' he said, smiling at her in the way that made her heart catch with love. 'If it were not for you looking after things at Harpers, I couldn't have done any of this, because Stockbridge is a good manager, but he doesn't have your flair – and it would have left a bitter taste in my mouth, Sally. I know it's putting a lot on your shoulders, but I believe you're capable of doing it and I want – *need* – to do all I can to help this country...'

'Mr Stockbridge does his share, as do Rachel and Beth and all the others we employ,' she said and hugged him. 'I know how you feel, love. Take no notice of me, Ben. I've got the store to look after, lots of friends and Jenny. I shouldn't complain and it's selfish of me to want my husband home with me when so many others are suffering. I see you often. I'm lucky...' Sally smiled at her husband, the owner of the store, who had given her the opportunity to be his head buyer and then married her.

'You're not selfish,' Ben soothed. 'It's only natural, Sally – but I'll be in touch as much as I can, my love, and we'll both rest easier when this is all over, knowing I did my part – small as it is...'

'You're wonderful,' Sally said, forcing a smile because she was close to tears and annoyed with herself. This was no way to send her husband off to wherever he was going. It wouldn't be easy for Ben working in all sorts of locations, moving about and dealing with the many problems she knew he must have. Sally was finding it difficult enough to keep the store supplied with stock, because Britain was struggling to be self-sufficient. What ships did get through the German net needed to carry essentials rather than the luxuries they normally sold at Harpers. She was having to find new small firms to supply her with different ranges. Keeping an Army on the move must be a million times harder.

Ben didn't tell her much about what he did, but she knew he was in touch with men he'd known in America and with friends of his late uncle, who had owned other stores in America, which now belonged to Ben's sister and cousin. Those friends were, many of them, influential and had a voice in Government as well as in the military. His sister Jenni's husband was a General in the American Army and she knew that Ben had been working on a deal that concerned some ex-American Army equipment over Christmas. He'd received several odd telegrams from Jenni, which he'd understood but made no sense to Sally.

'I'll write when I can – and I'll telephone you in the evening whenever I'm able...' he promised now and she smiled, kissing him softly on the lips, just as a wail issued from the bedroom.

'I know,' she said. 'Finish your packing, Ben. Jenny sounds as if she's woken up – I'd better see if she needs changing...'

'Yes, of course,' he said and returned to his task.

Blinking back the ridiculous tears, Sally went through to her daughter's room and saw that the beautiful little girl was wide awake and looking about her with those big intelligent eyes that were so much like her father's.

'Yes, my darling, you know, don't you?' Sally said and picked her up. Jenny was usually such a good baby, but sometimes when she decided to cry and scream it seemed that nothing could comfort her. Ben had spent hours around Christmastime walking the floor with her in his strong arms until she was soothed. She'd seemed slightly better since then, but now her little face screwed up and she made a wailing sound. 'It's all right, Mummy is here with you, and Daddy will come back as soon as he can...'

As if on cue, Ben walked in carrying his cases. He dumped them on the floor and came to them, taking Jenny from her and kissing her wet cheeks.

'Be good for Mummy,' he said to the baby, talking to her as if she could understand every word he said. 'Daddy loves you and he will be thinking of you, Jenny sweetheart. I'll soon be back with you and Mummy...'

Jenny's wailing stopped magically and she blew a bubble at him, her mouth forming a perfect O to show off her tiny teeth, of which she now had four.

'There, that's better,' Ben said and popped Jenny back in her cot, where she lay kicking and laughing up at him. 'I'd better go, Sally – if I delay any longer, I'll miss my connection, and I'll have to drive all the way there...'

Sally nodded silently. Ben was right, delay was pointless. He had a car arriving any moment to take him to the station and if he missed his connection it would mean frustration and perhaps a reprimand from his superiors. Even though he wasn't in a combat unit, he was still expected to obey orders.

'Yes, of course, you must go...' She moved forward, kissing him and stepping back before he could take her in his arms. 'Go on, Ben – leave now!'

Ben inclined his head, glanced at the cot once more and left without another word. She knew it was as hard for him to leave them as it was for her and Jenny to see him go.

Her daughter started to grizzle as soon as Ben had closed the door behind him. Sally picked her up and cuddled her, but she screamed, refusing to be comforted. Obviously, Sally's unease had communicated itself to her baby and she blamed herself rather than her child. Jenny was distressed because she knew her mother was upset.

Pushing her own emotions to the back of her mind, Sally sang softly to the little girl. It was one of the songs Ben often sang to her and after a few moments she quietened and was soon sleeping. Sally smiled and placed her baby gently back in her cot. She went through to the sitting room, leaving the child's door open slightly so that she would hear if Jenny cried out. It was six o'clock on Sunday evening and now that Ben had gone, she knew the hours would drag until Mrs Hall came the next day and Sally could leave for her work at Harpers. Thank goodness, she had work she loved and good friends, because otherwise she didn't think she could bear the enforced parting from Ben.

Sally had spent so much of her life alone and unloved. She hated having to be on her own now. Living with Ben, being loved and loving him had spoiled her, giving her a taste of happiness that she didn't want to lose. Suddenly, she laughed and shook her head. What an idiot she was! She was being too morbid! She mustn't dwell on her fears. She should find something to do!

There were plenty of new catalogues to look through for new stock – and she was constantly searching for new suppliers now, because her usual sources could not keep Harpers' shelves and rails fully stocked. They'd been fully stocked at Christmas, because of Sally's industry before the war began, and that had led to really good trading over the festive period. Many women had bought more than normal – perhaps more than they needed – because everyone feared the shortages that were undoubtedly on the way. The newspaper reports left no one in doubt that Britain would have to supply most of its own food and goods for the foreseeable future. The Germans were sinking too many merchant ships and that meant supplies stocked before the war would start to run out... everyone would need to tighten their belts.

Most of the male staff were already in one of the forces and some of the girls had joined the VADs, like Maggie Gibbs. However, Sally had plugged the gaps with older men, women and young girls straight from school. Her senior staff like Rachel Bailey, Beth Burrows and Mr Brown from the men's department trained the newcomers and standards were still high.

Sally frowned, a new worry on her mind now. How would they keep Harpers going once the new regulations and the shortages of raw materials started to bite? The clothes manufacturers she'd used from the beginning were finding it difficult to replenish their cloth, a great deal of which had come in from overseas. Some firms that had always used British wool were not feeling the pinch just yet, but silks, cotton, and other materials that were mostly imported or relied on imported ingredients were harder to come by.

'I'm sorry, Mrs Harper,' one of her regular suppliers had told her the previous week. 'I can only supply half of your order – I've been told that I have to regulate my orders so that everyone gets a fair share...'

'Yes, I do understand,' Sally had agreed. 'But Harpers have been one of your best customers – couldn't you make that two-thirds instead?' She'd smiled at him winningly. 'We sold rather a lot over Christmas...'

'The Government will be rationing us soon,' the representative had replied. 'Then I'll be forced to stick to the rules – but since it's you, I'll up your order to two-thirds. You've been good to me in the past, Mrs Harper, and I'll do my best for you now...'

Sally had thanked him. She knew that stocking her store was going to be an uphill battle for a while and thanked her lucky stars for the containers Jenni had sent from America before the war started. Some of the stock probably wouldn't have been her first choice in normal times... but they were far from normal at the moment...

Hearing her doorbell ring, Sally went to answer it, slipping the door chain on before she opened it to see who her visitor was. A smile touched her face as she saw the woman standing outside and she quickly removed the chain, opened the door and invited her in.

'Beth!' she cried. 'It is so lovely to see you...'

Beth Burrows was a good friend. They'd started at Harpers together and had remained the best of friends, even when Sally was moved up to the top floor and been made a buyer long before she could normally have expected such a promotion.

'Ben told my father-in-law he was leaving this evening, so I guessed you would be on your own,' Beth said. Sally embraced her and drew her in. 'Fred told me to come over, so I did. He's gone to meet a friend and play cards or something. I should have been on my own...' Fred was the storeman at Harpers and his job was to make sure the new stock got checked in and delivered to the right departments.

Sally nodded, because her friend's arrival had lifted her feeling of loneliness. 'Have you any idea when Jack will be home again?'

Beth's husband, Jack, was working on the merchant ships that brought the goods Britain so sorely needed into the country and, like other seamen, was constantly under attack. His life was precarious and Beth must live in constant fear of a telegram telling her his ship was lost.

Beth shook her head, worry in her eyes. 'He should be back in three weeks to a month – but you know how it is...'

'Yes, I do, Beth. You must be worried to death...'

'I do worry, of course I do,' Beth agreed. 'Jack says he's lucky and I'm not to worry. He's promised me he'll come home safely when this is all over and I have to believe him.'

Sally nodded. Every woman in Britain had the same nightmare at the moment. 'Come into the kitchen and have a drink,' she said. 'What would you like – sherry or a cup of tea?'

'Oh, I think a sherry this evening,' Beth said and smiled. 'I got a lovely long letter from Maggie today and I brought it to show you. I don't know if you've heard recently?' Sally shook her head. 'No, well, you can share mine. I suspect our Maggie is exhausted. They work those poor girls in the VADs to death, I think...' Maggie must be finding it harder than her work as a shop girl at Harpers.

'Yes, I'm sure it is very hard work and the uniform is ugly,' Sally said, 'but I understand how Maggie felt and why she wanted to join. When I read of all the casualties over there, I wish I could help those poor men...' Maggie was a volunteer to help the nurses and would be given all kinds of jobs to do out there.

'You already work hard enough,' Beth assured her. 'Someone has to keep Harpers going – think of all the jobs lost if it just went to the wall because of the war. No manager is going to work as hard to keep things going as you do, Sally.'

'No, that is true,' Sally agreed. 'I do go that extra mile to get the goods we need and I do seem to have a flair for it – though I still sometimes have to pinch myself when I remember how it happened.'

She smiled as she remembered something that her husband had told her recently. He'd confessed that he'd fallen in love with her at the start. His sister, Jenni, had liked Sally, but she'd realised how Ben felt and so she'd recommended her for the post of buyer. She'd seen him first looking in the window at Selfridges and they'd discussed the window display but she hadn't known who he was until that day at work when she was told the owner wanted to see them all and she'd realised that she'd seen him before.

'You took a big chance,' Sally had told her husband when he'd explained why he'd given her the chance to become so important to Harpers. 'I might not have been any good...'

'I sensed you had it in you,' he'd replied, kissing her. 'But I'll admit that I might not have done it if I hadn't fallen madly in love with you the first time I saw you looking in Selfridge's window.'

'You kept that to yourself a while...' Sally had teased, but she'd known why. Ben had been married to a woman who lay in a coma in a hospital bed – and he'd blamed himself for her terrible injuries. Ben hadn't said a word to Sally until after he'd returned from a sudden visit to America, during which time his sick wife had passed away. Only some weeks later did he speak of his feelings for Sally.

'I wanted to make sure you didn't disappear,' he'd explained. 'I couldn't tell you how I felt – you would have thought me mad and it would've been wrong. All I could think of was to make you love working for Harpers so that you would be near me...'

Sally had kissed him after he'd told her why she'd been promoted so swiftly. Once she might have felt a bit miffed that it actually had little to do with her abilities, but she'd proved her worth to Ben and to Harpers many times over. Jenni had always believed in her too and they'd given her a wonderful chance to prove her talent.

'I saw something of myself in you,' she'd confided. 'I knew you could do it.'

Beth recalled her wandering thoughts. 'You deserved it. You always had potential...'

'Or perhaps Ben just fancied me,' Sally said truthfully. 'Mind you, he kept that a big secret for long enough. There were times when I thought he didn't much like me at all...'

'Ben was in a terrible position,' Beth said, because she'd been told about Ben's previous wife and the terrible tragedy that had overtaken their lives before he became the owner of the Oxford Street store. 'He had an invalid wife to support, no backing and a store to run that he could barely afford – he must have had great faith in you, Sally love.'

Sally nodded. 'Yes, I suppose I know that deep down – and Jenni had been put in a similar position by her uncle, though I think it was even harder for her because he was critical when she made mistakes and she says there were quite a few. Both Ben and Jenni have been supportive even when I've bought something that didn't sell.'

'I don't think that has happened much.'

'Oh, there was a line of the hobble skirts that didn't sell through,' Sally said ruefully. 'They were popular and then they weren't and I'd ordered more – I had to reduce them to cost price in the after-Christmas sale.'

'They went then,' Beth reminded her. 'Everything was snapped up within days.'

'Yes, that's true. They were good skirts.' Sally smiled. 'I noticed a customer wearing one recently. She'd very cleverly put a little pleat in the back so it kicked out when she walked. If I'd thought of that, Minnie could have done it to all the skirts and they would have sold at full price...'

'True – Minnie is so clever with her needle,' Beth said. She was fond of the middle-aged woman, who did fancy sewing for Harpers, and was married to the manager, Mr Stockbridge. Theirs was a true love story, because they'd found love again after being separated for years. It was only after her sister's death that Minnie had found work and then discovered that her former sweetheart was the manager at Harpers.

'Yes, she is,' Sally agreed. 'We're lucky Rachel introduced her to us.' Rachel Bailey was their friend and the floor supervisor for the whole store, her expert eye making sure that everything was as it should be throughout the day.

Beth nodded, but her eyes clouded with concern. 'Rachel had that batch of letters from her William at Christmas; it seems they'd been held up and all came at once – and now it is happening again. She hasn't had a new letter for weeks and she's worried about him...' Rachel's husband was in the Cavalry division and she worried that he might be in the thick of the fighting somewhere in France.

'It's awful for Rachel,' Sally sympathised. 'And all the other women who have husbands fighting. I do hate this war, Beth.'

'We all do,' her friend agreed. 'But it is happening and all we can do is keep going despite everything.' An affectionate smile touched her lips. 'Just like poor Maggie.'

Sally nodded in fervent agreement. 'Maggie is so brave to put herself through all that, Beth. She doesn't say much, but I know from her letters that she is very tired and her hands get terribly sore. I sent her some special hand cream, but I don't know if it helped.'

'I miss her,' Beth sighed. 'I think what she is doing is wonderful, but I miss her...'

2

'Well, young ladies, this is the day you've all been waiting for,' Sister Harris boomed as her sharp eyes moved along the line of young women. They were all gathered in a meeting room at the Royal Sussex County Hospital in Brighton and a buzz of excited chatter went through the girls as they waited expectantly. 'Today is the day we allow each of you onto the wards as a probationary nursing assistant. I never expected some of you to make it this far and I'm surprised and pleased with all of you. Those of you that finished the course this far have worked hard and can be proud of yourselves.' She paused and turned to look at the man standing quietly to one side. 'This is Captain Morgan and he is looking for volunteers for the front line – but I shall let him speak for himself.' She stood back and indicated he should take her place.

'Thank you, Sister Harris,' Captain Morgan said and stepped forward.

Maggie was surprised when she saw the officer who had spoken to her at her first-aid classes, before she'd joined the VADs. He'd taken her and Becky Stockbridge home in his car, because Becky's purse had been stolen and she'd had no money for the bus fare. She'd known he was recruiting nurses for the Front because he'd asked if anyone was interested, but it was still surprising to see him here, addressing these young trainees.

'I know that all of you young ladies have worked like Trojans to reach the standards we set for you before we allow you to help our nurses and wounded – well done.'

Maggie touched her friend Sadie's arm and smiled at her. Pleased that they were both a part of the final team, she felt at one with her friend; they'd shared the hardships and won through. Over a hundred girls had started the course and no more than thirty-five had stuck it out, most falling by the wayside in tears over the harshness they had to endure from Sister's tongue. They had all suffered Sister's tongue lashings, but some had managed to get through despite it, and she and Sadie felt proud of themselves for surviving.

There was a murmur of relief from the young women around Maggie, some smiles and a few giggles. All of them had endured rigorous training and could now feel satisfied that they'd passed the first of many hurdles in their nursing careers. As yet they were only there to assist, but all those assembled had been chosen to try for the actual nursing training and were the best of their class. Despite all the hardships of the past weeks, Maggie hadn't let go of her goal, which was to help the men being injured at the Front, and she was proud and happy to be amongst the chosen few.

Captain Morgan's smile seemed to embrace and caress them all. 'Every single one of you will be aware that our men are being killed and injured each day and that you will be much needed to help care for the wounded. I know you've all been through a lot, but now I am going to ask you for more...' His gaze moved from face to face, seeming to dwell here and there as if looking for something special. 'Not everyone will want to volunteer for work overseas, of course, but we desperately need nurses and nursing assistants to go out there right now, to be close to the action.'

Maggie listened intently. She'd already been asked by her superiors if she would be interested in serving in Belgium and she'd said yes – this was the opportunity she'd been waiting for.

Once again, Captain Morgan paused to let his words sink in, then, 'The field hospitals are the front line for tending the wounded and they are overflowing. Also, it is my duty to tell you that nurses who volunteer will have to suffer uncomfortable living conditions. We try to make you welcome, but it's spartan to say the least. However, it's where we have to face up to the most appalling wounds and do what we can to save lives – and it's often hopeless.' His gaze moved round the room, seeming to gather them all into his confidence. He had a warm manner and it drew the women to him. 'I fear that too many will die no matter what we do...'

'My trainees understand that they must be prepared to face hardship, Captain,' Sister Harris said, frowning. 'None of them would expect anything else.'

'I'm sure you've trained them well.' He smiled at her and she nodded her approval. 'However, nursing here in the safety of a well-equipped hospital and out there on the front line are two different things...'

One of the young women put her hand up. 'May I ask a question, sir?'

'Of course. I will answer if I can.'

'Are the nurses out there in danger of being killed?' She sounded a little tentative. Maggie listened to the answer with interest but she knew that nothing would change her mind.

'We do not send young women up to the trenches. We have stretcher bearers who bring the wounded back – but it can happen. A stray shell or a deliberate attack from the air can cause casualties. Nurses have died. Accidents can happen around muni-tions – and the Germans don't care if nurses are in the transport convoys, they drop their bombs on anything that moves, and shoot at them from their planes...' Maggie nodded and smiled, because she had long ago accepted that such an undertaking could not be without danger.

'How do volunteers get there?' another young woman asked.

'What is it like out there?' put in her companion.

'It isn't easy to get there, though we provide the transport, but there is danger, and not all of you will be able to bear the tension – or the conditions when you arrive, which can break even the strongest spirit. You'll be living in wooden huts or tents, with no proper sanitation, no proper baths and you often have to cross muddy fields to get to your stations. You will live with mud, blood and hardship every day. We're often short of medicines and some-times even food.'

'We don't care about that, sir,' Sadie piped up. 'We just want to do our bit for the men...' Maggie nodded agreement.

'Good.' Captain Morgan smiled. 'That is as I expected. No one will be criticised or thought less of if they prefer to serve nearer home. However, we do need you – so please raise your hands if you wish to volunteer...'

A forest of hands went up, including Maggie's and Sadie's. Captain Morgan's smile grew wider, because none of the new nursing assistants had kept their hands down.

'Excellent,' he said, nodding his approval. 'I don't always get that response, but Sister Harris told me you were a tough bunch and that is just what we need. All I can say is thank you.' He paused, then, 'Any more questions?'

Several young women asked for more details: what they would need to take, what they could tell friends and relatives, if they could write home. Captain Morgan answered them patiently until Sister Harris put up her hand and said that was enough.

'Anyone who is prepared to go will get a fact sheet, money for travel and an itinerary, also advice on what you need to take with you, what you'll be able to buy out there and what you won't.' She gave them what passed for a smile. 'Kindly allow Captain Morgan to leave us – he is a busy man.'

'I just want to congratulate you all,' he said and turned to shake hands with the sister before leaving the stage.

'You will all report to my office and be put on the list of volunteers,' Sister Harris told the nurses with a pleased look. 'Your orders will come through in a week and in the meantime, you will have three days leave, starting from six this evening. Now you can go to the wards you were assigned to and see what it feels like to do a bit of real nursing...'

'Phew,' Sadie whispered as they moved off. 'The old trout can actually smile, though I thought her face might crack...'

'Sadie!' Maggie said and pushed her but laughed.

'Miss Gibbs – or should I say Nurse Gibbs?' Captain Morgan asked from just behind her left shoulder.

Maggie swung round with a smile of surprise as the captain approached her. She hadn't been sure he would remember her, much less speak to her directly. 'Good morning, sir. I'm not a proper nurse. I need another couple of years training before I can call myself that – but I only signed up to assist during the war...'

'When you get out there, you will find yourself doing everything the nurses do before you know where you are,' he said. 'I know we throw you all in the deep end, but we can't help it. We're desperate for both nurses and nursing assistants. A lot of the girls are willing when they go out, but the appalling conditions, the terrible things they see and the sound of the guns combines to break them and some of them last only a few weeks.' He looked grave, as if wanting them to understand what they were taking on.

'We're from the East End of London,' Sadie piped up. 'We're tough, sir. Nothing ain't gonna break us – if the dragon sister couldn't, them bloody Germans can't...'

'Sadie is right,' Maggie said, smiling at her friend. 'We've already seen hell and spit in its eye, sir.'

'Tell me that in two months' time and I'll believe you,' he said and smiled at her. Then, changing the subject: 'I saw your friend Miss Stockbridge a few days ago. Her father allowed me to take her out for tea and she says she will write to me...'

Maggie was surprised. She hardly knew him and thought it would be the same for Becky Stockbridge, but since he'd been invited to hers to tea, their friendship had clearly progressed. She wondered that her friend had not written to tell her of her encounter with the dedicated doctor. She and Becky had been best friends while Maggie worked at Harpers, but perhaps Becky had other friends now. That thought made her a little sad and she decided to send Becky a postcard and see if she replied.

'Is Becky well?' Maggie asked. Her friends from Harpers all seemed a long way away, but she thought of them often. Harpers and her life there were still dear to her, though she wouldn't have given up her experience here. 'I'm looking forward to seeing her.'

'I'm sure she will be delighted to see you,' Captain Morgan said. 'I shall not delay you any longer – but you may meet me again when we get where we're going...'

Sadie looked at Maggie as they walked to their assigned wards together. 'He's a bit of all right – friend of yours, is he?'

'No, I've only met him once before. He gave a similar talk at our first-aid classes – but he was helpful to us that night,' Maggie said. 'He's not my friend, though. I think he's a little sweet on Becky – she was one of my friends in London – but she's a bit young for him and her father won't let her marry for years yet.' She smiled fondly. 'I have a boyfriend. As I told you, my Tim is in the Royal Flying Corps. He was sent over to a base in France and I haven't seen him since he gave me my ring – the one I wear on a ribbon under my uniform – but he writes me a postcard when he can and I know he's getting leave soon. I'll just have to hope he gets leave while I'm visiting my friends in London...'

'Yeah, lucky you,' Sadie said. 'We can travel up to London on the train together, Maggie. I can't wait ter get 'ome ter see me family.' She looked proud. 'They'll be made up to know I've passed me exams.'

Maggie nodded. 'I don't have a family, but Beth is my friend and she's as good as a sister anyway.' Maggie's parents were both dead now and the memories were still a little raw, despite it being a while ago now.

* * *

'Oh, Maggie love,' Beth said and hugged her when she walked in carrying her suitcase late the following evening, which was a Thursday. 'I'm so glad you're home. I've been worried because you didn't write...'

'I know and I'm sorry,' Maggie said. 'I wrote you three letters but only had the chance to post them the day before yesterday so you may get them while I'm here or after I've gone...'

'Has it been that hard?' Beth asked, and Maggie nodded.

'These last few weeks have been hectic. Sister Harris was a real gorgon, Beth. She had us hard at it every minute of a long day and we had to study at night to pass our first exams. Neither Sadie nor I were confident of passing, so we didn't go out anywhere, even to walk on the seafront or to post letters. When we finished our shifts, we just wanted to sleep...'

ggie, that is hardly fair on you or the others,' Beth
y did you sign up? We all miss you at Harpers...'

d I miss you – but it is so worthwhile, Beth. I've met some
nderful people and I'm really looking forward to the next
stage.'

Beth's gaze narrowed. 'Don't tell me you're going over there?'

Maggie's eyes avoided hers. 'We're not supposed to say much –
but I suppose I can say yes.'

'Maggie! Why on earth did you volunteer?' Beth looked upset,
even cross.

'Because I'll be needed,' Maggie responded defensively,
understanding her friend was worried for her. 'There are
hundreds – thousands – of wounded, ours, French and others,
Beth. The nurses are working so hard, some of them break
down mentally and physically. They need help – and some of
those wounded men might be ours. It could be Stanley who
used to help Fred, or it might be Marion's sweetheart... or Tim...
or Rachel's husband.' Her bottom lip trembled. 'I'd want
someone to care for Tim if he was wounded...' Tim was Fred's
younger son and Beth's brother-in-law and they were all fond
of him.

'Yes, I know how fond you are of him,' Beth said and bit her
lip. 'It might even be my Jack if he got taken there after an attack
on his ship. I'm stupid to go on at you, but it's because I love you.'

'I know,' Maggie said. 'If I'd still got a family, my mother or
sister might say the things you did, Beth, but I haven't – so I'm
glad I've got you, Tim and Fred.'

'Fred received a letter this morning,' Beth smiled. 'Tim will be
home tomorrow for three days – so you will have a couple of days
together...'

'That is lovely,' Maggie said and rushed to hug her, feeling
surprised and happy that she would be seeing Tim. 'I have missed

you terribly, Beth. Please don't scold me any more. I'm doing what I have to and I like it, even though it's hard.'

'Yes, I know,' Beth replied and hugged her back. 'I'm so glad you're here. You must go and see Sally. She might bring her little Jenny in to Harpers – such a lovely child.'

Maggie nodded, glancing at Beth. There was no sign that she was having the child she longed for, so Maggie said nothing. Beth didn't talk about it much, but she'd seen her looking at Jenny when they'd attended her christening on one of Maggie's brief leaves and knew how much Beth longed for her own child.

'Is Jack expected home soon?' she asked, hoping to change the direction of Beth's thoughts.

'I think it should be soon,' Beth said and her face lit up. Her husband, Jack, had joined the Merchant Navy when war became inevitable, knowing that was where he could do the most good. 'I got a telegram from America a week ago, where his ship had been sent to pick up important cargo, and he just said, "Soon now, love Jack" – so I think it means he'll get leave when his ship docks.'

'I'm so pleased for you,' Maggie said and hugged her again. 'I'll call in at Harpers and visit everyone tomorrow.'

* * *

At Harpers' store, Maggie made the rounds of the departments, saying hello to everyone, and finished up in the one she thought of as hers. Beth was serving a customer with a leather bag and the new junior – a girl Maggie didn't know – was wrapping a piece of silver jewellery with loving care. Marion Kaye had just sold two scarves and was the first to finish. Maggie went up to her and had a chat. Marion had written several times, so they had kept in touch while Maggie was training. Marion had joined Harpers some months before Maggie left to take up her volunteer work.

She was a friendly girl with a big family and a boyfriend she loved.

'How is Reggie getting on?' she asked. Marion's boyfriend, Reggie, was in the Army but as yet he was still training and had not been sent overseas.

Marion's face lit up. 'He had leave last weekend and he was wearing full uniform at last, which pleased him,' she said. 'He thinks they might be off soon, but he says he's been told he will get two weeks leave then, so he'll come home first.'

'That is wonderful,' Maggie said, thrilled for her. 'Two whole weeks – you won't know what to do with yourself...'

'Yes, I shall.' Marion smiled. 'I've asked for leave so we can spend time together.'

'I don't blame you,' Maggie murmured sympathetically. 'Have some fun while you can.'

'Yes, we shall.' Marion's smile faded. 'We don't know when he'll get leave again.'

Maggie understood what she wasn't saying. Reggie could be killed on active service, like any soldier serving at the Front, and it could be the last time they were together. She nodded and touched her hand gently, but a customer approached and Maggie stood to one side, watching the new girls work while Marion was busy.

Becky was showing a customer hats and the new girl was assisting her. Maggie nodded her approval, because Becky had soon got the hang of things and she sold her customer three hats and left Shirley to pack them while she took charge of the money and change.

Miraculously, the department was suddenly clear of customers and Maggie went to talk to Becky and Shirley for a moment. It was obvious they had bonded and Maggie felt a little envious, regretting the closeness she'd had with Becky, but then her friend looked directly at her. 'You will come and have supper with us this evening?' she said. 'It's ages since we saw you and I know Minnie and Papa would love to see you...'

'I think Tim will be home this afternoon...'

'You must bring him with you, of course,' Becky said. 'Do say yes.'

Maggie nodded. 'Yes, we'll come, even if we don't stop long,' she promised and then, with a little wave to Marion, she left the department and made her way upstairs to the office. Stopping en route for some minutes to speak to Rachel.

'Oh, Miss Gibbs, Mrs Harper is expecting you,' Sally's secretary, Ruth Canning, told her and got up to open the door for her.

Maggie smiled at the secretary and thanked her. Sally was sitting at her desk and her little girl was in a cot beside her. She'd had the cot moved in so that she could bring her baby into the office sometimes rather than leaving her at home each day, and she jumped up to run around the desk and embrace Maggie. They'd been friends from the first day they'd met when applying to work at Harpers and although Sally was now the boss's wife, she was never any different with Maggie.

'I knew you were making your way round the store and told Ruth to bring you right in,' Sally said, smiling in delight to see her. 'I've really missed seeing you, Maggie. I think what you've been doing must have been terribly hard.'

'Yes, it is,' Maggie agreed, 'but I love it, Sally. I know it's the right thing to do for the moment.' All the formality the staff normally maintained during working hours had gone out of the window; they were just two young women united in friendship and mutual hatred of the war.

'I hope you won't forget us and go off to be a nurse when this awful war is over?' Sally said, looking at her anxiously.

'No, I don't think I shall. Only a few of us will be able to carry on then, because there are far more volunteers than are needed in peacetime.' Maggie smiled and breathed in deeply. 'I love the smell of Harpers – perfume and leather and silk. All I've been living with is carbolic and disinfectant.' A little laugh escaped her. 'Sometimes I think I must have been mad to give all this up, Sally...'

'Beth thinks you are. She fusses over you like a mother hen,' Sally said, eyes sparkling with mischief. 'I know Rachel is anxious for you, too. But I think it must be quite fun. If I was single, I might have done the same...'

'You're just the sort they want too,' Maggie told her earnestly. 'We've lost two-thirds of the girls that started with us – but those of us that are left are tough. Sadie thinks we've seen the worst with our dragon sister, but I think it will be much harder out there in the field hospitals...' A little shiver went through her, because she knew life would be very different out there.

'You're being sent overseas?' Sally looked at her in shock. 'Isn't that dangerous?'

'Perhaps a little. None of us even thought about that side of it,' Maggie said. 'We just know we're needed and there's no more to be said – the men have to endure terrible dangers and their living conditions are horrendous. They need whatever help we can give.'

'Oh yes, it must be awful for them, and the nurses and doctors too,' Sally agreed. 'Ben was telling me only the other week that the situation out there is dire as far as the hospitals are concerned. They are gradually sorting things out, I understand, but be prepared to live rough, Maggie. I think the soldiers and the nurses all have to take their turns bathing in those great big wine vats the French use. They have separate areas, of course, but the sanitation is basic and the toilets will be a row of wooden seats over a trench, if you're lucky.'

'Yes, we've been told we're not about to stay at the Ritz.'

Maggie laughed. 'I'm expecting that kind of thing to be basic, Sally, and we'll mostly be sleeping in tents. I'm not worried about that – it's if we run short of medicines for our patients that concerns me...'

'That's one of the things that Ben has been asked to help sort out,' Sally told her. 'It's his job. He has to source supplies and get them there – and to discover what is needed most. So, let me know what is needed if you can and I'll pass any information on to Ben.'

'We're only allowed to say certain things on our special postcards,' Maggie replied, 'but we could work out a code. If I say things are wonderful, you'll know they're dire, and if I say there is plenty of fresh air, you'll know we need everything you can send us.'

'Oh yes, that's clever,' Sally said. 'It won't tell the enemy anything, but it may help Ben to know what you need. You won't be able to tell us where you are though.'

'No, but it will be much the same everywhere out there.' Maggie laughed a little nervously. 'It is all exciting and a bit frightening, but I cannot wait to get out there and do my best.'

'Oh, you will do well. I'm proud of you,' Sally said and picked Jenny up. The little girl was awake and waving her small fists at them. 'Do you want to hold her?'

'Just for a little while,' Maggie said and took the babe with a smile. 'She's beautiful, Sally, and getting bigger every time I see her.'

'She is growing fast.' Sally smiled lovingly at her child. 'I wouldn't be without her for the world. Shall you get time to visit us at home?'

'Becky invited me to supper this evening,' Maggie said. 'Tim may want to go somewhere tomorrow, but I'll pop in and see you again when I have time.'

Sally ordered coffee and biscuits for them and Maggie stopped to chat for nearly an hour before taking her leave. She needed to shop for items she'd been told she might need: a warm cape for evenings, soaps and flannels and stockings, an extra pair of sensible boots suitable for wearing in mud, any cosmetics she wanted, extra supplies of underwear – of the warm variety – writing paper, ink and pens and some fruit sweets or mints in a tin and some biscuits. All the things it would be impossible to find when she was in France or Belgium at the Front.

'If you take some cigarettes, the soldiers will be grateful, so pack them even if you don't smoke,' Sister had instructed. 'Also, take a favourite book, something you can read over again or one you can pass on when you've finished it. Everyone needs to share out there, nurses, and it's good if you have a few extras to help others...'

Maggie smiled to herself. Sometimes she felt a little nervous of the future but overall she was excited. It was going to be an adventure!

* * *

Tim was waiting when Maggie got home with all her parcels. He came out to meet her and she ran straight into his arms, dropping everything. She hugged and kissed him, tears trickling down her cheeks as they both hung on for dear life.

'I couldn't believe my good luck when they sent me home with a troop ship to bring back a new plane,' Tim said. 'I thought I'd rush down to the training hospital to see you for a few hours, but you're here...'

'It's my pre-embarkation leave,' Maggie said. 'I don't know where I'm going, but if we're lucky it might be near you.'

'We're based only five miles from the nearest field hospital,'

Tim told her with a smile. 'I doubt we'll be so lucky, but I can pull a few strings with friends and find out where you are and then, when I get leave, I can buzz down on the motorbike. A lot of the hospitals are just further down the line. The chaps clubbed together and bought a bike. We all use it and we try to be fair, take turns so that everyone can get into the village or the nearest town for a few hours' downtime...'

'It would be wonderful if we're near you.' Maggie looked at him with shining eyes. 'Can you tell me the region you're in?'

'Not allowed to,' Tim said, 'but it's in France and we're flying over the border between Belgium and France daily.'

Maggie's smile lit up her face. 'I don't know for sure, but someone hinted that we'd be close to the French border. I know that could stretch hundreds of miles, but we might just be lucky.'

Tim touched her cheek and then bent his head to kiss her tenderly. 'We'll make the most of this leave, darling, and then we'll leave it to providence to see if we can find each other over there.'

'Oh, Tim,' she said and sighed. 'I love you so much...'

As he kissed her passionately, she wished for a moment that she'd told him she would marry him when he'd first asked her. It had been after Minnie's wedding and taken her by surprise. Caught up in her plans, she'd asked him to wait, because the service did not accept married women. Now, she thought perhaps she ought to have said yes and kept it a secret. At least then they might have had a little time together as husband and wife – and yet she knew that she was being driven to do what she considered her duty. As a wife, she could not have served and Tim would have wanted her to stay home, stay safe. One day they would be together, but first they had to get through this wretched war, which seemed to have reached a stalemate in the trenches, with constant fighting but little actual progress for either side.

'I love you, Maggie,' Tim told her. 'Keep your head down, my love – don't volunteer for front-line duties and think of me.'

'I shall think of you always,' she promised. 'You have to keep safe for me, Tim. Remember I'm counting on you to come home to me...'

3

Sally felt a bit restless in the days after Maggie had left. She went to work, looked after her baby and sat listening for the telephone in the evenings, hoping for a call from Ben. Her young friend was doing something so worthwhile and about to have adventures in France or Belgium and she envied her in a way. Of course, she could never regret her marriage or her wonderful baby or her job at Harpers, which kept her on her toes most of the time, but now and then, with Ben away at some secret location on the south coast, she felt lonely. She missed the companionship she'd shared at the flat with Maggie, Beth and Rachel. It had been soon after they all started working for Harpers and just after the death of Maggie's mother; she'd been glad of their company.

That morning, she'd taken her baby into the office. Jenny was sleeping in her cot, her sweet face flushed and calm and Sally scolded herself for her feelings. It should be enough for her to have a loving husband, who was mostly based in London, and she felt disloyal for even thinking that she might have enjoyed following in Maggie's footsteps.

If she needed more to do with her time, Sally should join one of the many volunteer groups, but not a sewing or knitting circle. She couldn't think of anything that would bore her more.

She was being foolish! Sally's time was fully occupied with Harpers and her child. Yet she wouldn't mind helping with something if she could – and there were hours when she was alone and the time dragged.

Sighing, Sally left the office, deciding to go shopping. She thought she might as well stock up on some baby lotions, creams and cotton wool, as well as food. Ben would come home when he could – so he'd said when he rang last, which was some days ago – and she would be buying steak then, if she could find any, but for herself cold ham or omelettes and salad were an easy option.

Emerging from a chemist with her basket full, she almost bumped into a woman entering.

'Marlene! Lovely to see you! How are you?' She smiled at the woman who ran and co-owned her friend Michael O'Sullivan's pub. 'Have you heard from Mick? He visited before he left to join his unit, but since then I've had just one card...' Mick was a business friend who had helped Sally in the past. He owned shares in three restaurants, but had joined up the moment war became inevitable.

Marlene nodded, smiling warmly. 'I had a postcard yesterday. He said he was training hard and enjoying himself – but I think he will be missing his restaurants. The food is awful where he's stationed, so he says.' She winked and Sally laughed.

'Poor Mick, he does like a good meal.' Sally drew her aside as the busy shoppers milled around them. 'You look wonderful, Marlene, are you enjoying life?'

'Yes, as much as possible in these dark days,' Marlene grimaced. 'Which reminds me, I was going to visit you as soon as I could find the time – but I may as well ask you now. I'm setting up a visiting group. We want a team of ladies willing to visit wounded soldiers in hospital or one of the nursing homes, to help with things like writing letters and fixing problems for them. I thought of you, because you're better at fixing things than anyone I know.'

'Thank you.' Sally laughed. 'Would you like to come back to my office for coffee, Marlene? I don't want to leave Jenny too long, though my assistant, Ruth, is keeping an eye on her for me, and we can talk.'

'I'd like that very much,' Marlene agreed. She smiled and nodded to herself. 'I invested that fifty pounds you gave me and four hundred and fifty for myself. Mick was chuffed to bits that you'd invested with him. It really pleased him and it meant that I still had my little emergency fund...' Marlene had been fifty pounds short of the money Mick needed and so she'd offered the money she'd saved to help her out.

'It was hardly anything...' Sally said, feeling a little embarrassed, because it had been such a small amount and a little thing to do for her friends. 'I would have invested more with Mick if I'd had it available...'

'Yes, I know,' Marlene agreed as they walked back down Oxford Street together. It was what was often thought of as the wrong end, being near Soho, and some people had thought the store would fail because of it, but just before the war it had been thriving and was still holding its own despite the difficult times. 'I used to avoid this end, but I often come down here now that Harpers is here. I like to shop with you for my clothes. I've had two plain dresses made elegant with some beautiful embroidery.'

'Yes, Minnie Stockbridge is excellent at refurbishing a plain dress. She is our manager's wife now and a wonderful seamstress,' Sally said, looking thoughtful. 'The war hasn't affected us too much yet at the store and we still have plenty of stock but one of my suppliers told me they haven't been able to get some of the silk they use from Italy and some others have hinted that things may get even tighter next year.'

'Yes, I know,' Marlene agreed. 'Some of my suppliers have been cutting my orders by a fifth for the restaurant – particularly on the stuff we have to import. We just don't realise how much we do rely on foodstuffs from France, Spain and Italy – even America sends us grain and other things we need, though it is the fancy cheeses I like to serve that may become impossible to get.'

'Yes, food supplies may be difficult soon,' Sally said. 'Ben's sister brought us a huge container of tinned food before the war started. We would never have got through it all, so we've been selling it in the food department at Harpers. It was supposed to be just cakes and chocolates, but the tinned fruit and jams have gone very well. I suppose people are just buying as much food as they can afford in case the war lingers on.'

'Papers,' a young lad's voice broke into their conversation. 'Germans torpedo HMS *Bayano*. Many of the crew lost. Bodies washed up on the Isle of Man...'

'Oh dear,' Sally said. 'Did you hear that, Marlene? Another ship has been sunk.'

'I don't think it is a case of if the war lingers, but rather how long,' Marlene said sorrowfully. 'I believe this awful conflict will drag on for much longer than anyone dreamed at the start.'

'Yes, I believe you're right, though I hate the idea. Ben never did think it would be over by Christmas.' Sally sighed. 'You can tell me over coffee what you think I can do for these wounded men.'

* * *

Sally was feeling more cheerful after Marlene left her. She'd felt a bit selfish because her life was so comfortable. However, visiting the men in hospital and sorting their problems out was a worthwhile job that would aid their recovery and therefore the war effort. Writing letters was one of the easier tasks, but Marlene had explained that the soldiers often needed so much more. Some of them had financial difficulties brought on by their injuries. They needed help securing places in the appropriate nursing homes so that they could be close to family and loved ones, and they needed help finding the right people to get their false legs or arms and the best doctors to treat horrendous facial scars.

'You'd think those things would happen automatically,' Marlene had said, 'but unfortunately not. The hospitals are so busy dealing with the seriously injured that other appointments get pushed back unless someone fights for them.'

'I'd be more than happy to help,' Sally had said and looked pleased. 'I suppose sometimes the best specialists are at the other end of the country and you have to liaise between the various medical teams...'

'Yes, that's where I thought you could help,' Marlene had replied, beaming because Sally had gone straight to the crux of the matter. 'One of the best consultants at treating facial burns is in Newcastle and he needs to be persuaded to come down to London to treat a patient when he has a ward filled to the brim up there.'

'So, someone needs to talk to this consultant,' Sally had said, nodding her understanding. 'Persuade him he is needed down here.'

'We've tried writing letters and phoning, but Doctor Alexander isn't listening...' Marlene had explained. 'If we could meet tomorrow at the London hospital, I can introduce you to some of the men – and you'll see the problem for yourself...' She'd frowned. 'It isn't nice to see, Sally, but I think you've got the stomach for it.'

'I hope I have,' Sally had said, meeting her eyes frankly. 'I've never been tested, Marlene. My life has been protected for a while now and I'm even a little spoiled these days – perhaps it will do me good to see what others suffer.'

* * *

Sally was very affected by her tour of the hospital with Marlene the next day. She'd known of course that there were many men with terrible wounds, but she hadn't really understood how bad they could be. Their plight touched her heart and she was determined to do whatever she could to get this obstinate Mr Alexander to visit London. Surely, he could spare a little time for men with such terrible wounds.

Forcing the awful sights of awfully disfigured men from her thoughts, Sally returned to her desk. She would visit once a week, take small gifts and do whatever she could – and she would try ringing this Mr Alexander in Newcastle. However, she had appointments all afternoon and Mrs Hills, her housekeeper, and Pearl were looking after Jenny and giving the apartment a thorough cleaning while Sally was busy.

'You've quite enough to do without hospital visiting,' Mrs Hills had scolded her when she'd told her where she was going that morning. 'It won't do, Mrs Harper, upsetting yourself over things you can't cure. I'm sure Mr Harper would say you had more than enough to do while he is away.'

Pearl still came in to look after Jenny three afternoons a week, but she'd taken part-time work at one of the many hospitals crying out for nurses to return to work – even those that had left the service to marry were being accepted in the present crisis. Mrs Hills had been a brick, increasing her hours to enable Sally to spend more time at Harpers. In the evenings, Sally often felt restless and alone, but she couldn't complain, almost every wife in Britain was experiencing the same feelings of loss – and most of them had men serving abroad. At least Ben spent a few hours at home with her at the weekends when he could get leave, but it was the middle of March and he hadn't been home for a while now.

Sighing, Sally looked at the new catalogues for the summer season fashions. She flicked over the pages, looking for something that jumped out at her, but nothing much seemed to have changed. It was all the fault of this war, of course. The manufacturers obviously thought women would go on wearing their old dresses so they hadn't launched anything very different this year, but at least there were some pretty new hats she could order for Beth's department. Hats were no problem, because the materials were easily sourced in Britain and the styles would suit all tastes, from the more manly look to the frivolous flowers and netting.

Sally smiled, got out her notebook and started to write out her order.

4

Marion Kaye went straight up her next-door neighbour's path and then around the side of the house to the back door. She was about to knock when it opened and her little sister, Milly, came flying out, hugging her about the waist and laughing.

'Reggie is home,' she said in a rush. 'And he brought me a present.'

'Well, aren't you the lucky one?' Marion said, laughing as she allowed Milly to draw her into Mrs Jackson's warm kitchen. She caught the delicious smell of apple pie baking and saw the family clustered about the big pine table which was filled with food and dishes. Her heart leaped for joy as Reggie turned to look at her and she saw the love and tenderness in his face. Reggie was on his feet as soon as he saw her and came to her with a grin on his face. It was so good to see him after nearly two months when he'd been training hard and hadn't been allowed even a twenty-four-hour pass. He looked so tall and handsome in his uniform that her heart turned over. 'You didn't write to let us know,' she said, too emotional to say much, 'but it is a lovely surprise.'

'How is my best girl then?' he asked with a cheeky grin and Milly punched him in the leg.

'You said I was your best girl,' she accused with a pout.

'And so you are,' Reggie replied good-naturedly. 'You're my best little girl and Marion is my best big girl.'

Marion laughed as her sister's face showed she was trying to work that one out. 'That will teach you to be careful when you flirt with my sister,' she said teasingly and hugged his arm, looking up at him with mounting pleasure. 'It's lovely that you're home, Reggie. We've all missed you such a lot.'

'How much?' he asked with a twinkle in his eye and held his hands apart a few inches. 'This much – or this much?' He opened his arms as wide as they would go and Marion shook her head at him.

'Don't pander to his vanity, lass,' his mother said, looking at him fondly. 'You'll only make him worse.'

'I missed you a lot,' she said and gave him a little dig in the ribs. 'How long do you have this time?'

'Not as long as I'd like,' he said regretfully, 'but I intend to make the most of it.' His eyes promised much.

'Good.' She gave him a special smile and then looked at his mother. 'I came to collect Milly and thank you for having her. I wouldn't be able to keep my job if it weren't for you, Mrs Jackson.' After Marion's mother had died in the infirmary the previous year, Mrs Jackson had offered to look after the little girl when she came home from school until Marion got in from her work at Harpers.

'You'd manage somehow – besides, I like having her here. She helps me get tea ready for this lot – and they eat me out of house and home.' Mrs Jackson indicated her large family and then laughed to show she didn't mean a word of it. 'I can still find a bit of tea for you, Marion. Why don't you sit down and have a bite to eat?'

'I've got to make tea for Kathy and Dickon,' Marion said, speaking of one of her sisters and her youngest brother. 'I'll have mine with them. I know you've fed Milly, because you always do – and I'm very grateful.'

'Have you heard from Dan or Robbie recently?' Mrs Jackson inquired about Marion's elder brothers, who were serving in the forces, dismissing her gratitude as unnecessary. With her husband and family all in essential work and all contributing to the family finances, a slice of bread and strawberry jam or a piece of her pie with mash was nothing to Mrs Jackson. Besides, her tins were always filled to the brim with cakes and biscuits and the little girl didn't often eat much more than a sandwich and a slice of cake with a glass of milk.

'Not since last month,' Marion said with a frown. 'It worries me a little, but neither of them is good at writing letters, so I don't suppose it means anything.' She looked at Reggie as he pulled his jacket on. 'Have you finished your tea? Only you should...'

'I've had all I want for now. Ma will keep the apple pie warm for me to eat later if I want it. I'd like to come wiv yer and help yer, love. We shan't get much time together. I've only got thirty-six hours' leave.'

'I thought you might have longer?' she sounded wistful even to her own ears.

'Not this time.' He looked regretful.

'And I've got work tomorrow,' Marion noted with a sigh. He'd had a few days' leave at Christmas, but mostly it was just a short pass and that meant they had hardly any private time. 'Of course, you can come, Reggie. I'll make a cup of tea. I'm cooking sausages and mash this evening with some cabbage and fried onions. Dickon enjoys them with his mashed potatoes.'

'Yeah, me too,' Reggie agreed and held the door open for her. 'Ma used to cook them often, but they give me dad a queasy stomach now so we don't have them, because he can't resist if he smells them.'

Marion nodded. Fried onions were addictive and so tasty with things like sausages and mash, turning an ordinary supper into something delicious, but they didn't suit everyone. Marion's mother had never been able to stand the smell of them frying, though her family loved them. The fleeting memory gave Marion a pang of sharp grief, because her mother's tragic death was still so raw that any small thing could hurt terribly.

Once inside her own kitchen, Marion turned to Reggie and he took her in his arms and kissed her passionately. Milly had run off to play with her doll and the pretty bead necklace Reggie had bought for her.

'I miss you like hell!' he whispered as he held Marion close. 'I wish we were wed, Marion. It's hard wanting you so much and knowing we have to wait for ages...' As the eldest girl and with no mother to care for her family, she knew she had no choice but to be the one who cared and provided a home.

'Yes, I know – I'm sorry, love,' she told him, smiling up at him. 'I'd love to say yes, but I have the others to think of – and there's no one around to give me permission to wed you, Reggie.'

'We could ask Dan next time you hear from him.'

'Yes, we could,' Marion said and sighed. 'I couldn't afford to lose my job, Reggie – if we had a baby...'

'Yeah, I know.' Reggie let her go and looked resigned to waiting for the girl he loved. 'I'm daft, Marion. I know you're stuck for the time being. There's just you to look after Kathy, Dickon and the little one, but I'd give you most of my wages if we were wed.'

Marion smiled lovingly at him. 'It's not just money, Reggie. You know that – but with you being in the Army and Dan and Robbie away...'

'Yeah.' He sighed and felt inside his jacket, giving her a small parcel.

'You shouldn't, Reggie...' she began and then smiled as she opened it and saw the pretty silver earrings in the shape of leaves. 'These are so lovely. I'll always treasure them.' She looked up. 'We ought to save for the future, Reggie – for the day when we can wed.'

'I've got money put by for that. I've been saving for years. Ma was always on to us boys to put some of our wages away each week and I did – so I can afford to marry, Marion. I know I promised I'd wait another year or so and I will. It's just that I love you so much...'

'I love you too and I wish—'

The door opened then and Kathy entered, closely followed by Dickon, his battered canvas satchel over his shoulder. He'd used it for school for years and now it held his docky tin and flask for his midday meal at work at the shipyard, where he was training as a fitter. Dickon wasn't sixteen yet, but already he was doing a man's job. Kathy was fourteen and wanted to leave school next term, though Marion hoped she would stay another year and give herself a chance of a better job in the future, as her mother had wanted for them all. Milly was nearly seven, but shy and uncertain, only now beginning to gain a little independence since she'd started proper junior school rather than the infants' classes she'd attended previously. Marion felt responsible for keeping them together as a family and encouraging them all to make the best of their lives, as their mother might, had she lived.

She thought Dickon looked tired and wondered if doing a man's job – as he'd been determined to do when Robbie left home at the tender age of sixteen and a bit to join the naval cadets – was more taxing than he'd expected. He never complained, but she didn't expect him to admit he'd taken on more than he'd bargained for.

'What's for tea?' Kathy asked. 'I'm starving, Marion.'

'Sausages and fried onions with mash and a little cabbage.'

Marion gave Reggie a wry smile and put her apron on.

Kathy filled the kettle and Marion began to peel the onions, tears streaming, even though she did them underwater to mitigate the effect, and then the potatoes. Soon the saucepans were boiling merrily and the sausages were in the pan sizzling away. The tempting aroma began to fill the kitchen, making everyone hungry.

'I've got enough sausages if you'd like some tea?' Marion offered Reggie, because he was sniffing the onions frying appreciatively, but he shook his head.

'Ma cooks enough for the Army,' he said. 'Do you need any wood chopping?' When Marion shook her head, he nodded. 'I'll pop back home and leave you all to enjoy your food – and I'll come over later. I'd like to take you to a dance, but by the time you've had tea it will be late...' He paused as she offered him a forkful of soft delicious fried onions straight from the pan, then took them into his mouth and chewed, rolling his eyes in appreciation and making a sign of excellence with his fingers. 'You'll make a lovely wife. You'll come down the pub later for a little while?'

'Yes, I'd like that,' Marion said and gave him a loving smile. Dancing or the Music Hall was for weekends when she had plenty of time to get ready and could stay up later. A walk to the pub and back was all they could manage on a working day, but it was enough for her.

Reggie was a kind, generous man and she wanted to be his wife more than anything, but she already had her brother and sisters to look after, as well as Robbie, who could come home for a visit at any time. If she and Reggie married, she might have a baby and with Reggie away all the time, she wasn't sure she could cope with the extra responsibility. It would also mean the end of her job at Harpers. Marion had recently received another rise in wages and was now getting twenty-five shillings a week. She could manage nicely on her wage, especially with the extra Dan had given her when he was home last. She'd refused to take any of Robbie's pay, telling him he should keep it and save it, but he'd promised he would give her some of his savings when he came home on leave – only he hadn't been allowed leave yet, because he was training intensively.

Marion worried about her brothers more than she'd let on to Mrs Jackson. She loved them both and the terrible fighting going on all over the world scared the life out of her when she thought of anyone she loved being hurt. She didn't think Robbie was out there at the Front yet, but it wouldn't be long before he was posted overseas, and Dan was on the ships. The enemy were shelling the British merchant ships mercilessly and her brother might well be in danger, but he'd lived away from home before the war so she didn't expect to hear from him much. Robbie was a different matter and he'd sent cards at first, so it was a bit odd that he'd stopped a few weeks back, though perhaps the training for the cadets was just too non-stop for him to make time.

From the letters that Maggie Gibbs sent her now and then, Marion knew how hard it could be training to do a new job. Maggie had found her nursing training very tough for a long time, though when she visited the department at Harpers, she'd been excited to be leaving for her duty overseas. Sometimes, Marion wondered what it would be like to be a nurse and help injured men. She didn't think she could do it, even though she'd enjoyed the first-aid classes she'd attended for a while. It had upset her too much to see her mother and Milly when they were sick. Marion thought she might be a bit too soft to be a nurse. Although, you never knew what you could do until you were faced with a crisis.

Bringing her thoughts back to the present, she turned the sausages just in time to stop them burning. Dickon didn't like his sausages burned, though Robbie had always said he liked them a bit black on one side. It was amazing how different two brothers could be...

Smiling, Marion served up heaped plates of buttered mash, cabbage, fried onions and the perfectly cooked bangers. Kathy and Dickon attacked their plates with gusto and Marion started to eat hers. Milly sidled up to her and asked if she could have a piece of sausage, so she cut it off and gave it to her.

'What did Mrs Jackson give you for tea?'

'Corned beef sandwiches,' Milly said, 'and custard with plums, cos the apple pie wasn't ready, but she says I'll have a bit tomorrow.'

'That was nice then. Did you eat it all?'

Milly nodded and smiled. 'I like your sausages, Marion...'

'Eat it up then – oh, you have – do you want another bit?'

'Yes please.'

Marion gave her the rest of the sausage, leaving just the one for herself. She took the little girl on her lap and fed her a forkful of onions and mash. Milly licked her lips and smiled, then said she'd had enough and wriggled to get down.

'You spoil her,' Kathy said. 'Do you want me to cook you another one?'

'No. If I'm hungry I'll make a bit of toast later.' Marion smiled. 'You used to sit on Mum's lap and ask for treats from her plate when you were Milly's age, Kathy.'

Kathy nodded and wiped a hand across her nose, on the verge of tears. She still wouldn't talk about her mother, even to Marion. 'We learned how to cook a chicken casserole in cookery class today. There are lots of variations you can do, and you can use all sorts of meat, fresh and leftovers. I think we could have a casserole more often, Marion, and it would be cheaper than what we're havin' every night – save you some money.'

'Is that what your teacher says?'

'Yes. They teach us economy and cooking.'

Marion smiled at her serious sister. 'You'll make someone a good wife.'

Kathy looked at her for a moment. 'I'm not sure I'll ever marry,' she said and got up to clear her plate, her back to Marion. Her shoulders were hunched as if she was tense and they shook as a sob left her.

'What's wrong, love?' Marion followed her, turning her to look into her face. The misery in her sister's face shocked her. 'What did I say – I thought it was all you wanted, a family to cook for...?'

'A family,' Kathy said, and the tears welled in her eyes. 'But men are pigs. I don't mean your Reggie; he's nice – but lots of them are...' The tears welled over as a big sob shook her small frame. 'How do you know, Marion? How do you know they won't be like him?'

'You mean like our father?' she asked and Kathy nodded, another deep sob leaving her though she struggled to hold it in. Their father was a bully, who had beaten their mother so severely that she died of her injuries. If he ever returned the police would arrest him.

'You just have to be careful,' Marion replied. 'Pa drinks too much – and he was angry with Ma...'

'She didn't do anything to deserve what he did,' Dickon said and stood up. 'I'm going to the club to play darts wiv me mates.' He grinned at her and she nodded, knowing it was his habit to go out with friends now.

'Don't be later than nine o'clock,' Marion said. 'We have to be up early for work, Dickon.'

'Yeah, I know,' he grunted. 'I shan't let yer down, Marion. I ain't like him...'

'I know.'

Marion struggled against the tears. Kathy had held her grief inside for months, but Dickon was sullen and angry over what had happened that night. It had upset him when Robbie went off to join the Army cadets and she thought he resented being the only male in the house, felt that he was trapped by responsibility to her.

Marion took her sister's hand and led her to the battered old sofa. They sat down, arms around each other. 'I know it was terrible for you, Kathy. You heard it all – Ma's cries and his excuses – but don't let what he did sour your life, don't let it change you, love.'

'I hate him. I don't want him here ever again.' She would certainly report him to the police if he returned and tried to threaten them.

'Nor do I,' Marion agreed. 'The police want to talk to him, Kathy. He could be arrested if he comes here – if they find him, they'll put him inside for a long time for what he did.'

'No, they won't,' Kathy said. 'He'll get away wiv it. My friend Vera's mother said so. She said men are all rotten sods and they get away wiv murder...'

'That's just a figure of speech,' Marion told her with a smile. 'If he comes near us again, I'll go straight to the police I promise you.' She touched Kathy's cheek. 'Ma wouldn't want you to be upset, love. She loved you – she loved us all. The reason she stopped with him was to keep us all together.'

'Yeah, I know.' Kathy offered a watery smile. 'I'm sorry. It's just... I always wanted a home and family to cook for, but now I think I'll just be a cook in a café or somethin'...'

Marion put her arms around her, holding her close. *Pa, what have you done?* she thought. Damn him! He was entirely to blame. If he'd put his head around the door then Marion would have gone for him with the poker. His wicked acts had almost destroyed her family and it was taking all her strength to hold it together.

'I'll tell Reggie I can't go to the pub and stay here with you...'

'No!' Kathy looked up sharply. 'You must go, Marion. He's only got a few hours. I'll be all right with Milly. I'll make a nice vegetable casserole for tomorrow – and I'll use those extra sausages to give it some flavour. You'll see, it will be lovely.'

Marion had thought they would have them cold with tomatoes and bread to take to school and work, but she nodded and smiled. 'Yes, you do that, Kathy love, and I'll bring some crisps home to go in your lunch packet tomorrow.' Tomato sandwiches and crisps would have to do, though Dickon wouldn't think much to that. She too would have preferred her sausage cold for lunch, but she couldn't deny Kathy the chance to cook when her sister was so upset. 'Put plenty of onions in, because that will make it tasty and they're cheap...'

Kathy smiled and got up, happier now that she had a purpose.

Marion followed her to the sink and did the washing up. The shadow of her mother's death still hung over the family, even though Marion had done all she could to cheer them up at Christmas. Perhaps they ought to move house, and yet she liked being next to Reggie's mother. No, she couldn't move, because it would cause too many complications and yet she knew that none of them would ever truly be happy in this house again.

Perhaps when Milly was a bit older, she could look for another home for them all – perhaps when she and Reggie decided to get married, things would be better...

5

That weekend, Sally hugged Ben as if he'd been away for months, though it was only five weeks or so, and then stood back to look at him. It had shocked her when he'd just walked in the door without a word of notice, but she'd been too happy to see him so hadn't complained that he might have let her know. He looked so smart in his Captain's uniform, but older and more serious. She thought that he had a lot of responsibility in his job for the Government, perhaps more than he'd expected.

'How was it?' she asked. 'Did you miss me?'

'Every minute of every day and night,' Ben said and smiled down at her, his eyes filled with love. 'How have you been, my darling – and our little princess?'

'She has another tooth through,' Sally said proudly. 'She is very well – sleeps most nights, but sometimes she's a bit fretful. I think she misses her daddy.'

'I certainly missed her,' Ben said and went through to Jenny's bedroom to pick her out of her cot.

Jenny gurgled and kicked, clearly delighted to have her doting father back.

'You've grown so much, my baby; I shall soon need help to pick you up,' Ben joked and turned to look at Sally. 'I'm afraid I shall be off again sooner than I thought, love.'

'Oh, that's disappointing,' she said calmly, though her heart had fallen to her smart black button boots. 'Where are you being sent and when?'

'I can't tell you the first, but I may not be able to ring you as often and I may not be here for several weeks, even longer than this trip, which means you'll have all the responsibility of the store alone.'

'That is no trouble.' Sally nodded thoughtfully. 'Mr Marco's apprentice and Marion worked hard on the windows for Easter.' That had been the previous week and it was now Saturday the tenth of April, Good Friday being on the second of that month. 'We've had a fairground scene and a group playing cricket, as well as one dedicated to our boys over there, and we've been collecting money for the troops, too. All the staff have put in and we contributed fifty pounds – we shall send tobacco and sweets.'

'That's a great idea, Sally,' Ben said and looked at her with love. 'Trust you to think of it.'

'Well, it wasn't my idea really,' Sally replied. 'I read that the Queen herself had sent a Christmas tin to the soldiers, so I decided we would do something of the kind at Easter. I contacted the wife of an officer who shops at Harpers and we adopted her husband's troop – so we'll send them parcels whenever we get the funds. '

'My lovely Sally. Always thinking of others.' He smiled at her. 'Meanwhile, I have one week at home.'

'We'll make the most of it then.'

Sally told Ben about her visit to the hospital and the difficulties in finding enough surgeons with the right skill to help them as they lay in bed that night, having made love and talking first of their child and Harpers. He lay stroking her back and kissing her naked shoulder, listening and making a few pertinent remarks here and there.

'There is a man named Mr Alexander in Newcastle. I'm told he's excellent, but he's very busy and he won't spare the time to come down.' Sally sighed. 'I've visited the hospital a few times now, just to take fruit, magazines and write a few letters. I don't have the time to do much, of course – but there's one man in particular, Captain Maclean, I'd like to help.'

'Is he a friend?' Ben asked and kissed her earlobe.

'No, I don't know him, but he has a sad story. His face has been terribly burned and his girlfriend took one look and ran out. The nurses say he is very bitter.' She pushed closer to Ben. 'I don't know why, but his story has been playing on my mind. He seemed to have no hope of anything beyond an existence in hospital. If he had something to make him fight for his life...' She sighed and shook her head.

'Poor chap.' Ben sat up and sipped a glass of water from beside the bed. 'I can understand why you'd want to help him, Sally. Have you tried ringing this Mr Alexander?'

'I've rung about twenty times and I always get this same woman, who tells me he doesn't have time to speak to me – or to visit.' She sighed and sat up against the pillows, clasping her knees. 'I was wondering – do you think we could bring someone over from America? Do you know anyone – or does Jenni?'

'Jenni most certainly does,' Ben said. 'There is a very good man – Thornton, I believe his name is...' He wrinkled his brow. 'But do you think anyone would risk running the gauntlet of the German U-boats to come over?'

'He might – if Jenni got to work on him.' Sally looked thoughtful. 'If I went up to see this consultant in Newcastle and asked him to come down, I could drop a hint about bringing an American over...'

Ben looked at her and laughed out loud. 'Prick his vanity, you mean? It might work as a bluff. Why don't you contact Jenni first? Ask her if she knows Thornton well enough to twist his arm a little?'

'Do you think he might – if we paid his expenses and for his time?'

'A sea trip takes days – could he afford the time and would he want to risk it?' Ben was thoughtful. Since the Germans had declared that all ships bound for Britain were fair game, it had made travelling to the United Kingdom hazardous for visitors.

'Yes – but Americans are still coming over – not as many or as often as they used to, but some are risking it.'

Ben nodded and smiled. 'They don't have a war over there yet and the Germans threaten and bluster, but they haven't actually attacked an American passenger ship yet, as far as I know. It would be expensive to bring him over – but use some of our contingency fund if you need to, Sally. Men like this Captain Maclean deserve the best.'

'I'm going to try Mr Alexander first,' Sally said in a determined way. 'I can't bring your American surgeon over for every man in London who needs him. I have to persuade Mr Alexander to give us some of his precious time on a regular basis.'

'Well, good luck with that,' Ben said and caressed her silken smooth rump with his hands as his passion stirred once more.

'I'm going to try,' Sally said as she sat astride him and bent down to kiss him deeply, her hands caressing his bare shoulders. 'But it will have to wait until you go off wherever you're going, because while you're here I want to be with you as much as I can...' She kissed him again as he stroked the arch of her back. 'I love you so much, Ben, so much...'

Her laughter rang out as he pulled her down to him and began to kiss her passionately once more.

* * *

Some nights later, Ben stood looking out of the window at the passing traffic. It was true that London was a city that never slept and nor could he. He had been thinking about her determination to help the badly injured men she'd seen in the hospital. It was just like his Sally to go out on a limb for someone she didn't even know, who had aroused her sympathy. She surely had enough to do with Harpers and being a mother, but that was his Sally. It was a part of her – a part of what had drawn him to her in the first place. He smiled, because he wouldn't mind betting this Mr Alexander would bend if he met the irresistible force that was Ben's wife.

He hadn't told Sally that he'd spent part of the past few weeks flying over France and Belgium looking for suitable routes for the convoy of the medical supplies the field hospitals desperately needed. His tiny plane had been shot at the last time they had been on a reconnaissance flight and he'd ruled out making drops that way. It could work a couple of times, but they couldn't deliver anywhere near what was needed, which was why Ben had been searching for alternatives.

This next tour of duty would be more dangerous; he was leaving for France at the end of the week, accompanying a convoy of goods the soldiers and nurses desperately needed. The last two convoys sent by conventional means in trucks had been attacked by German pilots diving and shooting at them from above, and most of what they carried was destroyed; it meant lives were lost and Ben had been asked to plan a route that was safer – if one could be found. He'd decided that they would take the supplies part of the way in fishing boats from the Channel Islands and then go ashore in rowing boats to a remote part of the French coast. The supplies would then be transported on pack ponies to their destination, just like the Cornish and Devon smugglers of old. Some French partisans were due to meet them at the beaches – and would show them the safe routes Ben had seen from the air. He would accompany one contingent of supplies and several others would set out for other destinations at the same time. That way they split the risk and at least some of the supplies ought to get through.

The idea had been discussed for several days before being approved by headquarters. Some officials thought it too dangerous and slow, but Ben had pushed his idea, because too many ships were being caught near France and came under terrible fire, and any vehicle seen on the main roads would be bombed. Merchant ships had been damaged and one partially sunk when it was almost at its destination, needing evacuation and all goods were lost. Even buses requisitioned from London had suffered a similar fate travelling by road, so Ben had come up with the idea of the rowing boats and the ponies, travelling across fields rather than by road. A small fishing boat wouldn't be noticed or suspected of carrying important supplies; the ponies could go by way of remote villages and lanes – and they could travel by night. It would still be dangerous, though the more obvious routes were the ones the Germans were attacking from the air. It would be slower, potentially dangerous, and was a big risk, but he couldn't see it was a worse risk than the more conventional routes which were regularly bombed and ambushed.

Turning, he looked at Sally and saw she was fast asleep. It was hell having to leave her so soon, especially after he'd promised her that he would be based in London for a while. Their week had half gone already and it seemed like five minutes. It was amazing how precious time became when there wasn't much of it. After this, his posting was officially London for a while, providing he made it back from this mission...

Sally was stirring, opening her eyes and looking at him sleepily. 'What's wrong, love? Can't you sleep?' she said softly.

'I thought I heard Jenny,' he said, 'but she's fine.' He went back to the bed and crawled in beside her, taking her into his arms. Her skin was warm and delicious next to his and he felt his desire stirring once again.

'Did I ever tell you how gorgeous you are and how much I love you?' he asked as he gathered her to him.

'All the time,' she murmured and nibbled at his ear. 'You're not bad yourself, Ben Harper.'

* * *

Sally counted the days and then the hours. Ben was with her almost every moment of every day and she sensed there was something that he wasn't telling her, but wouldn't ask. If he couldn't or didn't choose to tell her, she mustn't press for details. Their love was based on trust and understanding and they were so close she picked up his thoughts much of the time and that's why she knew this next parting was serious in some way.

That morning after they got up, Ben spent half an hour just sitting on a stool in Jenny's bedroom watching her sleep. Sally saw the look in his eyes and her blood ran cold. Ben was absorbing every detail of her face so that he could take it with him. She could feel his eyes on her too, drinking her in when he stood up, coming to Sally and taking her into his arms. He didn't kiss her but just held her close, his face against her hair.

'You smell wonderful,' he said. 'It isn't perfume, it's just you, my darling.'

'I love you, Ben,' she said, looking up at him. Her throat was tight with emotion and she could only whisper, 'Come back to me safe, please.'

'I shall,' he promised and his voice was strong, his look confident. 'It's only a trip to the coast, Sally.'

She nodded. He was keeping something inside and it was killing him to lie to her so she reached up and kissed his lips tenderly. 'Whatever it is, you have to do it – and I love you for who and what you are.'

'I know – that's why I can go.' He smiled, bending his head to kiss her again. 'Take care of our little one, Sally. I'll be back as soon as I can...'

She watched as he picked up his suitcase and left the apartment. Ben didn't look back. If he had, she would have begged him not to go, but perhaps if he'd looked back, he couldn't have left.

Hearing a little cry from her daughter, Sally went to the cot and picked her up. She was wet and needed changing. Thank goodness for babies and their needs! You had to look after them and that meant you couldn't brood or collapse into tears.

Lifting her head, Sally got on with her day. Whatever happened, she had to continue her life for Jenny's sake – and there were others who needed her help. The staff of Harpers were relying on her to keep the shop going. Mr Stockbridge was the manager, of course, and helped as much as he could, but Sally was the lifeblood of the store. She was the one whose ideas made it bright and vibrant despite some shortages on the shelves. Then there were the injured men she'd pledged herself to help if she could – men like Captain Maclean, who was lying there longing for death. She didn't know why she couldn't get the look of desperation in his eyes out of her head.

After talking it through with Ben, Sally had made up her mind; she would ring Newcastle again and if there was no change of attitude from his secretary, she would go up on the train and see if she could badger Mr Alexander into coming down to take a look.

* * *

Sally shivered in the bitter wind as she got down from the train in Newcastle. It had been a long journey and it was far colder up here than back in London. She'd shed a few tears alone in her bed the previous night. Ben hadn't told her anything, but she sensed it wasn't just the south coast of England this time. Her instincts told her that Ben would be in danger but she'd suppressed her fears. He had to do his job and she had to do hers.

She'd left Jenny with Mrs Hills, who was staying in the apartment for a couple of days so that the baby wouldn't be too unsettled.

'She'll miss you,' Mrs Hills had told Sally before she left, 'but she's taken to the bottle well and I promise you I shall make sure she's fine.'

'You have the telephone number of the hotel I'll be staying at overnight?' Sally had asked. 'I'll ring you in the evening as soon as I can.'

'Yes, of course, but she will be perfectly all right, Mrs Harper. I've had three of my own, remember.'

Sally had fretted as she caught her train in London. She knew nothing about the northern city other than it took more than five hours to get there. Her conscience was troubling her as she thought about leaving her little girl with Mrs Hills. Was she neglecting her child? Supposing something happened and she was hundreds of miles away...

No, of course nothing would happen. Jenny did look for her mother and she might grizzle a bit if she wasn't there to give her a cuddle when she woke, but Mrs Hills was like a doting grandmother to her and knew how to comfort her. Pearl loved her too and, being a nurse, would know if she needed medical attention. So, she was fretting for nothing!

Sally squared her shoulders. She'd taken this task on herself and if she could possibly do it, she would secure the services of this elusive consultant surgeon by hook or by crook. A little smile touched her lips. He was just another man, surely, he couldn't be too much of a monster?

She hailed a taxicab and asked to be taken to the offices of Mr Alexander in Westgate Street. The man looked at her as if she'd landed from Mars and in the end she wrote down the address for him.

'Howay, why did you not say?' he asked scornfully, clearly dismissing her as an ignorant Southern woman.

Sally waited for him to take her case, but he didn't so she half threw it into the back of the cab. He looked at her stony face and when they arrived at the modest office, he wrote down the price of her fare. It was fair, she knew, so the man was honest but just scornful of a woman whom he saw as a rich Londoner.

When Sally walked into the office, a sour-faced woman looked up from her work. 'Name?' she barked at her. 'Appointment time?'

'Mrs Harper. I've rung several times and I made an appointment for this afternoon. I believe I am half an hour early.'

'So it appears,' the woman said and glared at her. 'And didn't I tell you that Mr Alexander hasn't the time to come down to London?'

'Yes, I know – but this is an exceptional case,' Sally said. 'If Mr Alexander will just take a moment to hear me out...'

'And is this case of yours more deserving than fifteen children covered in first-degree burns?' the woman demanded fiercely. 'Trapped, they were, in the orphanage and six of them died of their injuries – fifteen are so badly burned they may yet die. And then there are our own men, soldiers burned giving their all for their country...'

'Yes, I do understand that,' Sally said, 'but Mr Alexander is needed just as much in London – could he not spare just one day a week for us?'

'And if I did – what would happen to my patients here?' the voice had a definite northern accent but was far more understandable than the taxi driver's had been.

Sally whirled round and found herself facing a tall thin man, perhaps forty or so, with greying hair at the sides. His eyes were narrowed and angry, his mouth hard, and yet he was an attractive man with something that she immediately recognised as class and confidence.

'I'm not asking you to desert them, sir,' Sally said in a respectful tone, because this man commanded it just by his presence. 'I'm just asking you to consider giving us one day a week – even if you worked on a Saturday or Sunday. I'm sure we could find a nursing team to give up their day off to assist you...' She held her breath, knowing she was pushing it, perhaps being too bold or even impertinent. Yet in her efforts to help the men so terribly wounded, she felt it was worth risking the rough edge of his tongue.

His eyes were like wet steel as he looked at her. 'Supposing I said I prefer my own team?'

'I should say that you're just making difficulties.' Sally glared right back at him, suddenly angry. 'If you won't come to London, will you help them here if I arrange transport here and back?'

'You're a persistent young woman,' Mr Alexander said and his mouth firmed into an annoyed line.

Sally's heart sank because she knew she had only one last card. 'I've heard you're the very best in your field and I'll do anything to help these men,' she said and crossed her fingers behind her back. 'Even if I have to bring a surgeon over from America...'

'Rubbish,' he said and his gaze was piercing, but there was a hint of something more, as though she'd touched a nerve somehow. He hesitated a moment, then, 'I will visit this Sunday – and if I consider I can help this patient, I shall have him brought here by my own ambulance, but I make the decisions. I decide if he is a candidate for my time.' His eyes flashed with sudden fire. 'Is that enough for you, Mrs Harper?'

She felt the force of his personality and held down her surge of elation. This man was worth all the time and energy she'd invested. She felt it instinctively and was glad she'd gone that extra mile – or several hundred miles, as it happened.

'Thank you so much! It's more than I dared hope for,' she said and smiled. 'I am sure you will think Captain Maclean a worthwhile case, as are others. I am very grateful to you for seeing me and listening.'

'I've no doubt they all are,' he said gruffly. 'But I can't split myself into six, Mrs Harper.' He gave her another piercing look. 'I'm going to visit my clinic. You will accompany me – and then tell me your patients are more important than mine...'

* * *

Sally closed her eyes as the train moved off on its long journey back to London the next morning and she could feel the tears trickling down her cheeks. She knew that she would never forget the sight of those children lying there, side by side in neat rows.

Their injuries were horrific, equally as terrible as Captain Maclean's and perhaps even more pitiful.

She'd seen the way those that were conscious and able to understand lit up when Andrew Alexander walked to their bedside and asked them in his gruff voice how they were. He had a special way with him that brought comfort and even a laugh from critically injured children and that laughter broke Sally's heart.

Afterwards, he'd walked her back to the canteen and bought her a cup of coffee. 'Now, Mrs Harper, do you still think I'm a stubborn ignorant pig of a Geordie?'

'I never did, sir,' Sally had protested, even though she'd seen the glint of rough humour in his eyes. 'But if I had, I should be ashamed now – and I do understand why you were too busy to answer the calls of a foolish woman...'

'Nay, not foolish,' he'd said and his smile was the same caress that he'd bestowed on his children. 'I do not blame yer for being a woman – but you're a very persistent woman and I admire your resourcefulness.' He'd looked at her oddly. 'You must be a busy woman, Mrs Harper – tell me, why did you take the time to come up here – is Captain Maclean a relative?'

'No. I just felt strongly that he – and others like him – deserve the best, and you are the best, aren't you?' Sally had looked up at him challengingly.

'That makes you either very stubborn or quite special,' he'd replied thoughtfully. 'We shall see...' Suddenly, his eyes had sparked with mischief. 'And I'll do my best, Mrs Harper – but only on condition that you stop calling me sir. My name is Andrew...'

'And mine is Sally,' she'd said and smiled. 'And I'll try not to be a nuisance in future, but I can't promise I won't telephone.'

'I'll be offended if you don't,' he'd said and she'd seen the humour in his eyes once more. 'You've got your way, Sally Harper.

I'll be coming down when I'm able, if you have any patients for me, so don't you go fetching that fancy surgeon over from America, can't abide those chaps who charge a fortune for their work.' His gaze had met hers consideringly. 'You would really have done it, wouldn't you?'

'Yes, and I'll be happy to contribute to your work for the children, Andrew – tell me what you need for them and I'll do my best to supply it.'

'Now that is the best offer I've had all year. I'll be bringing a list with me on Sunday and don't think I won't ask.'

Again, she'd seen that twinkle in his eyes and she'd liked him. He was a stern man, but he had a heart of gold and she was glad that she'd persisted and forced him to meet her. Andrew Alexander was not only a brilliant constructive surgeon far advanced beyond most of his fellow surgeons, he was an interesting man and Sally was glad that she'd secured his help for her terribly injured men.

Her tears had gone now and her mind was back with Harpers and her baby once more. She'd telephoned Mrs Hills the previous evening and been assured everything was well, but she wouldn't be at ease until she was home and could see for herself.

Not for the first time, Sally understood how lucky she'd been when she applied for that job as a sales assistant at Harpers. Ben had fallen in love with her and she with him and it had given her a wonderful life. She had so many people to think of and care for and she couldn't wait to get back to her work and make sure the business did not suffer more than need be because of this war.

They'd lost so many of Harpers' young men to the Army. As she sat on the train homeward, Sally's thoughts were with those she knew to be serving their country. Salesmen and the young lad from the porter's basement – and Mr Marco, their clever window dresser. She missed him more than she'd ever thought she would and knew she wasn't alone. Only a couple of days previously, they'd received a postcard from Sussex, where he must be training, to tell them he was fine and would come to see them when he could; he'd said he was thinking of them, and Sally had made sure his card got passed round the departments, because everyone missed their charming and flamboyant window dresser. Harpers' windows were still well dressed, but not with quite as much flair in Sally's opinion. She helped where she could, but there was no doubting Mr Marco had a special talent. She just hoped he would come back to them when the war was over and the last time they'd spoken, she'd told him to keep his head down and not be a hero.

'I expect they will put me behind a desk,' he'd joked. 'I'll be a pen-pusher, Mrs Harper, that's the closest I'll come to the war, you'll see. The only danger I'll be in is of permanently inky fingers.'

His sense of humour had caused her to laugh as he'd intended and made the parting easier, but she did miss their little chats. Mr Marco had always been so encouraging about the stock she chose, telling her she had a natural talent for it and she supposed he was right. Ben and Jenni had thrown her in at the deep end, leaving her in charge of the buying while they returned to America, and at the time she'd been nervous of making a mistake and being demoted again.

'I could never have done that to you,' Ben had told her once when she'd revealed her fears. 'I knew you had talent from the start when we spoke about Selfridge's window displays – but even if you hadn't, I wanted you near me and it was the best way, to make you an important part of the firm.'

'Oh, Ben,' she'd whispered huskily. 'I never guessed how you felt, not once.'

'I couldn't let you,' he'd said. 'I wasn't free and I daren't tell you how much I cared for you.'

Sally's eyes pricked with the tears she refused to shed. Both Ben and Mr Marco were in the Army now and she had to be strong. She had to keep Harpers afloat during these difficult times so that when her husband and her friends returned, they would have a job to come to. Once again, the success or failure of Harpers was in her hands.

6

Marco looked at the officer. He'd been asked to meet Major Richardson informally for a drink at the man's private club in London and a little tingling at the nape of his neck was warning him that he might live to regret this day.

'You're wondering why I've asked you here?' Major Richardson said and smiled, reminding Marco of a crocodile before it snapped up its prey. 'You are of mixed race – Italian grandfather, French mother, and British father, I understand.' The piercing blue eyes narrowed. 'What made you volunteer instantly the war started?'

'I wanted to fight for my country. I have good friends here; my work is here and I want to protect all we stand for in this country.'

'Good show – but you were born in America?'

'My father was in the diplomatic service and my mother travelled with him,' Marco said. 'I don't talk about it generally as his work was confidential – but you know all there is to know about me and my family, don't you?'

'Yes, done my homework, don't yer know.' The Major smiled. 'You are fluent in several languages, including Italian, French,

German and English – isn't that so?' He hesitated, then, 'You were singled out for special duties some weeks ago I believe – did anyone tell you what they might be?'

Marco frowned, then nodded. He'd been called into the captain's office and asked how he felt about doing undercover work. When he'd agreed, he'd been told to return to the ranks and that he would be contacted in due course.

'I understood I might be needed to do secret work, sir. I'm not sure what that means. So far, I've been given the same duties as other men in the ranks but told to be ready to move on.'

'Yes, as I thought.' The Major nodded. 'You were chosen for your fluency in languages, as I said earlier, also your mixed birth – and I understood you were prepared for something rather more delicate than lying in a trench shooting a gun?'

'I was told my German and French could be useful...' Here it came! Marco's spine tingled. 'I also have a smattering of Polish and Russian...'

'Ah...' Major Richardson now smiled the smile of a contented crocodile who had caught and digested his lunch. 'Just so – and exactly the man we need for the job. We've been told you're a reasonable mimic and can sing a bit?'

'Yes,' Marco said and waited. He was fairly certain now that he knew what was required of him. 'I play the piano and sing but not well.'

'You could pass as a nightclub singer in France – or entertaining the German troops in a front-line camp...'

The question was loaded and left Marco tingling from his nape to his toes.

Marco looked at the Major thoughtfully. He'd known the approach would come soon and the invitation to this exclusive club had made him alert. This was why he'd been picked out and approached almost as soon as he'd joined the ranks. They had given him time to train and settle in as an ordinary private and now he was to be told his mission.

'Yes, sir – if that is my role...'

'You would be rubbing shoulders with the enemy at times – and your particular talents fit you for this assignment – but you need to be always on your guard and watchful.'

Why didn't he just come out and say it? Marco believed in calling a spade a spade. He looked the Major in the eye.

'You want me to be a spy for the British in France, sir? As I understand it, you want me to penetrate the German ranks as a French cabaret artist who doesn't care whether they are the enemy or not as long as I earn a few extra francs...' A man of loose principles and few morals. It was the perfect cover for Marco and one he knew he could assume with ease.

'Got it in one, private. I knew you were the man for me as soon as you were pointed out. You'll be instantly promoted to Captain, naturally. I do not know what idiot put you in the ranks, but thank God someone had a quick eye and pointed you out to me. We've been watching you for a while, Marco, and we need men of your calibre. It's dangerous, dirty work and I shan't lie to you – if your cover is blown, the Germans will shoot you, but they may well torture you first for information you may have, so shooting would be a relief...'

'Yes, sir, I imagine they might,' Marco replied grimly. He felt the ice at his neck, but his expression did not falter.

'And you cannot give that information no matter what they do to you – are you prepared to die for your countrymen?'

'For my friends – and the memory of someone I loved,' Marco said without hesitation. He might have nerves tying his stomach in knots but he wasn't going to show it. Besides, what did he really have to lose? With Julien, his young lover's death, his life had become empty and cold. 'When do I leave, sir?'

'We'll give you a crash course and then get you in under the cover of darkness close to the border with Belgium. You will probably be taken most of the way by fishing vessel; the enemy don't bother with them as much as the naval ships, but then the rest of the way you'll go in by rowing boat or dinghy and you'll be met at a prearranged rendezvous.' He paused. 'You are Marco Bellini – you may as well keep the name you prefer as it fits – and you have a position as a cabaret artist in the Fallen Angel. It is a nightclub of dubious reputation, close to the lines – and, even though it's off limits, German officers have been known to visit; they drink there and enjoy the girls – and men; it's that kind of club. You may be asked to perform at a place of the officers' choosing. If you go behind enemy lines, we cannot protect you...'

Marco looked at him in silence for a long moment and then inclined his head. 'I wouldn't expect you to, sir. I'm on my own out there and my duty is to protect what I know and pass on information I gather by mixing with German officers – the higher the rank, the better, I imagine.'

'Yes, we'll give you a few names you can contact, some French, some English – you'll need more than one in case your immediate contact is killed – and we need regular information, at least every few days, which may be risky for you and others.' Major Richardson paused. 'The village was overrun by Germans early in the conflict but they abandoned it on retreating. It's a sort of no man's land at the moment; quite close in one direction to the German lines and to a British field hospital in another direction, and some of your contacts are there, others in the village. That means several lives could be forfeit if you break under torture – so you can't, understood?'

Marco swallowed hard. 'I understand, sir. I'll listen and report to my contact.'

'If you are tortured, the pain may be too much,' Major

Richardson went on grimly. 'A remedy will be provided – cyanide crystals give a quick, relatively painless death. Some operatives choose to swallow them if they think they will betray others.'

'I imagine so, sir.' Marco faced him without a flicker and saw the appreciation in his eyes.

'Good chap.' Major Richardson smiled. 'I realise we're asking a lot – on average, a spy has a shorter life than a private at the Front. It's nerve-wracking and you need to be a strong character. I believe you are strong enough to accept this – so I'll wish you good luck.' He took a sealed envelope from his pocket and pushed it towards him. 'Your orders, Marco – and have a drink with me here after the war – yes?'

'I certainly hope so, sir.'

'Oh, you'd best sign this – Official Secrets Act.'

'Yes, of course, sir.' Marco did so with a flourish and then saluted.

'Good luck, Marco. God speed.'

Marco saluted and left, knowing he'd been dismissed. The mission had come right out of the blue and taken his breath away. A crash course in how to be a spy and then into France under the cover of darkness and a new life – a life that could end suddenly and brutally if he made a mistake. Yet if anyone was suited to the task, Marco knew quite clearly that he was the man. He could act the part of a decadent cabaret artist as naturally as he breathed. His talent at the piano was small, but he often entertained at theatrical parties – and that was how he'd been spotted of course. He wondered how long he'd been under surveillance. They knew all about him – his feelings for Julien, the young man he'd loved and lost to suicide; everything. Because they thought he had not much to live for, he seemed an ideal candidate – but Marco had realised that life was more precious than he'd imagined it could be without Julien. He had begun to recover enough to make new friends and to want to live.

However, it would be a battle of wits and no one enjoyed that more than he. After all, he'd been playing a part most of his life. His private life had always needed to be kept secret, even more so when he joined the Army, and he'd found the charming smile and teasing manner got him through life smoothly. This was no different – just more dangerous, and that would add spice.

A smile touched his lips as a thrill of excitement went through him. Pitting his wits against high-ranking officers in the German Army would be interesting, a deadly game of chess with huge stakes – if he won, he gained information for the British; if he lost, he could lose everything, including his life. He wondered what the odds were on his surviving and chuckled as he thought of discussing it with Ben Harper after it was all over. It would be something to look forward to if he survived. The war had suddenly become a game and one he believed he might be quite good at.

7

Maggie looked at Sadie nervously. Their steamer had avoided being hit by the enemy U-boats as they crossed the channel to Calais, despite some of the girls being seasick and wailing half the night as heavy waves pitched against the sides of their boat and they all prayed to arrive safely. Now they had disembarked and were being sorted into various groups for their journey onwards to the field hospitals that would be their home for at least the next six months. So far, their luck had held and the two of them were being sent to the same field hospital in the fiercely contested war zone just inside Belgium on the border with France.

'At least we'll be together,' Sadie had whispered as they were given their orders by a grim-faced sergeant. 'I reckon we shall need friends once we get out there.'

'Yes,' Maggie agreed and hugged her friend's arm. Now that they were here in France, she was even more pleased that they had been posted together. It was all strange and bewildering, from the embarkation on board ship to being delivered like so many sheep at the other end, together with a load of noisy boisterous soldiers; some of them newly trained recruits heading for action for the first time.

'They're respectful to our faces at least,' Sadie said when a group of the soldiers suddenly burst into loud laughter and then started to sing popular songs, 'but I wouldn't mind betting that some of that laughter is directed at us... The tall one with the ginger hair can't keep his eyes off you, Maggie.'

'I dare say they've had a drink or two on the quiet,' Maggie replied thoughtfully. 'After all, they are going to the Front and their lives are at risk. Some of them will never go home alive...'

The two girls looked at each other soberly. Back home, it had all seemed an adventure. They'd been warned what it would be like, but it was for real now and more than a little frightening; every so often they could hear guns firing and the buzz of planes overhead. Some were Allied Forces and friendly, but others weren't and they'd already witnessed one attack from the air, when little explosive devices had been dropped ahead on the road, causing one lorry to turn over.

At the start of the war, the only nurses available or wanted by the British soldiers were the Queen Alexandra Imperial Nursing Services, a mere three hundred in number but beloved by the soldiers. The very first volunteers, many of them girls from wealthy families, had been asked to nurse French and Belgian wounded, but now the tide of wounded had driven out these fears and the new girls would be nursing their own men. Maggie was glad, though she still remembered some of the French she'd learned at school and would have been happy to nurse any wounded man that needed her help.

For a moment, Maggie thought of the peace and comfort of Harpers. The store would be busy, filled with customers shopping for their families, hunting for bargains and new clothes. She felt a sharp pang of loss, because she'd loved being a part of all that –

and this was a strange country and, so far, it felt cold and unfriendly, and like most of the other nurses and soldiers she was uneasy and wondering why any of them were here.

'I reckon he's tryin' ter catch yer eye, Maggie.' Sadie nudged her in the direction of a young soldier, who was staring at them.

'Well, he is out of luck,' Maggie said and smiled at her friend, her nerves settling. She was here because she cared and wanted to help.

Meeting the eyes of a young soldier who looked about sixteen, though the age at which young men could join up was nineteen, she smiled at him reassuringly. Like many other young boys, he had probably lied about his age to get accepted and the need for men was so great that the recruiting officers sometimes took all comers if they could pass for the required age. He was clearly frightened of all the things that had unsettled her and somehow that made her feel calmer. He and others like him were why she and Sadie were here. In a few days, some of these men might be lying in a hospital bed and she would be helping to look after them.

To Sadie, she said, 'It doesn't matter who looks. I'm spoken for, remember?'

'Don't tell anyone else,' Sadie warned. Sadie had noticed Maggie's ring hanging round her neck when they'd shared a cabin on the way over and she'd had to tell her that Tim had given her an engagement ring, swearing her to silence first. 'If Sister found out you were engaged, she'd have you back on the next ship before you had time to draw breath...'

'That is so silly,' Maggie said and yet knew it was true. Sister had warned them close relationships were forbidden for the duration of their service.

'We do not want to spend money training and kitting you out only to have you throwing up with morning sickness five minutes after you get there,' she'd warned sternly. 'Marriage, babies and nursing do not mix.'

It made sense, of course it did. Much as she might wish she'd been Tim's wife before their parting, Maggie was here to do a much-needed job and had she married, she might well have been expecting her first child.

As the nurses and new recruits were shepherded into a convoy of vehicles – some Army trucks, some borrowed baker's vans and even an old London bus – Maggie's heart did a little flip. It was partly excitement and partly fear because she could hear guns booming in the distance and knew that they were headed towards them. They were going to a position no more than ten miles from the front line.

Looking at Sadie, she smiled and whispered, 'We're here – it's beginning.'

'Yeah, exciting, isn't it? I can't wait to start.'

Maggie looked at her and nodded, her nerves settling as she saw that Sadie was really looking forward to the work they'd trained so hard for. It was time for Maggie to put thoughts of Tim, Harpers and home away. For the next six months – if she managed that long – she was here to care for the wounded men and that was just what she planned to do. 'I can't wait either,' she said. 'I'm glad you're here with me, Sadie.'

'Yeah, me too,' Sadie said and squeezed her arm. 'We can do this, Maggie love. We shan't crumble and have to go home before our term is up.'

'No, we shan't.' Maggie jutted her chin. 'We're here for as long as they need us.' She lifted her head determinedly. Sadie was right. They were here to do a job and that was just what they would do, just as her friends back home were doing their jobs, keeping Harpers going so that their families and friends could carry on with their lives as best they could.

* * *

Beth turned sleepily as her husband stirred beside her in their bed. She smiled because they'd spent the previous evening dancing and then Jack had made love to her, holding her and caressing her hungrily, as if he'd been starving in the desert.

'I've missed you so much, my love,' Jack told her as he opened his eyes and reached up to bring her down to him, kissing her again softly, caressing her mouth with the tip of his tongue. 'What are you thinking about?'

'You, how much I love you – and Maggie, too, wondering how she is coping out there,' Beth said. 'It was sad you didn't get to see Tim last time he was home for a few days.' The brothers had just missed each other, which was one of the misfortunes of war.

'It can't be helped. We all have our work to do.' Jack kissed her lips, stroking her cheek tenderly. 'Meanwhile, I've got three weeks to be with you and that's a little miracle.'

'It's only because your ship was hit and has to have a refit,' Beth said and shivered in his arms. 'I'm glad I didn't know anything about it, Jack. I should've been worried to death.'

'The Germans got lucky and just caught us in the tail,' Jack said. 'Our boys moved in on them and blew them out of the water and then nursed us home all the way across the Atlantic. It was a bit hairy at times, and frightening if I'm honest. The seas got a bit wild and we took on a lot of water, but Captain Marlowe was determined to get his ship home. So now we've got some shore leave while they patch her up again.'

'Yes, and that's lucky for me,' Beth agreed and snuggled up to his warm body. 'I just think we're so fortunate that it wasn't worse...'

'If it had been, we shouldn't be here to tell the tale,' Jack said.

'If they'd hit us broadside, the ship would've gone and a lot of us with it.'

'Yes, I know...' Her father-in-law, Fred, read the papers all the time and she always knew when he'd seen articles about merchant ships being sunk or damaged because he got that worried look in his eyes. Of course, he never told her, but she usually found the paper out in his shed and read the stories for herself. Beth hadn't known about Jack's ship being damaged and she was glad, because she would have been terrified.

'What shall we do this Sunday?' Jack asked, changing the subject. 'Would you like to ask friends here for lunch?'

'I'll ask Sally and Ben, if he's back,' Beth replied. 'Rachel might come, though she often invites her late husband's mother to lunch on Sundays. So, it will probably be us and Sally, Jenny and Ben, if he's home, and Fred, of course, unless Tim gets leave again unexpectedly. I know Maggie won't because she said her posting is for at least six months.'

'I heard a lot of the nurses have to come home sooner because of the awful conditions and what they see out there – they just break down after a while,' Jack said.

'Maggie won't,' Beth said with conviction and sighed. 'I wish I could stay here with you, Jack, but I have to go to work – but it's my afternoon off today, so I'll be home early.'

'Good, we'll go out to dinner this evening.' He smiled at her. 'See if you can get a few days off while I'm home, love. I know it isn't easy – but I'd like to make the most of it while we can.'

'I do have a few days holiday due so I'll ask if I can take them off now,' Beth replied and kissed him. She threw back the covers reluctantly, wishing she didn't have to leave. Yet she would hate not to have her wonderful job at Harpers, because without it she would be lonely. She would speak to Rachel Bailey about taking a couple of days off and arrange it with Mr Stockbridge, and then draft in one of the other senior ladies to cover Beth's position.

Smiling, she avoided Jack's arms and pulled on her dressing gown. She could hear Fred moving around downstairs already. He would have the kettle on, she knew, and more than likely her toast would be waiting by the time she got down. She needed to get to work and sort out her leave so that she could be with her husband while he was home...

8

Marion finished wrapping the small gifts she'd bought for Milly's birthday and hid them in her wardrobe. She'd managed to save a little money and had a present from all of them, as well as one Reggie had bought when he was home last, and a little something extra just from her. Her little sister was excited about her birthday, due that weekend, and Mrs Jackson had promised to bake her a lovely sponge cake as well as knitting her a pretty yellow cardigan with pearl buttons.

Reggie had been home for a short pass three weeks earlier and told Marion that he believed the next time he came home would be the last for a while.

'Is it time?' she'd asked and her heart had caught with fear, because the look in his eyes told her that Reggie was being sent overseas, even though he couldn't – and wouldn't – tell her. 'Have you finished your training?'

'Nearly,' he'd said with a look of pride. 'Captain Forest said we were one of the best new units he'd seen and that we were a credit to our friends and relatives.' A lot of the young men joining up at the same time were being put into the same units with others from their town or village and called themselves the 'Pals' regiments, but as yet none of them had been sent overseas. The first to go had been the regulars and some of the men who'd been part-time soldiers before the war. The new recruits would all be posted overseas soon and Marion dreaded the day when Reggie would be one of them. However, she wouldn't dream of telling him of her fear. She was proud of him, and like so many other sweethearts and wives, she would wave him goodbye with a smile.

'That's good,' she'd said and kissed the man she loved on the cheek. 'I'm real proud of you, Reggie. Where do you think you'll be sent when the training is finally over?'

'I don't know, love, and I probably couldn't tell yer if I did,' he'd said with a grin. 'Anyway, they'll give us at least a twenty-four-hour pass when the time comes.' He ruffled his dog's fur. Marion smiled. She'd hated the beast for a start but in a way, it had been responsible for getting them together when it stole their sausages. 'Some of the chaps have their dogs with them in training camp, but I don't reckon that's right – I couldn't take my old fellow over there to get shot at. If I didn't come back – you'd see he was all right, Marion? Ma might want to get rid of him.'

'You will come back,' she'd said fiercely, 'but yes, I'd have him – he spends half his time here with Milly anyway.'

'Yes, she loves him.' Reggie had thrown a look of affection at the little girl, who was playing happily with her doll.

'You'll come home before you leave for the Front, won't you?' Marion had asked.

'Of course – and if you could get a few hours off while I'm home it would be great.'

'I'll ask Becky to swap her half day off with me or one of the others,' Marion had promised. 'Shirley won't mind either, but you need to let me know when you're coming so I can arrange it.'

'I'll send yer a postcard, love, when I can,' he'd told her. 'You keep sendin' yer letters to the same address I gave yer, Marion. I'll be lookin' fer them, girl.' He'd hugged her then and she'd felt the sting of tears, though she hadn't let herself cry because that would only upset Reggie.

Fortunately, the last few weeks had been really busy for her, because she'd been doing two jobs, which meant she hadn't had time to mope over Reggie. She spent an hour each morning consulting Mrs Harper and the others on the window-dressing team, helping to decide on the new ideas, and, when the windows were changed, the whole day helping to arrange and display the goods and background pieces. She wasn't sure the windows were quite as clever as they had been when Mr Marco was at Harpers, but they did their best and everyone seemed to admire them.

Smiling, she crossed the day off on her calendar. Only four more days and Reggie would be home for his next leave, which was longer than he'd expected. They'd given them three days this time and she knew in her heart it was because he was being sent overseas. She couldn't wait to see him walk in at the kitchen door, especially since she knew that after his embarkation leave, he would not be home for months on end.

* * *

Mrs Burrows looked happy when Marion walked into the department that morning. She nodded to Marion as she took the dust covers off the hats and started to rearrange them. Shirley was already dusting counters and Becky was checking her stock of scarves and gloves, making notes in her stock book.

'Is everything all right?' Marion asked anxiously, because they'd had some stock go missing when a girl called Janice had worked in the department.

'Yes, fine,' Becky said. 'I've got a box of new stock to unpack this morning so I'm just checking everything before I start.'

'New stock – lucky you,' Marion replied. 'We had a box of hats last month, but I'm not sure when we'll have more.'

'Oh, I don't think you need worry,' Mrs Burrows told her, overhearing their conversation. 'Hats are not going to be in short supply apparently, because we have plenty of the raw materials in the country.'

'Really?' Marion brightened. 'Some of the customers were worried about that, I know.' Women did like a new hat, especially in the spring and summer; it cheered them up when times were hard.

The Government had mentioned the dreaded word rationing a few times lately and although no measures had been taken yet, everyone was expecting it might happen, because if too many ships went down, victims of German attacks, and their cargoes were lost, the country would soon experience shortages. The farmers had lost men and horses to the war, which meant that the work was harder, and that women and children were much in demand on the land. For the moment, those workers left were doing a heroic job and managing to feed the population, though sometimes there were long queues outside butchers and greengrocers. Home-produced products were already being unofficially rationed by manufacturers because they had to make sure everyone got a fair share and that was why the newspapers carried warnings of what might come. Things like sugar were sometimes in short supply and housewives tried to stock up whenever the shops had a delivery, but most shopkeepers only allowed a one-pound bag to each customer at a time and kept some under the counter for those special customers they favoured.

'Well, I don't think we need to worry too much,' Mrs Burrows said with a smile. 'We may not get everything we used to or as much as we'd like, but Mrs Harper usually manages to get her share or a bit more of whatever is going.'

'She's wonderful,' Marion said and looked at her supervisor. 'The way she looks after her baby and the shop – there aren't many ladies who could do that.'

Very few women ever had the chance to do such an important job and Sally Harper was held up to everyone as an example, and all the young women employed in the store admired her, because it showed them it was possible. Even though a few whispered that she'd only got the job because the boss fancied her from the start, most thought she deserved all she had.

'I agree with you,' Mrs Burrows said now to Marion. 'Mrs Harper is a marvel – but that's why Mr Harper put her in charge of the buying in the first place. She has made a lot of friends in the trade over the past couple of years and she'll keep us going somehow.'

'It would be awful if Harpers closed down because of the war,' Marion said, feeling worried. 'Whatever would we all do?'

'Mrs Harper won't let that happen. Besides, the Government will make sure we all get enough to live on, because people have to live and have clothes to wear – but luxuries may be in short supply. That's where Mrs Harper's expertise at sourcing things and her charm at getting the representatives on her side come in,' Mrs Burrows assured her. 'In her way, Sally Harper is as much a hero as the men fighting out there.'

'Yes, she is,' Marion agreed. She hesitated, then, 'I wondered if I could have all day off next Monday please, Mrs Burrows. I've had a telegram to say Reggie is coming home on Friday night and he'll be home until lunchtime on Monday.'

Beth Burrows thought for a moment, then, 'Could you come in in the afternoon – after he leaves?'

'Yes, I wouldn't mind that at all – and I'd work this Friday afternoon to make up for it.'

'Then that would suit me,' Beth told her with a smile. 'My husband is home too, and I'm trying to take a few hours off here and there. I'll have to speak to Mrs Bailey, of course – but I can take Friday afternoon off and come in on Monday morning. I can put Shirley on your counter but oversee her.'

Marion smiled in delight. 'That's ever so good of you, Mrs Burrows. I really appreciate it – only it's probably his last leave before he gets posted over there...'

'Then of course you must have time off – and don't worry if you're late in,' Mrs Burrows said quickly. 'We all have to help each other in times like these, Marion.'

Marion saw a customer enter the department and head for her counter. She nodded to her supervisor and went to greet the young woman.

'How may I help you, miss?'

'I'm looking for a hat,' the young woman replied a little uncertainly. 'It is for my wedding. We're having it at the Registry Office, because my Terry is being posted overseas soon, and I'm wearing a cream and navy suit.'

'Oh, I have some lovely hats that would go with an outfit like that,' Marion said and smiled at her. 'You'll want something pretty and special for your wedding.'

'Yes please,' her customer responded eagerly. 'We should have had a white wedding this summer, but Terry has two weeks' leave and he wants us to be married before he goes.'

'Yes, I'm sure he does,' Marion said, sympathy in her voice. She knew just what the young woman was thinking, because it was in her mind too, only there was no possibility of a wedding for her before Reggie went away, because they had to think of Milly, Kathy and Dickon. Marion, as the eldest, was responsible for them until her brother, Dan, came home – and because he worked in the Merchant Navy and was in danger, she didn't know when, if ever, he would return.

A little frown touched her brow as she recalled his last visit, when her mother had died of a brutal beating at the hands of their father. Marion didn't want Pa to come home ever, but her mother's death made her responsible for the children and so she couldn't just get married to suit herself. She would have to wait until Dan returned for good, or Reggie did, and moved in to help take care of them.

'Do you think this suits me?' the young woman asked, trying on a cream straw hat with a big navy ribbon bow. 'Or is this better?' She removed the straw hat and put on a navy silk creation with a big red silk rose at the front.

Marion studied her and then gave her opinion. 'I think the navy hat with the splash of red is very pretty on you.' She looked round for inspiration. 'Or this one.' She produced a cream silk hat trimmed with a spray of pink roses and tulle. 'This one is really special and wonderful for a wedding – but it is nearly three pounds...'

'Oh, that doesn't matter. I've been saving for ages,' the young woman said and tried it on. 'Yes, that is lovely and will make it special – just what I wanted. I'd like that navy straw one as well, because that will do for everyday.'

'That is four pounds and ten shillings altogether,' Marion said, and the customer smiled.

'Thank you, I'll take them.' She paused and looked at the scarf counter. 'I should also like some cream lace gloves, do you think your colleague has any?'

'I believe so,' Marion said and beckoned to Shirley, telling her what the customer wanted. Shirley fetched two pairs to show her while Becky served another customer with silk scarves.

'Lovely.' The young woman looked delighted with the gloves

she was shown. 'It's so nice to find just what you want in one department without having to go all the way to the other end of Oxford Street. I work in an office just a few yards from here and I've been looking at your windows every day.'

'What do you think of them?' Marion asked, mentally crossing her fingers. 'We lost our window dresser at the start of the war – he's in the Army – but we're doing the best we can.'

'I loved that display of a country scene with the beehives and the slogan about us all working as hard as the bees for the war effort last week,' the young woman said. 'But one of the best ever was that magical underwater grove you had the other year – it looked just as if it was under the sea.'

'That was the lapis lazuli window,' Marion confirmed. 'It was Mrs Harper's idea and I loved that too.' She packed the hats in their boxes and Shirley brought the lace gloves in another pretty black and gold bag.

The customer paid her money, received her change and beamed at Marion. 'You make it a pleasure to shop here,' she said. 'Terry bought me a lovely necklace from that window I mentioned and I shall certainly shop here again.'

She picked up her purchases and walked out, looking pleased with herself.

Mrs Burrows came up to Marion afterwards. 'That was nicely done, Marion. The cream silk was one of our most expensive hats.'

'Yes, but it was for her wedding. She's having it at the Registry Office, because her fiancé has to leave for the Front.' Despite herself, Marion knew there was a tinge of envy in her voice, because she would have loved it if she could have married Reggie before he left to serve in the Army.

'Ah, I see,' Mrs Burrows nodded. 'Well done anyway. It's nice to see our customers happy and our girls working together.'

9

Rachel Bailey finished her tour of the ground floor, her keen gaze lighting on a cardboard box lying where it shouldn't be and a junior was immediately sent scurrying with it to the basement where it belonged. Fred Burrows was a little short-handed because of the war, but, all the same, the box should not have been left lying about. Rachel enjoyed her job as the floor walker, or supervisor, going from floor to floor keeping her eye on things. It was she who told Mr Stockbridge, the manager, if any of the staff were away ill or not doing their jobs properly, and she made certain that all the counters were presented as they should be, advising on any she considered looked untidy or not up to standard.

Satisfied that the ground floor was both busy and smart, she went up to the department she still liked to think of as her own, though Beth Burrows was in charge there now, as it was her first job at Harpers.

The department was busy as always and Beth was selling a gentleman a silver bracelet. He'd chosen one of the most expensive and also asked to see one of the more elegant of their leather bags. At the start, they'd stocked a few expensive crocodile and snakeskin bags, but Sally Harper hadn't replaced that stock recently, sticking to leather bags instead. Skin products had to come in from America or overseas somewhere and she said the ships were better employed bringing in food and other more essential goods. She was trying to purchase as much British produce as she could these days.

Letting her practised eye move around the department, Rachel thought how well everything was kept here. If every department was as tidy and well run, she would hardly be needed. However, she waited until Beth Burrows was free, and her customer had left, because she enjoyed having a few minutes to talk to her.

'You've been busy this morning?'

'Miss Kaye has sold several hats,' Mrs Burrows told her. 'They've also been busy with scarves and gloves – but that was my first sale this morning. It was a birthday present for the customer's wife and he was very generous – spent over ten pounds.'

'We could do with more customers like him,' Rachel said and smiled. 'I understand Jack is home – if you need cover for a few days, let me know and I'll arrange it with Mr Stockbridge. Mrs Stockbridge wouldn't mind helping out, I know. She's very sensible and could easily do the scarves or hats.'

'Mrs Stockbridge is very kind to stand in for us,' Beth said, speaking formally, as was the custom on the shop floor, though to her, Mrs Stockbridge would always be Minnie. 'I've exchanged Friday afternoon with Miss Kaye – but I should like to take my outstanding leave of three days next week, if that is possible.'

'We'll make sure it is,' Rachel told her. 'You need to spend some time with your husband.'

'Yes, I do,' Beth agreed. 'I think that lady is coming back for a bag she looked at earlier this morning.'

'I'll see you later.' Rachel nodded to Beth, Becky Stockbridge and Marion Kaye and went on her way. She would call in on Mr Stockbridge and ask for Beth's holiday to be scheduled and then she would go up to Mrs Harper's office on the top floor.

'Good morning, Mrs Bailey.'

She smiled at one of the young lads from Fred Burrows' department in the basement. He was carrying a load of parcels and heading for the lift. Rachel moved to open it for him and he grinned in appreciation.

'Thank you, ma'am.'

'How are you getting on, Mr Hardy?' she asked as they entered the lift together. 'I trust you enjoy your work here?' Bob Hardy seemed a good worker, keen and energetic.

'Yes, Mrs Bailey. I like Mr Burrows and the job is good – but I'll be off to join up in the summer.' He winked at her cheekily. 'It was a bit of all right Sheffield United beating Chelsea at the Old Trafford last Saturday. That's my grandad's team and them Chelsea lot think they're the bees' knees – took 'em down a peg for once.'

'So, we'll be losing you too in the summer.' She frowned. The young lads came for a few months, but as soon as they were old enough to join up, they were off, eager to fight for King and country. She wondered how many of them would come back whole and healthy to work for Harpers again.

Her thoughts turned to her husband, William. Although she'd had a letter from him a month previously, it had been three months out of date, delayed since before Christmas and she still didn't know if he was safe. April was nearly over now and she hadn't had up-to-date news of him for four months. It was so hard having no way of knowing for certain...

'I'll be back when the war's over,' Bob Hardy told her and grinned. 'I like working with old Fred, so I'll likely be asking for my job back then.'

Rachel frowned at his disrespect, because it was one of Harpers' rules that everyone was addressed by their surname and not by their Christian name. It wasn't easy for Rachel to remember when talking to Beth Burrows, who was her friend, but she stuck to the rules in working hours, and young Mr Hardy should do the same. However, it wasn't her place to reprimand him and she wouldn't report him this time as she was sure Fred Burrows had encouraged the use of his Christian name.

The lift pinged and Bob Hardy got out with a nod to her. Rachel continued to the top floor and made her way to Sally Harper's office. As she did so, Mr Stockbridge came up to her, smiling. She stopped to speak to him, asking about his wife.

'How is Minnie? I haven't seen her for a couple of weeks.'

'She is very well,' Mr Stockbridge replied, looking a bit like the cat that got the cream. Minnie had certainly made a difference to his life and Rachel found herself envying her friend. Minnie was so lucky to have her husband at home, though of course he was a little above the age needed for the forces. 'She told me to ask you for lunch this Sunday, Mrs Bailey – I do hope you can come?'

'I should like that very much, Mr Stockbridge,' Rachel said and smiled. Her weekends were often lonely now that she did not have the company of her young friends or her husband. If it were not for her work at Harpers, she would not have known what to do with herself.

'I shall tell my wife to expect you.'

Rachel smiled inwardly as she moved on. He did so love saying that phrase – my wife!

Sally Harper's secretary was busy typing, but she nodded to Rachel to go in. Rachel knocked at the door and was invited to enter. Sally was nursing her baby on her lap and looking at a sheaf of papers. She smiled as she saw who it was and held up her daughter to be seen before putting her back in her cot. Jenny gave a wail of displeasure at this but settled almost immediately.

'Rachel, what can I do for you?' Sally asked with the smile that made her so loved by most who knew her. Rachel reflected that there was so much joy in a smile and people often didn't smile enough, especially since the war.

'I just wondered if you'd heard from Mr Harper?' she said with a lift of her brows.

'No – not for more than two weeks,' Sally Harper replied and her hand twitched nervously. She put her papers down, betraying her inner agitation. 'What about you – it must be months since you heard, Rachel?'

Rachel smiled because Sally was a good friend and she'd never stuck to the rules about Christian names; she hadn't when she was a sales assistant and she didn't now she was the boss's wife. Rachel relaxed. In Sally's office she was off duty and could speak as a friend to the young woman she both admired and cared for deeply. 'I had a batch of letters four weeks back, but they were out of date; delayed in the post it said on the envelope. So, I still don't know if he's all right...'

Rachel's first marriage had ended with her husband's painful illness and subsequent death. She had thought that she would never have a chance of happiness again but then she'd met William. Their relationship hadn't gone smoothly at first but then she'd realised that she cared deeply for him and their marriage had been brief but happy.

'Yes, that's what I thought.' Sally gave her a sympathetic look. 'Have you time to take coffee with me?'

'Yes please. I was hoping you might ask – if I'm not disturbing you?'

'No, not at all,' Sally said. 'I do have loads of work to do, as we all do – but I could do with a break and we don't talk enough.'

'No, we don't,' Rachel agreed. 'Beth is happy – she has Jack home for a few days.'

Sally frowned. 'Considering what happened, he was lucky to get home, Rachel. It makes you wonder...'

'Perhaps it is best not to,' Rachel said with a little shudder. 'I sometimes lie awake at night torturing myself and it does no good at all.'

'No, of course it doesn't,' Sally agreed, 'but we can't help it, can we?'

'No.' Rachel bit her bottom lip and then straightened up, patting her upswept dark blonde hair into place. Her hair was very long now and she didn't need padding as some other ladies did to achieve the full rounded style that she knew looked both smart and elegant, though William liked it when she took her hair down and let it fall to beyond her shoulders. 'I refuse to give in to useless worry, Sally. I know that William will write when he can.'

'He has probably sent you dozens of letters and they've all been delayed or gone astray,' Sally agreed, showing her sympathy.

'Yes.' Rachel gave a wry laugh. 'It doesn't say much for our Government's organisation skills if letters can go astray so easily, does it?'

'No, but it seems to be that way. We're holding our own at the moment over there. That's what the papers say.' The British had a firm blockade on German ports; not too long ago, the Navy had scored a victory with the sinking of the battleship *Dresden* and at Hoboken in Belgium two German submarines had been sunk. However, the Germans were sinking British ships too and to the ordinary citizen it was hard to know which way the war was going.

'Can you believe a word they write?' Rachel asked in a sceptical tone. She looked up as Ruth brought a tray of coffee in. 'Thank you so much, Miss Canning.'

'You're welcome, Mrs Bailey. I'm afraid there are only plain biscuits, Mrs Harper – they didn't send any chocolate ones this time...'

Sally grimaced as her secretary departed. 'I particularly ordered chocolate and iced biscuits. Sometimes I wonder if they listen at all at that place.'

'Maybe it is the war,' Rachel offered, but Sally shook her head.

'No, I asked the manager if they still have chocolate ones and he assured me they have – it's that dizzy secretary of his.'

'I don't mind a nice plain biscuit,' Rachel said and laughed. 'Not everyone is as well organised as your staff, Sally.'

'No, that's true,' Sally murmured and looked pleased. 'Oh, these are quite nice – they taste of almond.'

'So, they do,' Rachel said and smiled. 'Thank goodness for you, Sally Harper. I'm not sure what I'd do if it were not for you, Beth and Harpers, and Maggie, of course. I'm worried about her. I hoped for a letter, but I've heard nothing since she left, have you?'

'No – but that doesn't mean she hasn't written,' Sally replied. 'She's the one out there in danger and hardship, but I sometimes think the women waiting at home in agony for news suffer most.'

'Yes, very true,' Rachel agreed, sighing. There was nothing harder than having to carry on as normal not knowing how the men one loved were managing over there. It was so unbearably lonely when one turned the key on the door at night and drew the curtains. When the Archduke of Hapsburg was assassinated, no one had thought that it would cause such a terrible conflict or that the war would drag on for so long. However, there was no use dwelling on her loneliness, so she smiled at Sally and said, 'How are you getting on with your hospital work? I can't imagine how you find the time to fit it all in.'

'I can only visit now and then,' Sally said regretfully. 'Mr Alexander has taken two of our men to help them.' She hesitated, then, 'I usually visit on a Sunday. How would you like to come with me one week, Rachel? We could talk to the men, do whatever we can – and then have lunch if you're free?'

'I've been invited to lunch with Minnie this week,' Rachel told her, 'but I'd love to come another time, Sally – and yes, I think I should like to help out. I dare say I have more time than you do.'

'We'll go together the first time and then you can visit when-ever you have the time.' Sally smiled at her. 'Please, do have more coffee, Rachel.'

'No, I should get on now.' Rachel stood to leave. 'I will come with you to the hospital, Sally. I shall enjoy doing what I can.'

* * *

Rachel finished wrapping the new blue cardigan she'd made for Hazel that evening. She would have to drop her mother-in-law a line and let her know she wouldn't be coming that weekend but would definitely see her the next. Most Sundays she asked her to lunch or went there to visit, because she'd known she would be alone – just like Rachel.

Rachel had read William's last letters fifty times, knowing that his cheerful writing hid the loneliness and unease he was feeling. William wasn't particularly enjoying his experience of Army life and she'd sensed it on his last visit home. He'd never been meant to be a soldier, which was why he'd become a Minister of Parlia-ment – but patriotism had prompted him to volunteer and now he was enduring a life he did not care for, leaving Rachel alone in the home they shared and she wasn't finding it easy after living with Maggie and her other friends for more than two years prior to her marriage.

She put the parcel for Hazel's birthday to one side and reflected that fortunately at work she was busy and fulfilled. Harpers had had a really busy period over Christmas and the early spring was just as good, and though the first three weeks of April had been a little slower, if she was any judge, this week had picked up again. The stock levels were running at a lower level than Sally Harper liked, Rachel knew that, but there was nothing they could do about it. As yet they'd managed to keep their standards up and Rachel thought her friend had done very well. Whether she would be able to continue to keep the level of stock high enough in the future was a matter of conjecture. Rachel wouldn't have changed places with her for double wages; it was just too big a problem.

She looked at the letter she'd read so many times before. There was no point in reading it again; it wouldn't bring William home or tell her where he was and if he was still alive. Her heart caught with pain as she thought about the alternatives. Could he be injured and lying in hospital – but surely someone would have let her know? No news was better than one of those dreadful telegrams so many wives were receiving to say that their husbands were dead.

'Oh, William,' Rachel sighed. 'I do wish you were here...'

She got up to make herself a cup of hot milky cocoa. Sitting here brooding wasn't going to help her. She would take her drink up to bed and read a book. No point in feeling sorry for herself. Thousands of women all over the country were doing just the same as her, waiting for news and imagining the worst.

10

Sally had just finished feeding Jenny one evening a week or so later when she heard someone at the hall door. It was opening! Only one other person had a key to the apartment. It must be Ben! She'd heard nothing from him for at least three weeks, when he'd rung to say he was fine, and she'd been sick with worry, because normally he phoned every few days.

She jumped up and went rushing through to the hall, a flood of sheer relief charging through her as she saw Ben standing there. However, her first feeling of delight was muted a little as she saw that his arm was in a sling.

He came slowly towards her.

Instead of flinging herself on him to hug him, she held back warily, afraid of causing pain. 'You're hurt,' she said, almost succeeding in keeping the tremble from her voice.

'I was lucky. It is just a flesh wound,' Ben said and smiled at her wearily. 'One of the nurses bound it up for me. She said that it will be sore for a bit but I should get my own doctor to look at it when I could.'

'Oh, Ben, my love...' Sally's voice caught in her throat as she moved closer and kissed him softly on the mouth. 'Come and sit down. I've been so worried. We've missed you terribly. Was it very awful?'

'It was a bit touch-and-go for a while,' Ben admitted and then he grinned at her, looking much like a schoolboy caught out in mischief. 'But we did it, Sally. We got the whole consignment through to the Front without losing any of it. We resupplied the whole line of field hospitals with all the supplies they're so short of – and it was great, just as we planned.' He looked hugely pleased with himself. 'No one really believed it would work; they said it was a mad plan – but we did it.'

Sally cried and tears of mingled anger and relief trickled down her cheeks. 'Damn you, Ben Harper! You promised me you would be here in London and safe...'

'Well, now I shall – at least for a while,' Ben said and looked at her contritely. 'I need a bath, a sleep, and then food, in that order – will you forgive me, Sally, if I put you last for once?'

'Idiot,' she said, blinking back the stupid tears. She shouldn't give way to tears. What did any of it matter as long as he was here, safe? 'Do you want me to ask the doctor to call?'

'I'm all right. Perhaps I'll go to his surgery tomorrow,' Ben replied with a yawn. 'Draw a bath for me will you, love? I just want to look at Jenny. I've missed seeing her and you, Sally.'

'I'll run your water,' Sally said, blinking back her tears, and left him to stand looking down at his daughter in her cot.

Her emotions were mixed, torn between relief and love, and anger that he'd put himself in danger. He was supposed to be masterminding the way supplies were delivered to the Front, not taking them out himself. And yet she knew that Ben would never hold back. If a dangerous but necessary job needed doing, Ben Harper would consider that it was his duty to go himself – and perhaps that was why she loved him so much.

'It's odd,' he said as much to himself as her as she turned to head to the bathroom. 'I thought I saw Marco at one of the field hospitals on the border. He was talking to a nurse, but he wasn't wearing uniform.' He frowned. 'I waved and called his name, but one of the doctors wanted to speak to me and when I looked again, he'd gone. He was nowhere to be found and the nurse told me she'd been speaking to a French nightclub artist. He'd come in because he'd had a slight accident.'

'You must have been mistaken then,' Sally said. 'You were probably tired and saw what you wanted to see. He's still training in Sussex.'

'Yes, but that doesn't mean...' Ben shook his head, but still looked puzzled. 'Like you said, I was tired. It was a harrowing trip and the end of a long day.'

'You've done a wonderful job, Ben, but now you need to relax and let me look after you.' She hovered at the bathroom door, wanting to linger but needing to run that bath for him. He smiled and looked down at his child.

'Just what needed doing, Sally. We carried the banners of the Red Cross, but we didn't use them. It was a case of sneaking in under cover of darkness, but we did it.' His words dismissed what he'd achieved, but that was his way.

Sighing, Sally reflected on the cruelty of war and the way it affected everyone's lives as she went into the bathroom and turned on the taps. Ben was never going to be content to sit at home while others were fighting for King and country. She would have to live with the possibility that Ben might not come back one day, just as Beth did, and so many others, all dreading the black-edged telegram. All the women who worked for Harpers had loved ones at the Front or preparing to go out there and Maggie was out there too, doing her bit – just like the nurse who had patched up Ben's wound.

Sally brushed away her tears impatiently. They were all heroes: Maggie, her fellow nurses, out there risking their lives; her husband, Jack, Mick, Marion's brothers and husband-to-be, Rachel's husband, Tim and every other man who had volunteered to fight. That included Marco, who was training with the Army on the south coast. Ben couldn't have seen him in France, because hardly any of the volunteer divisions had been sent to the Front yet, and that postcard had only just arrived, posted in Sussex.

She sighed as she swished the water round, spreading the scent from the lavender essence she'd added, and wishing that all of them could be safe at home and enjoying the lovely spring weather. She remembered the cheerful letter and gift that had come from Jenni for Ben's birthday – Ben would want to see those when he was rested. Mick had also managed to send a postcard. At least Ben was here to share the lovely weather they were having at the moment. She would invite some of their friends to dinner one evening and make the most of the time they had together.

Smiling, Sally turned off the taps and put some clean warm towels ready for Ben, but when she returned to the living room, her husband was curled up in an armchair with his daughter asleep on his lap, both of them far away in the land of nod. He'd taken his left arm from the sling to lift Jenny but was holding her securely with his right.

Sally stood looking at them both with love for a moment and then went to put the kettle on. She could run another bath when Ben woke and, in a moment or two, she would take her baby back to her cot and let her husband rest. Like so many others in this terrible time, he had certainly earned it...

* * *

'So, you got Alexander to come down then,' Ben said as they ate lunch the next day, and she told him about her trip to Newcastle and the result. After Sally had removed Jenny to her cot, Ben had woken for long enough to make his way to bed and promptly fallen asleep again. She'd made him a ham sandwich and a cup of tea when he woke for a short time later, but he'd left most of it uneaten. It was about five in the morning when he'd got up and stumbled groggily to the bathroom. Ben had spent more than an hour soaking in fresh hot water. When he finally emerged, he looked better but was still tired and returned to bed, where he was soon sleeping once more. His exhaustion brought home to her how hard it had been in a way words couldn't, though he'd told her as much as he could remember when he woke up enough to dress and talk. 'Did your grumpy surgeon do what you wanted?'

'Yes, he came down after he took me to see his patients – some children with horrific burns. It's no wonder he didn't want to come, Ben. He already has enough to do.'

'Well, he can't do it all, no one can,' Ben told her. 'So, the offer about bringing an American surgeon over still stands.'

'For the moment we're fine,' Sally said. 'I've since been contacting other doctors who are experts in the field, in England and in Wales. Mr Alexander has been brilliant. And others are going to do what they can. Two of them responded instantly. It was just a matter of organising it. The hospitals don't have time to make endless phone calls and work it all out, but most of the consultants are only too willing to help if you tell them about a deserving case.'

'No one is better at organising than you,' Ben said and demolished the cold boiled ham, egg and chips she'd prepared. He sighed with content. 'And this is food for the gods, Sally. I haven't eaten anything decent since I left.'

'It must have been awful out there…'

'No, not too bad,' he disagreed. 'Most of the time, everything worked well. We used all the little back lanes and avoided the enemy for seventy per cent of the time – and then just in the last couple of days we ran into a patrol near the German lines and our French escorts had to fight our way out of a tight corner. That's when I got the little nick in my arm.'

'Does it hurt very much?'

'It's sore,' he said ruefully, 'but I can still move it, so I was lucky. Three of the French partisans were killed in the skirmish. Fortunately, we saw the enemy patrol first and were ready.'

Sally felt chills down her spine. The thought of Ben being shot at was terrifying and she felt sick. It was worse somehow than if he'd been with the Army. 'You could have been killed...'

'Yes, I know...' he said and looked remorseful. 'I've been told not to do it again. Apparently, I'm too valuable to risk.'

'You are to me,' Sally choked, barely holding back the tears.

'The British Government seem to think the same,' Ben quipped wryly. 'My contacts back home mean more than my deeds of daring.' He made a face at her. 'I've been told that it was a good idea, but next time I have a similar brainwave, a regular Army man who knows how to fight will go in my place.'

Sally's eyes were wet with tears, but she blinked them back. She looked at him consideringly. 'Do you mind very much?'

'Yes – and no,' Ben admitted. 'It was something I felt I had to do at the time, but I felt a bit of a fool when, instead of praise, I got a dressing-down from my superior officer. He says he has plenty of men who can shoot better than me and he needs my influence and my expertise.'

'Will you hate me if I say I'm glad?' Sally said, smiling through her tears.

'Never, my love. When I was hit, I realised what might have happened and I promise I won't go off on any more mad adventures. I've been ordered to stick to what they hired me for.' Ben looked rueful and Sally realised that he'd been made to feel it was a reckless venture rather than a brave act.

Sally felt a surge of relief. 'I think what you did was rather wonderful and very daring and brave.' She looked at him with love and approval. 'I don't want you to do it again, but what you did was pretty marvellous.'

'Thank you, darling. You've made me feel so much better – as you always do,' Ben said and laughed, looking at her with mischief in his eyes. 'My superior officer made me feel like a naughty schoolboy, but it was a bit of a mad idea and I wanted to see if it worked, before I sent others in.'

Sally nodded and understood that he'd wanted to show his courage and do something worthwhile, but he'd been raked over the coals for going on the wild venture himself instead of sending a more experienced man.

'Well, I'm glad,' she said. 'I don't mind how often you have to work late hours, Ben – but don't do that to me again unless you're forced.'

'I won't,' he said, but something in his eyes told her that if the chance arose, he would take it. How could she complain when it was a part of what made him the man she adored? She just had to be thankful he'd come back safe and hope that he wasn't asked to do something dangerous in the future.

'I shan't go in this morning.' She smiled and bent to kiss his cheek as she removed his plate. 'I'll show you Marco's card after you've finished. I don't think it could have been him you saw, Ben...'

'I'm pretty sure it was,' Ben replied, frowning. 'I've thought about it and I'm sure it was him – or his double. What's more, he didn't want me to see him – now why was that, do you think?'

'He couldn't have been avoiding you, Ben. Marco is your friend...'

'Yes, I know.' Ben nodded and looked thoughtful. 'I'd trust him with my life, so that means...' He smiled to himself and nodded, as if a light had clicked on in his head and he understood something. 'Yes, I'm pretty sure I'm right – but perhaps I didn't see Marco at all, Sally. Just someone who looked like him.'

Sally stared at him. She knew that look – and now he wasn't telling her what he really thought.

11

The small town, or overlarge village, depending on your point of view, was no more than a few kilometres from the border with Belgium and the boom of the guns could be heard from early in the morning until they ceased at night. Even then, the sharp crack of a rifle could sometimes be heard as one side or the other took a potshot in the dark or put a dying man caught on the barbed wire between the trenches out of his misery. On his arrival, Marco had been surprised that a nightclub should exist in what he would have thought to be a sleepy place. However, the club served the men of the area with rough red wines and plain food, and had thrived in the months since the village had been overrun by the Germans. Before that it had probably been not much more than a large inn that put on a little music now and then – but it now had a stage and was patronised by the enemy, and the owner, Paul Mallon, was not one to ignore a gift horse. He'd brought in girls who sang and danced a bit – and was glad to get Marco, with his mediocre musical talents, to entertain the customers.

When the Germans had been pushed back to the border, Paul Mallon had kept his little club going and he was rewarded by the return of the enemy officers whose base camp was just the other side of the border. They came across whenever they pleased, night or day, because the British and French troops were bogged down in their trenches and couldn't patrol this far up, though it was strictly no man's land, controlled by neither side.

As Paul had told Marco that first night, 'If the British or French troops push the enemy back again, I shall serve them.' He'd shrugged his shoulders. 'It matters little to me – German money is as good as French.' A man with such an attitude was hardly to be trusted and Marco was on his guard around his employer. His job had come through Paul's brother-in-law and, his main contact, Pierre, had warned him to be careful of him.

'He is married to my sister, Giselle, but I don't trust him. Be sure not to leave anything lying around, Marco; he may search your room when you're out...'

As yet, Marco had done and seen nothing of any interest to the British. Pierre had asked him to pass a message on to one of his contacts, but he'd had nothing important to report since then.

The smoke-filled club seemed hot and stuffy that evening as he slipped out of the side door into the small area at the back of the club. The night was pitch black as Marco left the heat and noise of the Fallen Angel, keeping to the shadows and avoiding the yellow light of the street lamp. Fortunately for his purpose, there was only one that worked in this dingy back courtyard, which made it a perfect breeding ground for crime: robberies, sexual assault on any girl unwise enough to venture out of the smoky atmosphere of the club alone and brutal beatings had all happened here. It was a seedy area and one that Marco would normally have avoided like the plague, but for a spy it couldn't have been better.

He waited in the shadows until he heard the voices and knew that the men he'd seen leaving this way earlier, had finished their clandestine coupling in the dark, indulging their selfish vices against a backdrop of the bloody battles being fought just a short distance away. They were making their way back to the club and the heady atmosphere of decadence, wine and song.

'You are a sweet boy,' a deep guttural voice spoke first in German. 'I like you and so I shall overlook your little slip.'

'Johannes,' the second voice was that of a much younger man, a German soldier Marco had seen earlier in the club. 'I'm sorry I flirted with Hans…'

'I am not speaking of your foolish indiscretions with others,' the first voice said, harshly now. 'You are not my love, only a boy I use – understand that and you know your place. You were telling that waitress where you were going to be sent next week – and that could give valuable information to the enemy, don't you realise that I could have you shot?'

'She is only an ignorant peasant girl.' The young man's voice was scornful. 'What harm can she do?'

'If she knows your company is being moved up to Ypres on Tuesday, it gives the enemy a chance to ambush you and it tells them that we are reinforcing. Are you so stupid that you understand nothing?'

There was the sound of a sharp slap and a cry of pain from the younger man. 'Why did you do that?'

'To sharpen your wits, Shultz. I had you promoted to lieutenant. I could have you sent back to the ranks with a click of my fingers – and worse. This is my last warning, for God's sake.'

The last words were spoken in disgust and then the back door of the club opened, revealing a sliver of red light and the figure of the officer disappeared through it. Marco heard the sound of a sob and then retching, as if the younger man were being sick.

'Oh, God, oh God.' The voice was a cry of pain. 'How I hate him. I wish I could gut him like the pig he is…'

Knowing the officer by sight only, Marco understood the younger man's revulsion. He was a bully, uncouth in his habits at the table, his uniform stained by wine that he spilled when drunk. Kurt Shultz was young and good-looking and it was clear he was being blackmailed into a liaison he did not care for.

Hidden in the shadows, Marco smiled. He'd picked up quite a few snippets from careless officers in the club as they drank, flirted with half-naked girls before taking them upstairs or disappeared into the darkness of the walled yard at the back with the man of their choice. The German officers who came here were all taking a chance, breaking the rules because they liked the relaxed atmosphere of the Fallen Angel, slipping through the lines in the dark of night. They came looking for a place to hide their depravity and indulge their vices.

Marco had been approached many times by high-ranking officers, any one of whom could have supplied him with the information he needed to pass on to his French and British counterparts. He'd refused them with a shrug or a smile, even though he might have found some attractive in a previous life; he'd refused because none of them were the sort who would let important information slip. Now, he'd found someone who might supply him with the kind of information he needed.

He moved forward, out of the shadows, lighting a cigarette. The young lieutenant turned his head to look at him. Marco took out his silver cigarette case and offered him a cigarette.

Shultz hesitated a moment and then moved towards him, raising his head. 'Marco, is that you?'

'Yes,' Marco answered, moving closer.

'How long have you been out here?'

'I just came out an instant ago – from the side entrance,' Marco said. 'I wanted to smoke alone for a moment or two. It's good to be quiet sometimes, to have some peace, isn't it?'

'I wish I could be at peace,' Shultz replied. 'The bastard won't leave me alone – I hate him!' The lieutenant knew he must have overheard and Marco realised it was his opportunity.

'His kind always is,' he said and smiled, lighting a cigarette for the younger man. 'You should keep away from him – or just say no.'

'I've tried. He forces me – blackmails me – you don't know what kind of a pig he is. If I refused, he'd probably have me knifed in the back or sent on a mission that I would never return from.'

Clearly, Kurt was afraid of the officer.

'I've met men like him,' Marco said, his gaze steady. 'Can't you find friends to protect you?'

Shultz shrugged his shoulders. He was tall and slim, handsome and very young, his face soft and vulnerable in the faint light of the street lamp. Marco felt a pang of regret that he had to use him but knew that he would never get a better chance.

'I can't protect you from him – he's a German officer and I'm just a singer and half French at that – he would still bully you, but I could warn you to leave when I see him come in. I could be your friend...'

Shultz looked at him uncertainly. 'You are like me, Marco. I knew it, but the others said you weren't – you've refused all offers. Is it because we're Germans?'

'No, I didn't like any of them,' Marco said. 'I choose those I wish to love.' He smiled at the young man. 'As I said, I could be your friend – show you where to hide when that pig comes in another night. I'd let you use my room...'

'Does that mean you like me, Marco?' Shultz's voice had dropped lower and was husky with passion. He was clearly recovering from his feelings of fear and revulsion at being forced to pander to a man he hated.

'Yes, I like you,' Marco said and realised as he spoke that he did. There was something about the young German that reminded him of Julien and the memory caught at his heart.

For a moment, he was tempted to turn away, find another fool to milk for information, but his duty to his country kept him standing there smiling in a way he knew Shultz found attractive. Marco could always find men eager to be his lover, but he seldom took up the offers that came his way. He'd discovered that he preferred a deeper love, rather than mere lust, as a young man and his affairs had been few; he had loved only once. The pain of Julien's death still struck hard at times. He might have loved this man in other circumstances and so he would give him a chance to walk away.

'We can be friends or...'

Shultz moved in closer. He smiled and blew a gentle puff of smoke towards Marco. 'What if I choose to be more?'

'Then it is your choice,' Marco said and didn't move as Kurt's head bent towards him and his lips caressed his.

'Yes, we shall be close friends,' Shultz said, and then drew back. He was smiling now, as if he'd found an inner strength. 'But not tonight, not after that pig – when I have washed off his filth, I will return. Perhaps tomorrow...'

'Good,' Marco said and smiled. 'I shall look forward to it.'

As Shultz headed back inside, Marco stood outside in the dark, smoking, feeling the guilt seep into his soul. Shultz didn't deserve to be used the way Marco was planning to use him, but he'd sworn to get as much information from the enemy as he could and this was the surest way. Shultz was vulnerable, he would respond to love and kindness and Marco would give him that – but he would also betray his secrets to save the lives of others. It was the reason he was here, to do what little he could to aid the Allies and shorten the war. Perhaps it was also to find himself, to find a reason to feel something other than regret again.

12

Maggie came off duty just as it was getting light. She'd been working all night and she was bone-weary; her back and shoulders felt as if she carried a four-stone weight and all she wanted was to collapse onto her bed in a heap and sleep for a week.

She headed towards the line of wooden shacks that served the nurses as home. Inside, they were basic: a narrow camp bed and a metal locker for each girl – four of them in this hut; she'd been told they were extremely lucky to have so much. The first volunteers had slept in tents and straw mattresses on the floor for weeks until someone had managed to ship out the beds and a few soldiers had thrown up the rough wooden huts for the Angels, as they called the nurses that looked after them.

The washing facilities were just as Maggie had been warned. Both the nurses and the soldiers had to use old French wine vats and once filled they were used over and over again until the water was filthy and cold, when it was painstakingly emptied out by a team of soldiers. The toilets were just a line of buckets, under a long wooden seat, and these also were emptied by the soldiers;

the unlucky men were most often those on a charge for some minor disobedience. The smell was vile and it was a small wonder that the girls complained about catching fleas; the men were covered in fleas and lice when they came in from the trenches and it was impossible not to pick them up, whatever they did to keep clean.

Maggie thought she hated that more than anything else. Tending the critically wounded was shocking and it often brought the girls close to tears as they saw the horrendous injuries, but they got used to it. Men with legs, arms and even half of their faces blown away by the terrible explosions that happened all the time were common sights. Burns and bullet wounds were almost acceptable after a while, but it was the sight of brains hanging out of a man's head, or a young lad trying vainly to hold his guts in as the blood poured out of his stomach and his life drained away that made them want to vomit.

After a while, they learned to endure even those awful sights and to do what they could to comfort the dying. There was often nothing much they could do but hold a man's hand as his eyes clouded and the colour drained from his face, or sit by his bed and listen as he talked of home and loved ones. Perhaps a sip of water that like as not he couldn't swallow or a puff of cigarette smoke. Strong drugs that would have taken away the pain were scarce and used mostly for those men that had a chance to be patched up and sent home. It was heartbreaking, courage-sapping work, and it was no wonder that only the strongest of them survived longer than a few weeks. Already ten of the girls that had travelled out with Maggie and Sadie had been sent home after they couldn't cope and cried so much that Matron told them to pack their bags and go.

'Our men deserve better than your doleful faces,' she'd told them severely. 'If you cannot smile and control your feelings, go home and bind up splintered fingers, which is all you're fit for.'

Sadie was just dressing when Maggie walked into the hut. Thankfully, it was no longer as cold as it had been when they first got out here, but early in the morning it could be chilly and Sadie was pulling on an extra pair of long drawers.

'You'll be hot once you get on the wards,' Maggie said. 'We had twenty new men brought in last night and it's packed in the ward, the atmosphere is like a hothouse.'

'I'll risk it.' Sadie grimaced as she pulled on her thick stockings. 'I hate these things, but they keep your legs warm and I'm cold.' There was no heating in the huts and the girls piled blankets and coats on their beds at night to keep warm.

'You're not going down with a chill?' Maggie looked at her in alarm. Sadie hated having to use the wine vats for washing and like some of the other nurses she'd discovered a small stream and went there to wash in its cold water. The soldiers had told them about it first and shown them a secluded spot, which by mutual agreement the men left to those nurses that wanted to use it. 'I told you it was too cold to bathe in the stream yet.'

'Nah, I'm tough.' Sadie made the boast but coughed and Maggie frowned at her. Most of the nurses had coughs or colds and those sensible enough asked for a day off and went into the village of Saint Angelus, which was behind the Allies and about twenty-five kilometres away from the German lines. 'I just ache all over.'

'Try and get some sleep and I'll be back later,' Maggie said to soothe her.

She left Sadie snuggled down in bed, still moaning and set out for the hospital tents that served as wards for so many injured men, her thoughts busy. Sadie ought to go to the village to recuperate, where she could be sure of getting help. The village women were welcoming and opened their homes to the nurses, giving them warm baths in clean water in front of the kitchen fire and a bowl of hot stew or whatever food they had, and most wouldn't accept a penny for their kindness but there were other ways to show their thanks, with gifts from the parcels the nurses received from home.

Maggie had received as many food parcels as any of the nurses and she saved some of her chocolate to take to Madame Marie Heron, at her little farm on the village edge, where she stayed on her day off. Madame Heron was also a dressmaker and she loved Belgian chocolate but it was scarce and so Maggie took her a bar from her little hoard when she visited. Of course, it was English rather than Belgian chocolate, but Marie thought it delicious, especially the milk variety.

'You should keep it for yourself, ma petite,' she'd told Maggie, but when Maggie insisted, she'd broken it in half and they'd shared it. 'This is very good – your family send from home, yes?'

'Yes, it's Fry's milk chocolate,' Maggie had said and smiled. 'My friends send me all sorts, but this is nice because it has a sort of biscuit inside.'

'We used to have chocolates from Belgium,' Marie had replied, 'for special treats – birthdays and Christmas, you know. It was so delicious when Papa brought home the bonbons...' She'd sighed and looked sad. Her father had been killed in the first few days of the war, when a German plane had dropped a bomb on the barn he was working in and he'd died instantly. Her husband was fighting with the patriots, so Marie, her ten-year-old son, her twelve-year-old daughter and her fifty-six-year-old mother kept the farm running; she had various cousins and nieces who all visited and helped out when they were harvesting the grapes.

Maman, as everyone called her, cooked the most delicious stews, sometimes fish with mussels, shrimps and other river fish that were strange to Maggie but tasted good when served with vegetables and Maman's delicious sauces; sometimes they had meat, usually pork if they killed a pig, and very occasionally beef or poultry.

The French country people tended to cook many different things, using ingredients Maggie didn't know or recognise, but she ate them, because she was hungry and their food tasted better than what she was given at the nursing station. Her friends made her welcome and she enjoyed the time she was able to spend with them, talking, sharing their stories and telling her own of home. Marie marvelled at all the things Harpers sold and was fascinated by Maggie's description of hobble skirts, which she'd never seen, because the fashion had never reached her village.

Marie had never been far from her village. She dreamed of going to Paris one day and shopping in real dress shops, buying a dress straight off the rails. Her own dresses were black, with white lace collars for Sunday. Maman made the lace and she sold some to her neighbours, earning a little extra income by her industry. When Maggie admired some of her work, she was presented with a large piece, which could be made into a wedding veil or a Christening robe for her first child. She offered payment, but Maman shook her head and Marie advised her not to press it.

'Maman likes you very much or she would not give you such a gift,' Marie had explained. 'The veil was intended for my younger sister, Yvonne, but she died when she was sixteen and never used it...'

Maggie had felt moved to tears by the story and humbled that she had been given such a present. She felt she'd done nothing to deserve it and couldn't think what she could do or give the generous lady to repay her for her gift – until the parcel came from Sally Harper. Sally had sent her a big box of Belgian chocolates and a wonderful sea-green silk scarf.

I'm sending these for your birthday,

Sally had written on a pretty card.

I know it isn't your birthday yet, but there's no way of being sure you'll get them on time so I thought I'd send early. We think of you all the time, Maggie love, and hope you're well – do send a postcard soon if you can...

Maggie smiled wryly. That meant Sally hadn't received the last three postcards she'd sent. The post was so haphazard, but it couldn't be helped. She would send a thank you for these and hope it got there this time.

The chocolates she would give to Maman next time she visited the farm and although the scarf was beautiful, Maggie decided she would give it to Marie for her birthday, because it was coming up very soon. Marie had never had anything as pretty in her life and Maggie had lots of nice things. She wouldn't tell Sally what she had done, though she was certain that her friend would approve if she did. However, if she'd mentioned it, Sally would be certain to send more gifts.

Maggie wrote her postcard that evening, using the code they'd agreed.

Thank you for the lovely gifts, much appreciated. Things are great here, as usual. Thinking of you and looking forward to a summer holiday at the sea when I'm home. Love, your Maggie. xx

Sally would know that meant the conditions were as awful as they'd expected and that she wasn't near the coast but in the French countryside. She'd told Sally half-jokingly that she would write the reverse of the truth on her card and she thought it would work but had no way of knowing, because most of her cards never arrived where they should. Although she'd had a gift from Marion Kaye, some mint humbugs, a bar of perfumed soap, and a packet of cigarettes and a note that said she hoped Maggie was well and she'd had her card. The cigarettes were for the men. Maggie didn't smoke and Marion knew it, but she also knew the nurses kept a packet in their apron pockets to give dying men a puff in their last moments as comfort. The cigarettes showed Maggie that at least the card she'd sent Marion had arrived safely.

She'd sent Marion a thank you straight away but hadn't heard since. It was the way things happened out here. You got a bundle of mail, parcels and letters from home and then nothing for weeks. Perhaps that was why she'd had nothing from Tim. He'd promised to write and it was odd that he hadn't sent her anything for her birthday.

Maggie felt a strange sensation inside. Where was Tim? He'd promised he would find her and visit as soon as he could, but apart from one brief card, she'd heard nothing in ages. She knew that if he was as busy as they were, he didn't get much time, but that didn't stop her worrying. She knew he was flying dangerous missions and sometimes she woke in a cold sweat, worrying about where he was and what he was doing.

* * *

Maggie woke refreshed from several hours' sleep when Sadie entered the hut and flopped down on her bed with a grunt. Startled, Maggie looked at the little silver watch pinned to her nightgown; she wore it in bed at night so that it didn't get lost, and on her uniform during the day. A lot of the nurses lost things and no one knew who was doing the pilfering, so Maggie made sure she never left her watch lying around.

'Are you all right?' she asked as a muffled groan came from Sadie's bed. She got out and went over to her friend, who was lying with her eyes closed and moaning. Maggie felt her forehead. 'You're hot,' she remarked, but got no answer.

'Sister... sent me back...' Sadie moaned and buried her head in the pillows. 'I ache all over...'

Sadie clearly had a nasty chill. Maggie pulled a warm blanket over her and went off to get them both mugs of hot tea. She had time before her next duty started and she would feed Sadie toast and butter with marmalade and hot tea, and an aspirin. Her friend needed a little nursing and the doctors were far too busy to come out to nurses who had taken a chill, so it was up to Maggie to look after her.

Sadie was unappreciative of her efforts and tried to push her away, but Maggie managed to get some medicine into her and three hot drinks before she was due on duty. The canteen manager had come up with a stone flask of hot cocoa for Sadie after Maggie fetched the first two hot drinks and she left it by the bed with instructions to drink as much as she could.

Sadie mumbled something rude, but when Maggie returned to their hut after her own duty, Sadie was sitting up in bed looking better.

'Thanks for the cocoa,' she said sheepishly. 'I may have been a bit rude earlier?'

'You were, but it doesn't matter,' Maggie said. 'Why don't you go and stay with Marie and Maman for a couple of days? Sister told me you're banned from duty for at least two days – she doesn't want you infecting the rest of us.'

'Thanks so much,' Sadie muttered and rubbed at a nose that looked increasingly red. 'It's nice to be wanted...'

'If we're all ill, who will look after the men?' Maggie said and grinned at her. 'You can take Maman those chocolates – and you're not to eat one, even if she opens them and offers them to you.' Sadie had been eyeing them lustfully ever since they'd arrived.

'You're mean,' Sadie grumbled, then turned over in bed and went back to sleep.

However, in the morning when Maggie woke, there was a note on Sadie's bed to say she'd gone and the chocolates had gone with her. Maggie smiled, knowing that her friend wouldn't be able to resist if Maman offered one of the delicious morsels, but it didn't matter. Sadie needed a rest and she needed to be fussed over. She wouldn't have given in if Maggie hadn't pushed her and Sister Mayhew hadn't banned her from working, but she would come back refreshed and all the better for her little break.

* * *

Sadie came back on the following Monday and Maggie saw at once that she could hardly contain her excitement. Sadie's cold had gone and her eyes were bright, her hair shining clean after the bath she'd had in front of Marie's kitchen fire.

'So, what put the sparkle in your eyes?' Maggie said, and Sadie laughed.

'You know me too well,' Sadie replied and gave a naughty giggle. 'I've met someone, Maggie – Pierre is with Marie's husband working for the French partisans. They came on a flying visit to the farm and, well, I've fallen in love...'

'Sadie! You can't have,' Maggie said, looking at her in disbelief. 'You were only there three days.'

'One look was enough,' Sadie said and giggled. 'His eyes are like melting chocolate – and by the way I didn't eat any of those you sent Maman. She offered me one, but I gave it to Pierre. He hadn't tasted any for more than a year and he said it was wonderful.'

'Then it was well given,' Maggie replied. She eyed Sadie in amusement. Her friend must have really taken to the young Frenchman to have given him her chocolate – but love? Surely that came slowly, little by little? 'So, you really like him then?' she said, and Sadie smiled dreamily.

'He's gorgeous, fantastic – he makes my heart race and my knees go weak...'

'That sounds promising,' Maggie joked. 'When will you see him again?'

The smile died from Sadie's eyes and she sighed. 'Who knows? He's with the partisans, so it might be months before I see him again – or never...'

'Did he say anything – did he say he liked you?' Maggie asked.

Sadie nodded and smiled. 'He said he'd never met anyone like me and that he would never forget me. Only he can't promise to come back because...' Sadie shook her head sadly. 'I know why, Maggie. It's this bloody war.'

Maggie looked at her and then went to sit next to her and take her hand. 'I know, love. Now you know how I feel wondering where Tim is all this time. He promised he would try and visit me, but he hasn't and that makes me wonder where he is and what he's doing...' Her eyes felt moist as she felt her desire to cry.

Sadie nodded and then hugged her. 'They're both strong, brave men,' she said. 'We just have to believe they will come back to us, Maggie.'

'Yes, I know,' Maggie said and sighed. 'I'm tired out, so I'm going to get some sleep.'

'Maman said thank you for the chocolates and she hopes you will visit very soon.'

'Yes, I shall,' Maggie replied, yawned and turned over.

She dreamed as she slept and as she dreamed, she saw Tim's face and he was smiling at her.

'I'll see you soon, love,' he said. 'Remember I love you – I've always loved you and I always shall...'

13

Beth was with Fred when the telegram was delivered. They were just sitting down to their tea on the Saturday afternoon when the doorbell rang and Fred went to answer it. He came back with the small buff-coloured envelope in his hand and his face had gone as white as a sheet.

'Oh, Fred!' Beth's hand went to her heart. A telegram could only be bad news – which of his sons was it? She could hardly breathe as he opened it, stared at it in silence for a moment and then looked at her.

'It's Tim, Beth, not Jack.' He sat down abruptly on the nearest chair and she ran to him kneeling by his side, taking his hand in her own. 'My Tim's plane has gone missing over the sea...'

'No...' Beth held on to his hand tightly, her own sense of relief tempered by the grief of Tim's death. Her hand was shaking almost as much as his and the tears were running down her cheeks. She couldn't stop them. 'Oh, Fred, maybe they'll pick him up...' Her heart ached for him. He'd thought Jack was lost when the *Titanic* went down, but miraculously Jack had been saved and had saved others, and been lauded as a hero by his employers and the people he'd rescued. Perhaps another miracle could happen for Tim. 'There are a lot of ships out there – if he went in the sea, he may be safe on a ship...'

'It happened three days ago and nothing has been heard since.' Fred's expression was bleak. 'He's gone, Beth. No one could live for three days in that sea; it's too cold...'

Beth clung on to his hand. She could see the grief in his face, though he was trying to control it rather than upset her, and of course she was upset, because she was fond of her brother-in-law – and there was Maggie. If Tim was lost, Maggie would be devastated.

Beth swallowed a sob. How were they going to tell Maggie that the man she loved might be dead? It would be too cruel to just send her a letter.

'What will that poor lass do?' Fred was echoing what was in Beth's thoughts. 'She's lost enough in her life – first her father and then her mother and that other chap let her down.'

Beth nodded. 'Maggie had thought she loved Ralf, but she told me the last time she was home that she'd never loved him the way she does Tim. He is very important to her – just as he is to all of us.' Beth swiped at the tears that had started to trickle down her cheeks. 'Oh, Dad, what are we going to do? We can't write to Maggie and tell her Tim is lost – not until we're certain it is hopeless.'

'No, we mustn't do that,' Fred agreed and she saw the tears standing in his eyes, tears he was holding back in his concern for her and Maggie. 'The poor lass is doing her bit for our men out there and suffering terrible hardship. It will kill her to know Tim's missing – so we'll keep it to ourselves until we're certain. The telegram says he's missing. We'll wait until we have confirmation of...' His voice broke and he couldn't continue as his head bowed and he covered his face with his hands, shoulders shaking with grief.

Beth hovered for a moment, unsure of how to comfort him, but then she put her arms around him, holding him as he wept out his pain.

'He's my little lad, my baby...' Fred mumbled into her shoulder. 'It's not right, Beth – I should be the one to die first, not my son...'

'It's not your fault,' Beth murmured and stroked his arm. 'It's this awful war, Dad.' She bent and kissed his hair, which was thinning at the temples. 'Don't give up hope yet. It is still possible he might have been picked up...' It was a forlorn hope, she knew – a man alone in that vast sea, at the mercy of the bitter cold and strong currents. Tim would have needed to be picked up fairly quickly to have a chance of survival and the likelihood was that he would have died in the wreckage of his plane.

Fred eased himself back from her, forcing a tight smile. 'I'm sorry, Beth. I shouldn't have given way like that – it's my duty to be strong for us all.'

'No one can be strong all the time,' she said and smiled at him lovingly. 'You love him – we all love Tim. No one could help it. I'm going to go on hoping and praying for him, Dad. I shan't give up until they tell us for sure.'

Fred nodded his head and wiped his face on his shirtsleeve. 'Jack will be home again in a few days. He'll know more – have more idea how we can find out what Tim's chances are...'

'I'll ask Sally Harper to help us,' Beth said, making up her mind. 'Ben and Sally know a lot of important people – and they will help us get more details of what happened.'

'Yes, you do that,' Fred replied. 'Why don't you go and see them this evening – and I'll go and visit some of my friends down the pub?'

Beth hesitated, but she sensed that he was trying to put a brave face on and carry on as normal, and perhaps that was the best thing to do, because sitting around the house crying wouldn't do anyone any good.

* * *

Sally was just ironing some of Jenny's things when the doorbell rang. She went to answer it and her smile of pleasure when she saw Beth turned to concern as she realised her friend had been crying. Her eyes were puffy and she looked so upset that Sally's heart caught with fear.

'Is it Jack?'

Beth shook her head, gulping back the tears as she said, 'Tim's plane went down over the sea three days ago. Nothing has been heard since...'

'Oh, Beth – poor Fred and Maggie!' Sally felt upset as she understood what Beth and their friend would be going through. 'Maggie doesn't know, though, does she?'

Beth shook her head. 'They aren't married so the telegram came to Fred.' Beth hesitated, then, 'We've decided not to write and tell her – at least until we know for sure.'

'I'm not sure you should then,' Sally said. 'She has been out there nearly two months, which means she still has more than four months before she gets leave. It's an awful way to tell her – in a letter. We really need to tell her face to face.'

'Yes, of course that would be better,' Beth agreed, 'but how can we? We can't go out there to tell her...' She saw the thoughtful look in Sally's eyes. 'You wouldn't even think of it?'

'I'm not sure if it could be arranged,' Sally said slowly. 'I don't see why not, though. I mean, Ben was telling me about a woman who arranged a private ambulance and went out to the field hospital to fetch her badly wounded husband home. She knew his commanding officer and he'd told her Captain Luke Jefferies was lying there close to death and that medicines were short, so she hired the ambulance, took a load of medicine with her and a private nurse and doctor and went out to fetch him. If she could do that – someone could visit Maggie and tell her...' She shook her head. 'No, I don't mean me.'

'I should hope not!' Beth cried. 'Ben would never let you, it would be far too dangerous. You could be shot at or killed – and it would be so difficult to get a pass to get there.'

'I don't see why someone couldn't do it,' Sally replied, and Beth could see her mind working, piecing together the things she'd need to do to achieve her aim. 'I'll ask Ben if he knows anyone heading out there.'

'Yes, he might be able to arrange it,' Beth said. 'Once, we know for sure...'

'No, we shan't do it until we're sure that Tim is lost. He might be on a ship, Beth, perhaps a foreign vessel that hasn't let anyone know yet...'

'Yes.' Beth sniffed and wiped her eyes. 'That's what I tried to tell Fred, but he's convinced Tim is gone, says he feels it inside.'

'He may be right,' Sally said sombrely. 'We can only pray, Beth.'

'I wondered if you could find out a bit more for us,' Beth said. 'The telegram from the War Office is so basic – and it would be better to know the details...'

'Ben knows a lot of people,' Sally confirmed. 'I'll talk to him when he comes back from his meeting and ask him to find out what he can for you.'

'Yes, I hoped you would,' Beth said and blew her nose hard. 'I didn't know what to say to comfort Fred – what can I tell him?'

'Nothing, just be there when he needs you,' Sally replied.

'Words don't help much, but a loving hug and a cup of tea is a comfort – which makes me think it's time I put the kettle on. Would you rather have coffee, tea or cocoa?'

'I think a hot cocoa would be just the ticket,' Beth answered, smiling now. 'You're right, Sally. We shall all be devastated if Tim is gone forever, but we have to comfort each other...'

Sally hugged her around the waist and smiled. 'You've always got me,' she said, 'and we'll be there for Maggie – we're all she's got, Beth, and I think she will need us more this time than ever before.'

14

Jack was below in the engine room when the order came down to slow engines. He looked at his second mate and frowned because they were nearing the shores of France. They'd made good time from Gibraltar and were carrying goods for home consumption as well as supplies for the troops, which they intended to drop off at Calais. It meant going in close to the French coastline and they often had to run the gauntlet of German fire, both from their frigates and the little fighter planes that buzzed them from the air, firing at anything that moved and dropping incendiary devices. Their weapons were more of a nuisance than a hazard; it was the surface fire or even worse the U-boats that sneaked up undetected and took a ship out from below.

'What do you reckon is going on up there?' Jack asked. They were not close enough into port yet for them to be stopping to unload cargo – so what could they be slowing down for?

'No idea,' his mate said. 'Why don't you fetch us a mug of tea and take a look?'

'You can manage here for the moment?' Jack asked. It wasn't truly his job to look after engines, but Jock, the first engineer, had gone down with a bug of some kind on the way back from Spain and the Bosun had asked for volunteers to help Malcolm until the first engineer was on his feet again. Jack had worked in all parts of the ship since joining the Merchant Navy and he quickly offered his services. He'd been a steward on board the luxury liners he'd worked in before he took over a hotel, but there wasn't much call for that kind of work on board a working ship, so Jack went wherever he was called and was happy enough scrubbing decks or cleaning engine parts or simply doing lookout duties.

It wasn't unusual for his shipmates to ask him to make a brew. It was well known that Jack knew his way round the galley and he gave the cook a hand sometimes, helping to feed and serve the men. 'Jack of all trades, that's me,' he often said and grinned at the men he felt were friends. On board ship you became close to people and they were either your friends or your enemies. Fortunately, the *Maid of Portsmouth* was a friendly ship and Jack hadn't made any enemies. Everyone got on well and took a share of the work, no matter what it entailed. Jack was popular on board and he often made a bacon sandwich and a brew to take up to the night watch if he had nothing better to do. For Jack, making tea and feeding someone who was cold and hungry was better than sitting staring up at the bunk above him and wondering what Beth was doing at home.

Some of the men drove themselves half mad wondering if their wives were seeing other men while they were away. Jack never considered it. He knew his Beth and was well aware that her only concern was that she worried for him.

He smiled as he made his way to the galley and asked Cookie if there was any tea going. The huge pot was filled with hot strong tea and he was told to help himself. He filled the mugs and put in milk and sugar, stirring it well.

Glancing out of the window, he saw that men were hanging over the rails.

'What do you reckon is goin' on, Cookie?'

Bob Saunders, known as Cookie to his shipmates, pulled a face. 'The lookout spotted some wreckage from a plane in the water. He thought there was a body still caught on a bit of it and they were going to try and haul it in.'

Jack nodded; his face grim. It happened often enough in these waters. The pilots in those flimsy planes went down regularly and ships seeing wreckage always tried to take on board anything that could identify the plane and, in rare cases, pluck someone alive from the sea.

'Not much chance he'll be alive after last night's storm,' Jack said and frowned. He had an icy feeling at his nape and something made him take the tea on deck instead of heading back to Malcolm in the engine room.

As he moved nearer to the men who were hauling something on board, Jack's inner feeling of foreboding increased. He knew it was a chance in a million, but he couldn't shake the feeling that the man being pulled from the wreckage of his plane was his brother, Tim. No, that was daft, it couldn't be and yet he had this tingling at his nape.

'That tea for me?' one of the midshipmen said and took a mug from him. Jack hardly noticed as someone else took the other mug.

'Poor bugger never stood a chance...' one of the others said. 'At least we can give him a decent burial.'

'Has he got any papers on him?' another asked.

Jack walked as if in a dream to where someone had laid the body of the young man on the deck and covered it with a blanket. The body had its jacket on still, but most of its clothing had been pulled off by the sea; it happened to bodies that were in the sea for some hours, if they managed to be kept afloat by being tangled in the wreckage.

His heart racing, Jack knelt down on the deck and pulled back the blanket someone had put over the dead man for decency. The shock of seeing what he'd feared was so great that he gasped and started shaking. It couldn't be! No, it was impossible – not his little brother. He'd known Tim could be shot down, of course, but he was a lucky little blighter and Jack had always thought he bore a charmed life, but even with the changes death and the sea had made, Jack knew his brother.

The tears were running down his cheeks as one of his mates put a blanket around his shoulders and gently eased him to his feet.

'What's wrong wiv Jack then? It ain't the first time we've fished a dead 'un from the sea.'

'His brother's in the Royal Flying Corps – I reckon it must be him,' another voice said.

'His name is Tim.' Jack found his voice at last. 'Thank you for pulling him out, Pete. My father will be grateful to have him back...' He choked back his emotion, his fists balling at his sides.

'Bloody hell, mate!' another of his friends said. 'I'm sorry – it's a rotten chance that we pulled him out like that.'

'No – it's better than leaving him to the sharks,' Jack said and shuddered. He looked at their Captain, who was watching silently. 'You'll let me look after him, sir? Take him home to my father?'

'Yes, Burrows,' Captain Marlowe said. 'As you know, we would normally bury him at sea after taking what identifying marks we could, but your brother's body will be placed in the hold and, when we reach port, arrangements will be made for you to take him to a local undertaker so that his body can be made decent for your father to see him.'

'Thank you,' Jack said and bent to pick up Tim's body, but two of his friends got there first.

'We'll see he's all right,' Pete said. 'Best you don't see too much, Jack. Wait until the undertaker has had a go to make him decent.'

Jack knew that often the bodies fished from the sea had been attacked by sharks and their flesh torn to the bone. His friend was trying to spare him.

Captain Marlowe ordered Jack back to the engine room. 'We're nearing the port. Look sharp, Burrows, you're needed below. We've taken enough risk as it is. Keep a sharp lookout the rest of you, we don't want to get caught by a U-boat or we'll be the ones in the water.'

Jack saluted and did as he was told. He felt numbed with grief and shock and was glad to have a job to do.

As he climbed down below, Jock looked up in expectation. 'Where's me bloody tea then?'

'Sorry, Malc. I was ordered back below,' Jack said and went to his station as the orders began to come through. 'I'll get you one later.'

He worked mechanically, blocking out the thoughts and the emotion. Grief would come later when he had to go home and tell his father and Beth – and then there was Maggie. Poor little devil, it would break her heart and Jack wondered how they were ever going to tell her.

15

Marion listened sadly to the news that Tim Burrows was now officially dead a few days later. She didn't know him personally, of course, but he was engaged to Maggie and so it made her want to cry. Mrs Burrows had brought the news and looked so red-eyed and pale that both Mrs Bailey and Sally Harper told her she should go home, but she said Fred had come into work and she would too.

'Jack is seeing to everything,' Mrs Burrows explained, her face pale but determined. 'He has been so strong ever since he got home and he did everything right from the start, organised the funeral, Fred just left it all to him, because it was too much.'

'I'm so sorry, Mrs Burrows,' Marion said and her throat caught with distress. She hated to see her supervisor in such pain and wished she could do something to help, but she knew from experience that grief was personal and you couldn't share another person's pain, even when they were members of your own family. Kathy had taken their mother's death inwardly and still couldn't talk about it. 'It was a terrible thing to happen – and for your husband to be there when...' She couldn't go on because her supervisor looked as if she might faint from grief. 'I'm sorry, I didn't mean...'

'Jack says it is a good thing it happened that way,' Mrs Burrows said, raising her head as the tears fought to escape. 'He thinks that God intended us to know the truth – and at least we know for sure. Most men lost at sea are just that. We have Tim back and Fred will have a grave he can lay flowers on. We have to be grateful to Captain Marlowe for that, because the general rule is that bodies found at sea are given a Christian burial at sea. Because it was Jack's brother, he allowed him to bring him home to us...'

Marion nodded. She didn't know quite what to say. Becky Stockbridge had dissolved into tears and run off to the stockroom to recover herself. All she could say was poor Maggie, poor Maggie, over and over again and Mrs Burrows had glared at her.

'None of you is to write to Maggie Gibbs about this,' she said now. 'Mrs Harper is trying to find someone who will take the news to her in person. We don't want her to hear it in a letter – do you understand? It would be too distressing to learn about Tim that way.'

Becky Stockbridge had returned to the floor after her tearful exit and looked at her in distress. Clearly, she felt she wanted to tell her friend, to tell her how sorry she was, but Mrs Burrows was adamant.

'I know you care for Maggie,' she said, and her voice was strong. She was in command of her emotions now. 'But Mrs Harper and I are the closest to family that Maggie has and we want the news broken gently. When she has been told then you can write – do you understand?'

'Yes, Mrs Burrows,' Marion said, but heard the murmur of protest from Becky. She felt a lump in her throat and wished she didn't have to work, but they couldn't all go home – and if Mrs

Burrows and Fred Burrows could come into work then she could hardly complain.

'To your places now, girls,' her supervisor said as she saw a customer enter the department. She went to her own counter and began to rearrange the jewellery.

Marion was the first one to be busy. She didn't know whether to be pleased or sorry, but she was soon drawn into the customer's discussion about the merits of a red straw and a cream and pink silk tulle hat. She pushed her sadness to the back of her mind. Life had to go on despite what had happened – but it was the first of Harpers' people to be killed, as far as she knew – Tim Burrows wasn't strictly one of Harpers' staff, of course, but he was Fred's son and everyone liked Fred Burrows.

Marion was acutely aware that she had three of her loved ones serving in the armed forces. If Mrs Burrows could lose her brother-in-law, then Marion could lose one of her brothers or her Reggie. A cold shiver went through her and she caught her breath. It had brought the war very close and the mood was sombre throughout the store as the day wore on and the sad news spread. Tim Burrows was the first casualty of the people close to Harpers, but they all knew that he would not be the last to be lost in this awful war and it brought it very close to home.

* * *

'Why should we have to do as she says?' Becky muttered to Marion when they had a moment to spare from their work. 'I'm as much Maggie's friend as she is.'

'Yes, you are her friend, but Maggie thinks of Mrs Burrows as her sister and if she and Mrs Harper think it's best to send someone out there to tell her, then we have to wait until she knows.' Marion looked at her hard. 'Think how you would feel,

Becky, if you heard that something had happened to Captain Morgan from a stranger.'

Becky blushed and shook her head. Marion knew she wasn't actually courting Captain Morgan, but Becky had told her that he had sought her out when he was last on leave in London. She'd been excited and Marion knew she'd invited him to Sunday lunch at home with her father and Minnie and he'd been writing to her for a while now. Marion could always tell when Becky had had a letter from him, because there was a glow in her eyes.

'No, I shouldn't like it very much,' Becky admitted. 'Do you think they will tell us when we can write?'

'I am certain they will,' Marion said. 'You really shouldn't even think of writing until Mrs Burrows says it's all right.'

'I suppose.' Becky shrugged and went off to serve a customer with a scarf and a pair of white lace gloves. It was clear she was still resentful, but Marion hoped she would be sensible when she thought it over.

Marion's heart ached for her friend and she couldn't imagine how awful it would be for Maggie. Marion had a big family and there was always someone needing something from her – but if she lost either of her brothers or Reggie, she thought she would want to curl up into a ball and die. Maggie had no close family and it would be even worse for her.

* * *

Sally was in her office when Ruth told her that an Army officer had called to see her. She got to her feet and smiled as she saw who had walked in the door. He was wearing the uniform of a lieutenant in the engineers and looking very smart and handsome and healthy. It was her good friend Michael O'Sullivan – or Mick as he preferred to be called – and she hadn't seen him for ages.

'Mick! How lovely to see you!' she cried and held out her hands to him. He took them and kissed her cheek. 'How are you? Are the restaurants still busy? I'm sure they are. It is such ages since I saw you – and I've been thinking about you and wondering how you were...'

'I'm doing fine, Sally darlin',' he said and grinned at her. 'How are you – and young Jenny? I hope she's still thriving?'

'She's beautiful,' Sally told him. 'But tell me – what have you been doing?'

'This and that – mostly what I'm told,' he replied with a grin. 'Marlene gives me your news when she's seen you – and I like to think of you safe here at Harpers...' His smile dimmed. 'It's a terrible war, Sally, and I'm glad you're out of it – and Ben too.'

'He hasn't been entirely out of it,' she said and drew him further into the office. 'Sit down and have coffee and let me tell you all about his adventures.'

Mick nodded and allowed her to give him a comfortable chair. Over coffee and biscuits – chocolate ones this time – Sally told him all her news, ending finally on the sad circumstances of Tim Burrows crashing into the sea in his plane.

'It's sorry I am for the young lad and all of those boys. Too many of them are hardly out of school trousers before they're lying in the ground.' Mick shook his head over it and looked grave. 'Wasn't he courtin' one of your friends?'

'Yes, Maggie Gibbs,' Sally answered. 'Ben and I have been discussing it. We have to get the news to her somehow, Mick. Beth doesn't want her to read it in a letter or hear it from a stranger. I've said I'll find someone to take her the news if I can – but it's so difficult for a civilian to get to the field hospitals on the border between France and Belgium. I don't even know which one she's working in.'

Mick looked at her thoughtfully, then back at the closed door.

'Now, don't you be tellin' anyone or you'll get me shot – but I am bound that way very shortly. My chaps are in great demand over there, so they are. I can find out where she is and go and tell her myself, if you'd like that?' His Irish accent was faint but charming and she smiled at him, drawn to him and grateful for his friendship, which seemed to surround her with comforting warmth.

'Mick, could you?' Sally looked at him hopefully. 'I'll have to ask, of course, but I know Beth and Fred would be grateful – and I'm sure Maggie will remember you. I've spoken of you to her so many times – and I could give you a letter from me.'

'Sure, that will be the way,' Mick said in his easy Irish manner. 'I'll take her anything you want – and give her your love.'

'It's so kind of you,' Sally said and her eyes were wet with tears. Mick O'Sullivan was such a good friend to her. At one time she'd been aware that he cared for her, might even have fallen in love with him herself if she hadn't met Ben. Mick had never pushed the boundaries of their friendship though, never stepped over the line, and she trusted him implicitly. 'I can never thank you enough, Mick. I'll ask Beth and Fred if they want to send letters too, but I know they'll be grateful. When shall I see you again?'

'I'll call on you at home this evening. Much as I adore you, Sally – it is Ben I need to speak to – your husband is a great help to us in the engineers, arranging for deliveries of the right materials and making sure they get to us on time.'

Sally nodded. 'He's in a meeting all day, but he should be back by seven this evening. Why don't you have supper with us? It won't be a fancy meal like they serve in your restaurants, but Mrs Hills will have something cooking for me when I get back.'

* * *

Beth's eyes filled with tears when Sally told her what Mick had offered. She gave her a quick hug, thanked her and then went down to tell Fred. He looked relieved and told her to thank Mrs Harper on his behalf.

'She's a busy lady and yet she always goes that bit further to help,' he said. 'We're lucky to have her, Beth love.'

'Yes, we are,' she agreed and wiped the tears from her eyes. 'I have to get back to the department – and I'm going to write a little note for Maggie.'

He nodded and smiled, but the sadness in his eyes tore at her heart. He'd lost his youngest son and nothing could take away that pain.

* * *

Mick spent half an hour talking with Ben in the front room while Sally cooked the vegetables to accompany the delicious beef and mushroom pie Mrs Hills had prepared for her earlier. She gathered it was about some supplies Mick needed shifted from one place to another, and as she went to summon them to eat, she saw them shaking hands and looking pleased about something.

'Mick was telling me he's doing well with his restaurants despite the war,' Ben said. 'He's managed to source some good suppliers of game and fresh produce from Scotland and changed his menus to fit what he can source these days.'

'I think we all have to do that,' Sally agreed and smiled at Mick. 'I've got a really fantastic range of Scottish plaids coming in this autumn and winter. One of the men I helped recently had good contacts up in Scotland and I was given preferential treatment.'

'It's not what you know, it's who you know,' Mick said and grinned at her. 'And Marlene told me you'd worked a minor miracle for some of the wounded, arranging exchange visits of various specialists and consultants.'

'It was just a matter of helping the staff with some organisation,' Sally told him with a smile. 'They are so busy, they don't have time to phone round the various hospitals the way I can – besides, it's not just me, there are quite a few of us, each doing what we can. Rachel Bailey has started visiting on her half-day now and I know she's very popular with the men. And I've found the new contacts I've made up and down the country very useful. I've found a wonderful new milliner and a small knitwear firm down in the Welsh valleys who have been looking to expand for a long time. The managing director – or rather his daughter, Gwyneth – told me that she'd been trying to build up the courage to contact us for ages and then a friend of the family told her that I'd helped get him the right treatment and she decided I couldn't be too much of an ogress and came to London to see me.'

'That range is very good quality too,' Ben said and lifted his glass to toast her. 'Shall we eat – that food smells delicious and I'm sure Mick is as hungry as I am.'

'Yes, let's eat,' Sally said and laughed. 'Ben knows I would talk business all night and you're our guest.'

'He's right I am hungry and that pie does smell good,' Mick said and smiled as Sally passed him three letters. He took them and placed them inside his uniform breast pocket. 'I'll see the young lass gets them, Sally. And I promise I'll break the news to her as gently as I can.'

16

It was so much warmer now that it was almost May and summer here in France; it made everyone's lives easier, despite all the hardship and the shortages. Maggie knew she felt better when the sun shone and Sadie was much recovered now, all memory of the coughs and chill she had in the early spring gone. They were becoming accustomed to the mud, which had dried into hard ruts now, and the sparse comfort of their huts. However, some of the patients didn't do well in the heat. For them, lying on a stretcher for hours before being brought down the line to the hospital could be uncomfortable. Flies buzzed round the wounds and that annoyed some of the injured men, though those with the worst damage probably were aware only of the terrible pain.

A few months back, a daring plan to resupply the field hospitals had ensured they had plenty of medical necessities for the past few weeks, but they were beginning to run low on certain things again and the strong painkilling drugs were rationed to those that had a chance of recovery once more.

Maggie sighed as she saw the lorries beginning to come in

with their cargo of severely wounded soldiers. Orderlies took the stretchers from the back of the lorries, farm carts, and the various vehicles the Government had commandeered to transport those that could walk with a bit of help. Once they had unloaded, they left immediately, because there was always another load of injured men to bring in. The transport went on whenever a lull in the fighting allowed the stretcher bearers to go in and recover men from no man's land, that stretch of killing ground between the lines.

The men lucky enough to recover sufficiently told the nurses their harrowing stories. Some wounded men made it back to their own trenches unaided, some leaned on friends, some were carried over the shoulder of a mate who refused to leave them behind – others lay on the earth and wept, their cries keeping the men in the trenches on edge as they waited for the chance to go in and fetch them back between bombardments. Still others were caught on the barbed wire the enemy had set up around their defences, screaming all night as they struggled to free themselves but were unable to get out, dying slowly of their wounds. Then the sound of a rifle would break the stillness of night and the screaming stopped. The sudden silence was a relief to those that listened, even though it meant another life lost.

In the midst of sickness, filth and fear, death was sometimes your friend. Many a soldier carried a prayer book in his breast pocket and felt comforted to know it was there – because when the cold, rain, mud, heat, dust and stench of their lives became unbearable, the glimpse of Heaven offered in those prayers seemed to provide a way out of the nightmare. Only the strong and the angry never thought of death as peace. The strong scorned it and spat in the face of danger and the angry cursed the enemy and dreamed of driving their bayonets deep into the flesh of the men in the opposite trenches.

'It's the only way,' one young soldier had told Maggie when she helped patch up a wound to his face. He'd been lucky enough to receive only a flesh wound and would make a full recovery in time. 'I don't want to be sent home, nurse – I want to kill the bastards that murdered my mates...'

Maggie had nodded and smiled. She knew they were supposed to encourage that sort of attitude; it was what was required, because the men had to fight and the angry ones didn't think of getting a Blighty wound or deserting. They were the first over the top, charging towards glorious revenge or their own deaths. The strong ones gritted their teeth and did what was necessary for King and country, and the weak ones lay shivering and shaking and praying it wasn't their turn to die as they were ordered over the top. Now and then a very frightened soldier would refuse to climb the ladder to the top of the trench and, depending on the officer in charge, he would either be put on a charge of mutiny or sent over with a bayonet at his back.

Maggie had heard it all from between the chattering teeth of the sick and dying. She had lost count of the young soldiers who had died as she gave them whatever comfort she could. Sometimes, they were the lucky ones. It was the others – those that would survive – that suffered so much terrible pain and agony day after day. Even when they had sufficient anaesthetics, the pain from surgery was almost beyond bearing. Sweating, with suppurating wounds, they lay in every available space, weeping and begging for their mothers. Maggie and the other nurses went from one to the next, comforting those they couldn't help and treating those they could. Bandages were changed, drinks given, foreheads wiped and hands pressed. It was all they could do most of the time and for many of the men it was their smiles and a cheerful word that kept them going, giving them a tiny ray of hope.

'You're an angel,' one of the men had told Maggie that morning as she held him so that he could drink a few sips of water. 'When I get leave, I'm going to buy you the biggest box of chocolates you've ever seen, nurse.'

'Oh, that's lovely,' Maggie had told him with a smile. 'I shall enjoy those, Sergeant Johns.' It had been hard to keep her smile in place but she'd managed it. Sergeant Johns was unlikely to go on leave again. She knew that when she went back on duty that evening, he would probably be dead, but she'd thanked him for his intended gift and held the tears inside.

Maggie turned away from the hospital convoy and walked towards the little row of huts where she slept. She was tired and her back hurt and the ache in her heart was even worse. It was weeks since she'd heard from Tim. He hadn't written and he hadn't visited – both of which he'd promised he would do faithfully as often as he could, which meant he wasn't able to do the things he'd said he would.

Aware of a cold knot at the base of her stomach, Maggie tried to fight the knowledge that had been with her for a couple of weeks now. She had no way of confirming it, but the emptiness inside told her that Tim had gone. Her heart felt heavy with loss despite Sadie telling her she was imagining things – and she looked for a letter from England every day. If Tim had been killed, his father must know – so why didn't he write? The not knowing and yet feeling it inside was killing her, eating at her guts, but tears wouldn't come. Perhaps if she knew the truth...

'Nurse Gibbs,' the voice had a slight Irish lilt to it.

Maggie turned and looked at the officer walking towards her. She recognised his uniform as the engineers, those brave men who were always first on the scene, building bridges, digging trenches and putting up the makeshift accommodation like her hut.

'Please, may I speak to you for a moment...'

Maggie felt the shaft enter her heart. She vaguely recognised the officer – his name was Michael O'Sullivan and he was a friend of Sally Harper's. Sally had called him Mick and she'd liked him a lot, trusted him as a good friend. Now she knew why she hadn't had a letter. Sally had sent a friend to tell her.

Here it was at last! The confirmation of what she'd known instinctively.

Tears stung Maggie's eyes and she waited for him to come up to her.

'Nurse Gibbs – may I call you Maggie?' He smiled at her and she saw the warmth in his look and the kindness. 'Is there some-where we can go for a cup of tea?'

'It isn't worth drinking,' Maggie said and her voice sounded too harsh. 'Please just tell me – it's Tim, isn't it?'

His soft eyes looked at her with sympathy. The old Maggie would have collapsed against his chest, but she'd seen too much death. 'Has someone told you? Sally thought you should hear it from a friend.'

'No one told me, I just knew,' Maggie said and her throat was so tight that the words were no more than a whisper. 'Tim is dead... in the sea...' She could barely see him for the tears she refused to shed. 'Was it in the sea – do they know for sure?'

'Tim was reported missing in action, but the wreckage of his plane was found in the sea and his body was recovered for a Christian burial at home. His funeral is this week, I understand.' Mick moved towards her as she swayed, her head swimming as the force of her grief hit her. 'I'm so sorry. I'm sure you can get leave, go home to be with your friends...'

Maggie stared at him, numb with misery. Tim was gone. She wouldn't see him again, wouldn't have the chance to be his wife – would never know what it was like to lie in his arms. Why hadn't they got married when he was on leave? Why hadn't they spent the night in bed together? The regret was so strong that it tasted like iron in her mouth. She wanted to scream and shout, to protest that it couldn't be true. It wasn't fair! Why had she lost Tim? Why did she lose everyone she loved?

Bitterness and pain swept over her. She turned away as if to leave, stumbled and almost fell. Sally's friend stepped forward and caught her, holding her tight to his chest. She smelled a faint tang of musk, the wool of his uniform and something that was uniquely his; it was comforting and instead of trying to break free, she let him hold her as she suddenly let go and the tears poured out of her and she sobbed into his shoulder.

'You should let me tell your matron – she would give you compassionate leave,' he said against her hair. 'You shouldn't have to bear this alone.'

Maggie looked up at him. She gave him a little push and he let her go but offered her a clean white handkerchief. She took it and blew her nose but didn't give it back. 'Thank you for coming to tell me, Lieutenant, and thank you for your concern – but Matron needs us all. Men are dying every day here – not just one but fifty or more – sometimes a hundred. She can't let her nurses go home when they are so desperately needed here.'

Mick looked into her face and she knew he could see that she was determined. Her tears had dried and her expression was blank, cold, the way she felt inside. He nodded, a frown on his handsome face. 'I think you need friends, but I'll be around for a week or so – just ask for me if you need me.' He smiled at her gently. 'Private Hadlow is on the hospital transport most days; he would get a message to me – and I'll come again if I can, even if you don't ask.'

'Thank you. I'll be all right. I want to work.' Maggie wiped her sleeve across her face. 'Now I should get some sleep.'

'Yes, of course.' Mick hesitated and then handed her a parcel tied up with brown paper and string. 'From Sally Harper and Fred and Beth Burrows.'

Maggie stared at it, seeming unwilling to take it for a moment, then nodded and accepted it from his hands. 'Thank you. I'll write to them when I'm able.'

He stood for a moment, uncertain, not wanting to leave her.

She appreciated his kindness but couldn't bear it. 'Please go, Lieutenant. I am all right now. I do have friends here and my work. You can't do anything more for me – but you've been kind and I shan't forget...'

'I shan't forget you, either, Maggie Gibbs,' he said and smiled at her. 'You're a lovely girl, so you are – and your patients are lucky to have you. If the Germans get lucky and put a bullet in me, I'll be sure to ask for you, me darling.'

It was an attempt at lightness. Maggie nodded but didn't respond with a smile. Instead, she turned and walked away, aware that he watched her until she disappeared into the row of huts that were currently her home.

Maggie felt numb all over now. She was blocking out her grief the way she'd learned to do when she'd first seen young men die. If she thought about Tim and what his death meant to her, she would just lie on her bed and weep. So, she wouldn't think about it – she wouldn't accept it. She would just put it all out of her mind. When this war was over, when she returned to England at the end of this nightmare, then she would think about the life that awaited her. She couldn't even begin to think what she might do in the future because at the moment it was dark and bleak and she didn't want to think at all. She would do what all the nurses did out here: eat, sleep and work and forget everything that had once made life beautiful.

* * *

Mick watched the young woman walk away. She was so vulnerable, but beautiful, proud and magnificent in her grief. He'd remembered her vaguely as a young girl, but she was a woman now. A wisp of a girl shouldering the weight of the world and his heart grieved for her.

He shook his head. As an engineer his own life was often in danger. There was no way of knowing if he would ever get through this war alive – but if he did, he would seek out Maggie Gibbs and see what he could do for her. She was everything the men out here admired and he wanted to help her – to shoulder some of the pain she'd been forced to bear, but he knew he couldn't. Maggie didn't know him, probably wouldn't want his comfort or his help – but he wouldn't forget her, and if he could help her one day in the future, he would.

Turning away, Mick went back to the lorry that had brought him in. He had a job to do up at the Front and by the end of the day he might be amongst the wounded being tended here or dead.

Whistling, Mick nodded to the young private who had obligingly brought him here in the battered old lorry he kept going with bits of wire and crossed fingers.

'Ready to go, Lieutenant?'

'Yes, thank you, Private Hadlow.' He climbed into the passenger seat. 'I owe you one.'

'Packet of fags,' the soldier said and grinned. 'Think a lot of her, do yer?'

Mick smiled. 'She's one hell of a girl,' he replied.

'They all are,' Private Hadlow said. 'I wouldn't have their job for all the tea in China.'

Mick nodded. He had been deeply touched by the young girl's bravery and carried the memory of her stricken eyes with him as he left. He would write to Sally Harper and let her know straight away, though she might not hear for a while since the letters sometimes took weeks to deliver.

17

Sally got a letter from Mick some weeks later, towards the beginning of June. She smiled, because he must have pulled strings to ensure it got through so quickly. Normally, the post could take weeks from over there, but Mick was used to getting things done. He'd probably sent it with someone who was coming home on leave. It had been delivered to her office with a lot more post, but she'd vaguely recognised Mick's scrawl. She opened it and read that he'd seen Maggie, passed on their messages and that she'd taken it hard.

The poor lass cried, but that's only natural. I'd have been more worried if she hadn't. However, I could see she has taken it deep inside; what it means probably hasn't sunk in yet and she was determined to go on working. I tried to persuade her to come home, but she wouldn't consider it. She says she's needed out here and it's true; there are so many wounded men, they can hardly cope as it is. If she asked for leave, she wouldn't know what to do, so perhaps it is best she stays and keeps on working. Your friend is a brave young woman, Sally, and she's doing a wonderful job here – they all are. The men call the nurses the real heroes – their sweet angels who make living bearable and dying easier.

I have to stop now, because I'm needed. They need a... building and I'm the man for the job, they say. Take care, Sally, and I'll call when I'm home again. Give my regards to Ben and my love to young Jenny. I've given Marlene a birthday gift for her so you'll be seeing her soon.

My fondest love as your friend, Mick.

Sally folded the letter, putting it away in her handbag. It had told her just what she'd expected. Maggie wouldn't come home for the funeral – she would rather stay out there where she was doing her job, the job she'd trained for and was so much needed. If she'd returned, she would have had to face reality and she'd decided to tuck her grief away and go on working. Sally didn't blame her. She thought she might have done the same in Maggie's place, but Fred and Beth had thought she would come home and they might be upset. Sally would do her best to make them understand, but both were grieving hard for Tim's loss and might not see that Maggie just couldn't face them or her own grief.

'Is something wrong?' Ben asked from the doorway of their bedroom.

She went to greet him with a kiss. 'I've had a letter from Mick. He has told Maggie about Tim and she was obviously distressed – but she won't come home – she says she's needed out there...'

'Yes, I'm certain she is,' Ben agreed with a frown. 'That doesn't mean she's right to stay, Sally. Bottling up her grief will only mean she suffers more in the end.' His eyes had a faraway look and she knew he wasn't thinking only of Maggie.

Ben had been concerned earlier in the month by the sinking of an American passenger ship, the *Lusitania*. He'd told her that one of the passengers had actually been a friend of the American President, Woodrow Wyatt, and she knew he'd worried for Jenni, who had spoken of visiting them when she'd written earlier that year, and he'd told her not to think of it in one of his regular letters to her.

Sally nodded, looking thoughtful. 'Yes, I know – but Maggie has already had too much pain for such a young woman to bear. She lost her parents, was let down by that fellow Ralf and she loved Tim all the more because of it. I don't think she could face Fred or Beth at the moment.'

Ben put his arms around her, holding her close. 'I know how I'd feel if someone told me you were gone, Sally. I'd want to bury myself deep and keep everyone else at arm's-length. It's a pity you couldn't have been the one to break the news, love. Mick did his best, but she might have opened up to you more.'

'I wanted to go, but Beth begged me not to – and I thought you wouldn't let me.'

'I wouldn't have wanted you to risk your life,' Ben agreed. 'With Maggie out there, you did the best you could, darling.'

Sally nodded. 'I know – but was it good enough?'

* * *

'Maggie isn't coming home?' Beth looked at Sally in shock. 'How can she do that? I thought she loved Tim? Surely she wants to be here with her family – and to attend his funeral.'

'I think Maggie is hurting too much to think straight,' Sally told her softly. 'Please don't think the worst of her, Beth. She doesn't mean to hurt you or Fred – she just can't face anyone at the moment, and she is needed out there. So many young men are injured and dying that she feels it would be wrong to take leave

for her own personal grief.' She hesitated, then, 'She would probably not be given leave even if she asked.'

'She could have had a few days for compassionate leave,' Beth
argued and looked upset and angry. 'Jack's been given another
week to see his brother buried and so could she. Though, of
course, his ship is being refitted again so that helps. They picked
up more shell damage on the way home from Calais.' She was too
upset to think of Maggie's point of view. 'I don't know what Fred
will say; he delayed it a couple of days just to give Maggie time to
get back – I imagine he'll be deeply hurt...'

However, when Beth relayed the news to her father-in-law, he
just nodded his head in acceptance. 'I don't think she means any
disrespect, Beth. The young lass is just too upset to face what has
happened and she wants to stay there, where she's needed.'

'I suppose you're right,' Beth said, but her disappointment was
sharp. It felt like a slap in the face. She'd expected her to rush
home so that they could comfort each other and she'd thought
Maggie would cling to her and she would be able to make her feel
better and assure her of their love and that she was still a big part
of their family, but it seemed to Beth that Maggie had shut them
out, given them the cold shoulder – as if they were nothing. Even
Rachel had remarked on it, saying she couldn't understand why
Maggie didn't ask for compassionate leave and come home.

Her first distress had cooled, but, in her heart, she still felt
hurt and rejected, though common sense told her Maggie was
doing what she had to do.

18

It was in mid-June that Marion saw the girl standing outside her door as she approached her house. She was of medium height, her hair shoulder-length, blonde and wavy, and her red coat smarter than was normally worn round here. She turned as Marion came up to her, a tentative smile on her face and then she extended her hand as Marion noticed the suitcases piled near the front door.

'You must be Marion,' she said. 'I'm Dan's wife – he did tell you about me?' She frowned as Marion didn't answer immediately. 'I'm Sarah and we were married last time Dan got home...'

'Married?' Marion felt the shock run through her. She moved forward and grasped Sarah's hands. 'I'm sorry. Yes, of course he told us about you, but I didn't know you were married.'

'It was very quick, a special licence. He only had twenty-four hours before he had to go back, so we got married.' Sarah's coat opened slightly and Marion saw the swollen mound of her belly. She was more than a few months pregnant. 'The trouble is my father doesn't approve of Dan – and he threw me out...' Sarah blinked, tears standing in her eyes. 'I thought my father really loved me, but it seems that was only while I was his little girl and did as I was told, when I grew up and fell in love, he resented it – and Dan wasn't good enough for him. I don't think any man would be...'

'Oh, Sarah, love,' Marion said, instantly understanding the significance of the suitcases. Dan must have anticipated this might happen and he'd told Sarah to come to his sister. It was probably why he'd told Marion there was a girl he loved, thinking she might need to know in the future. 'Of course you can stay with us. You can have Dan's room. Robbie was using it after Dan left home, but he can share with Dickon when he's home on leave – or have mine and I'll move into Ma's room, but you must have Dan's. It has a double bed and a nice outlook over the garden.'

Sarah looked relieved. She flicked her long lashes to get rid of the tears and smiled properly. 'Dan told me how kind you were, but I was nervous of coming – after all, it is your family home.'

'And it's your home now, because you're family.'

Marion picked up the largest suitcase and carried it round to the back door. Sarah followed with the two smaller ones. Once they were inside the kitchen, which was much warmer, Marion made up the range fire.

'I'll make a cup of tea and then take you upstairs. My little sister, Milly, is next door at the neighbour's house. I'll fetch her once you're settled in, Sarah.'

Leading the way upstairs, Marion opened the door to the room Robbie had been using before he left to join up. She was glad it was her habit to polish right through the house once a week, because it still smelled fresh. Looking round at the shabby furniture, she turned to Sarah apologetically.

'I'm sorry it isn't smarter – but perhaps Dan will buy some new stuff when he gets back.'

Sarah smiled at her. 'It's much nicer than the lodgings I went into after leaving my father's house, Marion. Thank you for letting me have it. I can probably buy a few bits myself – if you don't mind me changing things?'

'You can do what you want in here,' Marion told her. 'Are you all right for money? I don't have much spare but...'

'I've got a little bit in the bank,' Sarah told her. 'My mother left me a small legacy, so it doesn't matter that my father cut me off without a penny. I could find a job, I'm good at typing and book-keeping, but I can't work like this.' She'd taken off her coat and Marion thought she must be about six months pregnant.

'You mustn't even think of going to work,' Marion said. 'I'm sure Dan will come home when he gets leave and he will make sure you have money to look after you and the baby.'

'Yes.' Sarah smiled. 'He gave me ten pounds when he was home. I spent it on my lodgings, but they were so awful I found the courage to come here.'

'I'm so glad you did,' Marion said. 'It will be lovely having you here, Sarah. I often worry that Milly will be too much trouble for Mrs Jackson, but she could come here to you if she wants now.'

'Yes, of course. I'll be happy to get her tea – and to help you with the housework, Marion. It must be a lot for you to do, working at Harpers and looking after this house and your family...'

'It isn't always easy,' Marion replied. She liked Sarah, who, at first meeting, seemed just right for Dan. 'I think it will be better now you're here – Kathy helps me, of course, but Milly is too young to do much and Dickon likes to go out with his friends in the evening. He brings in coke and wood for the range, but that's about his limit.'

'Dan told me he had a big family,' Sarah said and looked a little wistful. 'I was an only child and after my mother died, Father made me the centre of his world. He spoiled me, gave me nice things, but he wanted me to stay a little girl – be grateful to him. I think that's why he hated the idea of my getting married and having Dan's child. He couldn't prevent the marriage, because I'm old enough to do as I wish, but he forbade it. I thought he would change his mind, when he knew it was a fact and that I was having his grandchild – but he told me to pack my bags and leave, so I did.'

'What else could you do?' Marion consoled her with a look of sympathy. 'I wish you'd come to us straight away, Sarah. I hate to think of you living in those terrible lodgings. Dan would have hated that for you.'

'I thought you might resent me moving into your home...'

'No, I don't – I really don't,' Marion told her and went over to give her a quick hug. 'I love Dan and I'm glad he's got such a lovely wife – and that you've chosen to live with us now your baby is so close to being born.'

'I'm glad I came now,' Sarah said and looked happy. 'It was silly of me to worry, because Dan said you would welcome me but...' She sighed. 'Well, I'm here now and it's up to Dan to decide what happens next.'

'Surely you will stay with us for the duration of the war,' Marion told her. 'After it is all over and Dan is back for good, then you can decide.'

Sarah nodded, but looked uncertain. Marion decided to leave it there. Dan and Sarah would talk things over when he next came home on leave and they could all move on from there. Marion was quite happy to have Dan's wife and baby living in her home and she thought the rest of her family would be pleased too. After all, they had plenty of room for her with their parents' room empty. For a moment Marion had considered giving Sarah that but decided against it. Let her have Dan's old room and if Robbie objected when he came home, he could move into hers and she'd have Ma's room. Kathy wouldn't even go in their mother's room to clean; she said it was haunted by her mother's screams and couldn't bear any reminder of what had happened that terrible night their father had battered her. She and Milly shared a room as had Dickon and Robbie until Dan left home. Marion had a small room to herself, but she wouldn't mind having her parents' old room if Robbie would rather have hers than share Dickon's again. For a while she'd worried her father might return and claim it, but it seemed he knew he wouldn't be welcome – and if he did come near them, Marion would go to the police. He was guilty of her mother's death and by rights should be in prison, though she'd heard quite a few men had been let out of prison if they swore to join the Army. Perhaps that was the reason her father had escaped justice all this time. He was working on the merchant ships and so many men were being injured and killed that the police might have called an amnesty on criminals for the duration of the war.

'I'll leave you to unpack,' she said to Sarah. 'Just put Robbie's things into the hallway for now and I'll find a place for them. I'll get the kettle on and fetch Milly and then we'll all have a cup of tea before I get our supper.'

* * *

'Who is she and why is she here?' Kathy asked when she came into the kitchen a little later. Sarah was still upstairs unpacking, but Kathy had been told they had a visitor by one of their neighbours and from the look on her face she wasn't pleased.

'She is Dan's wife, Sarah,' Marion told her. 'She seems very nice, Kathy, and she had nowhere else to go – and she's having Dan's baby.'

Kathy glared at her. 'Why should we have to look after her?

Dan just went off and left us to the mercy of that man.' In her bitterness, Kathy refused to name her father. 'We've had to struggle to survive with little help from him – why should we have to take on his wife and child?'

'Please don't be bitter,' Marion said, looking at her sadly. 'I know it's been hard and I've had to ask more of you than perhaps I should – but Sarah is nice and she will help in the house.'

'She's still one more mouth to feed – and you don't get much for yourself now, Marion,' Kathy said, looking angry.

'We manage fairly well. Besides, Sarah has a little money of her own – and I'm sure Dan will send her money to help out.' Marion frowned. Her eldest brother had taken over the tenancy of the house after her father went off as a fugitive from the law. He'd been paying the rent ever since, having arranged for it to be taken from his pay in the Merchant Navy each month, so in actual fact it was Dan's house – and therefore his wife's. Marion felt a little trickle of unease as she realised that she was no longer the mistress in her own home. Sarah could, if she wished, assert her authority and even ask them to leave... However, Marion had no intention of reminding either her sister or her sister-in-law of that fact. Dan might have taken over the rent, but that didn't give him or his wife the right to order her and her family out of the house. Besides, Marion knew that he would never do such a thing – but Sarah was an unknown factor.

'Just be nice to her,' she advised her sister now. 'Sarah needs our help – and I like her.'

Kathy sniffed but didn't say anything more. It was just as well she hadn't put Sarah in their mother's room, Marion reflected, or she would never have calmed Kathy down.

'I'm sorry I've been such a long time,' a voice said and they both turned to look at Sarah, who had just entered the kitchen. 'Marion, I packed your brother's things into my suitcases and put them in the hall. I thought that would make them easier for you to store or move.'

'That was very thoughtful of you,' Marion said and smiled at her. 'This is my sister, Kathy. Come and have a cup of tea. I've got lamb chops, mashed potatoes, mint sauce and cabbage for supper. I hope that will be all right for you?' Marion felt a little ashamed that she couldn't offer something special, but they didn't often have a roast chicken or a joint midweek, because it was too expensive and took too long to cook.

Kathy nodded at her but didn't speak.

'It sounds delicious,' Sarah said and laughed. 'The best meal I've been offered in weeks. My landlady was a terrible cook.' She had a pretty laugh and Marion smiled with her.

'I'm not too bad – but my neighbour is much better. She cooks wonderful pies and treats for her family – and sometimes she makes one for us.'

Sarah smiled and nodded. 'Are your neighbours all friendly?'

'Yes, they're very good to me, especially the ones next door. I'm engaged to Reggie Jackson and Mrs Jackson looks after Milly every afternoon when she gets in from school.'

'You haven't fetched her yet?' Kathy looked at Marion accusingly. 'I'll go and get her now. She will think you've abandoned her.' She threw a darkling glance at Sarah and went out.

'That is my fault,' Sarah said. 'You were busy looking after me and your sister must be anxiously waiting to be fetched.'

Marion laughed and shook her head. 'Milly is probably happy playing games with Paula – she's a nurse – or one of Reggie's brothers. He has two brothers and both of them work in reserved jobs on the docks and still live at home. Both of them tried to join up but were told they couldn't because they're needed where they are. Paula's sisters are all married now and Mrs Jackson says having Milly around is like a breath of fresh air to her.'

'So, your Reggie is the only one serving in the Army from his family then?'

'Yes, but they all do volunteer work in the evenings.' Marion told her. 'John drives a van for the WVS and Malcom does fire watching at various important locations on three nights a week.'

Sarah nodded in understanding. 'Your sister isn't very pleased that I've come to stay...' she said hesitantly.

Marion bit her lip, hesitating for a moment. 'Don't take too much notice of her, Sarah. Kathy will see sense before long – but she's still grieving hard for my mother and she blames Dan for not stopping our father before it was too late. It wasn't his fault. Even if he'd been here sooner, it would still have happened; he couldn't be here every minute of every day. In a way it was Ma's fault, because she should have taken us children when we were small and cleared off while our father was at sea. She could have made a new life for us all somewhere else, but she never did.'

'Dan told me it all, I'm really sorry, Marion, but sometimes you have to be brave and take that first step,' Sarah said, looking sad. 'It was hard for me to leave my father's house, but he threatened to kill my baby – that common brat, as he called it...' Her eyes filled with unshed tears. 'He thought Dan could never be good enough for me and that's why he refused to accept our marriage. He said if I gave up the child and divorced my husband, he would take me back and leave me everything, as he'd promised long ago, but if I persisted in giving birth to the brat, he would kill it.' Sarah looked at her bleakly. 'I thought he loved me – but that isn't love, is it, Marion?'

'No, it isn't, Sarah,' Marion said and held out a hand to her. Sarah took it and held it briefly. 'You're welcome here – and this is your home as much as ours. Perhaps more so as Dan pays the rent.'

'It's your home,' Sarah said. 'I'm just grateful that you've let me share it until Dan comes home and sorts things out.' She smiled at Marion. 'I would never want to push you out of your place, Marion. This is your home, and your decision is the one that matters.'

Marion's last doubts flew away as Sarah looked at her earnestly. She wished her brother had told her of his marriage, but she liked Dan's wife and could only think she would be a happy addition to their family. 'Good, I'm glad we've got that sorted. I know Kathy will warm towards you in time, Sarah. She's out of sorts with the world at the moment and we all have to be patient with her.'

As she spoke, the door opened and Milly burst in. She stopped short, looking at Sarah doubtfully for a moment. Marion held out her hand and Milly took it, looking up at her.

'This is Sarah – she's Dan's wife and she's having his baby,' Marion explained. 'Won't that be nice – a new baby in the family? Perhaps Sarah will let you help her bathe her baby one day and you can knit some bootees for her like I showed you.'

Milly's puzzled look disappeared and she sidled up to Sarah, staring up at her. 'Can I touch your tummy?' she asked. 'My friend's mummy lets her listen to the baby's heart beating, she says it kicked her and she thinks it's a footballer.'

Sarah laughed and bent down to Milly, holding out her arms to her. 'Sometimes my baby kicks me,' she said. 'Do you think he will be a footballer?'

'It might be a girl,' Kathy said with a sour look.

'I like playing football,' Milly said. 'It could be a girl and still play football with me – couldn't it?'

'When he or she gets big enough,' Sarah told her, smiling. 'You know, when I was a little girl, I liked playing football too.'

'The teachers at school say I can't play in the team because I'm a girl,' Milly pouted, 'but Reggie and Malc and John say I can play as good as any boy and they would have me in their team if they had one.'

'I don't see why girls can't play if they want to,' Sarah agreed. 'I played hockey and netball at my school – but we often enjoyed kicking a football when the teachers weren't looking.'

'You're all right,' Milly decided and giggled. She turned to Marion and pulled at her skirt. 'What you cooking, Marion? I'm hungry.'

'Didn't you have any tea with Mrs Jackson then?'

'A slice of apple pie with cream,' Milly said and rubbed her tummy. 'It was lovely, Marion, but I still love your tea.'

'Yes, you can have a bit of my chop and some mash with mint sauce,' Marion said, laughing. 'If you eat that you can have a bit more.'

Milly smiled. 'I just want a taste because they smell so good.'

'They do, don't they?' Sarah said. 'Milly, while we're waiting, I've got something upstairs you might like.'

'Something for me?' Milly's eyes widened. 'It's not my birthday – Marion gave me lots for my birthday.'

'Yes.' Sarah met Marion's eyes and asked the question. 'Is it all right? It is something that belonged to me as a child.'

'Yes, of course,' Marion said. 'You don't have to ask, Sarah. You're a part of this family now.'

Milly was giggling as she went upstairs with her new friend.

Kathy was sitting on the old sofa, making a point of reading one of her schoolbooks and ignoring what was going on.

'Will you set the table for us, Kathy?' Marion asked as the kitchen door opened to admit Dickon. He was looking pleased with himself and tipped up his wage packet on the table.

'There's an extra six shillings this week,' he said proudly. 'What do you think of that, our Marion?'

'Oh, Dickon, that is wonderful,' Marion said. 'Pick it up and take your usual half a crown too. You've earned it and you must keep it.'

'No, I'll take three shillings and you have the rest,' Dickon said. 'I want you to have it, Marion. After this, I'll have four shillings a week – but that's enough for me. You should use it to treat yourself or Kathy.'

'Thank you, Dickon,' Marion said, smiling at him. He was so proud of being able to bring home what was almost a man's wage now and she wouldn't spoil his pleasure by rejecting it. She would buy Kathy something nice this week and then save a bit of Dickon's money whenever she could and give it to him one day – perhaps when he wanted something badly and couldn't afford it. It was what her mother would have done. 'I think Kathy deserves a new pair of shoes.' She looked at her sister. 'I'll meet you from school on my half-day this next week and we'll buy you that pair of tan court shoes you saw and liked the other day.'

'New shoes from the shop?' Kathy stared at her in disbelief, because she'd always had nearly new from a stall on the market and this would be her first new shoes since she was a little girl and her mother had bought them as a birthday gift for Kathy. 'Really?'

'I've been saving and now I can buy them,' Marion said. 'I would have got them for your birthday, but you can have them now and I'll get something different when it's your birthday.'

'Oh, thank you, Marion,' Kathy said and the sulky expression was gone.

'Dickon's money made it possible.'

Kathy grabbed her brother and kissed him. He grinned and shoved her off. Laughing, Kathy set about setting the table. Her smile dimmed a little as Milly returned carrying a beautiful doll with a china face and the prettiest clothes they'd any of them ever seen, but she was too happy to be mean and told her little sister it was lovely.

'Are you sure you want to part with such a lovely thing?' Marion asked and Sarah nodded.

'Yes, I'm happy for Milly to have it. I've got small gifts for all of you in my room. I'll give them to you later.'

'You don't have to give us anything,' Marion said.

'I want to,' Sarah replied. 'It's so good of you to take me in.'

'You're Dan's wife,' Dickon said, and came forward to offer his hand. Sarah shook it and he smiled. 'Welcome to the family. Dan will be glad you're here, and so are we.'

Marion looked across the room at Kathy. She had a faint blush in her cheeks, but she lifted her head. 'Yes, welcome to the family, Sarah,' she said. 'If Marion and Dickon say it's all right, you can stay...'

'Thank you,' Sarah said and smiled. 'Gosh, I'm hungry – that mint sauce does smell good.'

19

Beth saw that Marion Kaye was looking a bit pensive when she tidied the hats that morning. She did her work well, as always, but she didn't seem quite herself, so at lunchtime when Miss Stockbridge and Miss Jones had gone for their break, she took the opportunity to ask her if something was the matter.

'Oh no, not really,' Marion replied and smiled. 'It's just that my brother's wife turned up on Friday night unannounced. She's very friendly and I think we'll get on, though my sister Kathy isn't too sure about her – but she's having a baby and I'm a little bit anxious about what she ought to do. I don't think she's been to a doctor...'

'Then that's the first thing you need to see to,' Beth said with a smile. 'Ask your doctor to take her on his panel – it's best to be registered and then he will advise about a midwife and all that kind of thing. I expect you'll want to be with her when she has the baby, so when you know the date it is expected you could book your holiday.'

'Yes, that is what I've been thinking about.' Marion nodded. 'I think that's a good suggestion. I'm not sure Sarah knows how to knit. She hasn't made any provision for the baby yet. I was wondering whether I should buy some wool in my lunch break so we can all start to knit things for her.'

'That's a lovely idea – and if Sarah doesn't know how, you can show her.'

'Yes, we can. My sister Kathy is a wonderful knitter. She does lovely lacy patterns and made me a beautiful cardigan one year. She loves it and the only reason she doesn't do more is that we can't always afford the wool...'

'It is expensive if it's just for pleasure,' Beth agreed, 'but home-made baby clothes are much cheaper than those you buy in the shops. We only have a small department here, but the things are exquisite – too expensive for many young mothers.'

'Sarah has a little money put by,' Marion said. 'I thought I would get her started and then she might realise she needs to start making things, otherwise she'll have nothing ready when the baby comes – in about two to three months, I think.'

'Well, that will be exciting for you all,' Beth replied with a smile. 'Ah, Miss Jones is back from her break, so you may go if you wish. There's a lovely shop just down the street that sells wool and patterns.'

Marion thanked her and went off to get her coat.

Shirley Jones smiled at Beth and came to stand by her counter.

'You're back a few minutes early,' Beth said. 'You don't need to start immediately.'

'I wanted to check my counter,' Shirley replied. 'I had three customers altogether earlier and they were all picking up the scarves and asking to see more. I was very careful, but I just wanted to check nothing was missing.'

'I'm glad to see you are so conscientious.' Beth nodded her approval as the girl checked her stock against what she'd sold.

She looked relieved when she'd finished. 'Everything is as it should be?'

'Yes, thank you, Mrs Burrows.' The young girl smiled happily. 'I should hate to lose anything. I enjoy my job here so much.'

'Stock does go missing – it may be that it has been taken for the window and not written down or on rare occasions it may have been stolen. That doesn't happen often in this department, though I know the ground floor lost a few items at Christmas in the rush.'

'Mrs Harper must be so cross when that happens,' Shirley said and frowned.

'She knows that it can't always be avoided, but as long as it isn't habitual or all from one girl's stock, no blame is fixed to the salespeople – though we must make every effort to ensure it doesn't happen.'

'Oh yes, Mrs Burrows,' Shirley said, her innocent young face earnest. 'I think it is terrible to take what doesn't belong to you. My mother says folk that do that should have their hands chopped off.'

'Oh, dear me,' Beth said and smiled at her. 'That is a bit drastic – but I certainly think they should be locked up in prison. We had a young woman here – her name was Janice Browning – and she stole from Harpers. We discovered it too late and she got away with it, but I often think about her and wonder what she is up to these days. I hope she isn't using Harpers' name to blind employers to the truth. If they wrote here for a reference, they certainly would not get one.'

Shirley shook her head, but customers were beginning to flood into the department again after the lunchtime break, which was sometimes slower.

Beth went to stand behind her counter, frowning as Becky Stockbridge came rushing in five minutes late. She glanced at her watch pointedly, but her own counter was busy so she couldn't say anything to the girl and Shirley was managing very well. However, Beth would have a word later on.

'I wanted a bag like the ones you used to have before the war started,' the very smart young woman Beth was serving said in complaining tones. 'These leather ones are all very well, but I need something special.'

'You were looking for crocodile or snake skin,' Beth said and sighed, because this wasn't the first disappointed customer she'd had recently. 'I'm terribly sorry, madam, but Harpers can't stock them for the moment – they all come in from abroad and the ships are needed to carry more important things, like food and ammunition.'

'Oh, the war.' The young woman sniffed in disgust. 'Everywhere you go, it's the same – we can't get this because of the war or we can't get that. Do you know, I couldn't find one pair of black patent shoes I liked this morning. I think it is outrageous.'

'Oh, I agree it is such a nuisance,' Beth said, knowing from experience that it was best to agree with difficult customers like this one. 'I wish I could offer you our usual range – and I'm sure we shall have them in again as soon as the war is over, but I do have a beautiful black patent bag and if you should find the shoes you want...'

'Show me,' the customer demanded, and Beth brought out one of their most expensive bags with a diamanté clasp. She saw from the gleam in the young woman's eyes that she'd hit the right note. 'Well, there was one pair of shoes I quite liked, but they were for evening wear – and so is this.' She thought for a moment. 'How much is it – two guineas? Yes, I think I'll take it.' She smiled suddenly. 'I can afford the shoes and the bag and I didn't think I could.'

Beth hid her smile as she turned away to find a bag and some tissue to wrap it. She took her customer's money and watched her walk happily from the department. A lot of customers complained when they couldn't buy what they wanted, but deep down they all knew that they were lucky to have as much choice as they still had at Harpers. The reason was that Sally was tireless in seeking out new sources of supply and in getting the best deals from her suppliers. Beth had noticed the shelves of some of the shops in Oxford Street getting a little sparse in places. It was obviously going to get harder as the war progressed and the country began to run out of raw materials.

Once again, Beth thought that she wouldn't change places with Sally Harper; it was never an easy job and it was just going to get more difficult.

'I'm sorry I was late back.' Becky Stockbridge came over to Beth when there was a quiet moment at the counters. 'I was searching for some gifts to send Maggie Gibbs.' She bit her lip, tears hovering. 'I wanted something really useful, so I bought her a pair of warm stockings, a tin of toffees and a box of Pears soap and then I wrapped it up and I had to wait ages in the Post Office to send it...'

'Well, that was nice of you,' Beth said and felt a stab of grief. 'I hope Maggie will appreciate your thoughtfulness, Miss Stockbridge – and, next time, I suggest you wrap things at home and queue in your own time. I shall overlook on this occasion, but you know the rules.'

'Yes, Mrs Burrows. I am sorry.'

Beth nodded but didn't smile and the girl returned to her counter looking chastened. Maggie still hadn't written to them and Beth was struggling to cope with the lack of communication from her. She had tried to understand her point of view, but it still felt wrong. Surely Maggie would want to be at Tim's funeral?

Fred was putting a brave face on it. He'd got a photograph of

Tim on his chest of drawers in his bedroom, but he'd hardly said a word about his son since the funeral. Beth had stood by his side in church that awful morning, feeling chilled and frozen even though it was a pleasant spring day. She'd placed a little posy of tulips on Tim's grave, tears trickling down her cheeks. Both Jack and Fred had stood white-faced but silent and neither of them had said a word against Maggie – but Beth still found it hard to accept that she hadn't come or sent any kind of message. How could she not if she'd loved him?

Jack had returned to his ship and if anything, her anxiety was worse than it had ever been. Coupled with her distress at what she saw as Maggie's rejection of Tim's family, it weighed heavily on her.

She struggled to put aside her grief and her anger as a customer entered the department and headed for her counter. Once she started showing the beautiful silver jewellery, her feelings became calmer and she pushed thoughts of Maggie to a far corner of her mind, but she could not banish the hurt deep inside her. After her customer had gone, Rachel came up to her and asked if she would like to have a coffee with her after work.

'Yes, why not?' Beth said. 'We don't see each other to really talk often enough these days...'

* * *

Sadie looked at Maggie's face as she entered their hut and sighed. She looked so ill, but she just wouldn't give in, wouldn't take a minute longer from her duty than was necessary. She was the first to volunteer for an extra shift and she hadn't taken a day off to stay in the village or at the farm for weeks – not since the news of her fiancé's death, and it was killing her.

'Here, love, have some cocoa,' Sadie said and gave her a mug brimming with the hot creamy chocolate drink. 'I went and got these for us, because I knew you wouldn't bother.'

Maggie gave her a wan smile and sat down on the bed. 'Thanks, Sadie, I haven't had anything since this morning.'

'You must eat,' Sadie said and shoved a ham sandwich in front of her. 'I got this too and it's not bad – eat and drink or I'll force-feed you...'

'You're a good friend,' Maggie said. She bit into the ham sandwich reluctantly and ate slowly. 'I just don't think about food. All I can think about is those poor men; so many of them every day. Earlier, Sister Martin wanted volunteers to greet the transport and look after the new influx of wounded – as you know, we don't have enough beds for them. They were lying on stretchers on the ground, some just on the earth. We went from one to the other, doing what we could – most of them didn't stand a chance...'

'I know.' Sadie nodded and reached for her hand as she saw the look of despair in her friend's eyes. 'We can only do such much, Maggie love. I know you want to save them all but no one can.'

'Tim didn't have a chance. I didn't have the chance to save him,' Maggie said, and her face was suddenly white with pain. 'When his plane went down, he just died out there alone and no one was there for him... I need to be there for these men, Sadie. I keep thinking if I can make it a little easier for them, perhaps Tim will know that it's him I'm thinking about, that I wish I could ease his pain and fear, and with every man that recovers, perhaps a little bit of Tim's spirit will live on...'

'Yes, love, I know,' Sadie said and went to put her arm about her shoulders.

'He must have been alive at first and he froze to death in the sea,' Maggie said, her voice breaking with grief. 'All those hours he was waiting for help, desperately clinging to life, and when it came it was too late, and Sally's letter told me it was poor Jack's ship that found him. It must be a chance in a million, Sadie – but perhaps it was meant, God wanted him to be found so that we would know for certain he was dead.'

'Oh, Maggie, don't think about it,' Sadie said and tears were trickling down her cheeks as she held her friend in her arms and rocked her to and fro. 'It wasn't your fault, love. You couldn't have saved him, Maggie, it was just bad luck that he went down so far from land that he wasn't found in time, and yes, perhaps it was fate or God who decreed that Jack's ship was the one that found him. Stranger things have happened. Either way, you couldn't have changed anything.'

'I know.' Maggie blinked hard. 'I'm sorry. I didn't mean to put this on you, to upset you.'

'I'm your friend. That's what friends are for,' Sadie replied and hugged her tight. 'I know how much it hurts, Maggie. I want to help you, but there's nothing much I can do except be here for you.'

'Thank you for being a friend,' Maggie said. 'I know I have friends at home, but I couldn't face them when he was buried – I wasn't ready. I'll write soon, to Fred first.'

'They will understand,' Sadie told her. 'Of course they will.'

'I had a letter from Becky Stockbridge, she says Beth wouldn't let her write before. She said how sorry she was and she's sending me a parcel.' Maggie wiped her face with the back of her hand. 'Beth and Sally and Fred sent letters, but I couldn't read them, it was too soon – but I'll read them and then I'll write.'

'That Lieutenant was here earlier,' Sadie said, skilfully changing the subject. 'He saw me as I was on my way to the canteen and asked how you were.'

'Oh, do you mean Mick?' Maggie nodded. 'He was very kind when he told me...' She caught back a sob and raised her head.

'Thank you for the food and the cocoa. I might come to the village with you this weekend – but for now I'm tired and I need to sleep.'

'I'm not surprised,' Sadie said and drew back the blankets. 'Get into bed and I shan't disturb you. I'm on duty in half an hour.' She stood looking down at Maggie as she closed her eyes. Maggie looked absolutely drained, as if she'd given her all, but she wouldn't stop, she wouldn't give in. She was hardly nineteen years old and this had aged her, drawing lines of grief about her eyes. It was as if she was punishing herself for Tim's death.

Sadie bent down and kissed her forehead as she slept. She was fond of Maggie, thought of her as a sister, and she would take care of her until she was able to look after herself again. Left to herself, Maggie would never eat and, in the end, she would collapse, but Sadie was determined to see her through. If she could get her away for the weekend she would, because it would do her the world of good to leave the pain and suffering behind for a while.

Sadie smiled. Her own love life was progressing slowly. She'd seen Pierre twice in the last few weeks and each time she liked him more and more. Their kisses had become passionate and she knew he would want more than kisses soon. His work was dangerous and Sadie was aware that it was foolish to give her heart, even more so her virginity, because she could end up losing everything, just as Maggie had. In fact, she could lose more, for Maggie still had her career and her reputation and if Sadie fell for a child, she would lose both, but love came where it would and she didn't have much choice because she'd fallen head over heels when they met for the very first time, and next time he was home and his kiss inflamed her, she wasn't sure she could say no.

Perhaps Maggie would meet someone else in time. Sadie hoped so, but she wouldn't dream of suggesting it, because Maggie would instantly reject the idea. She thought that lieutenant who had inquired so earnestly after Maggie was handsome and rather nice, and that Irish accent was dreamy, so perhaps there was hope for her friend after all...

* * *

Maggie opened her eyes to find that it was still dark. Not time for her to get up yet, but she couldn't stay in bed any longer. She'd slept for a few hours because she was worn out, and that was the only way she could sleep. Unless she did extra shifts and made herself so tired that the weariness claimed her, her mind wouldn't let her rest.

She'd loved Tim so much, more than she'd even known, and her regrets were bitter, like a lead weight inside her. Why hadn't she married him? Why hadn't she gone to bed with him before he left her at the end of their last leave? She'd wanted to, but they'd resisted and now it was too late. In that moment, Maggie wished so much that she was pregnant with Tim's child. It would have given her something of him, something to look forward to.

'Oh, Tim, why...' she whispered into the darkness and suddenly the hot tears cascaded and she was sobbing her heart out. 'Tim, my darling, I love you so very much.'

Maggie turned her face to the pillow and let the tears fall. She'd wept once in Michael O'Sullivan's arms and not since until Sadie had comforted her and she felt a few tears on her cheeks, but now it was like a dam had broken and her grief poured out.

After a while, the tears stopped. Maggie felt strangely calm as she got up and washed her face in some cold water from a jug on the washstand she and Sadie shared. Her friend's kindness had unblocked that knot of misery inside her and she was feeling a bit more like herself at last. The grief for Tim was still there, but Maggie could cope now. The pain was there in her chest and she knew that there would always be an empty place inside her, but her life would go on.

Suddenly, she was aware of being very hungry. She pulled on a clean uniform and apron. She would visit the canteen and ask for some bacon and eggs with fried bread if they had it and then she would write to Fred.

* * *

When Beth came downstairs on a Saturday morning two weeks later, she found Fred sitting at the kitchen table, tears streaming down his cheeks.

'Oh, Fred – Dad!' she cried and went to him at once. 'What is it?'

'Read that.' He thrust a single sheet of paper at her.

My dear Fred – or may I call you Dad this once? I had hoped that you would be my father when Tim and I married. We talked of how we would live with you and how we would make sure you were never lonely as you grew into old age and we hoped to give you grandchildren. Tim loved you so much and I have grown to think of you as he did: kind, loving and strong – someone he could always lean on in times of stress.

I am sorry I didn't come home for Tim's funeral, but I couldn't bear it. One day I will visit his grave and bring flowers, but for the moment I have to stay here. There are thousands of men begging for help and each time I am able to relieve their pain and grief, I feel that I am helping Tim as I wish I had been able to in his time of need. I believe that he understands and he will always be with me in my heart. And perhaps with each man that lives because of what we do, a little of my Tim lives on in them.

I am your friend and daughter for always. Forgive me, Fred.
Tears flow as I write and I cannot write more.
Your loving Maggie. xxx

'Oh, Dad...' Beth said and the tears ran down her cheeks. 'Poor little Maggie. I didn't realise... I was angry with her for not coming home but...' She shook her head, unable to go on and Fred reached for her hand and held it tightly.

'You mustn't be angry, Beth. She's a brave, dear girl, and we must love her and support her as much as we can.'

'Yes.' Beth smiled at him through her tears. 'We must and I'm sorry I doubted her for an instant.'

20

Sally read the letter from Mick and smiled. He'd been back to the hospital where Maggie worked a couple of times and, although he hadn't seen her, he'd spoken to her friend, Sadie.

> *Maggie has a good friend in the lass, Sally. She looks after her, makes her eat and drink, makes sure there's a cup of hot cocoa for her when she comes off duty. Sadie says she's taken it very hard and works long hours – longer than anyone else – but Maggie is determined to do all she can for the poor devils they bring in on every transport. Ah, it's the pity of it, to see those young lads lying there crying for their mothers and those gallant young girls holding their hands and giving them a sip of water and a puff of a cigarette. Most of them don't even make it into the tents…*
>
> *I shouldn't tell you, Sally darling, but it's best you understand what's going on out here. You might think your friend should come home, but she can't – she's too busy trying to save lives. Her young man didn't get a chance and maybe that's why young Maggie is trying so hard to save all the others*

– try to see it her way, and I know you will, because you've a good heart.

'Another letter?' Ben asked when he walked into the kitchen carrying his daughter in his arms. 'She was wet, so I changed her – is that all right?'

'Of course it is,' Sally said and smiled as he put the little girl into her arms. Jenny opened her eyes and laughed up at her. 'Are you hungry, my love? Shall I give you a little bit of soft bread dipped in egg this morning?'

'Is she eating solids yet?' Ben asked, surprised. 'It astonishes me how fast she is growing up.'

'She likes soft foods, but only a little as yet, and she still enjoys her bottle or anything milky,' Sally answered. 'Most things have to be mashed up, but she does like the taste of a boiled egg and she sucks it off the bread and butter.'

Ben looked at her adoringly as she settled Jenny in her high chair. 'I can't believe she's almost a year old.'

'Well, she is in a few days,' Sally said and smiled. 'I've bought her a beautiful soft toy from you. It's a Steiff and I was lucky to get it – the shop assistant told me it was the last they had in stock.'

'Isn't that a German maker?'

'Yes, I think so – but it's the best of its kind, Ben.'

He frowned. 'I'm not sure I want my child to have anything they made, what else did you buy her?'

'A silver rattle and teething amber and two pretty dresses.'

'Get her a silver mug and spoon from me and give the Steiff to a jumble sale,' Ben said. 'You can find her another toy made here in England, can't you?'

'Yes, of course.' Sally felt a little upset that he'd rejected her choice, but decided to ignore it. Perhaps she ought to have realised that he would reject something made in Germany, because that was how most people felt in Britain now that the war was biting and so many men dying. 'I can hardly believe she's a year old next week. It just shows how time flies, doesn't it?'

'Too quickly,' Ben said and frowned. 'Was that letter from Jenni?' His sister hadn't written for weeks now and it was causing them concern.

'No, it was from Mick. You can read it if you like, Ben; it's mostly about Maggie.'

'Is she all right? But that's a daft question, of course she isn't.'

'He thinks she's probably working too hard to compensate,' Sally said, looking at him anxiously. 'Why don't you send Jenni a telegram? Ask her to send one back. It just isn't like her not to write or get in touch all this time, it must be three months or more since she said she thought she might be pregnant.'

'That is what worries me,' Ben replied, his eyes dark with anxiety for his sister. Jenni was always keeping them in touch with her life, so ready to come over or buy stock for them, that the long silence was concerning. 'I'd go over if I didn't have so much work on,' he said and glanced at his watch as he took a piece of toast and bit into it. 'I'd better leave, Sally, I have a meeting at nine, sharp, with the Prime Minister.'

'Then you had better go,' Sally urged, because it was already twenty past eight. 'You mustn't be late, Ben. I don't have to get in until ten this morning – and Mrs Hills will be here by then. Pearl is coming this afternoon.'

'I'll be home early this evening. If Pearl is happy to look after Jenny, we could go out somewhere...'

'I'll ask her, but I'm sure she will.'

'I must go,' Ben said and bent to kiss her on the cheek.

Sally kissed him back and smiled as he left. Ben was moving in exalted circles these days and forever busy. She never questioned him about his war work, that was off limits, so they talked about Harpers and their own lives. Sally continually thanked her lucky stars that Ben seemed settled in London; his arm had healed and he'd been told not to risk his life on any more trips to the front line. Tim Burrows' tragic end had made her even more aware of how fortunate she was and she sometimes felt a bit guilty when she saw how hard Beth had taken her brother-in-law's death.

Sally reflected that she had very little on at work after her morning appointments and decided that she would take a couple of hours off to help at the hospital. She popped in whenever she had time to spare, often in the afternoon, but when Ben was away, she sometimes went in the evening. She did very little really, but the men were grateful for small gifts and for someone to write letters or simply rearrange pillows. At least she'd helped a few of them get the treatment they needed, because Sister Maine had told her that Mr Alexander had taken four of their patients up to his clinic so far, including Captain Maclean. It was something, but with so many injured and dying of their wounds, it could never be enough and Sally totally understood why Maggie was determined to stay out in France.

Sighing, Sally settled her little girl and then started to get ready for work.

* * *

'I hope you didn't mind my popping into your office,' Marlene said later that morning. 'I know how busy you are – I haven't disturbed you?'

Sally shook her head. 'I had a new representative to see this morning. He comes from Norfolk and had several lines in the footwear department to show me. I gave him a big order and I'm not sure who was more pleased – him or me.'

'I expect they need the orders to keep going in these difficult times.'

'Yes, but all the stores are looking for supplies – however, Mr Rowley says he wants to secure a market for his goods with Harpers. Until now he's sold most of his stock through local outlets and he's right that I might not have seen him in normal times. These boots and shoes are more for work and hard-wearing than fashion, but men need them to be that way these days and so do women when they can't replace their shoes as often as usual. I think the working girl will appreciate them, but some of our smarter customers will think them too plain.'

'Some of my girls would be glad of them. My waitress, Lily, was complaining she couldn't find a comfortable working shoe the other day, they were all too expensive for her.'

'Well, our new stock will be in next week and they sell from twelve shillings a pair for button shoes with a small heel.'

'That's still quite a lot, but she should be able to afford it. I'll tell her about them,' Marlene said and smiled. 'And now, I'll tell you why I've come.' Her smile grew broader. 'Captain Maclean is back in the same London hospital as before and he wants to see you.'

'How is he?' Sally looked at her in surprise.

'He's had several treatments on his face and, well, perhaps I should let you see the improvement for yourself,' Marlene said. 'It is really quite remarkable. Apparently, he has to return for further treatment in about six months, but they think he's had enough for now and want to let him rest a while.'

'Then I shall pop in and see him this afternoon when I visit the hospital,' Sally said. 'That is wonderful news, Marlene. Thank you so much for coming to tell me...'

'I thought you would wish to know, because you went out of your way to help him,' Marlene replied. 'You didn't know who he was and you had no connection – and that makes it all the more remarkable.'

'He was in desperate need of help, Marlene, and something about him, about his sad story, touched a nerve and made me determined to help him.' She gave a little shake of her head. 'When I was in the orphanage as a little girl, I used to see some of the other kids in floods of tears, because they'd been caned or put in a corner. I always wanted to do something to help, but if I spoke out, I was thrust in the coal cellar and left to reflect on my wickedness and my hands were caned. I suppose that now I have a little influence, I choose to use it for those I consider need protecting – and there was something about Captain Maclean that reminded me of a little boy who was severely beaten on his legs by the nuns. He was in so much pain that he couldn't walk for days.'

'Oh, Sally, that is terrible – I didn't realise.' Marlene looked horrified. 'I thought they were supposed to be God-fearing people?'

'It was all done in the name of religion, to teach us to be good,' Sally said, 'but I think most of them just enjoyed inflicting pain on us – and little boys the most. I caught it too, because I was too stubborn to give in.'

'So that's why you do so much for others.' Marlene looked struck.

'I'm not sure I do very much,' Sally replied with a wry smile. 'I think I have it pretty easy – but I do remember what it was like to be at the mercy of those harsh women.' She shook her head. 'When I was leaving, one of the nuns – a little kinder than some of the others – gave me a silver cross that was my mother's. She wouldn't tell me anything more – just that it had belonged to my mother – but one day I'll go back and demand to know the truth.'

'So, you never knew your mother?'

'I was never told anything until the day I left when Sister Martha gave me the cross.'

'That is wicked,' Marlene said indignantly. 'You were not treated kindly, Sally – but I think I understand you more now – what drives you.' She smiled. 'Well, I'm not going to take up more of your time. I need to get back to my restaurant and see if everything I ordered has turned up. You have to be so careful these days. They will short-change you or send you inferior quality if you don't watch it.'

'Are you finding it difficult to keep up your standards?' Sally asked. 'I know it isn't easy.'

'I think it must be as bad for you.' Marlene gave a little shudder. 'How you manage to keep this place stocked, I don't know. It must be hard enough in normal times.'

'It's a case of being willing to compromise,' Sally acknowledged. 'I have to find smaller firms who I didn't know about before the war. Many of them have increased their capacity somehow. I think they've drafted in their grannies, grandfathers and their children to keep the workshops going.'

'It's all the fault of this horrid war,' Marlene said. 'They promised us it would be over by Christmas, but by the look of the news, it could go on for years.'

'Oh, I do hope not,' Sally said and sighed. 'I want Mr Marco back to dress Harpers' windows and the other brave young men who are over there too – and I want Ben back here in the office, rather than having meetings with the War Office all the time.'

Marlene nodded sympathetically. 'It isn't long since Mick was home on leave, so we caught up on all our business, but things aren't the same without him around. I miss his smile, Sally.' Marlene looked sad. 'He's more like a son to me than a business partner these days and I think the world of him.'

'I can understand that,' Sally agreed. 'To me Mick is a really good friend and I miss seeing him around, though of course I didn't see him as much as you.'

Marlene nodded. They talked some more about the wounded men they were trying to help find something like a normal life and then Marlene left. Even before Marlene's visit, Sally had already decided that she would quit work early that afternoon and visit the hospital before she went home. By the sound of it, Mr Alexander had done wonders and she was hopeful that Captain Maclean would at least be able to meet the world now that his face had been put back together again. He would have scars, skin discolouration, and probably bumps or lumps still, but he would look more or less normal, instead of the misshapen monster his injuries had made him.

It was so cruel the way this war destroyed men's lives and yet left them living and forced to face the consequences of what had happened to them – loss of limbs was terrible enough but catastrophic injuries to the face and head could be even worse.

Sally sighed as she thought of all the people she cared about, caught up in this terrible war. So many young men and women too had decided to help their country. But Sally wondered about the ones she'd known so well, wishing she knew more about their welfare. They hadn't had a card from Mr Marco for a while now and it made her wonder just where he was and what he was doing.

21

The atmosphere of the nightclub was thick with cigarette smoke and the strong odour of human bodies, wine and beer. A group of German officers were occupying the front tables close to the piano at which Marco had been seated for the past two hours. He'd been playing the songs they requested over and over again, most of them packed with innuendo that could be taken two ways but which made these men roar with laughter, because they took them to be filthy, and of course they were, sung in a certain way. Marco knew exactly how to please his audience and he had them in the palm of his hand, which pleased Andre Renard, the manager of the club, because it led to more and more orders for the best champagne and that would please the boss, Paul Mallon, who only visited to collect his takings once a week and lived many kilometres away from the village.

'Play that one again, Marco,' one of the officers called and Marco struck the opening chord, but just as he did so a Frenchman dressed in rough working clothes limped up to him. He had been sitting glowering in his corner all night watching and drinking the rough red wine of the house, and now he slouched forward and spat into Marco's face.

'Dirty collaborator,' he muttered in French. 'You should be run out of town.' He lurched forward and grabbed Marco's wrist, his fingers pressing hard against his hand as the message was passed.

Marco understood and his hand closed over the small piece of paper. He put up a hand as if to steady the drunk and slipped it inside his shirt cuff. 'You're not fit to call yourself French,' he said mildly as the drunk stumbled away.

'Disgusting beast.' One of the officers grunted, got to his feet and offered Marco a handkerchief to wipe the spittle from his face. 'Do you want me to teach the bastard a lesson? I'll have some of my men give him a beating.'

'Why bother?' Marco said and smiled as he accepted the handkerchief to wipe his face. 'He is a fool – knocked senseless in a fight, they say. Let him go, he doesn't worry me. Shall I have this washed for you?' He offered the handkerchief.

'Keep it,' the officer smiled at him. 'I doubt the fool had much sense even before his brains were knocked out of him.' He returned to his seat.

Marco tucked the handkerchief in his sleeve, securing the note further inside his cuff.

The Frenchman had shambled off out of the club.

Marco played on for another half an hour and then stood up, announcing that he needed a break and would return soon. This was greeted with calls of disappointment and instruction to come back soon as the night was still young. Promising he would, Marco left them to watch the girls Andre had sent on to dance for their customers while he had his break; they were soon whistling and calling out, Marco forgotten as the scantily dressed girls tantalised and teased, wiggling their rears to loud applause.

Alone in his room, Marco took out the handkerchief and

threw it on the dressing table. He took out the note Pierre had passed him right under the noses of the Germans and read it.

Something big is happening soon. Can you discover more details from your contact and let Cecile know whatever details you can?

Marco read it twice and was about to tear it into pieces when the door opened and Kurt entered. To hide the note furtively would cause suspicion. Marco tossed it onto the dressing table carelessly and smiled.

'How are you?' he asked the young man he liked despite the fact that Kurt was the enemy. Over the past weeks they had developed a kind of friendship.

'I hope you don't mind that I came up,' Kurt said. 'Johannes just entered the club, so I came to hide.'

'Of course, I don't mind,' Marco said. He moved towards him and embraced him lightly. 'Will you stay tonight?'

'For a while,' Kurt said and looked at him hungrily. 'You don't have to go back yet, do you?'

'I was going to have a drink.' Marco showed him the bottle of good burgundy wine. 'It's better than they serve downstairs,' he said as he poured it into two crystal glasses.

Kurt took the glass he was offered, swirled the rich ruby liquid and nodded. 'It is one of the things I like about you, your taste for good things; it's something we share.' He smiled his appreciation.

'Yes, we both like the finer things of life.'

'What was the note that fool passed to you?' Kurt asked, his tone unchanged. He might have been asking what the weather was like outside. 'It was careless of him. Anyone could have seen it and you could have been arrested.' He looked at Marco hard. 'You take too many risks, my friend.' Kurt picked up the note Marco had been careful not to hide and read it. He nodded, but his expression did not change. 'I'm not a fool, Marco. That pig Johannes made that mistake – I may be a coward, but I am not a fool.'

'I never thought you were,' Marco said. His heart was racing. Was Kurt about to have him arrested? He'd been so careful, but something he'd said or done had alerted the lieutenant to what he was really doing here.

'Have I told you much?' Kurt asked now, still in that same toneless voice.

'Not very much,' Marco said. 'Not much more than I could have picked up listening to the customers.'

Kurt nodded and examined his fingernails for a moment in silence. 'I hate this war and I hate the German Army. I never wanted to join,' he said and looked up at Marco, his intense blue eyes meeting his gaze. 'I want to live in England when it is all over – I thought if you really liked me, we might have a life together?'

'I do like you – more than I ought,' Marco admitted. Kurt was good company and could be amusing. In other times they might have been very good friends, without the barrier that lurked beneath the surface. 'Perhaps when it is all over...'

'You're an artist in many ways,' Kurt went on. 'I admire that – I could love you, Marco.' He smiled and there was sweetness in that smile. At times, there was something that reminded Marco of a man he'd loved very much, of Julien. 'I can cook you know. I'm good at looking after things. We could have a home together one day.'

'Yes,' Marco agreed, 'we could – unless, you feel it your duty to report me as a spy?' He must not allow his memories of Julien to become entangled with this man – Kurt was the enemy and he must use him for the good of Britain. Sentiment must not be allowed to make him careless, even though he thought in other times there might have been a chance for them.

'Why would I do that?' Kurt asked carelessly. 'I hate those fat pigs out there and what they stand for, and I love you.' He moved closer. 'If you feel that we could have a life together in England, I could tell you much more than you will hear out there...'

'We can have a life together, Kurt,' Marco said and reached out to touch his cheek. 'Can you forgive me for deceiving you?'

'I wasn't deceived for a moment,' Kurt said and laughed softly. 'I told you what I wanted you to know – things I hoped would cause Johannes trouble and it did. He has been reprimanded for careless talk a couple of times.' A hint of malice gleamed in his glacial eyes. 'There is something big happening soon, Marco. Listen carefully and I'll give you the details to pass on to your contacts.'

'Thank you for trusting me,' Marco said. 'I'm not sure I deserve it.'

'But you do – you saved me that night. I was desperate. If you hadn't shown me kindness, I might have taken my own life.' Kurt smiled oddly and Marco's heart jolted, as he recalled the man he had not been able to save. Julien's suicide would never leave him in peace. 'Your engineers and tunnellers are preparing to take our lines by surprise. They think we don't know how near they've got to our front lines, but we discovered it days ago. Our tunnellers are working from the other side and at about midnight on Thursday we shall break through and then Oberst Johannes Hoffmeister intends to send his crack team through the tunnels straight to your lines. Any men caught in the tunnel will be killed and they'll overrun your trenches and kill as many as they can before escaping.'

Marco stared at him. This was big, something he would never have picked up listening to the careless talk around the tables. He might have heard laughter about the English getting a surprise, but this was so valuable that he was in two minds whether Kurt was telling him the truth.

'Yes, you can believe me,' Kurt said and leaned forward to kiss him softly on the lips. 'It is my gift to you, Marco. I'm leaving now by the back stairs. When your people congratulate you on giving them such valuable information, you will know you can trust me as I trust you.'

'You have to go?' Sometimes Kurt stayed on into the early hours, drinking good wine and, occasionally sharing Marco's bed.

'Yes, I need to get back, because I'm on duty.' Kurt smiled. 'Destroy that note, Marco. I'm not the only one who might decide to visit you this evening.'

Marco nodded and tore the note into shreds before setting it alight with a match in an ashtray. He was thoughtful as Kurt left, a little rueful. He'd thought himself clever, making the first moves on Kurt, but the German had been aware of his motives, perhaps, as he claimed, from the start. Kurt was no fool – just afraid of the man who had used him that night. It was hardly any wonder that he hated the German officer so much he would betray him without a quiver.

Finishing his drink, Marco went back downstairs. He would continue to entertain the officers in the club until it closed. Later, when he was rested and it was light enough to be sure he was not being followed, he would contact Pierre at the café. Kurt could have set a trap for him. He didn't think so, but he would contact the man Kurt already knew of so that if they were arrested his other contacts would remain safe. Marco was no fool either and he'd decided he would not risk Cecile this time. She was a nurse and more vulnerable; she was also more likely to break under torture. Pierre knew what it was all about. He'd been wounded more than once and understood pain.

If Kurt had just been playing with him, Marco would learn what pain could mean before tomorrow evening. He would make sure the cyanide crystals were hidden about his person just in case but pray that Kurt had meant it when he said he wanted them to live together after this damned war. It could save his life and, if the German proved himself a good friend, might be the beginning of a lasting friendship.

If he had been telling the truth, they were on the verge of something important. Marco would be able to pass on valuable information more often and on a larger scale than he'd dreamed of.

22

They were nearing the breakthrough point now and everyone's nerves were on edge. If the information received was correct, the Germans were tunnelling just a few feet away and due to open up the last section and surprise them in two days, but instead they would be getting the surprise.

Mick glanced back at the men behind him as he set the low explosive charge. Every one of them was a hardened soldier, armed and ready and used to this kind of nerve-wracking work. What could have taken another day or two to get through little by little would be weakened by the explosion and then he and the crack troops he was a part of would pour through the gap and down the tunnels, sweeping any opposition before them. It was what the enemy had planned for them, but because of the information received, the tables were turned.

Mick set the charge and ran back to where the others were sheltering behind a barrier of wood and stones. The noise was deafening and they all had their hands over their ears, heads down until the dust cleared.

When Mick looked up, he saw it had worked and they were

through to the German side of the tunnel and the intelligence had been good for once. You could never be sure you wouldn't be miles off course or completely on the wrong track when information was received, but this had proved true.

He was on his feet, leading the charge, scrambling through the dust and debris into the tunnels that had been dug by foreign hands. He could hear startled shouts somewhere ahead, because the enemy was uncertain what had happened. They knew something was going on but were confused and the first man to come face to face with the avenging British soldiers died without knowing what had hit him.

Fighting in such cramped quarters was the stuff of nightmares, because you scrambled over the man you'd killed and on to the next one, either killing or being killed. It was just down to who had the quickest reactions, who shot first or used his bayonet to clear the way. Mick was well into the German tunnels and he wasn't sure how many men he'd killed or injured before he met someone who was faster.

He fell with a bullet in his chest, vaguely conscious of the men behind him pulling him to one side as they surged past deeper and deeper into the tunnels. Before he lost his senses and sank into the darkness that enveloped him in a haze of pain, Mick thought there could be only one outcome. The enemy hadn't been ready and there were forty good men with him prepared to sell their lives dearly. They would win the day and kill numbers of the enemy before they retreated back to their lines. He probably wouldn't live to know the truth, but he was sure that in this stalemate of trench warfare, it would be hailed as a victory – small, but a victory just the same.

* * *

Maggie was one of the first to meet the convoy that afternoon. The trucks, lorries and waggons were overflowing with wounded men, as always. She greeted the driver of the first lorry and asked what category of wounded he was carrying.

'These were all involved in a fierce fight, nurse,' he said. 'It was close combat and you'll find stab wounds as well as bullet wounds. Most of this first lot are alive and with a chance of recovery, I would think.'

'Good, that's what we like to hear,' Maggie said. 'We'll take them inside tent C please, private. We have beds waiting there, some of our less severely wounded men went home yesterday.'

Private Reggie Jackson nodded. If you got what was called a Blighty wound, it meant you would be shipped home as soon as there was a ship available to take you. Blighty wounds were usually serious, but the men had pulled through the worst of it and were judged fit enough to travel, possibly after weeks of being nursed in the field hospitals. The dangerously ill patients were in tent A, because they often didn't last long and those that did were too sick to be sent home for weeks, perhaps months.

'Do you have a list of their names, Private Jackson?' Maggie asked.

'Yes, nurse.' He handed it to her and looked at her consideringly. 'I reckon I've seen you before – before this lot, back in England. Didn't you use to work in Harpers?'

'Yes, I did,' Maggie smiled at him. 'I don't remember you, I'm afraid.'

'Oh, I didn't work there,' he said. 'I'm Reggie Jackson – and I'm engaged to Marion Kaye. I think she pointed you out once and I saw you talking when I was waiting for her a couple of times.'

'Oh, dear Marion! It's a small world,' Maggie said and smiled warmly. She still had no sense of recognition, but she knew the name, because Marion had talked about him often enough. 'How are you doing, Private Jackson?'

'I'm doin' all right, nurse,' he said and grinned. 'This duty is the easy one. I get to drive these poor devils down here and grab a decent meal in the canteen before I'm back up the line.'

'Well, it's nice to meet you.' Maggie was checking the list. Her pencil hovered over a name and she looked up sharply. 'You have Lieutenant Michael O'Sullivan on your list – is he badly wounded?'

'He took a bullet in his chest,' Reggie Jackson said and frowned. 'A very brave man – he's a top man in the explosives team of engineers and he led from the front yesterday. If the ball had entered a fraction lower, it would have killed him, but it looks as if it hit his cigarette case and veered off into his shoulder area. At least that's what the doc said who patched him up when he was carried back into our lines.'

'He has been lucky then,' Maggie said, feeling relieved as she waved goodbye to him. She couldn't see the young officer who had brought her the news of Tim's death amongst the wounded, but several stretchers had already been carried into tent C. Maggie saw all the wounded off and then went to meet the next truck. When the more severely wounded were carried into their allotted tents, they would be tended to by the doctors and nurses on duty there; her duty this morning was to see the injured settled in the right wards, or tents, which was all they had to house badly injured men here. So, she couldn't go to investigate Lieutenant O'Sullivan's injuries just yet, because she had to oversee the rest of the new arrivals.

Lorry after lorry and several farm carts lined up to bring them in. Sometimes, it seemed that there were endless streams of badly wounded men. The next two loads of men were all very seriously injured, some of them had blast wounds, which meant they'd lost limbs, and in the case of one unfortunate youngster, the side of his face. Maggie instructed he be sent to tent A; he was unlikely to live long, but he would get care and attention from the nurses, even if there was nothing the doctors could do for him.

Maggie held his hand, walking with him into the tent and talking to him until his stretcher was placed on the ground in a shady sheltered spot where he could have peace. He was barely conscious, his moans of pain growing fainter. She felt the sting of tears as she realised that this one probably wouldn't even make it to the end of the morning. At least he had somewhere quiet to lie until he passed, she thought, and soothed his forehead with her fingertips.

'I'll look after him now, nurse,' a senior nurse told her. 'You'd better get back to the transport.'

'Yes, Sister,' Maggie said. 'I don't think he's really aware.'

'Perhaps just as well. Off you go.'

Maggie obeyed, though she was reluctant to leave the soldier, who couldn't have been much more than sixteen and looked far too young to have been sent up to the trenches. The volunteers were supposed to be eighteen, but quite a few sixteen-year-olds and even one fifteen-year-old had managed to enlist and been wounded and sent back to England to be patched up. She doubted this lad would make it home, though sometimes men did survive with what looked like impossible wounds.

She shook her head, refusing to give in to the tears that threatened. Her job was to comfort those she could with a kind word or a touch of a soft hand, a sip of water, or, as many of them asked, a kiss on the cheek. Maggie kissed those that asked, because it made them smile and most of the nurses were willing to give an innocent peck on the cheek to a man suffering terrible pain.

'You're a beautiful angel,' a young cockney soldier told Maggie as she helped him walk from the transport to tent C. He was one of the less seriously wounded men and as cheeky as they came. She gave him a wrapped toffee from her pocket and refused to kiss him, because he was full of himself.

'You'll be fine once nurse has patched you up,' she told him. 'It's a Blighty wound for you, private.'

'I'd rather they patched me up and sent me back up the line, nurse. My best mate was killed last night and I want to kill a few of the buggers for Ricky.'

'Well, you can do that when they send you back, but by the look of your leg, you'll be on the next ship home.' Maggie smiled at him. The real heroes always said the same, none of them ever wanted to be sent home. It was the ones that were stretched to the limit who welcomed the journey back home to recover – but after what they'd gone through, they were heroes too. Of course, they were all heroes just to go up and over the top knowing it could be their death. Most of the men told her it was the waiting that got to them. Once the order came to go over, it was almost a relief.

It was a busy day and by the time the last of the wounded had been brought in, men were lying outside the tents because they were all filled to capacity. The nurses and orderlies fixed canvas over them to keep off the worst of the heat in the middle of the day. Maggie went from one patient to another, soothing them, giving them whatever care she could. The doctors walked round looking at them. Some men were taken inside to replace those that had died and been carried out the back way ready for burial. Unless there was a ship going home that had the capacity to take them home for burial, they were buried nearby in a local church-yard. The field behind the church had once been a pleasant meadow with wild flowers growing; now it was a field of wooden crosses. Perhaps in time the wild flowers would return and make a field of poppies, Maggie thought as she put a hand to her aching back.

'Nurse Gibbs,' Sister Mayhew's voice cut across her thoughts. 'You've been on duty since seven this morning – take a break now. Get something to eat and drink.'

'I'm all right, Sister...'

'You look like death walking,' the sister said gruffly. 'You will take a break, eat and drink, and then report to tent C. That is an order.'

'Yes, Sister.'

Maggie did as she was told. It was well past the time she ought to have taken a break for her midday meal, but she'd been too busy to bother, but when Sister Mayhew gave an order, you obeyed. She smiled wryly as she remembered that at Harpers the time for luncheon was always set and restricted. She'd always had to hurry back if she went across the road to the café and bought a bun or a ham sandwich with her tea. All that seemed a world away from this... nightmare of death, blood and the stench of unwashed bodies that often lay in their own urine until the nurses could wash away the stink of battle and fear.

Maggie ate a sandwich made of sizzling hot bacon with mustard and lots of grease. It filled up her empty space and she couldn't taste the tea afterwards, which was good because it was normally stewed. Feeling better for the food inside her, she walked towards tent C. It was a relief to enter the ward, which was cool after the heat of the day and smelled of disinfectant and medicines. In here, the stench of battle had been washed away and the men lay in clean beds, looking relaxed and comfortable.

'Ah, there you are, Nurse Gibbs.' Sister Mayhew looked at her critically. 'That's better. I can't have my best nurses fading away for lack of sustenance. We need girls of your calibre here. Now, follow me as I make my rounds. I want you to help me change bandages and you can write up whatever I tell you, so pick up that board and look sharp.'

'Yes, Sister.' Maggie was so surprised at being told that she was one of Sister Mayhew's best nurses that she obeyed instantly without feeling tired or anxious.

In the third bed they visited, Maggie saw Mick O'Sullivan. He opened his eyes as Sister spoke to him, looking at them both a little hazily. Maggie smiled at him but wasn't sure if he knew her.

'Well, young man,' Sister said in her stern voice. 'This is what comes of leading a mad charge. From what they tell me, you were supposed to do your job and retire to the back, but instead you went surging ahead and cleared the way for the men behind you until you were deep into enemy trenches and someone managed to stop you. You were lucky your friends refused to leave you behind. Otherwise, it would have been a German nurse sticking needles into you, if they didn't shoot you.'

'Sure, a needle is a needle, be it English or German,' the faintly Irish voice said and a flicker of a smile played over his mouth. "Tis cruel you are, Sister.' His eyes were focused on Maggie and recognition came. 'But 'tis an angel standin' behind you, so it is.'

Sister shook her head at him. 'He's not dying, nurse. This one will mend – be careful or he will lead you astray. It's Irish charm and I should know – my husband is Irish.'

'Are you married, Sister?' Maggie was surprised as she'd been told it was strictly forbidden.

Sister Mayhew smiled. 'I married and gave up my profession, but when the war happened, I volunteered to come out here as my husband was fighting in the trenches.'

'Oh, I didn't know,' Maggie said a little uncertainly. 'No one has ever said...'

'Because most don't know,' Sister Mayhew said and winked at her. 'It's not allowed and you mustn't tell – on pain of death.'

'Oh, I won't,' Maggie promised and laughed. She'd always

thought Sister Mayhew was so stern and strict, but it seemed she had a sense of humour after all.

'We shall leave you to sleep, Lieutenant O'Sullivan,' Sister Mayhew said.

'Call me Mick, Sister darlin',' Mick said and winked at her.

'Avoid this one like the plague,' Sister Mayhew said as she moved on to the next one, but there was a smile in her eyes.

'I'll come and see you later,' Maggie promised softly and then followed Sister to the next bed. She sensed that the lieutenant's eyes followed her as she walked in Sister's wake, but she didn't look round.

Sister Mayhew kept Maggie busy until past six o'clock that evening and then sent her off duty. Lieutenant O'Sullivan was sleeping soundly so Maggie didn't disturb him but went to the hut she shared with Sadie and others.

Sadie was just dressing. She glanced at Maggie inquiringly. 'Have you eaten?'

'Yes, Sister Mayhew made me take a break and I've had sufficient, thank you.'

'I'm going for breakfast now,' Sadie said and grinned at her. 'I like Sister Mayhew – she's not the dragon everyone thinks her. It's sad though...'

'What do you mean?' Maggie asked, looking at her in puzzlement.

'Her husband was killed soon after the war started,' Sadie said. 'Everyone thought she ought to go home, but she just stayed on and got on with the job.' Sadie looked at her. 'She's a bit like you really, Maggie love – a damn fine nurse. She said she was needed here and there was nothing to go home for.'

Maggie nodded but didn't say anything. She'd wondered why Sister Mayhew had singled her out, sending her to get food and drink and then taking her in hand for the rest of the day. Now she thought she understood. Sister must have heard that Maggie had lost her fiancé, because things like that got known even if you tried to keep them a secret, and decided that she needed a helping hand.

Maggie lifted her head determinedly. Sister Mayhew had been out here since the beginning. If she could carry on despite the loss of her husband so could Maggie.

* * *

Marco walked down to the café in the village and ordered coffee from the café manager, Jean Macron, behind the bar. He reached for his change, but the proprietor shook his head.

'Pierre is upstairs,' he said, because the café was empty. 'He has news.'

'May I use your toilets?' Marco asked just in case he was being watched from outside and Jean shrugged towards the back door.

Marco went through and up the back stairs to the room directly above. Pierre was reading a newspaper and frowning, the strong odour of French cigarettes testament to how long he'd been there.

'Was the information correct?' Marco asked, straight to the point. He needed to know if Kurt's information was reliable.

Pierre grinned and then nodded. 'They took the enemy by surprise and inflicted some damage. It won't shorten the war, but at least it saved the British trenches from being overrun.'

Marco nodded. 'Good. Let's hope he comes up with something significant in the future.'

'He's running a grave risk – and so are you,' Pierre said, frowning. 'Be careful of Paul Mallon. I warned you before – but I've heard he has been passing information to the Germans. One of my associates was arrested and shot yesterday – so be wary. Never leave anything about that he might find.'

'He only visits once a week to collect the takings but I shan't be careless,' Marco assured him. 'I'd better go in case anyone comes in.'

Pierre nodded. 'I'm visiting a relative this weekend so I shan't be here – if you have anything, leave it with Jean or Cecile.'

Marco nodded. 'Take care, my friend.'

Smiling, he walked down the stairs and through to the café. When he entered, he saw two customers were drinking coffee, but neither were German and they didn't so much as look up. He was thoughtful as he strolled back to the club. Kurt's information had been good, perhaps soon he would have something really important to pass on.

23

There was a delicious smell of stew as Marion entered the kitchen after work that evening. For a moment, her thoughts went back to the time when her mother had always had a meal ready for them, but then she saw Sarah at the stove and smiled at her. Dan's wife had settled into living with them and proved her worth over and over again. She cooked and cleaned despite Marion telling her there was no need to do so much.

'I want to do it for you,' Sarah had told her. 'You've had so much to do, Marion, and little thanks for it. Now it's your turn to be spoiled a little – and remember, when the baby comes, you'll be looking after me for a couple of weeks.'

'I spoke to Beth Burrows,' Marion said, smiling at her fondly. 'She says I can have two weeks off at one go, though I'm not entitled to it – but she will arrange it with Mrs Bailey and I'll just lose pay for the four days that aren't a part of my holiday.'

'You wouldn't rather I booked up to go into the hospital?'

'It isn't particularly nice at the infirmary – and Mrs Henley from three doors down lost the baby she had there to infection. She said she much prefers a home birth with the midwives in attendance. You did call at Annersley House and book with them, didn't you?'

'Yes, I did, and Nurse Carrow examined me. She said I was doing well and I've got to attend the classes for new mothers once a week – so that means I'll meet people.' Sarah sighed. 'Your neighbours are lovely, Marion, but most of the young women are at work during the day.'

Marion nodded, because it was true. Many of the women in the lane went to work to help make ends meet. Some worked in canteens provided for troops on leave but away from home and some had landed jobs on the trams that trundled all over London. Nearly all the younger women had husbands working in the forces or other important jobs, but none of them earned very much and their wives and daughters were helping to do the jobs the country needed them to do while so many men were away. Older women looked after babies or very young children while the younger ones worked in canteens or factories, filling the jobs the men had left behind in their rush to join up.

Marion smiled and accepted a cup of tea. She had very little to do in the evenings now, so she was busy knitting clothes for Sarah and Dan's baby. Despite both Kathy and Marion trying to show her, Sarah hadn't picked up the skill and kept dropping her stitches, so Kathy and Marion had taken charge of the knitting. Sarah was better at sewing and embroidery and she'd made some pretty little dresses and a wonderful shawl, using Mrs Jackson's sewing machine. Milly had taken a shine to Dan's wife and divided her time between her and Granny Jackson next door, which meant Marion never had to worry about her youngest sister. Life had improved for all of them since Sarah's arrival.

'I should love a shawl just like that if I ever have a baby,' Marion told her when she showed her the delicate thing wrapped in layers of tissue after they'd eaten the delicious stew. 'It is so lovely, Sarah. I've never seen anything like it.'

'I saw one in Swann & Edgar's store,' Sarah replied. 'It was terribly expensive – about six guineas – and I made mine for two pounds.'

'Really?' Marion touched it reverently. 'If you can sew this well, Sarah, you could have a career making lovely clothes for people.'

Sarah glanced over her shoulder. 'I bought a piece of heavy yellow linen the other day. I was going to make a Sunday best dress for Kathy – do you think she would like it?'

'I think she would love it,' Marion said. 'It's not her birthday for months though.'

'It doesn't have to be,' Sarah said. 'I'm grateful that she has accepted me, Marion. I know Kathy wasn't sure about me at first, but she is much nicer to me now.'

'She has no reason to be anything else,' Marion retorted. 'You've saved us both a lot of work, Sarah, and don't think I haven't noticed the extra treats – we couldn't afford sponge pudding and custard or a lovely fresh cream cake every day. We made things like that last and we had them for special occasions. My house-keeping money doesn't run to treats like that often, so I know you paid for them.'

'A little money isn't a problem,' Sarah said and smiled. 'It annoyed my father to know that I had my own small legacy. He couldn't dictate to me as he used to and when I wouldn't give in over Dan, he got so angry that he practically pushed me out of the house. I sneaked in when he went out later that day and fetched some of the things I cared for, but he would have stopped me taking even those few things if he could.'

'He was so unkind to you,' Marion said. 'But I'll bet he's sorry now. I'll bet he wishes he hadn't been so nasty – look at what he's lost.'

'It was his choice,' Sarah said, raising her head. 'I wouldn't go back there now, whatever he offered me.'

'His loss is our gain,' Marion told her and gave her a gentle hug. 'I couldn't be more pleased to have you living here, love.'

'I'm so happy to be here,' Sarah said and looked at her anxiously. 'I haven't had a letter from Dan for months. I wrote and told him where I was – do you think he's written to my old address?'

'He might have done.' Marion hesitated, then, 'Would you like me to go to your father's house and ask if there are any letters for you?'

Sarah hesitated, then, 'Would you mind? It would have to be on your afternoon off, because it is too far for you to walk in your lunch hour.'

'You do so much here that I can spare the time for you, Sarah – and I'll know if he's lying. People nearly always get angry when they lie and you can see it in their eyes.'

Sarah sighed. 'He has probably destroyed the letters if they came, but at least we'll know. I'd go myself, but I doubt he'd open the door to me.'

'No, leave your father to me,' Marion said quickly. 'He might do something to hurt you, Sarah. I shan't risk it, I care about you and the baby too much.'

Tears welled in Sarah's eyes and spilled over. 'I'm so lucky to have a sister like you,' she whispered chokily. 'Some girls would have thought me too much trouble and turned me away.'

Marion kissed her on the cheek. 'I'm going to make us all some cocoa now. Dickon is out with his friends and Kathy is in bed reading – I think she's actually making a present for my birthday, but that's a secret and I'm not supposed to know.' She smiled, because Kathy was being very secretive.

'No, you're not and I shan't tell you,' Sarah said and gave a gurgle of laughter. 'Has Dickon got his key – or shall we leave the door on the latch?'

'Dickon has his key. I never leave the door unlocked when we go up.' Marion still lived in fear that her father might walk in on them unannounced. Dan had changed the lock after his father's last visit and Dickon always took his own key if he went out at night with friends.

Sarah nodded. Marion had told her about her father's violent rages and so had Dan. 'I'll pop up and ask Kathy if she wants some cocoa, shall I?'

'Yes...' Marion poured milk into a saucepan and put it on the range to warm. She touched the letters in her pocket – three of them from Reggie and one from Robbie; she would let Kathy share her brother's letter later. They'd come all at once, though some ought to have arrived weeks ago. Because she knew Sarah had heard nothing from Dan, Marion hadn't told her about her letters. She was saving them to read when she was alone in her room.

* * *

Reggie's letters were brief but filled with love and his thoughts of her and home. He told her over and over that he couldn't wait to be with her again and he wanted them to marry – well, perhaps they could now. Sarah's arrival had changed things. Marion no longer carried the whole responsibility for the family and it might be that she could help bridge the gap that Marion's loss of wages would make should she fall for a child. There was no reason why they should not all continue to live in the same house until the war ended and then they could split into two households. Once Reggie and Dan were home, they would sort it out between them.

> *I think you may know of Lieutenant Mick O'Sullivan; I was on the hospital transport last week and I took him down to the hospital where Nurse Gibbs is on duty. You know her – she seemed concerned for him and when I saw her last, she told me that he was doing well.*

Reggie had signed his letter with kisses and love as always and Marion smiled as she kissed the signature and put the letters away in her drawer. She would tell Mrs Burrows the news and she would pass it on to Mrs Harper. Marion liked Sally Harper, but she didn't feel able to approach her with a piece of personal news, better for it to come from Mrs Burrows, because she was a family friend and Marion was just an employee. Perhaps Maggie would already have written to her, but if she hadn't, she was sure that both her supervisor and Mrs Harper would be glad to know that Mick was getting on well.

* * *

Marion's half-day fell on the Wednesday that week. Instead of catching the bus home, she took one across the river to Southwark and got off just yards from the leafy avenue where Sarah's father's house was situated. It was an impressive house with a red door, a large black knocker and three floors, all the windows curtained with heavy drapes and hardly open. Far more expensive than anything Marion could ever afford, even when she and Reggie were married. No doubt Sarah's father felt that his daughter had married beneath her. She was glad that she was wearing the new coat she'd bought in Harpers' sale in January; with her staff discount it had been as cheap as something off the market and she loved it. She was also wearing a jaunty red hat with a feather. At least she looked respectable.

She stepped up to the door and knocked sharply. It was a moment or two before the door opened and a maid dressed in black with a white apron stood there, her attitude cold and forbidding.

'I am Miss Marion Kaye and I would like to speak to Mr Harkness.'

'I don't know if he will see you,' the maid sniffed as if Marion was something the cat had brought in and hesitated.

'I think you will find he wishes to see me – I have news of his daughter, Sarah.'

'You'd better step inside, miss.' The maid reluctantly allowed Marion to step inside the hall, glaring at her as she said, 'Wait there and don't move an inch.'

Marion smiled to herself. Did the maid think she was going to pinch the silver?

She heard a gruff voice bark something at the luckless servant and then a shout. The next moment, a man came storming into the hall. He was of medium height, stout with grey hair and fierce blue eyes and dressed in a smart blue suit and a white shirt with a black tie.

'Where is she?' he demanded, looking furious. 'If she thinks she can just sneak back here and I'll let her stay, she can think again...'

'Sarah isn't asking you to take her back,' Marion said, looking him in the eye. She wasn't afraid of him and he couldn't bully her as he had his daughter. Marion had sometimes been nervous of her own father but not this man, who seemed all fire and wind to her. 'She just wants to know if there are any letters for her.'

'Impertinent miss!' he growled at Marion. 'No, there are not – and if there were, I should burn them.'

'They are her property and you have no right to deny her,' Marion persisted.

'Who gave you permission to come here and make demands of me?' he asked, his voice rising to fury. He shook his fist at her, advancing to within inches of her face. 'Get out of my house and don't come back – and tell that girl, if she wants anything from me, she can crawl on her hands and knees.'

'Sarah only wants her husband's letters,' Marion said, bravely standing her corner. She raised her head, looking him in the eyes. 'She doesn't need anything from you – just what belongs to her.'

'Out! Out I say!' He seized a stick from a huge Chinese vase in the hall and brandished it at her. 'Wretch! I'll not be spoken to by a guttersnipe like you.'

'You are a rude, mannerless man and you don't deserve a lovely daughter like Sarah or a grandchild,' Marion said, tossed her head at him and left, shutting the front door behind her with a snap. She thought he might come after her and threaten her but he didn't and Marion had reached the end of the street when she felt a touch on her arm. She turned and saw a young girl dressed in the grey dress and white apron of a kitchen maid.

'Oh, Miss Kaye,' she said. 'I'm glad I caught you. I heard the shouting and when Carla told me who you were...' She took a rather crumpled envelope from her pocket. 'I grabbed this before anyone saw it. It's for Miss Sarah and I knew they would destroy it, so I kept it for her, but I didn't know where Miss Sarah was...'

'That is very kind of you. I'm not sure what your name is?'

'I'm Lily, miss. I was always fond of Miss Sarah – Miss Sarah was the only one kind to me in that house... How is she managing?'

'Very well, Lily. I'm sure Sarah will want to thank you – if you'd like to see her, you are welcome to come to my house.' Marion took a scrap of paper from the notebook she used at Harpers and scribbled her address on it. 'Don't let anyone else see that.'

'I won't and I'll come on my day off.' Lily's face lit up. 'Thank you so much, Miss Kaye – I'd better get back, but I'll come when I can.'

'Yes, I don't want you to get the sack.' Marion smiled at her. 'Although if you ever want to leave here, come to Harpers for a job. We're still looking for honest girls to work with us.'

'Oh, miss, they'd never take on the likes of me.'

'If you don't ask, you'll never know.'

Lily gave a little giggle and ran off.

Marion looked at the envelope she'd given her. She knew the writing at once; it was from Dan. Sarah's father would have destroyed it if he'd got hold of it, but Lily had taken it and saved it. Marion smiled. It had been worth the trip and she didn't care two hoots about the way Sarah's father had spoken to her. He was a foolish bad-tempered man and one day he would realise what he'd lost.

* * *

'Oh, Marion.' Sarah's eyes filled with tears as she saw the letter. 'Thank you so much – and I shall reward Lily if she comes to see me. I knew he must have written to me.' She tore open the letter and read it quickly, then looked at Marion, eyes shining. 'He hadn't had my last letters when he wrote this – but he says he has leave due to him and he hopes to be home when the baby is due, either just before or after anyway.'

'That's lovely,' Marion said. 'You must write again and tell him you're here with us and I shall too, and hopefully he will come here when he gets leave.'

'Oh, Marion, I was so afraid that something had happened to him...' She looked at the letter again. 'This was written nearly three months ago.'

'Perhaps your father destroyed the others,' Marion suggested as she saw the anxiety return. 'I know he has destroyed some, because I could see he was lying – but there might be a letter at your old lodgings. Would you like me to call there for you?'

'No, I can do that,' Sarah said. 'I didn't want to face my father, but I'm not worried about my landlord. I asked him to save any letters for me, so I'll go there tomorrow.'

'Yes,' Marion said. 'That's a good idea, but I'm sure Dan is fine.'

'He hasn't written to you either, has he?'

'No – but he would write to you more often,' Marion offered.

Sarah nodded, but Marion could see that she was still concerned. If no other letters had come since this one, it might mean... But, no, Marion would never believe that. She was sure she would know if anything bad had happened to either of her brothers or Reggie, but it was a little concerning. She would keep her fingers crossed that there was a more recent letter from Dan at Sarah's old lodgings.

24

'I'm afraid I'm unable to supply the particular tea service you asked for, Mrs Harper,' the salesman told Sally when she rang the firm and placed her three-monthly order. 'We do not have anything in the bone china line at all for the moment – it is so difficult for the manufacturers to get the right mix they need, so they've suspended those lines until further notice.'

'That is disappointing,' Sally said, looking down her list. 'I was hoping to buy a dozen tea sets and four dinner services from you...'

'Let me check,' the salesman said.

Sally frowned over her list until he returned.

'We still have three sets of dinnerware in stock, Mrs Harper. It is Shelly and a violets pattern.'

'Oh yes, I remember we had one last year. You have three the same?'

'Yes, Mrs Harper.'

'May I take them all please?'

'Yes, of course. In tea sets we have a rather nice line in blue and white willow pattern earthenware, if I could persuade you to try it? It is a rather nice quality.'

'Well...' She hesitated; it wasn't what she wanted or what her customers truly wished for, but if nothing else was available it would do to fill the shelves. 'I'll try three and see how they go.'

'I think you'll be pleasantly surprised,' he told her. 'The younger customer buys a lot of these sets, Mrs Harper. They cannot afford the more expensive porcelain – although bone china is always more popular with all our customers.'

'Well, we'll see how they go,' Sally said and placed her order. Whatever she managed to buy filled empty spaces on the shelves. She would have to ring around all the manufacturers and see what else she could pick up. It was time-consuming and harder than just ringing the firms she liked best and some of the stuff wasn't the quality she preferred, but in these difficult times, she had to fill the store with the best she could find.

Ruth knocked at the office door and entered when Sally said she could.

'Yes, Ruth, what is it?' she asked with a smile.

'There's a Mr Alexander to see you. I told him you were busy, but...'

'I'm never too busy to see him.' Sally jumped up and walked to the door and looked into the outer office. 'Mr Alexander, do come through. I'm so pleased to see you – and honoured that you came to visit me.'

'Sally Harper,' he said and smiled warmly. 'I've been visiting one of our patients. He told me you'd been to see him recently – and I think you'll agree that he is looking much better.'

Sally nodded. She'd been to visit Captain Maclean on the afternoon of Marlene's last visit and he'd been remarkably cheerful, the lost, bleak look gone from his eyes. His face structure had been rebuilt and although there was scarring, he now looked like a man again. He'd thanked her for her visit and Sally had made a vow to herself to drop in at the hospital at least once a fortnight in future. No matter how busy she was, visits and small gifts meant so much to the men who had lost so much on the field of battle.

'It is a miracle what you managed to do for him,' Sally said, taking his outstretched hands to press them gratefully. 'I cannot thank you enough – I hardly thought it possible you could do so much and I'm certain it has given Captain Maclean the will to go on living.'

Mr Alexander nodded. 'I can't make him the handsome devil he once was, but he looks halfway normal now and by the time we're finished, he'll be able to face the world without making the ladies scream and run away.'

'Only very foolish ladies would do that,' Sally said and he laughed, highly amused.

'I love it that you scorn mere mortals,' he told her with a quirk of his eyebrow. 'Of course, you took it in your stride.' His smiled teased. 'So now I've come to ask you to lunch with me. I have a couple of hours to kill before I return to my home town and I have a request for you, or perhaps your husband. I need more surgical supplies and I'm hoping either you or Mr Harper can help source them, perhaps from your contacts in America?'

'After what you've done for our patients, we could do no less.' Sally glanced at the work piled on her desk and smothered a sigh. This man had given up his time for her and she wanted to do all she could in return, even though she would have to work later this afternoon. 'I thank you for the invitation and I should be delighted to have lunch with you – where are we going?'

'I thought you might recommend somewhere?' he said, and Sally nodded.

'I know of a very nice restaurant and they always have a table for me – it belongs to a friend of mine and it's not too far away.'

* * *

Sally enjoyed the meal at Mick's restaurant as always. They still managed to produce a varied menu and the food was as well-cooked as ever. Somerset gammon steaks were one of the main features, cooked under the grill to perfection and served with mushrooms, chips and a delicious red cabbage that had been spiced with herbs and vinegar. It was followed by a spotted dick and custard that caused Mr Alexander to smile as he devoured his portion.

'I didn't think they had proper food in London,' he told Sally with a look of satisfaction. 'Trust you to know where to eat, Sally Harper.'

'Mick only employs the best cooks,' she said, with a gurgling laugh that drew the eyes of several diners. 'He will be delighted when I tell him how much you enjoyed the spotted dick – he says you can't beat good home-style cooking and all these fancy foreign puddings are not worth tuppence.'

Her companion chuckled. 'I think I should like your Mick – is he here?'

'Oh no, he is serving in France – well, to be precise, he is in a hospital bed there at the moment. My friend Maggie wrote and told me he is a true hero. He led an assault on enemy lines and was wounded.' She saw Mr Alexander's inquiring look and shook her head. 'I understand it is a minor wound in the chest and shoulder – he was lucky that it didn't enter his heart. A cigarette case deflected the bullet apparently.'

'They are often useful when it comes to chest wounds,' he agreed thoughtfully. 'I've heard of a good case stopping a bullet before. Your friend was lucky, Sally.'

'Yes, he was,' she said and smiled. 'He would say it was the little people – the leprechauns.'

'Oh, he's Irish, is he?' Mr Alexander smiled. His eyes quizzed her from across the table. 'And is he in love with you, Sally Harper? All the young men you keep sending me are half in love with you – I feel a bit that way myself...' His twinkling eyes mocked her, making her laugh and shake her head, because he was merely teasing.

'Now you sound as if you've kissed the blarney stone, Andrew. You know very well I'm married to a man I love very much.'

'Unfortunately, I do, and having met Ben when I was last down, I have no hope of displacing him in your heart,' he said with a look of mischief. Ben had called to see him at the London hospital on one of his brief visits and they'd had a long discussion. Ben had told Sally how much he liked the man and encouraged her to give him all the assistance she could.

'Has anyone ever told you, you are a terrible flirt?' Andrew Alexander was unmarried and liked to tease her; she imagined he had a flock of female admirers, because of his looks, rough charm and undoubted skill, and she took little notice of his declaration of love, understanding it was just his way.

'Dozens of times – as many times as I fall in love,' he said. 'It happens quite regularly, so don't let it disturb you, Sally Harper.'

'No, I shan't,' she said and her eyes were bright with amusement. 'I shall continue to send you men who need your attention – and Ben will continue to send you as many of your clinical needs as he can.'

'She wounds her admirers as she tosses them aside,' he said and kissed her hand gallantly. 'I shall pay our bill and then I must love and leave you, Mrs Sally Harper.'

'I enjoyed it very much, Andrew,' she said and kissed his cheek lightly. 'Don't die of a broken heart, will you? We need you too much.'

'It was an enjoyable experience,' he told her as they parted.

'Go back to your busy life and your husband and take no notice of this broken-hearted man.'

Sally laughed. Andrew Alexander was a man who worked hard and saw the most heart-wrenching injuries. Most men would feel sick to their guts and be unable to wield the knife that healed and helped the unfortunate patients, but he used humour and sheer determination to pull his patients through, giving no quarter and expecting none. Mick would be delighted to know that she'd taken a man like that to his restaurant and that the food had been heartily approved.

Smiling, she returned to her office and her desk. She had about thirty manufacturers she needed to ring and persuade or cajole into giving her the best of whatever was available.

It was around five that evening when the door of her office opened and Ben walked in. 'Still at it, love?' he said. 'Is Mrs Hills with Jenny?'

'Yes, she was going to stay later for me – I'm afraid I was taken out to lunch by Mr Alexander and I got behind with my work.'

'As long as Jenny is all right,' he said. 'You'll be pleased to know I had a long letter from my sister and she's fine – and she and her family are all coming over in June.'

'Jenni is coming – and her husband?' Sally was surprised. It was the first time Jenni's husband had come with her and she hadn't yet met him. Nor had she met Henry's son, the little boy Jenni loved so much but who was the child of his first wife.

'Yes, all of them – little Tom as well. Jenni says she's a bit worried how he'll react to the sea voyage, but he wants to come apparently, says he needs to face his nightmares.'

'Let's hope it helps him. I know he suffered a long time,' Sally said. 'I'm glad they're all coming this time. Will they stay with us?'

'We don't have room for all of them, so I'm sure she has

booked a hotel,' Ben said and smiled. 'It's quite a relief to hear from her, I can tell you.'

Sally nodded, because she knew he'd worried about his sister. 'Did she say why she hadn't been in touch?'

'No, not a word, which is odd,' Ben said. 'I know she got my telegram – but she still didn't say why she hadn't written.'

'I suppose she was just too busy.'

'Jenni is never too busy to write to you, Sally. She sent her love and I know she longs to see her namesake.' They'd named their daughter in her honour but spelled it differently.

'You think she has been ill, don't you?' Sally went to put her arms about him. 'I knew you were anxious about her, Ben. She is bound to tell us what is wrong when she's here...'

'Perhaps – it just isn't like her, Sally. Even her letter is restrained, not her usual style.' Ben looked at her. 'I hope this isn't too much for you, love? I sometimes think it is unfair of me to leave it all to you.'

'You have enough to do and I know your job is important,' Sally told him with a smile. 'Besides, I love it. It can be frustrating when I can't buy what I want or as much as we need, but I just have to keep trying other suppliers.'

He looked at her anxiously. 'Don't get ill, Sally. I couldn't bear it if you did.'

Sally laughed and shook her head. 'I'm blooming, Ben. You don't need to worry about me.'

'Good.' He smiled and took her in his arms to kiss her. 'I'll be away this weekend – don't look alarmed, I'm not going on some madcap adventure, my love. I'm just meeting some important visitors from overseas – and that's all I can tell you.'

'I don't need to know,' she said and hugged him. 'Just come back to me safe – that's all I ask.'

25

Beth read her letter with a slight frown. Maggie had written a long letter about someone called Sister Mayhew, who was wonderful, her life at the field hospital, and the constant flow of patients. Apart from her touching letter to Fred, she had hardly mentioned Tim. Perhaps she couldn't bear to, Beth thought and sighed. She no longer felt angry with Maggie for not coming home to the funeral, but she couldn't stifle her feelings of hurt. It seemed that Maggie had grown away from them and Beth had to learn to adjust. She read the letter for a second time:

The Germans have started to use a terrible new weapon. The men first saw it drifting towards them at dusk. It happened first at a place north of Ypres and they say it was like a greenish-yellow mist swirling towards them. No one understood what it was or what it could do, but we've had some of the patients transferred here and it is terrible. They are in such pain and distress, Beth, and the doctors say it has affected their lungs. We don't really know how to treat it, but we just do what we can to help and comfort them. The men have been told to hold wet clothes to their faces if they see such a mist again, and when they attack, as there is nothing yet to protect them. Sister Mayhew says the boffins will be working on something we can all wear to protect us, but I fear for those already affected and think they may not recover.

Maggie's letter continued in much the same way for another two paragraphs and only at the end did she at last mention Tim.

I know your hearts are broken, as is mine. I shall never forget Tim, but life goes on and it is such a struggle here that I have decided I must put my personal grief aside and devote my energies to caring for these poor men. They need us so much and I have decided to stay on after my six months is up...

'I don't understand her,' Beth said aloud.

Her father-in-law looked at her, his eyebrows raised. 'Is something wrong, Beth?'

'Read it yourself – it doesn't sound like Maggie at all.'

Fred frowned and picked up the letter, reading it silence and then nodding thoughtfully. 'Put yourself in her place for a moment, Beth. The poor girl is living through scenes that we can only imagine, daily. The suffering those poor men are enduring must be a torment to a young girl like Maggie. Remember, she is just nineteen. I think she is simply facing her grief in the only way she can – by working so hard that she blots it out of her mind.'

'I suppose so,' Beth said and sighed. 'I know it's hard for her, Fred, but surely she didn't have to stay longer than her tour of duty. She could have come home and let us look after her.'

'I think sometimes grief goes too deep for that, Beth love.' Fred smiled at her. 'I was lucky. I had you and Jack to lean on. If I'd had to face it alone...' A shudder went through him. 'That girl's out there in the middle of it, facing all sorts of things, and we should admire her courage. I'm not sure I would have been strong enough to do what she does. I'm glad that girl is getting on with her life, Beth, and she's right – those poor buggers out there need her more than ever now. That gas is wicked stuff and the Germans were protected from it with masks and helmets, so they just drove our men back from the trenches with their bayonets and guns. Fortunately, the Canadians hadn't been affected by it and they pushed the enemy back. Not before they'd advanced for nearly four miles, so the papers say.'

Beth nodded, looking at him sadly. Fred had wept for his lost son, but he'd carried on working, so perhaps Maggie wasn't doing much different. It still hurt that she hadn't come home to them, but Fred was right and Maggie was coping the best way she could.

'I'll send her some sweets and some Yardley soap; she likes the lavender one,' Beth said and smothered a sigh. Why did this war have to happen? Why wasn't Maggie still working at Harpers where she could see her every day?

'That's right, Beth.' Fred looked at her with approval. 'You tell her you're thinking of her and send her something nice. It must be hard for them to get anything out there.'

* * *

Beth was busy at her counter when Sally Harper entered the department that morning. She stood watching the customers and seemed to approve, chatting to Marion and Becky and young Shirley for a moment before coming to Beth when her customer left carrying the distinctive Harpers' bags.

'Is trade keeping up?' Sally asked her as Beth tidied away the bags she'd been showing her customer. 'I've managed a decent order of leather bags and silver jewellery. Thankfully, we have good British suppliers for those – and there is a new range of Scottish brooches I think you will approve. They are silver and have semi-precious stones like amethyst and agate set in them.'

'Did Mr Alexander tell you where to source them?' Beth asked smiling. She knew of Sally Harper's success with the eminent facial surgeon and also that he'd taken her to lunch the last time he was down.

'Yes, he did as a matter of fact. The supplier is a cousin of his – he does have quite a lot of family in Scotland, though he lives and works in Newcastle. I'm also getting a new range of Scottish shortbread for the sweets and cakes department. Rather special ones, I understand – Marlene told me about those.' She smiled. 'I'm lucky to have such good friends.'

Beth nodded. 'I noticed the bone china section was looking a little thin, Mrs Harper.' She always addressed her friend formally during working sessions. 'Are you having difficulty in sourcing new lines?'

'It hasn't been easy,' Sally Harper admitted. 'I have found a small potter down in Devon and he's going to send me some samples of what he calls studio pottery – vases and various mugs and teapots – but I'm also trying some earthenware tea sets.'

'Yes, I suppose that will suit some of the younger customers. We had two sets bought for us when we married. I don't like them as much as my bone china, but I use them for every day. You may find they sell as well as the ones you prefer, Mrs Harper.'

'Yes, well, I just hope our regulars understand there is a war on and it isn't easy to provide everything we did before it started to bite.'

'What about the clothes side?' Beth asked.

'We can stock our rails with British goods still – especially wool and cotton that is produced here, though the raw cotton is getting scarcer, but I can't buy enough real silk or many of the beautiful brocades our customers love for their evening dresses, which came from Italy and France. Instead, I'm offering an alteration service. Minnie came up with the idea. She can change the style of an old-fashioned dress where the material is still good, take sleeves out and add frills or remove them, trim the gown with ribbons that make it look new.'

'That sounds wonderful,' Beth acknowledged. 'It will keep Minnie busy and bring some trade in to help us maintain standards – but it must be wearing for you, constantly trying to find something new to replace whatever you can't find at your normal wholesalers.'

'That's my job – and after the war I'll remember all those small manufacturers who helped me out.' Sally nodded, changing the subject. 'Jenny has got most of her teeth now. Just in time to greet her namesake – Jenni is coming over with her husband in late June.'

'That is very brave of them,' Beth said. 'Are they not afraid of being torpedoed?'

'Jenni says she's been undecided whether to risk it, but her husband needs to come over on Government business and she and the child decided to come too. She says if we're having to put up with Zeppelin attacks and all kinds of shortages, she can risk a sea voyage.'

'Yes, perhaps.' Beth nodded doubtfully. 'Well, it's lovely they are coming,' Beth responded with a smile. 'I know you were very worried about her last month.'

'Ben thought something was wrong because she hadn't written or been in touch for weeks.' Sally looked thoughtful. 'I'm wondering if she has been unwell, Beth. It just isn't like her not to write or even send a telegram...'

'Well, you'll see her when she gets here,' Beth said and smiled. 'Oh, I believe this customer is coming back to buy a bracelet she looked at earlier.' Her gaze moved to a woman in a smart dress and coat approaching her counter.

'Then I shan't take up any more of your time,' Sally murmured. 'Come to supper on Saturday if you can – I think Ben will be home, unless he has another urgent meeting.'

Beth replied in the affirmative and Sally moved away as the customer approached the counter. She looked at her in a way that told Beth she'd made up her mind.

'Do you still have that bracelet with the turquoise beads?'

'Yes, we do, madam. Would you like to see it again?'

'Yes, please. It is a little more than I intended to pay, but it is such nice quality and one I looked at elsewhere was almost as expensive and nowhere near as nice.'

'Harpers always try to be competitively priced,' Beth assured her. 'But we never sacrifice quality. Even though there is a war on, we try to give our customers the best available.'

'Yes, Harpers has a good reputation. I know a bracelet from here will not fall apart as soon as my sister wears it.'

'If such a terrible thing happened, Mrs Harper would have it instantly refunded and complain to the manufacturer,' Beth assured her and the customer smiled.

'Yes, I shall take it. I'm sure Lizzie will love it.'

Beth wrapped the gift and took the money, giving her customer change. She glanced at the little silver watch pinned to her dress. The morning had flown and it was time for Becky and Marion to go for their lunch. She looked up as Rachel entered the department; they could have a nice little chat with the young girls at lunch and Rachel would help out if they had a rush of customers. Rachel was making it a habit to call in more often of late and Beth wondered if she felt lonely with her husband so often away. It did get lonely and she would ask Rachel to come and have lunch on Sunday...

* * *

Beth bought a bar of brazil nut toffee, a tin of humbugs and two bars of lavender soap for Maggie and wrapped them in tissue, before slipping in a note to say they were all thinking of her and hoped to see her one day soon. She didn't feel capable of saying more yet, even though Fred's sensible suggestions had eased some of the bad feeling inside her. She wrapped Maggie's gift in strong brown paper and took it to the Post Office before catching the bus home that evening.

Fred had arrived home before her, having caught the earlier bus. He had the kettle on and she could smell fish and chips warming in the oven.

'I thought we'd have an easy supper tonight,' he said. 'If you don't mind, Beth, I'm off down the pub this evening – meeting a couple of friends.'

'Of course I don't mind,' she told him with a smile. 'I've got some ironing to finish this evening and then I'll write to Jack.'

Beth still wrote her husband a letter every day and kept them until he came home on leave. He took a bundle of them in his kitbag each voyage and read them at sea.

'It brings home back to me like nothing else,' he'd told her on several occasions. 'I catch up on all the news, even if you've already told me.'

'You could come with me if you wanted,' Fred offered. 'Quite a few young women come in for a drink in the evening – and Mrs Jarvis is usually there.'

'Mrs Jarvis?' Beth questioned, because she hadn't heard him mention the name before.

'Mabel Jarvis is a widow,' Fred said with a little nod of what looked like satisfaction to Beth. She would guess that he rather liked the lady. 'She drinks a port and lemon of an evening but no more – just comes for the company.'

'You should ask her here to tea on a Sunday,' Beth suggested. 'If you'd like to...'

Fred looked at her in silence for a moment and then shook his head. 'No, I don't think so, not yet anyway. We're friends, but if I ask her here, it looks as if I want it to be more, I'm not ready for that yet, but thank you for asking, Beth.'

She smiled at him. It was Fred's choice. She often worried about him these days. When the war was over, it was Jack's plan to move into a home of their own. His hotel was ticking over, making a small profit despite the war and that was due to his manager, but one day Jack and Ben Harper were thinking of opening a restaurant and then Jack might sell the hotel. He said it took up too much of his time when he'd managed it and his manager was interested in buying it.

'We could have a nice house with a garden somewhere,' he'd suggested to Beth, 'and invest the extra money in Ben's new restaurant he's planning for after the war. The hours would be better for me there, I think – but I might keep the hotel as well. It just depends how things work out.' They still had most of Beth's nest egg put by for the future and it would come in useful when things were back to normal again.

Beth had thought Maggie and Tim might live with Fred for a while when they were first married, but if Jack bought a house it would leave her father-in-law on his own. She didn't like the idea of that and would have been happy to settle for what she had; they could always spend a little money on doing Fred's house up a bit. It would make Beth feel guilty to leave him alone. He'd been so good to her all this time and she was used to having him around, enjoyed his company.

'It's your house, Fred,' she reminded him now. 'I've been given a free rein to do as I like, but I don't forget that you gave Jack and me a home.'

'My home is always yours,' Fred said and smiled at her. 'You're like a daughter to me, Beth love. I'd have gone to pieces here alone after my Tim went like that if you hadn't been here...'

Beth moved forward and pressed his hand, her heart aching for him. She was so lucky. She still had Jack but Fred had lost his son and there was a hole in his heart that might never heal – and Maggie too. She'd lost the man she loved and her hope of a future as his wife. The last remnants of Beth's disappointment vanished as she realised just how much Maggie and Fred had lost. Whatever happened in the future, she must do what she could to help.

26

Marco was dressing for his evening performance when the door was thrown open and Kurt entered in a hurry, shutting and locking it after him. He looked terrified and he was breathing hard, his hand trembling a little as he put it out to ward Marco off.

'I told you I would give you something special,' he said and took some papers from his breast pocket. 'These are secret documents I stole from a briefcase – they detail plans for the coming offensive and the Kaiser's thoughts on Italy and various other information.'

'Good grief.' Marco took the papers from him, glancing at them briefly. He recognised certain words which backed up Kurt's claim, though his knowledge of written German wasn't good enough to read every paragraph properly. 'You took a huge risk, Kurt – if they'd caught you with these, you could have been shot as a traitor...'

'I know.' Kurt reached for the whisky bottle on Marco's dressing table and took a swig to calm his nerves. 'I was certain I would be stopped and searched...' He breathed deeply and then smiled. 'Will these be enough to get me to England after the war?'

'I am sure they will, with my recommendation to back it up,' Marco said, smiling in reassurance and wanting to make Kurt feel his gratitude and affection. Then, as he thought of something, he hesitated, looking at Kurt uncertainly. 'Can these be traced to you – how did you get them?'

'The fat pig was entrusted with a special mission,' Kurt said, speaking of the Oberst he hated so much. 'He was told to take a locked briefcase to headquarters and give them to General Lundendorff.' He smiled oddly. 'Instead of obeying his orders immediately, he drank a bottle of brandy and fell asleep. I stole these from his briefcase while he slept.'

'Will he know you were in his room?'

'No... Someone told me he'd been given an important mission – he was bragging about it to the poor young devil who has taken my place in his bed. I knew he was drunk so I sneaked in and took the papers – he'll never know who it was.'

'Did you break the lock?'

'I had the spare key. I've had it for months, waiting my chance. It's not the first time I've looked in his briefcase without his knowing – but I never knew what to do until now.'

Marco looked at him with understanding. 'You really hate Oberst Hoffmeister, don't you, Kurt?'

'He deserves all he gets,' Kurt said. 'Willy was crying and bleeding when he left that pig's room. I cleaned him up and gave him something for the pain – that's why he told me.'

'I hope for your sake and that young lad's that Hoffmeister doesn't realise what has gone.' Marco looked him in the eyes. 'Are you sure you want me to use these?'

'Yes.' Kurt looked at him unflinchingly. 'I want that bastard to suffer as he's made others suffer. Give those papers to whoever can do the most good with them – I'll take the risk.'

Marco hesitated and then nodded. He reached out and

squeezed Kurt's shoulder. 'This is important. It could make a big difference, perhaps even shorten the war if our people know what is being planned – and what the Kaiser is thinking. Especially where Italy is concerned – it seems the triple alliance isn't as stable as your leaders hoped.'

'Take it and remember what you promised,' Kurt said. 'I have to get back, I'm on duty in half an hour and I can't be missed.'

'Yes, go,' Marco said. 'Use the back stairs – and don't come for a few days. Make sure you're not followed.' He placed a hand on his shoulder. 'Be careful. I don't want you to get caught...'

'I won't lead them to you,' Kurt promised. He moved forward and kissed Marco. 'Thank you for making me feel decent again – and now I've paid you back, haven't I?'

'Yes, you have, more than. We're good friends, Kurt, perhaps we shall become much more to each other when all this is over – and I shan't forget my promise,' Marco said and smiled. 'Take care, my friend. I don't want to lose you.'

'Goodbye,' Kurt said. And for a moment there was finality in his eyes, as if he felt that they might not meet again. Marco knew a pang of regret. Yes, he had what he needed and he'd always meant to use the young soldier – but now he cared enough to feel anxious for his safety.

Marco frowned as he went swiftly from the room. Kurt had done something incredibly brave, but was it also foolish? He hoped it would not lead to trouble for the young man he liked and was beginning to feel real affection for.

Breathing deeply to calm himself, Marco looked around the room. He was due to perform in ten minutes. If he missed his cue, he would be looked for. Nothing must seem out of the ordinary. He couldn't risk carrying the papers with him in the club; they must be well hidden in his room. He went into the bathroom and removed the panel from the end of the bath, putting the papers inside and screwing the panel back into place. A clever mind would look behind the panel, but he had to hope his room wouldn't be searched before he could pass the papers on.

Back in his bedroom, he poured whisky into a glass and drank it. His hands were steady as he locked his room after he left it – not that it would keep out a German officer determined to search. He could only hope that Kurt was in the clear and make certain he passed that valuable information on first thing in the morning.

It took every bit of Marco's courage to go on and perform. He prayed he wasn't sweating or showing his nerves, because the club was packed with German officers, but thankfully Hoffmeister wasn't in the audience. Marco thought he might not have been able to carry on if he'd been staring at him with his close-set eyes. Kurt was right, the man was a pig in every way and he couldn't blame him for wanting his revenge, but he'd taken a huge risk. Marco just hoped it was worth it.

* * *

Marco would always remember that night as one of the worst he'd ever known. He was performing until three in the morning and then, when he finally got to retire, he couldn't sleep a wink. Every time he heard a car outside or a footstep in the street, he thought it was the Germans come to arrest him.

It was a relief to see the dawn. He dressed, went down and had a cup of coffee and a croissant in the bar, then returned to the bathroom and retrieved the papers. They burned a hole in his pocket as he walked downstairs again and spoke to his employer and one of the girls who worked in the club. Greta wanted to flirt and Marco did his best to indulge her, because to show any sign of nerves might alert a spy. He was in a French club and should have been safe, but there were always spies, people who would take bribes from the enemy for money or even food, especially with the German lines so close. It would be easy to slip through in the dark if one had the passwords and give information the Germans would pay for if it was useful.

Marco was allowed to leave the club at last and he strolled casually down the road. The papers he carried were so important that he knew he must give the information to Pierre. None of the others could see it safely on its way to England as securely as Pierre.

The café where Pierre normally hung out when it was safe was empty. Marco looked towards the ceiling and the man behind the counter nodded. No words were spoken or needed. Jean would understand that Marco would risk coming here for only one reason.

He moved towards the back, glanced over his shoulder again to make sure he hadn't been followed and then slipped through into the hall and up the stairs to the room above. Knocking, he said his name once and the door was opened.

Marco took the papers from his coat pocket and held them out.

'That important?' Pierre asked in English.

'If you're caught it will mean your death...'

'Merci, my friend,' Pierre said with a wry smile.

Marco nodded but said no more. Walls had ears and they spoke as little as possible. Pierre knew that Marco would only seek him out if it was really important.

'Good luck,' he said and went back down to the café.

Two men were sitting at the tables.

Jean had poured him a coffee and greeted him by asking him if he felt better. Marco made a show of adjusting his trousers as if he'd been to the toilets, said loudly that 'it was much better' and then went on to drink his coffee and pay for it.

'You sang well last night,' one of the men came up to him, offering him a cigarette.

Marco took it. He recognised the German officer, even though he was not wearing uniform. He was proud that his hand did not shake. 'Thank you – you are too kind, Captain Wenger,' Marco said. 'I'm glad you enjoyed the performance.'

'Oh, I like to watch you perform, Marco – you have such a talent for acting...'

Marco looked him in the eyes unflinchingly. 'I have a small talent, yes.'

'Amusing,' the officer said, his shrewd eyes narrowed. 'You are popular, but no one is sure of you, though I believe Lieutenant Shultz is a friend?'

'Yes, we share the same sense of humour and sometimes talk for a while.' Marco found he was holding his breath and forced himself to relax.

'Talk?' the officer raised his brows. 'Some say you are lovers – Hoffmeister is jealous of you. Be careful of him, Marco. He dislikes you and he is a bad enemy.'

'I imagine he would be,' Marco agreed. 'I try to avoid him.'

'Yes, that would be wise.' Captain Wenger turned away and then said casually, 'Poor Shultz may wish he had not angered the Oberst.'

Marco hesitated, then, 'Why? Or is that German business?'

'Oh, very much German business,' the officer said and smiled. 'Hoffmeister has been careless and some important papers have gone missing from his briefcase. He blames Shultz and has him locked up – I should not want to be in his shoes. I think that man delights in torture.'

'Shultz is in trouble?' Marco raised his brows, willing himself to remain calm, though underneath his heart was racing.

'Possibly – but he hasn't been officially arrested. Hoffmeister thinks he is to blame and will try to get a confession out of him to shift the blame. The poor devil will probably confess even if he is innocent.'

'Then I'm sorry for him,' Marco said and suppressed a shiver of distaste for the man who could tell him this news as if it were amusing. He knew a deep searing pity and something more – grief that it was his fault the young soldier had got in so deep, but he had to play it cool. Otherwise Kurt's sacrifice was for nothing. Would Kurt break? He'd been so certain Hoffmeister couldn't lay the blame on him, but it hadn't taken him long to work it out – how long before the trail led back to Marco? 'I'd be sorry for anyone the Oberst took a dislike to.'

'Yes – slightly amusing though, isn't it? Everyone knows that Shultz is a timid beast. Far more likely to be one of Hoffmeister's other enemies – he has enough.' He smiled oddly. 'Don't worry for your friend, Marco. I dare say someone will arrest the Oberst before he can do much damage.'

'One would hope the innocent will be spared,' Marco shrugged as calmly as he could, bringing every bit of acting skill he'd ever had to bear. His hands unconsciously bunched at his sides as he felt the urge to bury them in the face of this sneering officer.

'You're a cold fish, Marco,' the officer said. 'Some might suspect you of being involved – but why would you? You have nothing to gain...'

Marco smiled coolly. 'Indeed, what could I gain, Captain Wenger? I earn my living entertaining German officers – and the more you spend, the more I earn. What would I want with any missing items of Oberst Hoffmeister's?'

'Exactly.' The German officer nodded. 'Just what I said when your name came up as someone Shultz might pass the information to. I'm very rarely wrong about character in a man. I doubt you care for anyone or anything enough to risk your life.'

Now Marco allowed himself a shudder. 'Do we have to speak of such things, Captain? I know there are some brutes in your Army, but I think men like yourself and others are gentlemen and more refined...'

'Fortunately, we are not all like the Oberst,' Captain Wenger replied and smiled wolfishly. 'I do like you, Marco – but if I ever discovered you had lied to me...' He inspected his nails, which were scrupulously clean. 'Well, I'm sure we do not need to speak of such things.'

'I hope not,' Marco replied. 'Will you excuse me please? I have someone to see.'

'Please, do not allow me to detain you further.'

Marco left the café and walked down the road. He went directly to the little shop on the corner and bought a pot of flowers, spending some time chatting to the woman who sold her garden produce there. Then, without glancing over his shoulder, he returned to the club. Greta was sitting in the bar. He went up to her and presented her with the gift of potted geraniums.

'Happy birthday, Greta,' he said and smiled.

'But it isn't,' she began.

Marco leaned in and kissed her cheek. 'Just pretend it is and accept them,' he whispered. 'I'm being watched.'

Greta smiled and nodded. 'Thank you, Marco. It's a lovely present.'

Marco heard the door close. He knew he'd been observed, but whoever it was would report back to Captain Wenger that he'd bought a birthday gift for one of the girls at the club.

'To what do I owe this?' Greta asked a moment later.

'To your pretty face,' Marco said. 'Excuse me now, Greta. I have something to do.'

He left her sitting there staring at the pot of flowers, probably wondering what to do with them, and walked up to his room. Immediately, he knew someone had been in it – he could smell some kind of hair oil and it wasn't his. Someone had searched his room discreetly while he was out. Nothing had been taken and hardly anything was out of place, but someone had been looking for something – perhaps while he was talking to the German officer.

So, he was suspected. Did they have anything to go on or was it just because he was known to be friendly towards Kurt? Wenger had been warning him or trying to frighten him, perhaps?

Marco knew that it was important he held his nerve. It was likely that his work here was done. If he was under even the slightest suspicion, he would be a danger to the others. He would have to get a message to someone – not Pierre this time. It would be dangerous to go near the café again, because Pierre might be endangered. He could only pray that he'd got through to his contact immediately and delivered those papers – because it was likely the Germans would stop and search everyone in the village now that the papers were known to be missing, but for the moment it was probably best to sit tight and do nothing.

27

Maggie stopped by the lieutenant's bed and smiled as he opened his eyes and looked at her. His colour was better and his eyes looked clear of the fever that had pulled him down for a few days.

'Good morning, Lieutenant O'Sullivan,' she said. 'Are you feeling better today?'

'Yes, much better, Nurse Gibbs,' he said. 'Sister Mayhew frightened the fever out of me, so she did – told me she wanted me out of this bed, because she had more deserving cases...'

Maggie laughed and told him to open his mouth so she could take his temperature. 'You are a wicked tease,' she told him. 'Sister Mayhew has a soft spot for you and she won't make you go before you're ready.'

The officers often swept through this ward looking for men who were ready to return to the front line and simply lingering in bed for a rest. Despite the new recruits that were sent out regularly, the officers wanted their best men back. Men who knew what it was all about and didn't wet their breeches at the first sound of the guns and some of the young ones did, but then they were sending them out as young as fifteen to fill up the empty spaces caused by so many deaths and fatal wounds. The older men protected them as much as they could, but everyone knew they were far too young and should never have been accepted or sent to the front.

'I'll not be troubling you much longer, Nurse Gibbs,' Mick said and smiled at her. 'I've no doubt I'm needed elsewhere and as soon as the doc says I can go, it's back to duty for me.'

'You should rest while you can,' Maggie said and turned to move on, but Mick caught her hand. 'Is there something you need – something I can do for you?'

'I wondered if I could help you,' he said. 'I'm good at fixing things – finding stuff. If you need any soap or a bit of chocolate...'

She laughed and shook her head. 'I have good friends at home and they send me all those things, lieutenant. It's very kind of you but I don't need anything.'

'Well, maybe I could take you into the village for a drink on your night off?'

'What is that?' Maggie mocked. 'It's very kind of you, Lieutenant O'Sullivan, but I stay with friends when I do go into the village – but I do thank you for the thought.'

'Well, I had to ask,' he said, quirking an eyebrow. 'Sure, there isn't a man in this ward who wouldn't ask if he dared.'

Maggie laughed and shook her head, though she knew he was right. Ever since she'd come out here, she'd been inundated with offers to go for walks, a drink or the occasional dance in the village. She'd said no to all offers, because she had Tim – and even now, she wouldn't accept an offer – even from someone she liked. It was too soon and she didn't even want to think of getting to know another man.

'Perhaps one day,' she said and wondered at herself.

'One day but not yet,' he replied and smiled in a way that Maggie liked. 'Just so long as you know I asked.'

Maggie nodded and moved off to her next patient. He was lying with his eyes closed and she thought he seemed a bit flushed. She decided to leave him sleeping but report his change of condition to Sister Mayhew and moved on to the next bed, where the occupant was sitting up and grinning at her.

'Would you like a glass of water, private?'

'Nothing but a kiss will quench my thirst, nurse,' he quipped.

'Then you'll die of thirst,' she retorted and smiled to take the sting from her words. 'Sister says you're down for an enema today.'

'You do know how to make a man feel good,' he groaned and pulled a wry face.

Maggie laughed and moved on. It was a joy to work on this ward. Here the men were brought in sick and they recovered quite quickly, most of them being sent back up the line, or if they were lucky enough to be due leave, they might be shipped home. Either way, they'd had a brush with near death and felt lucky to be alive.

Maggie changed bandages, took temperatures and administered medication until Sister Mayhew sent her to have her break.

'You're looking better, Nurse Gibbs,' she said approvingly. 'I think you've proved yourself to be a good nurse – do you want me to recommend you for a spot of home leave?'

'No, thank you, Sister. I'm happy here,' Maggie said. 'I like working for you – but if I'm needed elsewhere, I'm ready.'

'I think I shall keep you here for a bit longer,' Sister Mayhew said. 'I want good nurses in this ward as much as anywhere else, so I'll be selfish and keep you to myself. Off you go now.' Just as Maggie was about to leave, she called her back. 'You're off this weekend, I think?'

'Yes, Sister – I'm going to a wedding in the village. Marie's eldest niece is getting married and she invited both Sadie and me.'

'Well, enjoy yourselves. There is no reason you shouldn't – remember that and don't feel guilty that you're not working.'

'Yes, Sister – and thank you.'

Maggie was feeling much better about life and she knew who to thank – working with these men who still smiled and joked despite all they'd been through had made her see that she wasn't the only one to know suffering and grief. They lost friends all the time and yet they carried on; they had to, and so would she.

* * *

There was an air of festivity in the village despite the sound of the guns, no more than ten or fifteen miles away, so the soldiers told them. When Maggie had first realised how close to the fighting they were, she'd shivered, fearing the Germans might break through and descend on them, but it hadn't happened yet. It seemed as if the war was fought over a small space called no man's land and although both sides made attacks on each other's lines they never seemed to get far. The first attack of what they now called mustard gas had taken everyone by surprise and the Germans had broken through for nearly four miles that day, but fortunately the Canadians had stopped them, driving them back, and stalemate seemed to have descended again, as far as Maggie could tell.

Here in the village it was as if the war was far away this morning. The villagers had put out tubs of bright geraniums and other flowers and Marie's house had garlands of flowers hanging on the door and from the windows. She was wearing the pretty silk scarf Maggie had given her as she welcomed the two English girls with kisses and smiles, delighted to see them and drawing them in as though they were family. She took them both up to see the bride, who was a pretty shy girl of eighteen. Since silk and satin was almost impossible to buy now, Magdalena was dressed in her mother's wedding gown of cream lace and had a crown of fresh flowers on her hair, her bouquet tied up with blue ribbons.

Sadie and Maggie gave her the lace handkerchiefs they'd managed to buy from a nurse who had purchased them in Paris while on leave, and Magdalena was delighted with her gift. Especially, she told them, since they were in a box with the name of a prestigious Paris shop and she'd always wanted something from there.

'Maison Fontaine is a wonderful shop,' she told Maggie. 'I have seen pictures and wanted to work there, but Maman kept me at home to help in the shop – but I will go there when the war is over and buy something.'

'You would like Harpers,' Maggie told her. 'I think the shop these came from must be similar, from what Nurse Rose told us, and I loved working there. I sold beautiful silk scarves and leather gloves – and sometimes hats.'

'Why did you leave? I would never have left if I'd had a job in a shop like that.'

'It was because of the war – because I wanted to help the men who were fighting for us.'

Magdalena nodded. 'I understand, because I know how I would feel if my Phillipe was wounded.' She sighed. 'He is only home for six days and then he must go back to his unit.'

Phillipe was a handsome young man of nineteen. He looked older than his years, perhaps because he'd been fighting with the French troops for a year now and that aged men quickly. They saw more horror and pain in a few months than most men would see in a lifetime.

However, that day was a happy day and the wedding went

well. Most of Marie's neighbours turned out to escort her niece to the church, leading her with strings of flowers and teasing the blushing bride as she was given to her bridegroom and the pair were blessed by the padre.

The ceremony was different to any wedding that Maggie had been to before, perhaps because it was a Roman Catholic ceremony, but although she didn't understand much of what was said and done in church, she shared in the general happiness and showered the happy couple with rose petals when they left the church for the reception at the village hall.

'I thought Pierre was sure to be here – he said he would,' Sadie whispered to Maggie when they took their places at the long table, which was miraculously covered with dishes of wonderful food: cheeses, ham, cold chicken, ripe tomatoes, peppers, green salads and fresh bread, accompanied by delicious relishes and, as the centrepiece, a large sponge cake decorated with soft icing and filled with jam and buttercream. Wine flowed and fragrant coffee was there for those that preferred it.

'No doubt he has been delayed for some reason,' Maggie soothed. She understood Sadie's anxious look because Pierre would not miss a cousin's wedding unless he was forced. Clearly, his work had taken him elsewhere – and it was such dangerous work that Sadie had every right to worry. 'He'll come later if he can, I'm sure.'

* * *

Pierre slipped into Marco's room and placed a finger to his lips, glancing around to make sure they were alone before he spoke.

'I have news,' he said. 'Shultz was tortured and died at the hands of that monster, but he did not talk. Hoffmeister has been arrested and shot. He was accused of treason and of murdering another officer to cover up his own guilt.'

'May God have mercy,' Marco said and crossed himself. For a moment grief stabbed at his heart and he felt guilt. It was his fault that Kurt had died in such a painful way. 'I never thought Kurt would be strong enough to keep silent through that kind of torture.'

'Apparently, he took cyanide crystals,' Pierre said. 'They are questioning where he got them, but they have no proof.'

Marco went to the drawer in his dressing table and opened it, taking out a small pillbox. Two of the pills he'd been given when he was sent out here as a spy had gone. 'I know where he got them – but they can't know...'

'Yet you are suspected,' Pierre told him grimly. 'Before he died, Hoffmeister named you as a British spy.'

'My God!' Marco felt a thrill of fear. 'Why in heaven's name did he do that? If Kurt didn't break, he couldn't have known.'

'It was probably just spite – or a suspicion,' Pierre replied with a shrug of his broad shoulders. 'Whatever, it means your time here is over, my friend. We have to get you out, now, today, before they come for you.'

'Yes, I have to go now,' Marco said. He slipped the pillbox into his pocket and pushed a few clothes into a canvas rucksack. 'Where do I go – have you any idea?'

'I've been sent to take you to the coast. A fishing vessel will take you offshore and you'll be met by a British ship.' He broke off as they heard shouting outside, going quickly to the window to look down into the street. 'They're here. I'll have to get you out across the roof; they will have the back entrance covered as well as the front.' He gestured at the rucksack. 'Leave that – you will have to manage without whatever it is.'

Marco nodded. His nerves were taut and he felt a sick anxiety inside, because he knew his fate if the Germans took him alive. He followed Pierre from the room as the banging at the front door began. They went to a small, discreet curtain that covered a narrow staircase leading up to the roof. The roof was flat at first but then rose to a peak but flattened out again where it met the neighbouring roof of a butcher and then the local baker. Keeping low, they scrambled across the roof to the next and then the baker's property. Here, a window was opened and a man dressed in a white apron beckoned frantically.

'Quickly,' he hissed. 'I'll get you away through my cellar while they search the club.'

'Thank you,' Marco said as he was helped inside. 'But you're risking so much, Jean.'

'Pouff,' Jean made a sound of disgust and spat on the floor. 'Those pigs raped my niece and the girl is now in a convent, broken and likely to die. I have no one but myself. If they kill me, I'll take some of them with me.'

Marco thanked him, feeling lucky that the sentiment in the village was mostly against the invaders. Even though the Germans shopped in their businesses and used the club as their own, they were not liked and it seemed that Jean knew more about Marco than he'd guessed his neighbours suspected. Was it one of them – a local – who had betrayed him to Hoffmeister? There was always one who would take the enemy's money and betray his neighbours; it was Sod's law.

Following Jean down to the bakehouse, Marco marvelled at the simple ingenuity of the cellars that led down beneath the bakery. The first was used to store old trays, sacks of flour and discarded furniture, but behind a false wall of wooden slats, there was a long and winding tunnel tall enough for a man to walk with his head bent.

'It leads to the church,' Pierre said and smiled as he lit an old-fashioned lantern. 'This has been here for centuries. I imagine it was used for smuggling in the old days.'

'You've used it before,' Marco said, feeling reassured as Pierre led the way. His nerves still prickled because it had been close. If the Germans had looked up or come ten minutes sooner, he would now be contemplating how soon he needed to take those cyanide crystals.

Poor Kurt, he would never get to London now, never live the life he'd craved of theatrical parties and fine dining. He'd wanted Marco to take him into his world and he'd died because of what he'd done. Had he lived Marco would have kept his word; perhaps they would have found a good life together or moved on after a time, but now he would never know. Marco prayed that the British had made good use of the information he'd given them and not dismissed it as unimportant – a man had died for those papers. Yet, as he pondered on what Kurt had done, plodding behind Pierre in the semi-darkness, Marco realised it hadn't been for any sense of high ideals or what was right and wrong. Kurt had taken the papers to impress him, and to bring disgrace on to the man he hated.

Well, at least he'd achieved a part of what he'd hoped for. The Oberst was dead, shot as a traitor in disgrace for losing important papers. According to Pierre's source, the verdict was that even if he had not passed them on, he was guilty because he had not properly protected vital information.

At last, the tunnel ended at the bottom of a winding stair. Pierre led the way up into the small, windowless room at the top – a room used for storing vestments, chairs and other objects used in the church.

'Someone will bring us food for the journey,' Pierre told him as he lit a candle. 'We'll wait until night and then we'll leave. They will let us know when the coast is clear – and if we're lucky, they will have transport of some kind. Otherwise, we walk.'

'You took a big risk for me,' Marco said and frowned. 'The Germans are not fools – whatever else they are. They will work it out that several of the villagers must have helped my escape. You realise what might happen?'

Pierre looked him in the eyes. 'We know the risks, my friend, as you do – but this is our home and we do what we have to, to survive, and we look after our friends. You didn't have to come here.' His teeth gleamed in the semi-darkness. 'Besides, you know too much. I either had to save you or kill you – and I decided I like you too much to shoot you.'

Marco looked at him and knew he wasn't jesting. Pierre would do whatever he had to do to protect the comrades who were resisting the enemy trying to subdue his homeland.

28

Marco lay hidden in the ditch as the patrol passed them by. As far as he knew the Germans were unaware of them and merely on a routine sortie, but it still made his heart pound as he kept his head down and prayed. It had been touch-and-go getting away from the village three hours ago. The Germans had still been searching for him and they'd heard shots. A roadblock had made it impossible for them to use any kind of transport, so they'd had to walk across the fields behind the church, using the ditches as hiding places. Fortunately, most were dry because of the warm weather, but some had stagnant water in them, which had soaked into their shoes and the legs of their trousers. Already regretting the extra clothes he'd left behind, Marco was cold, hungry and tired.

Pierre was blessed with being able to sleep for a few hours in the church vault, but Marco had been too restless. They'd picked a few apples from a tree and Pierre had bought milk and bread from a French farmer, but hot food was out of the question.

A sudden shout alerted the passing patrol and one of the Germans advanced towards where Marco was lying, his rifle primed ready. Marco could see his long boots and the breeches he wore when Pierre spoke softly in his ear.

'I'll try to draw them away. When it's safe, make your way to the coast as we arranged. You're only ten kilometres from the rendezvous, so you should make it tonight and you know where you're going.'

'What about you?'

'This is my job and my country,' Pierre said. 'Good luck, my friend.'

Without waiting for an answer, Pierre sprang up and fired at the patrol, taking down two of the men before they realised what had happened. He then began to run away in the opposite direction to the one Marco needed to take.

The German trooper shouted and started to run after him, firing into the night. His shot missed and Pierre kept on running. Now three others had joined the hunt and they all fired at the back of the fleeing man.

Marco saw the bullet strike, saw Pierre fall face down on the field. The Germans gathered round him, looking down at him. One of them kicked him and then another bent and turned him over. He laughed and said something that Marco recognised. Pierre was dead. The officer ordered them to pick Pierre's body up and they carried it off with them.

Feeling sick, hardly daring to move yet wanting to kill them all, Marco lay where he was until the sound of their laughter had faded into the distance. And then he cursed. Why had Pierre done that? It was a waste of life. Perhaps if he'd stopped where he was, the patrol would have passed them by – and yet he knew why his friend had taken the risk. He'd wanted to give Marco the best chance of getting away.

Tears stung his eyes as he forced himself up and started to walk and then to jog and finally to run. He needed the release of running to ease the shame and tension inside him. Marco was ashamed that he'd stayed put and let Pierre sacrifice his own life to save him and he was filled with rage at the stupidity of the men who had laughed when they'd killed him. He was burning with anger and it had formed into a hard knot in his stomach.

Two men he'd admired for their courage had died recently, one of them admittedly had brought it on himself by choosing to take revenge on a man he hated, but Pierre had been trying to save him. Marco just hoped the information he'd given was worth the deaths of two men – and there would probably be more. The Germans might take reprisals for his escape amongst the village men.

Gritting his teeth, he ran through the pain. His legs burned and his chest hurt, but it was good; he wanted to hurt; he needed the pain to stop him weeping. He wasn't sure whether he would make it to England, but if he did, he wanted to be sent back – and this time to fight. He wanted to kill, because Pierre had been killed for him and he needed to avenge him. He couldn't bear another death on his conscience.

* * *

'Queer sort,' one of the sailors remarked as they passed Marco lying in the hammock – they'd strung for him on deck, because he didn't want to go below. 'Said he didn't fancy being trapped below decks if we were hit, wouldn't have thought he was a coward.'

'He must be worth getting back if they sent us in for him,' the other man said and hawked, spitting over the side. 'It's all hush-hush – but I thought there was supposed to be two of them.'

'The Frenchie was killed,' the first voice said as they moved away.

Marco opened his eyes and looked up at the stars. He smiled

to himself because they couldn't understand that he needed to be able to breathe the fresh salt air, to know that he was himself again and no longer the decadent nightclub performer he'd pretended to be for the past few months.

His thoughts turned to the man he'd loved – Julien. His young lover had taken his own life when his father discovered his relationship with Marco. It had been hard to come to terms with that knowledge and though he'd blamed Julien's father he blamed himself too. Kurt had reminded him a little of Julien, but it was only a surface thing – underneath they were very different.

Some of the anger had gone now. The killing rage had faded, but he still wanted revenge for Pierre and for the others he knew would suffer because he'd escaped. It was more than likely that other villagers would be shot for helping a British spy escape.

Marco tried to ease the guilt inside him. He was doing the job he'd been asked to do – but it didn't help knowing that Pierre had been in love. He'd talked about a young woman – an English nurse called Sadie. She was pretty and funny and Pierre had intended to ask her to marry him one day. Now that could never happen and it was Marco's fault.

* * *

Marie told Sadie the news when they visited the village just over two weeks later. Pierre's home was some twenty-five kilometres away from Marie's village of Saint-Angelus on the borders of France and Belgium. He'd been shot by a German patrol while helping a British spy escape and after his body was returned to the village, six villagers were executed in the square for harbouring a known enemy.

Sadie stared at her in stunned silence and then shook her head. 'No, it can't be true,' she whispered. 'I don't believe you – not

Pierre... not my Pierre...' She turned, looking wildly at Maggie. 'She's lying, please tell me it isn't true...'

Maggie moved to take her in her arms and hold her as she shook with the force of her weeping. She kissed her head and held her tightly, looking at Marie over her head apologetically, but Marie needed no apology. Her eyes were filled with sympathy and sadness. She had been fond of Pierre, as were all the family.

'He died bravely, my little one,' Marie said. 'You must be brave too. Pierre was a good Frenchman and he did what needed to be done – it was a selfless act to help another brave man.'

'No – he shouldn't,' Sadie denied, her sobs increasing as Maggie soothed her. 'We were going to marry... he loved me...'

'I'm so sorry,' Maggie murmured against her hair. 'I know how it feels. I know it hurts so badly, Sadie.'

She couldn't tell Sadie it would get better, because so far it hadn't got much better for her. Yes, the sharp pain had eased a little, but the ache and the emptiness inside were still there. Maggie wasn't sure that it would ever get better and she wouldn't lie to her friend. 'I'm here for you, love, just as you were for me.'

Sadie pulled back and looked at her, her eyes dark with distress. 'You don't understand... Pierre... we were both a little drunk one night and he said we would marry soon...' She gave a strangled sob. 'I'm pregnant, Maggie. I'm having Pierre's baby...'

'Sadie!' Maggie stared at her in shock. If Sadie was pregnant, she would be dismissed from the service, sent home in disgrace – and her parents might not accept her if she had no one to marry her. 'Oh, Sadie, I don't know what to say...'

'The little one has the baby?' Marie exclaimed and went to embrace Sadie. 'You will come to us when they send you away from the hospital – you belong with us now.'

Sadie stared at her in silence, looking from her to Maggie.

Maggie nodded. It was perhaps the best thing for Sadie, if

Marie was willing to take her in and look after her while she had the child.

'You needn't tell anyone just yet,' she said. 'It will be our secret – and then you can come here to have the baby. Afterwards...' She shook her head, because they would talk about that when they were alone. Sadie had to make up her mind whether she wanted to keep her baby or leave it with Pierre's family and go back to England alone.

Marie was smiling and patting Sadie's arm. It was a good thing, she told them. All Pierre's family would welcome the news that he had a child. They would all want to help Sadie and to help bring up her baby.

Sadie let Marie chatter on. She was numbed, thoughtful, her eyes dark with sadness. Maggie knew that she would talk when they were alone, but her thoughts were perhaps not to be shared with Pierre's cousin.

She felt sad for her friend, but inside Maggie envied her a little. At least Sadie had lain in her lover's arms and known the joy of making love. She would have Pierre's baby and perhaps in time she would realise how lucky she was to have a part of her lover left to her.

* * *

'I shan't keep the child,' Sadie said when they were alone in their hut that evening. 'I'll go to Marie and have the baby – but then I'll give it to the family if they want it or to the nuns.'

'Are you sure?' Maggie asked. 'It is Pierre's baby – surely you must want to keep it?'

'No, not now,' Sadie said and she sounded angry, a little bitter. 'He promised me we would marry – why did he do something so dangerous? Why didn't he think of me? He must have known I might have a child...'

'He didn't know you were pregnant?'

'No, I wasn't sure at first – but we made love a few times; he must have known it could happen.' She caught back a sob. 'He should have thought of me – of what could happen. I've worked so hard.'

'But surely a baby—'

'No!' Sadie was determined. 'I'll talk to Sister Mayhew. She might know a way I can come back once I've had the baby.' She hit her pillows hard. 'I worked so hard for this – I can't lose it all now. If Pierre had lived, I would've been happy to leave, but now...' She sobbed in the darkness. 'I can't bear it, Maggie – why should I lose everything because he threw his life away?'

'How can you say that?' Maggie asked. 'He was doing important work...'

'But Marie said he'd done something very brave and foolish.' Sadie pounded her pillows angrily. 'He should have been more careful and thought of me. It isn't fair...'

'No, it isn't fair,' Maggie agreed, because how could she argue about that? It hurt to lose the man you loved and it wasn't fair that they should die because of this rotten war.

29

Marion knew something was wrong the moment she opened the kitchen door that evening. There was no sign of Sarah and no sign that any preparation for supper had been made. She took off her coat and ran upstairs, hearing the muffled cries as she reached Sarah's room. Inside, Sarah was sitting in her night-gown on the edge of the bed grimacing, her face screwed up with pain.

'Is it the baby?' Marion asked, going to her at once and taking her hand. Sarah gripped it so hard that Marion had to suppress a cry of pain. 'I thought it wasn't for another three weeks yet...'

'So, did I...' Sarah gasped, suppressing a moan of agony. 'I heard the postman and hurried to the door this morning and fell down the last steps.' She bit her lip. 'I didn't think anything of it, just a little bruise on my back and elbow, but then just as I was going to start supper this happened.' She gave a cry of fear. 'If I lose my baby...'

'Oh, Sarah love,' Marion said. 'You must have brought the labour on early by falling. Something similar happened to my mother when she had Dan – she had a little fall in the back garden and he was born a few weeks early, but he was all right and so was she.'

'You think I'll be all right?' Sarah looked at her hopefully. 'I've been sitting here terrified I was going to lose my baby.'

'No, I'm sure you won't.' Marion heard the kitchen door. 'That will be Kathy, love. I'm going to send her for the midwife and the doctor – and I'll put the kettles on.'

'I could do with a cup of tea. I meant to make a nice pie this evening...'

Marion laughed. 'I will make a cup of tea, but we'll be needing hot water for the midwife later and warm water for washing baby.' She pressed Sarah's hand. 'Don't be afraid to scream out if it hurts too much.'

Kathy was just taking her coat off. She looked scared as Marion told her that Sarah's baby was coming but put her coat back on and went out immediately.

Marion started filling kettles and saucepans with water and putting them on to boil. They could all have a sandwich that evening and a succession of hot drinks, because she wasn't going to cook supper when Sarah needed her.

Kathy returned in a panic by the time Marion had the tea made.

'Doctor's out with another patient and the midwife isn't in either...' she said and looked at Marion in fear. 'What shall we do?'

'Go next door and ask Mrs Jackson if Paula is home,' Marion said. 'She is a nurse and will have taken midwifery classes; she'll know what to do.'

Marion carried a tray of tea upstairs. She was encouraging Sarah to drink hers when Kathy came rushing up the stairs.

'Mrs Jackson says Paula's not home until nine this evening, but she's coming – she says not to worry...'

'Good,' Marion said and smiled at Sarah. 'It's all right, love. I'm here and Mrs Jackson knows what to do. She's had seven children herself and her daughter is a nurse.'

Sarah looked doubtful and nervous, but when Mrs Jackson arrived, her calm manner made them all feel better. She smiled at Sarah and told her to sit back and relax on the bed.

'Have your waters broken yet?'

'Not yet,' Sarah said. 'I'm getting pain every few minutes though.'

'About how long between?'

'Ten or fifteen... perhaps a bit more sometimes...'

'Then we've got plenty of time,' Mrs Jackson said. 'Either my Paula will be home or the midwife will turn up before you're in proper labour – it took me twenty-five hours to have my first, though Reggie was here a lot quicker.'

'Twenty-five hours...' Sarah looked aghast at the idea and Mrs Jackson smiled. 'I thought it would be quick – an hour or so...'

'For some lucky ones it is,' Mrs Jackson told her. 'Have they taught you any breathing exercises down at the clinic?' She panted a couple of times to illustrate. 'Just something like that.'

'I was just learning them...' Sarah breathed deeply. 'I can't remember what they told me.'

'Not to worry, when it starts for real, I'll sort you out,' she said. 'If I were you, I should drink your tea and let Marion get you a nice sandwich. By the look of you, it will be a while yet and you'll need to keep your strength up.'

'I thought it would be soon.' Sarah looked a bit disappointed as Mrs Jackson smiled and shook her head. 'So, not yet then...'

'I'll pop back and serve up my husband's tea,' Mrs Jackson said. 'Don't worry, I'll be back – and either Paula or the midwife will be here by the time you need help.' She went off with a nod and a smile, leaving the two young women to look at each other.

Marion laughed and squeezed Sarah's hand. 'She's right you know – Ma was ages having Milly. The midwife came and went three times before she was born.'

'Oh dear,' Sarah said. 'I wish it was over…'

'Could you eat a nice ham sandwich? I'll cut them small and put a little pickle in if you like – and I'll eat mine up here with you.'

'Yes, please,' Sarah agreed. She winced as a pain struck. 'I think the last one was only ten minutes ago…'

'Let me get you that sandwich,' Marion said and went down as Sarah clenched her teeth and muttered something unmentionable.

In the kitchen, Kathy was busy making toast for Dickon and a sandwich for her and Milly. She offered to make them for Marion and Sarah and Marion agreed. She placed the cups in the sink and then, hearing a yell from upstairs, ran up to her sister-in-law again.

'That was a sharp one,' Sarah said. 'They're coming quickly now, Marion. I think I wet myself and it hurts like hell…'

'Your waters have broken,' Marion said, noting the damp patch on the towels Sarah was lying on. 'That was quick.'

'Ouch,' Sarah cried out. 'It's like being kicked in the back by a horse.'

'Don't forget to breathe deeply – like this…' Marion panted as Mrs Jackson had told them earlier. 'That's it – that's what Mum did and she pushed when she got a pain.' It was odd but now that the baby was coming, she felt quite calm. 'You can do this, love.' She was remembering what the midwife had done and her mother giving birth, how she'd come through the pain and it had all been wonderful when Milly was born.

Sarah gritted her teeth and made a strangled pushing noise and yelled as she felt the worst pain so far. 'I think it is coming…'

she said and drew her knees up, her nightgown pulled up to her thighs. 'Is anything happening?'

Marion took a peek and gave a little squeal of excitement. 'I can just see the head... Oh, Sarah, it's coming. Breathe deeply now and push when you feel the need.'

Sarah panted hard and then felt a strong urge. She pushed and screamed and then fell back against the pillows in despair. 'I can't...' she gasped. 'I've never felt such pain – it feels as if I'm tearing apart...'

'The head is through,' Marion encouraged her and put her hands underneath the baby's head, supporting it with her hands. 'Next time you push I can help you.'

'I can't... I can't...' Sarah moaned. 'It hurts too much...' Yet even as she said it, she was beginning to pant again and then she felt the need to push and Marion held her hands ready, taking hold of the little slippery body by the shoulders and easing its passage into the world; suddenly baby came slithering out into her hands as Sarah screamed.

Kathy entered the room with their sandwiches and Marion yelled at her to fetch Mrs Jackson quickly. She backed out hurriedly and was heard pounding down the stairs and out of the back door.

'You've done it, Sarah,' Marion told her. 'You've got a beautiful little girl. She is perfect.'

Sarah craned to look. 'I want to hold her.'

'I've got to do something, cut the cord...' Marion said and frowned. 'I'm not sure what to do. I don't want to make a mistake. Let's wait for Mrs Jackson...' She gently wiped blood and moisture from baby's head and face with a towel and then wrapped it around the little body.

Sarah flopped back against the pillows and closed her eyes.

Within moments, they heard pounding feet up the stairs and then Mrs Jackson was back with them, a sharp knife in hand.

'Well, I never,' she said astounded. 'I thought you'd be hours yet, but we'll soon have the knot tied and then you can hold baby.'

'I wasn't sure what to do,' Marion told her.

'The midwives have proper instruments to clamp the cord,' she told Marion as she worked, 'but my granny always used to tie a knot like this, see, and then it's safe to cut the cord here.' She did so efficiently and wrapped the child in a warm towel Marion provided. 'Let mother hold her for a while and then you can wash her while I see to Sarah.'

Marion saw the look on Sarah's face as she held her daughter in her arms and kissed her head, which was still marked with her blood.

'She's so beautiful...'

'Yes, she is,' Marion agreed and smiled as Sarah nursed the baby for a few minutes.

'You'd better let me look after her,' Mrs Jackson said and poured warm water into a bowl. 'I can't see any damage down there, Sarah love, but you'd be best to let the midwife look at you when she gets here – and if she doesn't, I'll send Paula round. That sort of thing doesn't want leaving, though I don't think you need a stitch. Luckily she was small.' She bathed Sarah and then helped her into a clean nightdress. Together, she and Marion moved her gently from the damp sheets and put a dry one under her. Before Marion came home, Sarah had placed some old towels under her for the birth and that had saved most of the blood from staining the mattress.

The child was lying on a chair wrapped up warmly after Marion had bathed her in warm water and swaddled her in another clean towel. Now that Sarah was comfortable, she put the little girl back in her arms. Sarah smiled at them.

'I want to call her after you, Marion – and you Mrs Jackson.'

'I'm Pam,' Mrs Jackson said, looking pleased. 'Not that I deserve it – I quite misjudged her arrival.'

'It was probably the fall that brought it on early,' Marion said. 'Sarah tripped down a couple of stairs this morning and has had pains on and off since.'

'That will be it,' Mrs Jackson agreed. 'So, it's Marion Pamela Kaye – well that's a nice name. Let's hope your husband approves.'

'Oh, he will,' Sarah assured her. 'He thinks the world of Marion – and I do too. She's been so kind to me – there's no one like her.'

'I'll agree with that.' Mrs Jackson shook her head as they heard a knock at the door. 'That will be the midwife or the doctor – trust them to turn up when it's all over – but they can look you and the little one over, Sarah love, just to be on the safe side.'

* * *

It was an hour or so later that Sarah lay sleeping after giving baby her first feed and Marion was able to eat her supper. She was feeling a bit shocked at the speed of the birth and nervous now that it was all over. So many things could have gone wrong, but they'd been lucky and both the midwife and the doctor had told them Sarah and her baby were fine.

'I'll never be able to thank you enough,' Sarah said to Marion before she fell asleep, exhausted all of a sudden. 'If you hadn't been here...'

'I'm just glad I was and that you weren't alone in lodgings somewhere.' Marion smiled at her. 'You've got a lovely baby and I've got a gorgeous niece and I'm so happy. I only wish Mum had been here to see her. She would have loved her, Sarah.'

Sarah wiped tears from her face. 'I know you miss her,

Marion. Dan does too – but at least we're a family now. We've got a little person to bind us together now.'

Marion agreed, though she hadn't needed anyone; she'd taken to Sarah immediately but Kathy was enraptured with the new baby and told Marion that she was glad Sarah had come to stay.

'She looks a bit like Milly,' she said. 'I remember when Milly was little – before her hair went darker – and Sarah's baby looks like she did...'

Marion wasn't sure, but she smiled and nodded, pleased that Kathy loved her niece and was reconciled to Dan's wife living with them.

She was just about to make their evening cocoa and had sent Kathy up to discover if Sarah was awake and would like some when someone knocked at the door. She opened it and saw a neighbour from three doors down. 'Come in, Mrs Brown, what can I do for you?'

'Oh, Marion,' Mrs Brown said apologetically. 'I'm sorry to disturb you, but this was delivered to my house by mistake earlier today. I should've brought it before this, but I was out and then I heard you had a lot going on...' She handed a letter with an official postmark on it.

Marion saw it was addressed to Sarah and recognised her brother's handwriting.

'My brother's wife just gave birth to her first baby,' Marion said. 'Baby was early and took us all by surprise – but she's fine, a bit small, of course, but lovely.'

'That explains all the comings and goings,' Mrs Brown said. 'Well, I'm glad everything is all right – and if you need any help, I'm usually at home in the afternoons.'

Elsie Brown went scrubbing floors in an office block from four in the morning until eight o'clock and then did three hours washing up in a canteen to make her husband's small wage eke out. Ken Brown had been in an accident down the docks a few years back and though he'd recovered enough to manage the job of caretaker at the factory where he'd once worked harder than anyone, it didn't bring enough in to keep a family of five. None of their children was above fourteen and although the eldest boy would be leaving school to work on the docks that July, he wouldn't bring in more than a few shillings a week, so his mother would still have to work.

'That's very kind,' Marion said. 'I've asked for time off from work. I shall go in tomorrow morning and Kathy will stay home from school, but after that I should be able to take my two weeks' holiday to care for Sarah and the baby.'

'Well, my Jilly can run errands or do a bit of fetching and carryin' if yer want,' Mrs Brown said and smiled. 'I'll get off now – I can see you're gettin' ready to go up.'

Kathy entered the kitchen and smiled at their neighbour. She was friendly with Elsie's daughter, Flo. 'Sarah is still sleeping, so I didn't wake her – Baby Marion is sleeping too.'

'Calling her after you.' Elsie nodded and looked pleased. 'That's nice – not everyone would have done what you have, Marion.' She moved towards the door and then paused. 'Remember I'll help if I can...'

'Thank you, Mrs Brown,' Marion said. 'Everyone is so kind.'

After their neighbour had gone, Marion helped Kathy make the cocoa and they took theirs upstairs. Dickon was out again that evening. He'd come in for his tea as usual and retreated swiftly to the pub when he'd heard the screams from upstairs, telling Kathy he might stay at a friend's house that evening.

'I reckon Dickon's got a girlfriend,' she told Marion as they went upstairs. 'He's been so secretive lately – it's not like him...'

'He's too young to be courting,' Marion said with a frown. She felt a cold shiver at her nape. Since Sarah's arrival, she'd been too caught up in her and the coming baby to take much notice of Dickon and now she wondered – Marion didn't believe her brother was in love. She was more afraid that he was trying to enlist. He'd heard that several young lads of fifteen and sixteen had been signed on, even though they were officially underage.

He wouldn't do anything so daft – would he?

Marion made up her mind to talk to him in the morning. If he was feeling neglected or that she didn't need him... She couldn't forbid him to go if he managed to get accepted, but she would do her best to persuade him to at least wait for another two years.

Would the war go on for that long? She knew that a lot of people felt it was dragging on far longer than it should have done, but the lads of Dickon's age were afraid it would be over before they got their chance to kill a few Huns. Marion prayed it would be. She already had two brothers and her fiancé at risk – she couldn't afford to lose Dickon to the Army too.

Upstairs, she peeped in at Sarah and then the baby. Just as Kathy said, they were both sleeping well. She placed the letter from Dan on the table beside the bed where Sarah would see it first thing and smiled. Sarah had been fretting for weeks over not getting a letter from her husband, now at last one had come.

* * *

In the morning, Marion was down before Kathy and found Dickon pulling on his work boots. He looked at her sheepishly.

'Sorry I bolted, Marion – but I didn't fancy listening to Sarah... she's all right, isn't she?'

'Yes, and the baby, a little girl.' Marion looked at him intently. 'If I've neglected you recently, Dick, I'm sorry...'

'Don't be daft.' He grinned at her. 'You've got things to do –

and baby stuff to talk about. 'Sides, I'm a man now and I've got me mates.'

Marion looked at him and saw he was right. He was a man in everything but years. He did a good job and he gave her two-thirds of his wages, but she felt a pang of regret; he'd had to grow up too soon.

'I know – but you're still my little brother. Don't go away and leave us, will you?'

'They won't take me yet,' Dickon said and grinned. 'I went down the recruitin' office again last week, but they know me and told me to wait another two years. I would have to go off where they don't know me to get put on the register...'

'I know you want to join up, but we still need you here.' She looked at him anxiously. He was too young to fight!

Dickon nodded. 'Yeah, I know – Robbie told me I had to look after you all and so did Reggie. Don't worry, our Marion. I'll be around fer a bit longer – they say they need me down the docks, too. If we all go, there won't be enough men left to repair the ships, so maybe I'm doing more good where I am...'

Marion breathed a sigh of relief. 'I'm glad you realise that, Dick. Sometimes it needs more courage to stay home and do your duty than it does to go and shoot at the enemy.'

'Yeah, perhaps,' he said. 'Is there any bacon this mornin'? I'm famished.'

Marion smiled and went to the pantry. She would do him a special breakfast of bacon, fried bread, an egg and tomatoes. He deserved a bit of special treatment now and then and it would show him he was important to her and to his family.

30

Sally looked at the stocklist she needed and sighed. From her calculations, she would actually be able to buy about a half of what she'd wanted to order. This wretched war! However, she knew that in the scheme of things, her problems were nothing compared to the injuries the men were suffering. Harpers being less well stocked than she would like was insignificant when you thought about the men lying out there in those field hospitals with horrendous wounds. Her thoughts went briefly to Mick, thankful that he at least had recovered from his wounds. He'd proved a good friend these past years and the thought of him lying on a battlefield, slowly bleeding to death made her close her eyes for a moment – but then she smiled. Somehow, she knew Mick would come home. Many would not and some of those would probably be Harpers' men... and that dimmed her smile once more.

Nothing was as it had been, Sally reflected. These days, some food shops had queues. Whenever a fresh delivery came in and word got around, everyone rushed to buy whatever it was, whether they knew what the shop was selling or not. You saw a queue and joined it in the hope you could buy something nice to eat.

She shivered, pulling her cardigan tighter. The months just seemed to fly by. It was almost the end of June already, and Jenni was due any day now. It was cooler than it had been for a while. Sally wasn't sure where the summer had gone. She'd been so busy – and so had Ben. Perhaps the warm weather would return; you could never tell with the British summer. It could go from blazing hot to freezing cold in a day. Jenni's ship had been due a couple of days earlier, but they'd heard it had been delayed for various reasons. Ben was on thorns, anxious to see his sister, but fearful that her ship might be attacked. Sally reviewed the events of the past few months in her mind.

The war dragged on and the news veered from good to bad: in May, the Allied troops had stormed ashore in Gallipoli, but then the Auxiliary ship *Irene* had exploded at Sheerness with many dead. On 7th May, the American ship, the *Lusitania*, had been sunk after being torpedoed off the Irish coast; it had devastated the Americans when so many passengers were killed – including some close friends of President Woodrow Wilson. That incident had unsettled Ben, making him worry for his sister's safety when she came over.

Then, towards the end of May, the Liberal Government had ended when Prime Minister Asquith decided to form a coalition, and right at the end of the month the Zeppelins raided London itself for the first time. That in itself had been terrifying for those caught in the blasts and made everyone realise how terrible war from the air could be.

On 8th June, a young British flier had successfully downed a Zeppelin by climbing above it in the clouds and dropping his bombs. Tragically, it fell on a Belgian convent and killed two children and two nurses. He was later awarded the Victoria Cross for his brave act. In mid-June, the miners of Wales had gone on strike for more pay and on 25th June the Germans had sunk two American merchant ships off the coast of Ireland.

Ben was still haunted by the sinking of the *Lusitania* and Sally saw a permanent frown on his forehead these days. Some days, she hardly saw him and he was away at least one weekend in three.

'Mrs Harper...' Ruth popped her head round the door. 'There's someone to see you.' She was smiling and looked pleased.

Sally's nerves tingled as she stood up, looking expectantly towards the door.

'Marco...' she exclaimed as he entered wearing the uniform of a captain in the Army. 'You've been promoted. Congratulations! How lovely to see you!'

'Sally Harper,' he said and came forward to greet her, kissing her on either cheek in the French fashion. 'How are you – you look as lovely as ever.'

'I'm very well,' she said, feeling a little puzzled as she noticed he had a slightly tanned appearance. 'You're looking healthy – training must suit you.'

'Oh, well, running about on the south coast doing gym exercises...' Marco replied with a little shrug, which seemed a rather French mannerism. There was definitely a change in him, but she couldn't have said what it was or whether she liked it. 'It is very good for one. I find it a little boring, but we must do whatever they tell us.'

'I'm glad they haven't sent you overseas,' Sally said. 'We've lost at least two of our male staff – a young lad called Nick who was training under Mr Brown and Cyril Havers. He was on the china and glass counter if you recall?'

'Yes, I do. Cyril has been killed?' Marco frowned, because he'd known the young man well. 'Where did that happen?'

'At Ypres so I understand,' Sally said. 'And Fred Burrows lost his son, Tim – you may know he was engaged to Maggie Gibbs?'

'Poor little Miss Gibbs. I've always liked her,' Marco said, nodding in sympathy. 'I understand she is nursing now?'

'Yes, she is – and she didn't come home even for the funeral. She says she's needed where she is.'

'I'm sure she is,' Marco said, looking sombre. 'I'm very sorry to hear about our losses. We all know that too many men are dying out there, but it brings it home when it's someone you know, doesn't it?'

'Yes, very much so.'

For a moment, something in his face seemed to crumple and she thought he was close to tears, but then in an instant he had conquered it. 'I noticed the window dedicated to the women of the Voluntary Aid Detachment. Whose idea was that? Let me guess – did it come from you?'

'Marion Kaye and I came up with the idea together. We wanted to honour our girls as well as our men – we have two young women out there now in the nursing corps and, of course, there are many others doing a wonderful job, helping with canteens and driving the trams in their spare time.'

'I loved the look of it,' he said and gave her a little clap. His smile dimmed and he became thoughtful as he asked, 'Is Mr Harper around anywhere?'

'Ben is working, I'm afraid,' Sally replied. 'He will be home this evening – why don't you have supper with us?'

'That is the best offer I've had in months,' Marco replied with a twinkle in his eyes. 'I shall leave you – and take a few minutes to speak with Miss Kaye. I shall compliment her on the windows – and pass on a couple of ideas she might like if she gets stuck for inspiration.'

'I know you're doing your duty in the Army,' Sally said regretfully. 'But I do wish you'd never joined up...'

Marco looked at her oddly and then smiled. 'Do you know, Sally Harper – there are times when I wish the very same thing...'

* * *

Sally took her time nursing Jenny, changing her nappy and making her warm and comfortable, standing over her cot until she settled and slept. Even then, she waited a while before returning to the sitting room. It had been obvious to her that Ben and Marco had something important to discuss and she'd taken Jenny's cries as an excuse to leave them alone.

Judging that they must have had enough time by now, she walked slowly back, pausing outside the slightly open door as she heard the serious tone in their voices.

'I guessed what you must be doing when I saw you at that front-line hospital,' Ben said. 'Until I was briefed this morning so that I could fill you in on the new mission, I didn't dream you were in Pont le-Neuve. That was behind enemy lines at one time and I understand the Germans still think of it as their own, even though we drove them back ten miles, months ago.'

There was a smile in Marco's voice as he said, 'The Allies can't continually patrol that line that far up and so the Germans move back in and use the town as their own under cover of darkness. I call it a town, but it's little more than a big village really – perhaps three hundred people live there and another three hundred or so on the farms in the area. Some of them were born the Belgian side of the border but married into French families. It's always been a bit of a mixture – quiet, sleepy place with perhaps a dozen shops and a couple of inns – and if it weren't for that nightclub, it would probably have been ignored by the Germans.'

'You did so well to get that information back to us,' Ben said. 'I'm not sure if the Brass Hats will act on it all, but we're certainly going to.'

Sally decided she'd better not listen to any more because she might hear too much. She'd already heard more than she should and felt shocked as she realised for the first time where Marco's tan had come from – he'd been working undercover on the Belgian/French border!

Giving a discreet cough, Sally smiled as the men paused and then Ben changed the subject.

'I'm glad you approved of the window dedicated to our young women, who are doing such wonderful work, Marco – but I know Sally misses your special touch.' He looked up and smiled as Sally entered. 'Is Jenny settled now, darling?'

'Yes, she's sleeping,' Sally replied and nodded to the two men. 'Would you like some fresh coffee?' It was an excuse to leave them alone together if they needed more time to discuss what was clearly secret business, but Marco shook his head.

'I must go now, Sally. Thank you for a lovely meal – and a pleasant evening. I have someone I must see this evening – but I did enjoy myself and it was wonderful to see everyone at Harpers looking so well.'

'Those of us who have our normal jobs and lives are lucky,' Sally replied carefully. 'We have to thank all the brave men who are out there keeping us safe – and I know my husband is one of them, even though he still thinks he should have a gun and go and shoot the enemy.' She gave them a teasing look and they both laughed.

'Ben is a hero in his way,' Marco replied. 'From what I hear, you've been doing your part too, Sally, helping seriously injured men to face up to life again – and keeping Harpers going so that we all have a job to come back to when this is over.'

'I wish it would be over,' Sally replied. 'I do very little. I know there are others who do so much more and we don't even know about it...' It was the closest she could come to telling him she knew he was a hero too.

'We all wish it was over,' Ben replied and shook hands with Marco. 'I'll see you again.'

A look passed between them and Sally knew that they were involved in another scheme, perhaps to resupply the field hospitals, but if that was so, Ben would probably tell her a bit of it – but if it was secret, he would wait until it was no longer secret. She often learned about things the same day as the papers got hold of the story and she understood that there was a great deal about Ben's work that he wasn't allowed to tell her. She knew that much of it concerned deals with America, but that was as far as it went.

'Jenni's ship should have docked at Liverpool this evening, according to the last we heard,' Sally said, feeling she needed to say something after Marco had gone. 'I'm really looking forward to seeing her, Ben.'

'You heard, didn't you?' Ben said, looking at her hard. 'How much?'

'Just about where Marco was working and that he got some information for the British – no more, Ben, I promise you.'

'Good. I know you're not going to pass it on intentionally, but sometimes things slip out – you know you can't tell anyone what Marco is doing.'

'I wouldn't dream of it,' Sally said, 'and I promise I won't whisper it to Beth or anyone. If it got to the wrong person, it could cost his life.'

Ben nodded, serious. 'There are spies even here in London, Sally – people you wouldn't dream would give our secrets away. I laughed in disbelief when I was first briefed, but I know it to be true. I've known some of the men who were arrested and interrogated. Some people think we should have sided with the Kaiser...'

'How could they?' Sally couldn't understand that attitude. 'I don't want a war either, but we are at war and we must all be patriotic and loyal, even if we don't like what is happening.'

'Unfortunately, not everyone sees it that way,' Ben told her. 'We have a lot of brave men risking their lives for us, Sally, and not all of them are in the trenches...'

'Yes, I know, Ben.' She hesitated, then, 'Are you content with the part you're playing now?'

'Yes, because I know that what I do counts. I did think at first that I should be out there shooting a gun, but I've realised since that we all do what we do best – and seeing Marco out there, knowing what he must be doing, helped me to realise it. He wasn't using a gun, but his life was in constant danger and it will be again, so, protect his secret well, my love.'

'Of course,' she said and smiled up at him. 'I really don't know much at all and I'm glad I don't. It must be hard keeping a lot of secrets.'

'Especially when I have a bright and beautiful wife, I should like to talk to about them,' Ben confided with a wry look. 'Don't think I like keeping anything from you, Sally. I don't.'

'I know,' she said and put her arms about him, giving him a hug. 'All I want is for us to be safe and together as a family again. If your work is helping, then I'm content not to know. Jenni will be here tomorrow evening if her ship docks on time and she is going to want to know everything.'

'I think Jenni has some secrets to tell herself,' Ben said and frowned. 'I'm just hoping she and Henry are all right... I've never been sure he was right for her.'

* * *

Marco left Sally and Ben's apartment smiling to himself. Sally Harper was a minx and he suspected she'd heard a little more than she ought, but he didn't mind, because he knew wild horses wouldn't drag it out of her. She was a delightful woman and Ben was lucky to have a wife he could rely on like that.

Marco's thoughts were pleasant as he approached the Mayfair hotel where his meeting was due to take place. It was the fourth he'd had since his return from France, counting his talk with Ben; the first was mainly a debriefing, then he'd been summoned to meet the Prime Minister and been told the country appreciated his work and hoped he would continue to serve.

'I'd like to join the ranks and face the enemy on the battle-field,' Marco had told him, the anger still hard inside him. However, he'd been informed that they had other work for him and he would be liaising with a friend of his for the next briefing.

'I believe you worked closely with Ben Harper?'

'Yes, sir. We've been friends for years; we met when I was working in America for one of the larger stores in New York.'

'Then you'll understand that Mr Harper has been very useful to us with his contacts in America – his family were, and are, influential. His sister is married to an important general and has the ear of the American President.'

'That must be useful, Prime Minister...'

'Yes, it may prove to be so – though as yet we haven't been able to persuade our friends to join us in this fight. We have, however, received help of a substantial nature and much of it came through Mr Harper's contacts.'

'Yes, sir. I imagine we need money as much as anything to fight this war.'

'It's a damned costly business.' The Prime Minister had nodded and smiled earnestly. An earl and a man of education, he had overseen the war thus far but been forced to seek a coalition because of the increasing severity of the conflict. 'Well, sir, we are glad to have you back safely, but I'm afraid we'll be asking you to go back out there soon.'

Marco had shaken hands then with mixed feelings. It was an honour to be received by such a man, but he'd hoped to go back to France with a gun in his hands, to be a part of the British fighting force – though perhaps he was more useful in other ways. Whatever, he had a score to settle for Pierre's untimely death.

He frowned as he went into the hotel and gave the name of the General he was meeting that evening. He had a feeling he was not going to like the outcome, but he'd found himself unable to refuse Prime Minister Asquith when he was asked if he would continue his valuable work and so he would have to grit his teeth and get on with it wherever they asked of him.

31

Sally was ready and waiting when the doorbell rang and hurried to answer it, knowing it was her sister-in-law. She flung the door opened and held out her hands in welcome. 'Jenni, darling!' Sally rushed to embrace her, drawing her into the hall of their apartment. She kissed her cheek and Jenni kissed her back, but she felt a slight hesitation, as if something wasn't right and, drawing back, she looked at her again, seeing dark shadows beneath her eyes. 'You've been ill – why didn't you tell us?'

'I didn't feel like putting it on paper,' Jenni said and her eyes were filled with tears. 'I lost my son...' The words caught in her throat. 'I don't mean Tom – I mean my baby...'

'Oh, Jenni...' Sally put her arms around her carefully. She hadn't known for sure that her sister-in-law was pregnant. Jenni had mentioned she thought she might be about three months ago, but she must have miscarried. Now Jenni felt thin and fragile in Sally's arms and she trembled slightly, as if she were holding herself on a thin string. 'I am so terribly sorry. I know that doesn't help, dearest, but my heart breaks for you.'

Sally couldn't imagine how she would cope with the loss of

her baby. To never be able to hold her little Jenny again or kiss her or see her smile, it was unthinkable, and Jenni must feel the same, even though she hadn't carried full term.

'Thank you,' Jenni said. 'It was so devastating, Sally. I was ill – we thought it was just a little chill at the start, but then pneumonia set in and I miscarried; the doctors didn't know why...'

'Jenni love.' Sally embraced her again. She looked past her, but there was no sign of Jenni's husband. 'Henry isn't with you?'

'He had meetings in London this evening...' Jenni swallowed hard and Sally could see tears hovering. 'Tom is with the nurse we've employed – I couldn't look after him for a few weeks. I collapsed and went to bed after my...' She stopped, unable to say any more because it hurt too much. 'I never believed it could happen to me, Sally. Everything has always been so easy since I started working for my uncle – but it did...' She gave a sob of grief. 'I feel as if the world fell apart around me.'

'Of course, you do...' Sally looked at her with love and sympathy. 'What does Henry say?'

'Not very much.' Jenni's head came up and now her eyes sparked with anger. 'He said he was sorry when it happened – but then, after a couple of weeks, he told me I should pull myself together and remember that life went on...' Jenni gulped and wiped her cheeks. 'I wanted you so much then, Sally. Henry didn't want me to come to England; he said I wasn't well enough – but I knew I needed you and Ben.' For a moment, her eyes were bleak. 'I made a mistake, Sally. I should never have married him. Ben said he was a cold fish. I didn't believe him but he is...'

'Oh, Jenni, you don't mean that,' Sally said, because Jenni had known and loved Henry all her life, even when he was married to someone else.

'Yes, I do,' Jenni said and sniffed hard to hold back the tears. It was as if the rose-tinted glasses had suddenly been snatched away and she was seeing things with new eyes. 'I thought he would learn to love me...' She looked at Sally, her distress obvious. 'I knew he didn't love me when we married; he wanted a mother for Tom and Tom loves me...' Jenni gulped back her tears. Tom was the child of Jenni's close friend who had died in the *Titanic* tragedy and she'd taken on the role of mother to him voluntarily. He'd had nightmares about being shipwrecked and his mother's death and Jenni's heart had bled for him. When she'd married Henry, it had been for love, but it seemed he saw her more as a substitute for a paid nanny – and that must hurt Jenni so much.

'My dearest sister,' Sally said, holding her close. 'You must stay here with us for as long as you wish.'

'Yes, I'm going to,' Jenni said and raised her head, brushing the tears from her cheeks. 'I shall try to keep Tom with me – but Henry may insist on taking him back to America. I'm not going – not until I feel better, if then...'

Tom was Henry's son and Jenni couldn't force him to leave Tom in her care, even though he had little time for the boy. The decision would be his and even if it hurt Jenni, she could do nothing if Henry decided to take his son back to America.

'Don't let him use Tom to make you go back,' Sally advised. 'Give yourself time to think what you'd like to do with your life.'

'I'm Henry's wife. I'll have to go back eventually. It's important to him to have the right kind of wife and I know now that it was one of the reasons he asked me to marry him. For Henry's sake, there must be no hint of scandal or discord between us, at least publicly. I have tried to be a good hostess and mother, as well as a loving wife, but he wanted little in the way of love from me and gave me only a careless respect.' Her voice broke on a sob. 'I did try, Sally, I really did.'

'Perhaps.' Sally knew it would be expected, but her mind rebelled because she didn't want to see Jenni lead a miserable life with a husband who didn't truly love her. 'If you stay here when he goes back, Henry may come to realise that he misses you and begin to appreciate what he has...'

'Maybe,' Jenni said and smiled at her. 'I knew you would make me feel better. I do already.'

'Good.' Sally squeezed her shoulders. 'Ben will be home soon and...'

'You mustn't let Ben guess how unhappy I am,' Jenni said quickly. 'He has to deal with Henry and you British need whatever it is they're negotiating. If my brother knew how I feel, he'd half kill Henry...'

'Oh, Jenni love.' Sally smiled at her sadly. It was true. Ben cared for his sister a great deal and he might not be able to resist quarrelling with him. 'Do you think he won't know?'

'About my miscarriage? Yes, he has to know – but what I told you about making a mistake is between us, Sally. You have to keep my secrets, please.'

'Of course, I will,' Sally promised, but she felt doubtful. Ben was going to pick up on his sister's unhappiness immediately. He might accept that it was the loss of her baby, which was enough to make anyone unhappy for a long time, but Ben knew his sister too well and after a while he would pick up that things were not right with her and her husband, especially if she stayed in their spare room after her husband returned to the States. Jenni wasn't thinking clearly or she would realise that, but it wasn't surprising when she was in such a state. 'Come and have a cup of coffee, Jenni – or perhaps a glass of wine?'

'You have some of the coffee I sent?'

Sally nodded, because Jenni didn't think much of their English brands.

'Then I'll stick to coffee – if I start drinking alcohol, I might have too much...' She painted on a bright smile. 'And now I want to see your darling little Jenny. She must be growing by now.'

'She is and she's adorable,' Sally said proudly, glad to speak of happier things.

'Of course, she is – she has you and Ben for parents,' Jenni said and hugged her. At that moment, they heard a wail from Jenny's bedroom and they both smiled. 'Right on cue,' Jenni said and smiled for the first time. 'She knows her aunty is here – and I have lots of little gifts for her in my suitcase.'

* * *

'Jenni was a bit subdued this evening,' Ben remarked as they were undressing later in their bedroom. They'd taken his sister for a meal in one of Mick's restaurants and Jenni had eaten little and said even less. 'I know she is grieving – and losing a baby is a terrible loss – but I can't help sensing that something is wrong between her and Henry...'

'Perhaps it's just losing their son,' Sally said and shuddered at the thought. 'I feel so sorry for them both – for Jenni most of all, of course, but the child was his too. We would have been devastated had I miscarried our little one.'

'He doesn't seem to be showing any sign of distress,' Ben said. 'We had a business meeting earlier this evening, before I came home, and he didn't even mention it, bit odd that...' He shook his head, clearly disapproving. 'He was having supper with the Prime Minister and an interview with His Majesty tomorrow and seemed more interested in that than Jenni.'

'Perhaps he thought it inappropriate to speak of personal things at a Government meeting?'

'Perhaps,' Ben agreed. 'I'm not sure I could carry on if it happened to us – God forbid!'

'Yes, I know,' she agreed. 'How does anyone lose a baby and carry on, Ben?'

'Jenni is behaving as I'd expect her to,' Ben said thoughtfully. 'She's hurting and she never smiles unless it's at you – but Henry's no different to how I remember him before they married. I always thought him cold.' He frowned. 'I did warn her against marrying him. I know she had a crush on him for years, but he was never worthy of her...'

'I know,' Sally replied. She looked thoughtful. 'I've only seen him once, but I didn't like him. Perhaps I shouldn't judge, but if I'd met him before Jenni married him, I'd have told her to wait and think again...'

'You think the same as me,' Ben said and looked at her hard. 'Don't tell me if Jenni asked you not to – but she's said something, hasn't she?'

'I can't answer that, Ben.' She hated not being able to be honest with him but she had given her word to Jenni.

He nodded. 'I knew there was something wrong. Don't break your word, Sally. I'll talk to her myself and ask what the problem is – it stands out a mile.'

'Jenni says you have business with Henry...'

'I do and I shan't let my personal feelings interfere with that,' Ben said and then looked angry. 'Damn it! She's my sister. I knew there was something very wrong when she didn't write for so long. If it hadn't been for the war, I'd have got on a ship and gone over.'

'I think Jenni may want to stay here with us for a while after Henry goes home. I said we'd be happy to have her here in the apartment – and she can help me at Harpers if she wants. I can find plenty for her to do...'

'Will he leave the boy? Jenni felt responsible for what happened to Tom and his mother, because she gave her her own ticket for passage on the *Titanic*.' Ben frowned.

'That wasn't her fault; it was just fate,' Sally said. 'I'd love to have her here, but I think Henry will force his son to go with him.'

Ben put his arms about her and kissed her. 'I love you so much, Sally. You do know that, don't you? I might be late home sometimes and I don't give you half the attention I should these days, but I do love you.'

'I know,' Sally said and hugged him back. 'I love you too – and Jenni loves you, Ben. She needs us now and we'll be here for her, won't we?'

'We shall,' he agreed. 'I could kill that bastard...'

'She wouldn't want that,' Sally said. 'Get every last penny and concession out of him that you can – and after the war, you can tell him what you think of him.'

Ben gave a shout of laughter. 'That's my Sally! No wonder you had Harpers making a profit in its second year. I thought we might take twice as long to get out of the red, but my clever wife showed me the way it was done all by herself.'

'Not quite by myself – I had all Harpers' staff to help me,' Sally said and gave him a teasing smile. 'Be careful what you say to Henry, darling. If Jenni has something to do or say, it is up to her. We can give her advice and help if she needs us, but we can't interfere or pass opinions unless she invites it.'

'As usual, you give me wise advice,' Ben said and looked rueful. 'If I had my way, I'd give the cold fish a good kick up the backside or a bloody nose.' He glared. 'I think both.'

Sally laughed and started to tickle him. 'You're so fierce, Ben Harper. I think if they put you on the front line, the enemy would run away.'

'Tickle me, would you?' Ben grinned and pounced on her. 'Two can play at that game, Mrs Harper...' He found her ticklish spot and punished her until she begged for mercy and was scooped up in loving arms and carried to their bed.

After their lovemaking, Sally lay wakeful for a while, thinking how lucky she was. She would like Jenni to be as lucky and wished there was something she could do to make her sister-in-law happy. Sighing, she pushed the thought away. Jenni would have to make her own decisions about her husband and her life herself but both Sally and Ben would always be there for her.

* * *

'It's lovely having you here in the office with me,' Sally said when she and Jenni were sitting with a stocklist and a book of contacts in front of them. 'Are you sure Henry doesn't mind?'

'He has meetings the whole day,' Jenni said. 'I've promised Tom I will take him sightseeing this afternoon. Perhaps you could come too, Sally. I know he'd like to meet you and Jenny. He's doing schoolwork his father set him this morning; it was a condition of his being allowed to come that he did his work each day.'

Sally nodded but made no remark, although it seemed harsh to her that a young lad of not quite ten years was being forced to work so hard when he was on holiday in another country. If he was at home in America, he would be out of school anyway for a couple of months, but his father wanted him to study hard and get a scholarship to Harvard. She supposed it was often like that in the kind of family he was born into. Traditions had to be followed and sons were expected to follow in their father's footsteps, whether they liked it or not.

'Is Tom the academic sort?' Sally asked and Jenni shook her head. 'What would he rather do?'

'He says be a soldier like his father – but I think he would hate it. He loves art and music... his mother did too...'

'Well, you can be a soldier and love art,' Sally offered.

'Not in Henry's book,' she said. 'If you're dedicated to the Army, it should be your life – it is certainly Henry's.' Jenni shook her head. 'When Tom was younger, I could spoil him, give him the love his mother would have, had she lived – but now he is Henry's son and I'm not allowed to fuss over him. He is expected to behave in a certain way and no excuses.'

'That is a pity,' Sally said but made no further comment. It was not for her to pass an opinion on Henry's son.

Sally and Jenni spent the morning ringing up various suppliers and Jenni managed to find two new ones for Harpers. The managers were delighted to hear from the prestigious store and promised to send catalogues or travellers to show what was available. Most had some stock for immediate supply, though they were keeping orders to a certain size, because otherwise there wouldn't be enough to go around.

'I brought some samples of china, glass, textiles and jewellery over in my trunks,' Jenni told Sally when they'd finished for the morning and were about to leave for lunch. 'We're still producing at full pelt back home, so I bought what I could. I reckoned that any new stock would be welcome.' She laughed. 'Henry would've had a fit if he'd seen how many trunks with my name on them went into the hold, but I knew that you could do with whatever I could bring over.' She smiled and although still subdued it was more like the old Jenni. Working with Sally had done her good.

'Yes, we can,' Sally told her. 'I didn't expect you to bring anything, Jenni – this was a holiday...'

'I couldn't waste the opportunity. The trunks have to be vetted by your customs first and then I'll send them to you so that you can have first look.'

'It will be like a treasure cave,' Sally said and laughed. 'That's an unexpected gift, Jenni.'

Jenni shrugged. 'You know me, I can't resist a bargain.' She looked up as Ruth knocked the door and entered, looking doubtful.

'Mrs Harper, Mr Alexander is here. He wanted to know if you were free for lunch or coffee.'

'Ask him to come in.' Sally looked at her sister-in-law. 'This is the brilliant surgeon I told you about, Jenni.' She smiled as the Northerner entered and gave her a quizzical look. 'Mr Alexander – my sister-in-law, Jenni Richards.'

'Ah, the American who was going to bring over a surgeon to show me a thing or two,' Andrew murmured with a wicked twinkle in Sally's direction.

'I doubt I know anyone who could do that from what Sally tells me of your work, but I might have brought someone who would try,' Jenni said and offered her hand. 'I'm going to be in London for a while, Mr Alexander. I'd be glad to help your work in any way I can...'

'Now that's an offer I can't refuse,' he said and grinned broadly. 'If you two beautiful ladies have nothing better to do, you can have lunch with me and discuss something I have in mind for my patients.'

'We were about to leave for lunch,' Jenni said. 'I don't know about you, Sally, but I'm hungry.'

Sally nodded. Jenni looked intrigued and more relaxed than she had for a while. She silently blessed Andrew Alexander. If he and his teasing helped Jenni to forget her grief even for a short time, she would be forever grateful.

* * *

That afternoon, after a pleasant lunch with Andrew Alexander, Sally and Jenni took Tom to see some of the sights of London.

Sally had left her baby with Pearl, because she was a little grizzly and they were travelling on buses and trams with open decks on top to see things better. They ended up at the zoo, which Tom seemed to enjoy more than the educational tour of the Houses of Parliament and other famous landmarks they'd seen from the top of the bus.

They'd returned to the apartment for tea. Jenny had stopped crying and Tom played with her and some bricks on the floor for half an hour. He shook hands with Sally when he was ready to leave.

'Thank you very much, Aunty Sally,' he said. 'I did enjoy myself very much.'

'I'm glad.' Sally bent down and put her arms around him, giving him a hug. 'You must come again, Tom. I liked taking you to the zoo.'

He nodded and then suddenly hugged her back, a hint of tears in his eyes.

Jenni placed a hand on his shoulder. 'We had better go, Tom. If your father gets back early, he'll wonder where we are...'

'Yes,' he said and his bottom lip trembled. 'Goodbye, Aunty Sally...'

Sally's eyes stung as she watched them go. She'd seen the way his solemn face lit up when he saw the elephants, lions and the huge tiger. Obviously, his father didn't allow many such treats.

* * *

It was half past five the next morning when the doorbell rang at Sally's apartment, waking them from sleep.

Ben looked at Sally as he got out of bed and pulled on his dressing gown. 'Who the hell might that be?' he demanded.

Sally shook her head. She had no idea. Surely the War Office wouldn't send anyone for Ben at this hour without prior warning?

He left her getting out of bed to pull on a silk robe but was back in a few minutes to fetch her before she'd brushed her hair.

'You'd better come – it's Jenni and she is in a terrible state.' Ben didn't look great himself, his hair on end as if he'd pushed his fingers through it in distress.

Sally ran through to the sitting room. Jenni was sitting on the sofa, her head bent. She looked up, her face drawn and wet with tears as Sally went to her.

'I've told Henry I'm not going back to America ever,' she said dramatically. 'He was so cold – so uninterested in anything I wanted to talk about. I've told him our marriage is over...'

'Oh, Jenni, I'm so sorry,' Sally said. 'I know you must be feeling awful...'

'Don't be sorry,' Jenni told her and her look was determined. 'It's better to make the break now than go on in a miserable situation for years. We were never suited. I was just someone to fill the gap, a nanny and hostess to stand behind him and smile when he needed me to.'

'Surely not?' Sally said, but she could see that Jenni had made up her mind to leave her husband. 'If it's really what you want...'

'Ben was right. I should've thought more before I rushed off and married him.' Jenni looked rueful and her eyes were red-rimmed. 'The worst bit is that I have to leave Tom – and I'm all he has between him and the strict regime his father sets.' She blinked away her tears. 'But since I'm not fit to have charge of Tom and Henry's sending him away to boarding school, it won't matter.'

'Oh, Jenni, no.' Sally looked at her in distress. 'That poor child – it is so unfair...'

'That's what hurts. Henry is punishing me, but Tom will suffer for my failings as a wife and mother.'

'That's unfair! You're wonderful with him and he loves you – I could see that yesterday afternoon.'

'Well, I'm not to be allowed a say in his upbringing in future – because I can't be trusted. I took him to the zoo instead of making him work...'

'Henry couldn't have been so cruel,' Sally burst out, but she could see the truth in Jenni's eyes. 'No wonder you're leaving him.'

'I'm going to stay here, Sally. I can find work, at Harpers or elsewhere. I don't want anything from Henry – except Tom and he won't let me keep him...' She sighed. 'The row started over his son. He said Tom had to go home so he can work harder – he is sending him back alone, Sally, with just his nanny – and he doesn't really like her. I suggested he have a nice holiday with me before he started cramming for his school exams and that was when he told me I wasn't Tom's mother and it wasn't my choice.' Something glinted in Jenni's eyes. 'That made me angry. I was Tom's mother when he was crying all night, needing comfort – when the nightmares and the bed-wetting got on Henry's nerves. Now my opinion isn't important.'

'The pompous so-and-so,' Ben said from the doorway. 'I made coffee, Jenni love, but you can have some brandy in it...'

'Just the coffee,' she told him and smiled. 'I knew you would pick up that something wasn't right. I'm so glad I came to you and Sally – you two, and Jenny, of course, are my home.'

'Henry has no right to treat you like that – do you want me to talk to him for you, Jenni?' Ben frowned. 'However, he can take the boy; I can't stop him and nor can you.' Jenni shook her head at him.

'I know. It hurts me to part from him, but I have no choice – and I've accepted it,' Jenni replied sadly. 'I'm sorry for Tom and I'll miss him terribly – but even if I went back with Henry, I'd hardly ever see him.'

'Tom will miss you and you'll miss him,' said Sally sympathetically.

'Yes, that's true and perhaps Henry will let me write to him. I shall anyway, though he could stop it if he chose. He's angry at the moment, thinks I'm being emotional and foolish, but I'm not.'

'You're thinking straight,' Ben told her. 'Sally and I will stand by you, Jenni.'

'Henry might want to sell those shares in Harpers... I doubt you could find thirty thousand pounds to pay him back?'

'If he does, we'll have to find a friend to purchase them,' Ben said, but looked worried. 'I don't know if we've used the loan you raised on them, Sally...?'

'No, we haven't touched it,' Sally said. 'I thought about it and decided not to – and now I'm glad I didn't. You can buy them back, Jenni.'

'I suppose they're still in my name. Henry just loaned me the money.'

'Then give it back to him,' Sally urged. 'He won't want interest, will he?'

'He won't get it if he does,' Jenni said fiercely. 'No, I'm sure he won't – he isn't that mean.' Yet she looked anxious and Sally looked at Ben. When Jenni had given them the money, they'd kept it in case it was needed, never dreaming that something like this could happen. 'No, he won't ask. I'm his wife and it would cause a scandal. He can tell people I'm staying here for my health's sake and no one will question it for years, but if he tried anything nasty, I'd kick up such a fuss, he would regret it. I have friends who would sympathise with me...' She looked thoughtful, then, 'Maybe he'll let me keep it if he decides to divorce me.'

'No,' Ben said firmly. 'Give Henry his money and if he wants interest, I'll pay it somehow. I don't want him holding it over you. You will be the one he sues for desertion and if he does let him. We'll find a good lawyer to defend you. He hasn't treated you well, love, and if I have anything to do with it, he won't put it all on you, Jenni.'

'I'll find a job, you'll see,' Jenni said and smiled at him. 'It's being here with you that gave me the courage to make the break. I would've done it much sooner but I felt so alone...'

'You're never alone,' Sally and Ben spoke together. 'You've got us – and you always will have.'

Jenni smiled through her tears. 'I'm sorry to get you up at this hour.'

A wail was heard from the bedroom and Sally made a wry face. 'You beat her to it by half an hour, but she's right on time.'

Sally went off to see to her daughter and Ben looked at his sister. 'Henry won't take this lying down, Jenni. He'll try to get you back – if only because it looks bad to his friends.'

'He can try,' she said. 'I've had enough of being told to be sensible, Ben. I want to laugh and have a little fun. It broke my heart when I lost my baby – but I'm still young. I want to love and be loved – and Henry doesn't love me.'

'Perhaps in his own way he does,' Ben said, 'but you know I never truly liked him.'

'Next time I'll listen to you,' she said with a watery smile.

'That will be a first,' he said and laughed. 'I made a mistake when I married the first time, Jenni – but I struck gold when I found Sally. If you're lucky, it could happen to you.'

'Perhaps,' she said and smiled at him fondly. 'For the moment I'm just glad to be here with you three.'

32

'I found this in the order that came from the new supplier,' Jane Carghill told Sally when Ruth admitted her to the office the next morning. Jane had recently joined the staff as a senior salesgirl in the clothes department. 'It isn't much, but it is a fault.'

'Yes, a small one. Acceptable in a sale but not for normal sales.' Sally nodded as she saw what looked like a little knot in the weave of the wool. 'Leave me with it and I'll let you know what happens – you're sure this is the only fault?'

'Oh yes, Mrs Harper. We always check the stock carefully just in case. I went through every pack of knitwear myself.'

'Then I know I can trust your word. You have sharp eyes, Mrs Carghill.'

Jane Carghill left her and Sally sat in contemplation of the pretty jumper for a moment before ringing the sales manager of the manufacturer. He was instantly apologetic and told her he would refund her immediately and supply an extra garment.

'I can't apologise enough,' he said gloomily. 'It's the war, Mrs Harper. My best staff were all keen to join up and the new ones don't always spot a fault in time – last week we had a run of five hundred in our best line before the fault was noticed.'

'Are the faults always as small as this?' Sally asked curiously.

'Yes, they were all the same; it was just a little hitch in the machine and it's fixed now.'

'If you don't mind my asking, what do you do with the faulty garments?'

'We either sell them to the market boys for a few pence or we sell them for rags at the end of the year.'

'And supposing I said I would take that five hundred from you, what is your best price to me?'

'Are you thinking of having a sale?' the manager asked, a hint of excitement in his voice. 'Only we have a back stock of five thousand end of line and I was thinking about putting them out to the market boys at a shilling a piece just to clear my stockroom and get a little money in – but they only buy a few bits at a time...'

'Are the end of line perfect?'

'Oh, yes, Mrs Harper, but they're last year's stock or, in some instances, five years out of date. Perfectly good, but we only have them in certain sizes, you see.'

'Right, I'll take all your end-of-line stock and the five hundred imperfect items,' Sally said, feeling a spurt of excitement. 'I've had an idea, Mr Freebody – and, if it works, I'll be taking everything you can give me until the end of the war.'

Jenni entered the office as Sally ended her call. She looked at her face and saw the brilliance of her eyes. 'Now what are you up to, Sally Harper?'

'I've had what I think is a great idea, Jenni. If it works, I'll need your help, because we'll have to ring every knitwear company in the country and we'll have to be fast, because if my idea catches on, all our competitors will be trying the same thing.'

'That sounds exciting,' Jenni said. 'Tell me more.'

'Look at that tiny fault,' Sally said and showed her the garment Jane Carghill had brought to her. 'It's a second and I can buy it for one shilling – and there are five hundred of them. I'm going to sell them at two shillings and sixpence each, but I'm going to have a big notice telling my customers that for every garment they buy Harpers will donate one shilling to the fund for wounded servicemen, Army, Navy or Royal Flying Corps.'

Jenni stared at her. 'It's a good idea, Sally, but five hundred garments won't last long...'

'No, but there's another five thousand perfect garments, end of line and all at the same price to me.'

'Ah, now I begin to understand – it's a gamble, but I think you're on to something, Sally.' Jenni clapped her hands in delight. 'I always knew you were clever.'

'Normally, I would only buy a few things for the sale, but it's different now,' Sally explained. 'They cannot make enough new stock to keep everyone happy. I can't believe no one has thought of it before.'

'People might think twice about buying last year's stock unless it was very cheap at normal times,' Jenni agreed, 'but it's the twist of giving to the injured men that will make all the difference.'

'Well, it could cost me a few pounds if I'm wrong,' Sally said, 'and we shan't make much out of it, but it will bring the customers in and cause a bit of excitement – at least I'm hoping it will, and, of course, it will help those wounded men...'

'I'm certain it will bring the customers in, and anything to help the wounded is good in my book,' Jenni said. 'This jumper is fully fashioned and I'd like it myself. The fault is so tiny no one would notice – but you're right about us having to be quick if it works, because they will all want to do the same thing.'

'Do you think I should buy all I can get now?' Sally hesitated.

'What I'm investing so far is nothing, but if I went ahead and bought all the surplus stock, I could find...?'

'Perhaps two or three hundred pounds,' Jenni nodded. She looked thoughtful for a moment. 'It is a risk, Sally – but I think we should do it. Give me that list of suppliers and I'll pick out the ones you need.'

* * *

Ben looked at his sister and wife over supper that evening. He frowned and then nodded. 'Yes, I see it is a wonderful idea and if it catches on it will raise a lot of money for the wounded men – but it is a bit of a risk, Sally. Suppose some of the stuff turns out to be unsaleable at any price?'

'Then I've wasted your money and you can sack me,' Sally said promptly. 'I know it is a risk, Ben, but it is also a fantastic opportunity. Stock is low in most stores at the moment. There will be more raw material about again next spring after the sheep shearing, but most manufacturers are running low. New stock is limited – but they all had quite a bit of end-of-line stock and I bought all I thought sounded worth having. Some of it we've stocked before. I think it should be good value.'

'Well, I can only say good luck.' Ben smiled at her and saluted them both with his wine glass. 'I suppose we can stand a loss of a few hundred, even if things are tight at the moment.'

'Don't be such a pessimist,' Jenni scolded. 'It's a brilliant idea – just you wait and see.'

'I'm going to wait until I've got most of the stock in and then we'll put the notices in the window. I've spoken to Marion and she told me that Marco came up with a window for helping the wounded heroes, so we'll go with that at the same time as we open our sale to the public.'

Ben nodded and left them to talk about their plans as he disappeared into the sitting room to do some paperwork.

'I'm glad you were here,' Sally said a little ruefully. 'Ben didn't think it was such a good idea. If I'd asked him, I would probably never have done it...'

'Believe me, it will work,' Jenni assured her with a smile. 'I've got a feeling in my gut and I've had years of experience.'

* * *

The sales teams involved had all been sworn to secrecy. Marion knew what was going on because of the window display they'd planned together, but everyone else was in the dark. They all knew something different was happening, but the window was under wraps as always until the morning of the great reveal and then it went up to show a scene of nurses tending wounded soldiers, Royal Flying Corps officers and sailors. 'Support our brave heroes keeping Britain safe,' the banner across the window said and there was the Union Jack hung as a backdrop. Then there were displays of jumpers, twinsets and cardigans with the big notice in black and gold to echo Harpers' colours.

FOR EVERY GARMENT YOU PURCHASE FROM THESE RANGES, HARPERS WILL GIVE ONE SHILLING TO THE FUND FOR OUR WOUNDED HEROES. NOTHING IN THIS RANGE COSTS MORE THAN 2 SHILLINGS AND 6 PENNIES. PERFECT GARMENTS. ONLY AS LONG AS STOCK LASTS.

Almost immediately a small crowd gathered in front of the window, pointing and talking excitedly. Customers nodded at each other and came streaming in. There were large bins downstairs filled with the stock, where they could be accessed immediately, and another large sign to inform customers that more were available upstairs.

The tills started ringing almost instantly and continued the whole morning as the patriotic ladies of London streamed in to purchase garments that were perfect and cheap and yet every one contributed to a fund for the wounded. By that afternoon there was a queue out of the shop and down Oxford Street. Sally had brought more of the stock downstairs and kept the bins constantly filled.

'This is so exciting,' one customer trilled at her. 'I loved this style last year and you didn't have any further stock in – now I've bought three for half the price...'

'I'm so glad you're pleased,' Sally told the ladies who came up to her and congratulated her on what she was doing for the wounded of Britain.

'You are a heroine, Mrs Harper,' three of them told her. 'I can't believe what you've done – all these lovely things. So cheap and yet you're giving money to our men...'

'Harpers wanted to help,' Sally said. 'This is just a small thing, Mrs Simpson, but we shall be thinking of more ideas, don't you worry.'

'This always was my favourite shop and now I'll never go anywhere else,' the woman said fervently and smiled as she nodded to Sally and went off with her purchases.

Towards the end of the afternoon, Sally saw a man in a smart black coat and a beaver hat watching her. She looked at him, a feeling of recognition making her smile. He tipped his hat to her and then came towards her.

'Mrs Harper – you've stolen a march on us all, I think.' His eyes moved round the busy store, taking in the excited faces.

'I just wanted to make a few people happy and help the wounded at the same time.'

'Brilliant tactics,' he said. 'I salute you. Harry Selfridge doesn't often get beaten, but this time you've shown me the way.'

'I'm sure you will come up with something quite as good, Mr Selfridge.'

'Oh, I shall,' he said confidently. 'But you were the first.' He looked at her consideringly for a moment. 'Someone told me you used to work for me, Mrs Harper?'

'Before I came here, yes.'

'Why did you leave – may I ask?'

'One of your senior salesmen harassed me and when I reported it to my supervisor, I was told I was too sensitive.'

He frowned. 'Give me their names and I'll sack them instantly.'

'I've no wish for revenge. Coming to Harpers was the best thing I ever did.'

'Harpers' gain was my loss,' Harry Selfridge replied with a wry smile and tipped his hat. 'I suppose I can't tempt you back?'

'I think my husband might object,' Sally said and laughed, 'but thank you for the offer.'

He inclined his head and then walked away.

Jenni came up to her, grinning from ear to ear. 'Ben is going to have to eat humble pie tonight, Sally,' she said. 'When the great Harry Selfridge tips his hat to you, you know you've done something extraordinary.'

'I'll bet he'll have something better in his store by tomorrow or the next day.'

'That is possible,' Jenni agreed. 'He can't match what we've done, because we bought all the available surplus stock – but he will probably find a way to bring the customers in. However, he can't take away today's trading and we've sold more than half the stock you bought anyway. One more day like this and we've got to think of something else.'

Sally nodded and smiled. 'I doubt we'll see anything like this again, Jenni, but between us we ought to be able to come up with something.'

* * *

By the next morning, Selfridges had a notice in the window that for every pound spent in the store Mr Selfridge would donate two shillings to a fund for the war wounded. His trade increased, but there were no queues outside the shop, because he'd been unable to do what Sally had done. The beauty of her idea was that normal knitwear stock was low and it was the kind of thing many women went on wearing for years, even if fashions changed. It was slightly different from other clothing because sizes varied more in cloth garments and women needed to try on coats or dresses, and they also tended to make do with a skirt they had from a year or two back if they had a new jumper or twinset to smarten it up.

The newspapers had taken pictures and Harpers was blazed across the front pages of at least three of them, though *The Times* had relegated them to an inside page. However, Sally hadn't expected the papers to bother with her little initiative and felt pleased that it had made some headlines.

Sally had bought up the surplus stock in male knitwear the same day as she put her sale for women on. If the other big stores tried to purchase stock at knock-down prices, they were too late, and once she had exhausted her sale of women's specially priced knitwear, she put on one for men. It did well, though the queues didn't extend as far as the ladies' knitwear had done, but it was still popular.

Some of the other big stores had come up with ideas of their own. Discounts on old stock they already had with donations to the war wounded, and some just had tins dotted about the store to collect for the fund. Sally saw that Selfridges held a flag day and gave away sherry and wine in the shop, but Mr Selfridge stopped the two shillings out of every sale after a month.

Just over a month later, when Sally made a donation of nearly one thousand pounds to the fund for the war wounded, the organiser came to see her in her office to thank her personally.

'Harpers' contribution is magnificent, Mrs Harper,' she said, beaming at her, 'but because of what you did, we've had donations from almost every shop in London – and that amounts to several thousand pounds. Harry Selfridge asked how much you had donated and then doubled it. We cannot thank you enough for your efforts.'

'I'm delighted to have helped,' Sally said, smiling to herself. Harry Selfridge had made sure he won in the end. 'We're going to have another big push near Christmas. My staff are having a competition to come up with the best ideas and I'm giving the winners a five-pound voucher each to spend in the store.'

'No wonder your girls love to work here, Mrs Harper. My daughter just adores this store and she says she's going to work here as soon as she leaves school.'

'We shall be pleased to see her,' Sally said and smiled. 'Tell her to work hard and get her exams – because at Harpers, girls with good qualifications and skills have a chance to get on.'

'Yes. That is what my Millicent likes. She says there is more chance for a girl here than in most stores, though Selfridges also promotes women to supervisors, but you have a female floor walker and you became the buyer before you married Mr Harper.'

'Harpers tries to give women an equal chance. As yet, they do not get the same wages as the men, but one day I hope that will happen – or at least be more equal.'

'Well, you can't start a revolution on your own, Mrs Harper,' the woman said, smiling. 'Although after the war my Millicent believes women will get the vote – she's a real little suffragette.'

'Good for her,' Sally said, 'but she mustn't forget what our men are doing for us right now – and I'm sure she doesn't with a mother like you.'

'Well, I was with the Women's Movement, but we called a truce for the war. After all, if our men are willing to fight for us, we have to do our best for them, don't we?'

'We certainly do,' Sally agreed. 'I am so glad to have helped, Mrs Phillips. If there is anything more I can do, you must let me know.'

'You've already done more than most, but if I think of anything, I'll be back.'

Sally smiled. Her idea had paid dividends. Although Harpers had made very little from the sale of the cut-price knitwear, it had brought a great deal of goodwill to the store and they'd cleared everything. Sales were back to normal now and knitwear sales were down, but that didn't matter, because almost everything else was selling strongly. Harpers had now become the store of choice for many women and that was worth all the effort as well as the successful fundraising.

Because she was so pleased with the way things had gone, Sally kept back fifty of the best slightly faulty fully fashioned twinsets, two each in five sizes, and she sent them in a parcel to Maggie Gibbs serving with the VADs in Belgium. Sally had done a little for the wounded men and now she wanted to help the nurses on the front line and she decided that it would be her next campaign.

In the middle of all the sales activity, Henry sailed for New York, having sent his son on ahead with his nanny. Jenni spoke to him at the hotel for half an hour before he left and when she returned, her face looked drawn and anxious, but she hadn't said anything. She didn't speak about it all until a letter came for her from Tom at the beginning of August.

She showed it to Sally with a watery smile. 'Tom is going to write to me once a month and he says he will whatever his father tells him – he says he loves me and thinks of me as his mother, and he intends to visit me as soon as he can leave school and do what he wants.'

'Jenni, I'm glad,' Sally said. 'Tom loves you and he won't forget you – whatever his father says.'

Jenni nodded. 'Henry was civil when we parted. He told me he was sorry I was unhappy, but he has no time for sentimentality – and he says he will not try to divorce me unless we both wish it in a few years. He told me to keep the shares and the loan and says that if I come to my senses, I am welcome to return to his house.'

'I know it hurts – but perhaps you just have to accept that it's his way and let go, love.' Sally bit her lip as she saw the tears Jenni was holding back.

'Yes, I know.' Jenni smiled. 'I'll get over it – but it will take time. I'm lucky. I have my family and I'll survive.'

33

That evening, Marion was busy telling Sarah and Kathy how well Mrs Harper's sale had gone and how much they'd contributed to the fund for the wounded when the door opened and someone walked in.

'Dan!' Sarah gave a scream of delight and got up, almost knocking Dickon over in her rush to get to her husband. 'Oh, Dan, you are home – we've been so worried...' Sarah sobbed against his shoulder. 'I was so afraid that you might have been killed.'

'Didn't you get my letter from Gibraltar?' he asked with a frown. 'I got one from you and one from Marion telling me you were here and I wrote immediately to tell you I would be home soon...'

'The last letter we got was at least six weeks old,' Marion told him. 'Lily – she was one of the kitchen maids at Sarah's home – told us no more came in the time she was there, but she has left now and she's starting at Harpers in the café next week. She comes to tea on her day off, doesn't she, Sarah?' She smiled at her brother and his wife. 'We've been a bit anxious since the last letter though...'

'I was in hospital in Gib for some weeks,' he told them. 'I was wounded in the last run to... well, a friendly port, is all I can tell you, and the doctor put me ashore in Gibraltar to recover. I had to wait until a ship could pick me, and a few others, up.'

'Wounded?' Sarah looked at him fearfully. 'Where – does it hurt?' Her eyes went over him anxiously, looking for some terrible injury.

Dan smiled at her. 'It was just a bit of metal in my leg, damned painful for a while and they had to dig it out of me, but not life-threatening. We were attacked by a destroyer, but our Navy boys soon sent them packing. Unfortunately, six of us had deep wounds and needed to be put ashore at the nearest port.'

'As long as you are better now,' Marion said and smiled at him before changing the subject. 'You've got a beautiful daughter who is nearly six weeks old – are you going to congratulate your clever wife?'

'And Marion looked after me for two weeks,' Sarah said. 'She sacrificed her holiday to stay home and care for us.' He nodded to his sister appreciatively and then his eyes returned to her, dwelling on her affectionately.

'A daughter...' Dan's eyes narrowed as he looked at the woman he loved. 'I wasn't sure and I was afraid to ask if everything was all right... Where is she?'

'Take him upstairs and show him, Sarah,' Marion said and shook her head at Kathy, who was trying to attract Dan's attention. She smiled as the pair went off hand-in-hand. 'You can talk to him later, Kathy – they need a little time together.'

'I was only going to say welcome home.' Kathy looked a bit sulky.

'I know, love, but Sarah needs him to herself for a moment.'

'Tell Dan I'll see him in the morning. I'm off out,' Dickon announced.

'Don't be late home, love,' Marion said. 'Have a good time with your friends.'

'I shall. I'm in the darts team,' Dickon said proudly. 'That's why I have to practise every night. I'll bring you a packet of pork scratchings back if yer like, Kathy.'

'Thanks, Dick,' she said and smiled at him. 'I'll make your cheese and pickle sandwiches fer the morning if yer want?'

Dickon went out and Marion looked at Kathy. 'I'm sorry if I stopped you saying hello to your brother, Kathy. I don't mean to get on to you.'

'It's all right,' she said and shrugged. 'Sarah needs his attention more than I do. I'm going to start knitting a new dress for the baby. Sarah bought some lovely two-ply wool and I've got a pretty lacy pattern.' She sat on the sofa by the window and took out her knitting bag, frowning over the pattern she'd borrowed from Mrs Jackson. It looked intricate and, Marion thought, would take ages, which would please Kathy, because she liked doing fiddly things. Marion preferred one-row-pearl, one-row-plain patterns, quick and easy to finish, but there was no doubt that what Kathy did was lovely.

Because everything was clean and tidy, Marion decided she would write to Reggie and to Maggie Gibbs. Maggie would love to know about all the excitement at Harpers. It would bring back memories of her time there and perhaps make things a little easier for her. She'd also got some sweets, a new hair comb and some silk stockings for her friend. It was the sort of thing the nurses needed but wouldn't find easy to buy out there and Marion sent her something every three months. She sent Reggie a little parcel every month, but that was as much as she could afford from her wage, and she could only do that because Sarah had contributed towards the housekeeping.

Marion hoped Dan wouldn't want his own house just yet.

She'd got used to having Sarah here and it certainly made things easier for her.

* * *

'Are you sure you're happy here?' Dan asked as he looked down at his daughter sleeping peacefully in her cot. She was beautiful and he wanted to pick her up but was frightened of waking her. 'I can find a house nearby if you'd like?'

'Not until you're home for good,' Sarah told him with a smile. 'I like living with Marion and the others. It is comfortable and it makes things easier for all of us. When you come home at the end of the war, we'll find a new home for us and our little Marion.'

'It was nice of you to name her after my sister, but it may be confusing.'

'We call her little Marion,' Sarah said.

'Why not call her Pam?' he suggested. 'It's a nice name and you can't call her little forever.'

'Perhaps – but I don't want to upset Marion.'

'She won't care,' Dan said. 'Think about it, love, that's all.'

Sarah nodded, content that he was here with his arms about her and all was right with her world. 'Is your leg really better?'

'Yes, it is – they wouldn't have let me come home if it wasn't,' Dan said. 'I've got three weeks leave now and then I report for duty again.'

'That's wonderful,' Sarah said, sighing with contentment. She was so happy to have him home, looking strong and sun-tanned despite his wound. In a way she was glad she hadn't known he'd been wounded because she would have been terrified of losing him, and yet the shadow still lingered just behind her shoulder, as it did for most women in Britain, France and all the other nations fighting this war. Dan was here now, but next time he might be killed... yet she couldn't let herself think that way or she would go mad. She had to keep the faith and believe he would return to her when the war was over. She looked up at him, searching his face. 'Do you think the war will soon be over, Dan?'

'I wish I could tell you it would, but I don't see any end to it yet,' he told her truthfully. 'As fast as we beat the Germans and sink one of their ships, they seem to produce another. They're an efficient nation in many ways, but, with our allies, we just have to out-think them.'

'How can we when our government seem at odds half the time and things are always breaking down and going wrong – how can we beat an efficient nation like the Germans?'

'I don't know, but we've got some clever fellows on our side.' Dan sighed. 'We could do with some heavyweight help from the Americans. They are helping us in various ways, but they have a lot of ships and if they go to war with the Germans, it should make it easier. At the moment, the Germans have more of everything than we do...'

Sarah nodded. The papers said things like that, but it was different hearing it from her husband. 'Can we win? Or will they squash us too?'

'We'll win,' Dan said, his jaw jutting in determination. 'No matter how hard it is along the way, we British are too damned stubborn to give in. The Russians are pretty dogged, too. The Kaiser tried to make a separate peace with them earlier this month, but they rejected the offer – thank God!'

'Yes, we are a stubborn nation and the Russians have ties to our royal family,' Sarah said. Before the war, there had been lots of pictures in the newspapers of the Czar's family visiting with the British King and Queen, sitting in glorious gardens and by the river. 'My father always said so.'

Dan nodded, looking at her oddly. 'Are you upset over your father?'

'At first,' she admitted.

'I'm sorry he threw you out because of me...'

'I'm not.' Sarah smiled at him. 'For years I thought he loved me, so I tried to be the perfect daughter he wanted, but now I know all he wants is a puppet – a little doll he can dress in pretty things who will do what he says when he turns the key.'

'He is a fool if he thinks you're an automaton,' Dan said and laughed, kissing her softly. 'You're a beautiful loving woman and he doesn't know what he has lost.'

'I love you so much, Dan,' Sarah said. She went into his arms, kissing him passionately. Meanwhile, little Marion had woken up and was staring up at them with big blue eyes.

'She's awake now,' Sarah said, smiling at her baby. 'Pick her up, Dan, hold her.'

'Can I really? She won't break...'

Sarah laughed. 'I know. I was almost afraid to touch her at the start, but Marion showed me how. She's had plenty of experience with Milly.' She smiled at him. 'Your sister has been so good to me, Dan. I don't know what I would've done without her.'

'You'd have managed,' he said, bending to lift his daughter gently from her cot. 'But I'm glad you were here and I'm glad Marion looked after you – I know you're all right with her, my love.'

Sarah smiled, watching as he gently cradled his child. The look of wonder in his eyes was something to behold and it made her want to weep with happiness. She blocked her tears because Dan wouldn't understand; he would think she was sad when her heart was overflowing with joy. For the next three weeks she had all that anyone could desire.

* * *

Marion escaped to work the next morning with a sense of relief. She was happy to see her brother home, but it was a little awkward with all of them in the house. In her room, she'd been able to hear their lovemaking the previous night and it had kept her awake for some time. She hoped that Kathy and Dickon couldn't hear Sarah's little moaning cries, because they were both too young. It was good that they were so happy together, but it was a little embarrassing and Marion couldn't quite meet her brother's eyes when she offered him toast and a cup of tea.

However, her embarrassment was a small price to pay for Sarah's happiness, so she would put up with it for the three weeks Dan was with them. It had made her think about her own life and what it would be like to be married to Reggie. If being in bed together could be as nice as it sounded with Sarah and Dan laughing and making happy noises, she thought she might like to get married sooner rather than later. Her only previous experience was her mother's crying and screaming. Marion had known that wasn't as it should be, but until now she hadn't been sure it would be wonderful, but seeing the sparkle in Dan and Sarah's eyes as they looked at each other made her more impatient for Reggie to come home on leave.

She wasn't sure how long he would have to serve out there – she thought he was in France but didn't know for certain, because he wasn't allowed to tell her – but he'd mentioned Maggie and she knew where her friend was because they'd arranged a sort of code. Would they give him leave after six months, a year – or would it be longer? Marion felt an ache inside and wished he would come walking in like Dan had the previous night. It was a bit different for the men at sea, because they returned to port with cargoes every few weeks or months and often had a short leave before returning to their ship. Dan had longer this time, because he was recovering from a wound. It was unlikely that Reggie would be home soon, unless he was wounded and Marion did not wish for that – she would rather keep on waiting than see him hurt.

She smothered a sigh and got on with her work. Mrs Burrows was looking a little tired, she thought, and wondered if she dared to ask what was wrong with her.

34

Beth had got up feeling unwell. She'd been sick before breakfast and couldn't fancy more than a piece of toast and marmalade, even though she cooked scrambled eggs for Fred and Jack.

'Anything wrong, love?' Jack had asked before she left for work. She'd shaken her head, because whatever was upsetting her tummy wasn't important. She wanted him to see her smile as she kissed him, because he would be gone when she and Fred got home from work. She'd had a day off to be with him, but this leave was a short one. Jack's ship had been unloaded and cleaned and they were off again that evening, off with the tide.

'No, I'm fine, love,' she'd told him, touching his cheek with her fingertips. 'I love you so much – take care, won't you?'

'We do what we have to do, Beth,' Jack had replied without smiling. He hated her to talk of such things since Tim died. It had brought the dangers home to them all and Jack refused to speak or think about the risks he was taking every day of his life. 'I love you and I'll be home when I can – just get on with your life and enjoy what you can.'

'Yes, I shall,' Beth had said. 'I wrote to Maggie and sent her some things, like you said I should.'

'You have to accept her decision, Beth, for your own sake,' Jack had replied and for a moment she saw the grief in his eyes. 'Staying out there is Maggie's way of coping – we all have our own.'

Jack's way was to block it out. Beth and Fred didn't talk about ships going down or pilots being lost or the Army's reverses in Jack's presence. He didn't want to know and Fred respected his son's decision. He still read every single report of the troops' movement in the papers and she thought he kept a chart in his room, but he no longer had it up on the wall.

Beth had resisted talking to Fred about Jack's behaviour, but perhaps she would once he'd gone back to sea. It worried her that he'd shut it all so completely out of his mind, but she knew better than to say anything to him. When she'd been angry with Maggie, she hadn't wanted well-meant words of advice and nor would Jack. Beth and Fred visited Tim's grave regularly to take flowers, but she wasn't sure if Jack had been and she hadn't asked. Eventually, he would come to terms with his brother's death and until then she had to let him make his own way.

* * *

Beth saw Marion Kaye looking pensive as she served her customers. After they'd gone, she tidied her counter and checked her stock book, but it was plain to see that something was bothering her.

Making up her mind, Beth went over to her. 'Is there something upsetting you, Miss Kaye? Is there anything I can do to help?' she asked in a soft voice that wouldn't carry to the others.

'No, thank you, Mrs Burrows...' Marion Kaye sighed and seemed to come to a decision. 'My brother, Dan, came home yesterday. He had been injured and in hospital in Gibraltar and we were worried, because we hadn't heard anything, but he's all right now... It just made me think of my fiancé. It is months since I've seen him and I don't suppose he will get leave for ages...'

'No, probably not,' Beth agreed. 'I'm luckier, because my husband gets a short leave every time his ship docks, or mostly. Occasionally, he has longer, but mostly it is about three days, just for the ship to be cleaned and provisioned – and a bit more if there are repairs.'

'You must be pleased when he comes home, even if it is just a short time.'

'Yes, I am, but each time it seems harder to part,' Beth admitted. 'I think the soldiers serving abroad have the worst deal, because they don't often get home leave. They get stood down for a few days so they can relax or visit the nearest town or village, but they don't come back to England unless it is a longer leave, often, before they get sent somewhere else.'

'I think the Armies in Belgium are pretty static,' Marion replied. 'The British and French haven't had much luck in Gallipoli. From what I read in the papers, the Allies fight lots of battles but don't make much progress.'

'Yes, that is how it looks,' Beth agreed, 'but my father-in-law says that we're holding our own and making progress, even though it is slow, and might not seem that way.'

'Mr Burrows knows a lot about things like that,' Marion said with a smile. 'I like him. He's always pleasant and polite when I see him. Even after his son died, he didn't change.'

'No, he doesn't change, thank goodness,' Beth murmured, as much to herself as to the younger girl. 'Well, I'd best get back.

Don't give up on your boyfriend. Before you know it, he'll come marching down the lane and knock on your door.'

'Yes, I know.' Marion smiled. 'Thank you, Mrs Burrows. You've made me feel better.'

Beth nodded and moved away. The feeling was mutual. She'd been a bit down herself, but in doing her job she was cheering herself up. Her work was a welcome distraction, and, after all, Jack was a grown man and he'd been a tower of strength to his father during the funeral and before. If shutting all talk of Tim and the war out now was his defence, then it was his choice.

Returning to her counter as a customer entered the department, Beth realised she didn't feel sick now. Whatever it had been first thing that morning, it had gone.

It didn't strike her that she might be pregnant and it was only after she was actually sick for five mornings in a row that she realised she was having another baby.

* * *

Beth didn't write to Jack about her suspicions, nor did she tell Fred or anyone else that she thought she might be pregnant again. Fred looked at her oddly a couple of times but didn't say anything; he was waiting for her to tell him and she was waiting until she had time to visit the doctor.

'Well, I am glad to confirm that you are with child, Mrs Burrows,' Doctor Marsh told her after he'd examined her. 'We'll do more tests, of course, just to be certain, but I'm fairly confident that you are about two months along.'

That would coincide with a night after Tim's funeral when she'd comforted Jack and he'd taken her with a fast and furious passion that had slightly shocked her. Afterwards, he'd whispered an apology against her hair, but none had been needed. Beth had understood his mood. Grief made people do many things and it had made Jack more selfish and needy that night, but she'd given him what he needed without complaint – and now it seemed that the result of that frantic coupling was a child.

Beth hesitated before asking the question that nagged at her and yet terrified her. 'Will I carry it full term this time, doctor?'

'We shall do our best to see that you do, Mrs Burrows. Last time, if I recall rightly, you were under a lot of strain. Your aunt died and your uncle was accused of murdering her...'

'He attacked me because I had him investigated,' Beth said, her throat tight. 'My poor aunt – she waited all her life for the right man and then she married a rogue.'

'It often happens. Such men take advantage of vulnerable women,' Doctor Marsh said and shook his head. 'Her father should have seen her married to a good man when she was young – that is the safest and best way for a young woman, Mrs Burrows.'

Beth murmured something. She didn't agree with his old-fashioned ideas, but in her aunt's case perhaps her husband had taken advantage because she was alone and vulnerable. He hadn't got away with it, because Fred had hired someone to investigate him and the police had locked him up until he stood trial and was punished as a thief and a murderer. Yet it had been too late for Aunt Helen and that was something Beth could never forget.

'So, this time, we shall take better care of you,' Doctor Marsh's voice interrupted her thoughts. He patted her hand in a fatherly way. 'I suggest that you do not work past six months and after that get plenty of rest – until then take your time over things and don't rush about. Do you have an understanding employer?'

'Yes, I do,' Beth told him with a smile. 'Sally Harper is a good friend and she will tell me to take it easy.'

'I think you're well situated.' Doctor Marsh looked at her

thoughtfully. 'Some of my patients have no choice but to work until the last minute and they have to return to work as soon as they are fit enough – some do so before they're well and that is not a good idea. I hope you will take the time to enjoy motherhood, Mrs Burrows. It is, after all, a woman's proper function.'

Beth thanked him, assured him she would take care of herself and left his surgery feeling as if she were walking on air. She was having Jack's child and this time she was happy about it. The first time she hadn't been ready to give up her job, but she'd known when she'd seen Sally nursing her baby that she desperately wanted her own. She would be sorry to leave Harpers and would stay on as long as she was able to work safely so that Sally could find a new supervisor for the department, and, that being the case, she had best tell her employer first and ask her to keep it a secret.

* * *

'Beth, that is wonderful news!' Sally said and rushed around the desk to embrace her. 'I'm so happy for you – how long are you advanced?'

'Nearly three months the doctor thinks.' Beth's cheeks pinked. 'It must have happened when Jack was home for the funeral. I'm glad that something good has come from that terrible time...'

'It was awful for you – Ben and I felt dreadful too. We both think a lot of you and Jack – and Fred, of course...' She hesitated, then, 'When do you want to stop work?'

'I'd like to work until it becomes uncomfortable. The doctor suggested another three months or so, but I might do four...'

'Well, we'll see.' Sally looked thoughtful. 'I'll talk to Rachel and Mr Stockbridge, see if they think there is anyone within the store we could promote to take your place. I would rather promote from staff and take on more juniors.' She had quite a few capable young women working at Harpers now. They had gravitated towards it when she'd advertised for new staff, saying that women would be given real opportunity, and she was confident that many of them could step into Beth's shoes when necessary. However, Beth was special and it would still be a wrench to lose her, though their friendship would continue.

'Yes, because other stores don't train them as well,' Beth agreed. 'I know there is a young woman on the ground floor – her name is Sylvia Gower and she is very keen. She visits us now and then and asks lots of questions...'

Sally nodded and then spoke her thoughts aloud, 'I wondered if Rachel would like to take over the department again. I'm not sure we need a floor walker. I've been considering making that post redundant. I believe each floor supervisor should be responsible for keeping it tidy, clean and well stocked. Rachel told me that with at least three of our departments she hardly needs to visit...'

'I can't see why the department supervisor can't be responsible for it all,' Beth agreed. 'You might need to check some of them yourself or ask Mr Stockbridge until they get used to it – but I agree that it is not a necessary position.'

'I shall speak to Rachel about it,' Sally said. 'If she agrees, I'll ask her to take over the department again, but if not, we might try that young woman – Sylvia Gower.'

Beth sighed. 'I've made a lot of work for you, Sally.'

'Not a bit of it – I'm thrilled for you, Beth, and if you want to borrow any knitting patterns, I have loads. Come over and we'll go through them one evening.'

Beth thanked her and went back to the department. She wondered why Sally had decided to cut the position of floor walker. Was she struggling to keep the financial balance healthy and just a measure of economy or did she really feel it unnecessary?

* * *

Rachel listened to what Sally had to say later that morning and then nodded. 'Yes, I should like to take over when Beth leaves,' she said, because Beth had given her permission to tell Rachel about the baby. 'I'll be honest, Sally. I know it was a promotion and I appreciated it, but I miss working with the girls and the merchandise. My present job is not as personal and I sometimes feel it unnecessary.'

'And do you think I'm taking a risk in not replacing you?'

'I think it is something you should keep under review,' Rachel said and looked thoughtful. 'I sometimes feel that I am not needed – but occasionally I've had to speak to one or two of the supervisors. If you notice a change in the store's appearance or efficiency, then you must reinstate the post – but you could try to run Harpers without a floor walker. Either you or Miss Harper could walk the floor once a day and that should be sufficient.' Jenni had decided to revert to her maiden name now that she'd parted from Henry. She preferred it and those staff who remembered her from before the war were used to calling her Miss Harper.

'Yes, Jenni would soon put any slackers to rights,' Sally replied and made up her mind. 'I think that's what we'll do for now, Rachel.' She smiled at her. 'And now, tell me, have you heard from William?'

'Yes, thank goodness,' Rachel said and her face lit up. For a time, she hadn't heard and been worried to death, but then his letters had caught up. 'I had a new letter arrive yesterday evening, brought round by special messenger. He has been wounded and is being sent home to convalesce. He says it is not life-threatening and he'll be here on Friday week he thinks, though he will need to stay in hospital in London for the time being.' She smiled. 'I can't wait to see him.'

'I'm relieved you've heard from William, Rachel. Of course, I'm sorry he has been wounded, but at least you will get to see him soon – and hopefully it will not be anything serious.' Sally reached out to touch her hand. They were friends first and fore-most, even though Rachel worked for Harpers and Sally was the owner's wife. Sharing the flat for well over a year had formed a bond between them that ensured their friendship would continue no matter what else changed.

'I shall worry until I know,' Rachel said, 'but as long as he's alive that is all that matters.'

'Yes, of course it is,' Sally agreed. 'I think we all worry about our men – I know I live in dread that we'll hear another of Harpers' men has been hurt or killed.'

'Fred has had a letter from Ernest Jones' mother,' Rachel told her. 'He's had a slight wound to his arm, but he has recuperated over there and been sent back up the line. She is furious, because she thinks he should have got home leave and she asked Fred if he knew who she could complain to.'

'It does seem unfair he didn't get leave,' Sally agreed, 'but Maggie told me in one of her letters that some of the men actually refuse it. They see their friends killed and they want to go back and shoot Germans for revenge...'

'How awful!' Rachel shuddered and closed her eyes for a moment. 'I hate this war, Sally. It's so horrible. The papers report things that are inhuman – and imagine we should be pleased when an enemy ship goes down. I know we need to win this war and I'd rather it was an enemy ship than one of ours – but those poor men and their mothers and fathers...' She shook her head and looked sad.

'Yes, I know,' Sally replied, feeling sympathy for Rachel as well as all those killed or maimed by the war no matter their nationality.

'I expect I'm a little too emotional,' Rachel said. 'I do try to be objective, but sometimes it is hard.'

'Yes, it is,' Sally agreed. 'When I see some of the burn victims, I feel devastated, Rachel, but they are so brave – and we can only be the same. Life goes on and we're lucky that we have men willing to give their lives for us.'

'Yes, I know,' Rachel said. 'I suppose I feel guilty sometimes – guilty for being a woman and unable to fight...'

'The only reason we can't fight is because men won't let us,' Sally said. 'Ben has a pistol in his desk at home and I know how to load and fire it – if we were invaded, I would fight rather than let the enemy near my daughter.'

Rachel looked at her and then laughed. 'Yes, I believe you would, Sally Harper. I'm so glad I came to see you; you've really cheered me up.'

* * *

Rachel visited the hospital that evening. She took books, sweets, cigarettes and magazines for the men. She rotated the wards she visited each week now and had formed a friendship with some of the nurses. Sister Wright also had a husband serving in the trenches and she liked to talk to Rachel when she had finished her visit to the men.

That evening, she was just finishing her duty as Rachel was about to leave. They decided to go to a nearby café and have a pot of tea and a plate of toasted teacakes so that they could talk for a time.

'How is Mrs Harper?' Sister Wright asked as they were served their tea. 'I haven't seen her for a few weeks.'

'She told me she visited two weeks ago on the Sunday afternoon,' Rachel replied. 'She is so busy, what with the shop and her child, though she does have help at home.'

'Mrs Harper is unusual,' Sister Wright said. 'Most ladies are content to stay home when they have a child. I had retired when I married, but we were not lucky enough to have children and so when my husband joined the Army, I decided to do what I could to help once more.'

'I was surprised that you were married – I didn't think it was allowed?'

'Officially, I am not allowed to work as a married woman, but because nurses are needed so desperately, Matron allowed me to return. We are good friends.'

'Ah, I see,' Rachel said, and smiled. It seemed the rule that no married women were allowed to nurse was being ignored, at least for the moment and by certain authorities. It had always seemed nonsense to Rachel, but many men disliked their wives to work and she knew William might ask her to give up once he was home for good, but she would face that when it happened. 'Have you heard from Stan recently?'

'Yes, I had a letter this morning,' Sister Wright said, and looked happy. 'He will be home on leave for three weeks soon and then he's being sent somewhere else – a different posting. Of course, I have no idea where...'

Rachel nodded. She finished her tea and glanced at her watch. 'I should get home. I have to go to work in the morning.'

'Yes, as do I.'

They paid their bill and parted, going their separate ways. As she walked home, Rachel felt pleased that she'd decided to visit the hospital. Sally Harper had given her the idea and it had given her something to do now and then – and she'd made a new friend. At the weekend, she would be visiting Minnie Stockbridge for lunch and perhaps she would go and see Hazel in the evening. Many of her worries had slipped away since she'd heard from William and she felt lighter of heart. Perhaps he would soon be home...

35

It was Maggie's morning off and she'd planned to walk into the village that pleasant late September morning, and spend an hour or so with the French family she'd adopted, but when she saw the transports coming in, she changed her mind and went to greet them. They were packed with wounded men and she wondered if there had been another push to break through enemy lines; it happened every so often and resulted in a lot of extra casualties, though nothing much seemed to change. The two sides were firmly embedded in their trenches and no one was budging far.

'These men are very seriously wounded, nurse – some of them are probably too far gone,' the driver of the first lorry told her.

She opened the back and looked in, steeling herself not to recoil from the stench of blood and excrement and the odour of death. Even after months of working at the Front she hadn't got used to that awful smell. Some of the wounded had died on their way here and it was just a matter of taking them to a private spot for burial. The driver gave her a hand up and she climbed into the back and began to look into the faces of the injured; it was easy enough to pick out those that had passed away and she gave them a sorrowful glance as she passed by; they were beyond her help and the vicar would pray over them later.

She bent to touch the hand of a young soldier with a wound to the side of his head. Maggie was experienced enough to know that he had a chance and she summoned the orderlies.

'Take this one to ward B,' she said in a voice of authority. 'He is priority.'

'Yes, nurse.' She was obeyed instantly and without question.

She passed through the back of the lorry, picking out two more who had a chance of life and summoned more orderlies. The remainder of the men were either dead or had injuries that meant they would die whatever was done for them. The barely living would be taken to the ward reserved for hopeless cases and given something to help them pass, whether it be a cigarette or a powerful drug. At the moment their supplies were good, thanks to a recent initiative which had brought them much-needed medicines, bandages, splints and equipment and that meant they could ease the worst cases from terrible pain.

'Tent A for the rest,' she told the orderlies, who gave her a hand down. They nodded, faces impassive, no longer shocked by the order or the youth of the girl who gave it. What had been terrible was now the norm and they carried on with their duties, day in and day out, just like the men in the trenches.

'Right yer are, nurse,' one of them said with a cheeky smile. 'What about coming ter the dance wiv me this Saturday?'

Maggie smiled but shook her head. 'I'm already going to a party with a friend,' she told the disappointed soldier.

It was true. She just hadn't told him that her friend was Sadie. Sadie had stopped crying over Pierre and become restless. She'd wanted to go to the Harvest dance to celebrate the gathering of the grapes and Maggie had agreed, to humour her. It was a celebration of life and nature and their friends had begged them to come so they were going together.

'Life is for living...' Sadie had told Maggie defiantly. Her pregnancy didn't show under her nurse's uniform yet, though Maggie had seen the gentle mound of her stomach when she was in her nightgown. It wasn't enough to get her sacked yet, but it wouldn't stay secret forever. 'I'm going to enjoy myself.' Sadie had put off telling Sister Mayhew but she couldn't avoid it much longer.

'Have you thought what you'll do?' Maggie had asked and Sadie shook her head. She didn't want to discuss it and wouldn't talk about Pierre or the fact that she would be sent home once Matron found out her guilty secret.

* * *

Because of the extra cases of wounded, Maggie abandoned her plans and helped where she could, leaving only when she was ordered out by one of the senior nurses.

'I don't want you collapsing on me, Nurse Gibbs,' she said. 'Go and read a book or smoke a cigarette – but don't come back until you're on duty.'

'Yes, Nurse Moran,' Maggie said and smiled. She wandered away, visiting the primitive washing area to clean her hands and face of the blood spatter and then went off to the canteen to get some food and a cup of what passed for tea.

'Nurse Gibbs,' a cheerful voice said as she sat down with her ham and mustard sandwich. 'May I join you please?'

Maggie looked up and smiled as she saw the man who had asked. 'Captain O'Sullivan,' she said, noting the new uniform. 'I'm glad you've been promoted. You certainly deserved it.'

'Thank you,' Mick replied and looked pleased. 'Have they made you Sister Gibbs yet?'

'No and they won't,' Maggie said but laughed because the teasing look in his eyes was infectious. 'I am a very lowly nursing assistant and shall never rise to such dizzying heights.'

'Then they should be ashamed of themselves,' he said. 'I've seen you at work and no one could be more devoted to the patients than you are, Nurse Gibbs.'

'Oh, I should have to pass lots of exams to become a sister,' Maggie replied with a little shrug. 'I think I'd rather return to Harpers after the war. I volunteered because I knew we should be needed, but I loved being at Harpers with my friends and I'll go back when this is over.'

'And I'm sure they miss you.' His eyes seemed to caress her, giving Maggie a nice warm comfortable feeling. 'Your first six months must be up soon, I think?'

'Yes, it is, next month,' Maggie replied with a frown. 'I've told Sister Mayhew that I want to stay out here, continue with my work. She says she will talk to Matron, but she thinks I should go home for a couple of weeks' holiday, so perhaps I might.'

'I'm sure all your friends will be pleased to see you.'

'Mrs Harper has been so good to me,' Maggie told him with a little smile. 'She sent me a huge parcel of lovely knitwear so that I could give lots away to the nurses out here and they were all so pleased. Some of them had never had anything as nice and they couldn't believe they were free.'

'Sally Harper is a lovely woman,' Mick agreed, 'but I'm sure you have lots of friends at home.'

'Yes, I have Beth and Rachel and Becky Stockbridge, and there's Marion Kaye. Marion sends me things too and writes me lovely letters, so do Beth and Rachel sometimes. Becky doesn't earn very much yet and I told her not to send anything, because I really don't need it. I'm very lucky...' Maggie looked thoughtful. 'Sally Harper and Beth and Rachel became my family after my parents died – I suppose Harpers is like family too. I liked most of the staff, particularly Mr Marco and Fred Burrows.'

'Yes, I can see why you would; they are both decent chaps,' Mick agreed. 'So, you'll be returning to them when this is over then.' He nodded as if the idea pleased him.

'If it is ever over...' Maggie sighed. 'Do you think we're winning, Captain?'

'Not winning exactly, but at the moment we're holding our own and that's pretty good given the power of the German Army,' Mick said. 'It will take time, but we'll get there.' He hesitated, then, 'Would you allow me to call you Maggie – or am I asking too much?'

'Off duty that would be nice,' Maggie said. 'I know you're a special friend of Sally Harper's so I feel as if I know you – so that is fine, if you wish.'

'Yes, I should like to be your friend too,' Mick replied, his eyes never leaving hers. 'If you are ever in any trouble here, Maggie, you have only to ask for me and I'll find a way to help you.'

'I'm not in any trouble...' Maggie sighed deeply, 'but my friend is. She is going to need help soon. She won't admit it or think about it.' Maggie shook her head. 'It isn't my secret and she hasn't given me permission to say, but I might ask for your help...'

'Anything,' Mick said and smiled. 'I think you're a lovely person, Maggie Gibbs, always thinking of others, and I should be delighted to help your friend when she needs it.'

'Thank you, that relieves my mind a little,' Maggie confided. 'She may have to leave the service soon and she says she won't be sent back to England. I think the French family we know might take her in, but if they can't keep her after the birth...'

'I can give her money or whatever she needs,' Mick assured her, his gaze steady and steadfast, making her feel she could trust him. It was almost as if she'd known him for years and she felt safe and comfortable with him. 'Just tell me what you need, Maggie, and I'll do all I can.'

Maggie thanked him and glanced at the little watch pinned to her uniform. 'I have to go back to my hut and sleep. I'm on duty in four hours...'

'Then I shan't delay you.' Mick rose, but Maggie touched his arm and he looked back at her as she too stood up. 'Something I can do for you?'

'I was wondering if you would be at the grape harvest celebration this Saturday? Marie's family have gathered their grapes in and are about to start the winemaking, so she is holding a party.'

'Yes, perhaps – I could change duty with a friend.' Mick's face lit up. 'Will you be there?'

'I'm going with my friend, Sadie, but there will be dancing.' She looked at him shyly. 'We might dance if you liked...'

'Then I shall definitely be there,' he said and once again she felt the caress of his eyes. 'Go and get some sleep, Maggie. I shall see you on Saturday.'

Maggie returned to the hut she shared and discovered Sadie just changing her uniform. Sadie looked pale and tired, shadows beneath her eyes.

'You shouldn't worry too much about the future,' Maggie said and caught her friend's hand. 'We'll work something out, love. I'll help you all I can.'

'I'm not worried,' Sadie replied. 'I'm going to stay in this village until the child is born and then I'll give it to the family or the nuns. I want to be a nurse, Maggie – and I'm going to retrain from the start. I'll use a false name if I have to...'

Maggie was shocked, though she tried to hide it. How could her friend give away the child of the man she loved? 'Are you sure that's what you want, Sadie?'

'What would you do in my situation?' Sadie asked a little

truculently. 'I want to go on with my nursing, Maggie – there's nothing else for me back home.'

'But your baby... If I'd had Tim's baby, I would've kept it,' Maggie said firmly. 'Sometimes I wish I'd slept with him and fallen for his child – at least I would have that to love... a little part of him...'

'If Pierre had lived, I would have married him, but he's dead – so what are my alternatives?' Sadie said defensively. Maggie was silent as she thought about it. Sadie continued, 'I could try to pass it off on some other man, but the thought of another man touching me makes me sick – or I can keep it and pretend to be a widow – though the only jobs I'll find will be scrubbing or factory work. I don't want that, Maggie. Nursing was my way to a better life. I was a fool to let Pierre talk me into doing it... but I loved him...' Her voice broke on a sob and the tears slipped down her cheeks. 'I loved him so much and he offered me a wonderful life here on his farm. I've lived in the slums of London all my life, Maggie, and I won't go back to that.' She looked up at Maggie. 'Don't judge me, please. I don't want to give the baby away – but I can't face the alternative.'

'Perhaps you wouldn't have to,' Maggie offered but knew that Sadie had faced reality. Without an income, she would have to work and with a child the only jobs she would be offered were menial. Employers wouldn't be interested in a widow with a small child. Sadie sounded hard but she must be hurting so much inside; to lose the man she loved was grief enough, but then to be forced to give up his baby for the sake of convention was even worse, but it was the way things were. Either she had to pretend to be a widow and struggle on alone or give the baby away; it was a stark choice and Maggie wished there was an alternative but couldn't think of any she could offer. 'I can help with money until you can find work again,' she went on, because it was all she could do. 'And anything else I can—'

'I know you want to help, Maggie. It does help just having you to talk to,' Sadie said. 'Thank you for being my friend – and for understanding. Some women would be shocked at what I'd done...'

'I half envy you,' Maggie said honestly. 'If I had Tim's baby I would want to keep it.'

'I have to go...' Sadie left abruptly and Maggie knew her words had inadvertently hurt her friend. Sadie didn't really want to abandon Pierre's baby but she didn't know what else to do...

36

'I know you'll be running the risk of being recognised,' the officer said to Marco that September morning. 'Now that your last mission to help with the logistics of supplying the field hospitals is finished, we have decided it is time for you to return to France. We don't normally send our operatives back to the same area, but at least you'll be twenty miles or so away from where you were based. However, we do realise that it is likely you may be recognised by someone who saw you working at the nightclub. However, we need to re-establish contact with our agents out there and we're not sure who to trust now that Pierre and a couple of others were killed. We've had messages, but they could be from the enemy trying to trick us – if some of those captured talked, they may have all our codes.'

Marco had spent a few weeks working with Ben Harper and others, his local knowledge of various locations helping them to plan what had been a successful initiative to resupply vital medicines to those hospitals most in need.

'Yes, I perfectly understand, Colonel Rush,' Marco replied and flicked ash from the cigarette he'd been offered, along with the glass of aged Scottish whisky. 'What exactly do you need from me, sir?'

'We need you to contact those you knew who are still alive and ask them who has taken Pierre's place as their leader and then make contact. You will supply them with new codes we know haven't been penetrated and can trust. We want to organise some guerrilla raids with them – supply them with guns, explosives, that kind of thing. Pierre was planning several assassinations of high-ranking enemy officers before he was killed. Not everyone is up for that, Marco, but it could make a big difference to the outcome of the war.'

Marco frowned, wondering at the use of dirty tactics, but supposed all was fair in love and war. Something about the mission he was being given this time seemed to smell bad to him, but there was no thought in his mind that he might refuse it.

'Who are my contacts when I land?' Marco asked.

'Things have changed since you got out and our links to the French partisans have become tenuous. You're going to have to use your own judgement. We don't know who may have been turned and is playing as a double agent now. However, those that are loyal to the cause will trust you – that's why we need to send you back.'

Marco nodded. What the colonel was saying was true. He knew several people in the underground network and they would trust him; he also knew Pierre's cousin Marie, because she had come into town once and Pierre had introduced them. He was the obvious choice if the network was to be re-established – and yet Pierre had died to get him to safety. It made the loss of a friend's life seem worthless. However, Marco had no choice but to obey orders. 'Of course, sir. When do you want me to leave?'

'We'll get you there tomorrow night. They will be celebrating the wine harvest and your arrival will blend in nicely. You are

Marcel Robards and a second cousin of Marie Robards come to help in the winemaking.'

Marco nodded. Marcel was close enough to his own name to make it easy for him to respond to and he would not be in the immediate area of his prior posting, but he would more than likely have to visit Pont le-Neuve to speak to some of the operatives he'd known. That would be when the danger of being recognised as Marco the nightclub singer would be at its zenith, but Marie might have visitors who could also recognise him and he would need to be on his guard.

'Take the same precautions as before – nothing personal with you, no British clothes, cigarettes. We should be able to fix you up with some French ones.'

'I've got used to them anyway,' Marco said with a wry twist of his lips. 'No matches, lighters or watches. I know the drill, sir, and I still have what I brought back with me.'

'You'll need different clothes this time. You're a farm manager not a nightclub singer.'

'Yes, of course,' Marco agreed and got up as the officer rose. 'Anything else, sir?'

'No – just good luck.' Colonel Rush extended his hand. 'Sorry to have to send you back, Marco, but we need that group of French guerrilla fighters to continue with their resistance to the German occupation of border villages. They can get to places our chaps can't, harass the enemy...'

'Yes, sir. I perfectly understand.'

Marco frowned as he took his leave. Pierre had been part of a group resisting the Germans in whatever way they could manage, but he knew that his escape would have brought reprisals. There might be some locals who resented that and would betray him for food or money, even though the majority hated the enemy. This idea of assassinating German officers was a dangerous one. Pierre had never spoken of it to him, but perhaps he would not trust even a British spy with that information – and yet Marco was reluctant to pass that part of the message on. If such assassinations took place, reprisals would be taken against innocent men and women and that left a bad taste in the mouth.

Marco wrinkled his brow in thought. He would do what had been asked of him but he wouldn't suggest anything unless the new leader of the French resistance was eager for the mission – though he knew the names of men that were more accessible and would most certainly help throw the enemy into confusion.

* * *

The crossing was uneventful and Marco was met by the same group that had taken him in earlier that year. They looked surprised to see him return, because it wasn't usual to send the same man back, but said very little, simply nodding as Marco told them his new name and his destination.

This time they travelled in a shabby farm truck and went by the back roads, bumping over dried ruts in the hard-baked summer earth. It had been a good harvest and his guide talked of the winemaking to come now that the grapes were gathered.

'I'm looking forward to experiencing it,' Marco said and saw them look at each other and laugh.

'It is hard work treading the grapes,' his guide told him. 'If you've never done it, your legs will ache before you're half finished.'

Marco nodded and smiled. He didn't mind they were making fun of him; they were a friendly, uncomplicated bunch and he thought he would quite enjoy working with them if he had the chance. At least they knew what they were working for – to keep the enemy out of their country and protect their homes and their families.

Marco was here because he was loyal to the country, he called home, but he had no real home, he realised, and no family. Sometimes that made him feel empty inside and filled him with regret. He would like to know there was someone waiting for him. Of course, he had friends – Ben Harper, his wife and everyone at Harpers, but apart from that no one special. It seemed that everyone he cared for died or was killed...

Shutting out the sharp pang of grief as he remembered Julien, Marco concentrated on taking stock of his surroundings. He might need to know what the surrounding countryside looked like in the dark.

* * *

Marie greeted Marco with a kiss on each cheek and then another on the mouth for good luck. 'You are welcome to stay with us, Marcel,' she told him. 'I was so pleased when my aunt told me you were coming to stay. It is many years since we met and you were but a boy...'

She had greeted him at the bus station where his guide had dropped him off with the small haversack he was carrying in full view of any passers-by. It would appear to an onlooker that he'd arrived by bus, coming to stay with his cousin Marie.

'It is good of you to have me, cousin,' Marco replied.

'You come to learn how we make our wine, and it is my pleasure to show you,' Marie said as she led him to the horse and cart she'd arrived on. 'First we have a celebration this evening to thank God for the good harvest he gave us – and then we begin the hard work on Monday.'

'I understand it is hard work,' Marco said and smiled at her as he climbed up beside her.

She offered him the reins, but he shook his head and she laughed as if she thought it a good joke. Marco had never driven a horse and cart, though he had ridden a horse in Hyde Park. He thought he would have to learn and took note of the way Marie handled the reins and the instructions she gave to the horse.

'It is hard on the legs,' she told him as they approached the farmhouse and yard, 'but you are young and you can learn – and driving the horse, too. I shall teach you.'

'I've ridden but not driven a cart...' he apologised.

'No matter, we can show you everything.' Marie smiled at him. 'You are a brave man, Marcel. Pierre told me he admired you...'

'He was the brave one, Marie. I owe my life to him and the others who suffered because of me – and I'm truly sorry for what happened.'

'What you did may save many lives,' Marie said and shrugged. 'Pierre knew what he risked – and this is France. It was his country.'

'Yes, I know how he felt,' Marco said. 'I don't want any of you to risk your lives for me – if my cover is blown, you must give me up as an imposter. Pretend you knew nothing...'

'Pouff.' Marie snapped her fingers. 'It would be the same.' She drew a finger across her throat. 'I would kill as many as I could first.'

Marco laughed. He rather thought he was going to enjoy this assignment far more than the last one.

* * *

'You look lovely,' Sadie said as they finished dressing that Saturday afternoon. 'I don't think I've seen you wear that dress before?'

'I haven't...' Maggie's smile faded for a moment. 'It's the one I wore for a friend's wedding – the night Tim proposed to me. I was saving it until he got leave and then I couldn't face wearing it after he died...'

'You're feeling a little better, aren't you?' Sadie asked, looking at her curiously.

'Yes. It still hurts to think of him, but it is getting easier to remember the good things,' Maggie said. 'I know I'll always miss him and wish he hadn't died, but life has to go on and we've seen so much...'

'Too much,' Sadie agreed and hugged her. 'Let's forget it tonight and have a good time.'

'Yes, let's.' Maggie smiled at her. 'I'm looking forward to the dancing and the laughter – they're all so friendly and warm to us. It's like being with a big family, Sadie.'

'Yes, it is,' Sadie agreed. 'I've been thinking about what you said, Maggie, and I'm going to ask Marie if she will let me stay with her once I'm forced to leave nursing – until the baby is born anyway.'

'You know she will,' Maggie said and squeezed her hand. 'I can visit you sometimes and then we'll make plans – because we're not going to lose touch when we go home, are we?'

'No, never,' Sadie urged. 'We'll always be friends, Maggie. I love you as much as any of my sisters – no, more. They wouldn't have understood the way you have...'

Maggie put a finger to her lips. 'No more worrying tonight. Let's just enjoy ourselves.'

They left the hut smiling at each other and waved to the young soldier who was taking half a dozen of them to Marie's farm in his truck. He gave them a cheery greeting and helped them in the back, jumping back in the driving seat and setting off with a joke about not drinking too much.

All the nurses were giggling and laughing, talking about the young men they'd promised to meet at the dance that evening, which would be held out in the orchard behind the farm. As they approached, they could smell something cooking, and there were lights strung in the trees, little lanterns twinkling like big glow worms. After the blood sweat and tears of the hospitals, this was so peaceful and lovely that it touched their hearts.

Girls and men piled out of a couple of vehicles; their laughter sweet on the perfumed night air. Marie was there to greet them all and to welcome them to the party. A tall man dressed in the clothes of a French farmer in his Sunday best stood by her side. As they approached, Maggie felt a jolt of recognition and warning bells jangled in her head; she felt a prickling sensation at her neck and something told her to be careful.

'Ah, ma cherie, Nurse Maggie Gibbs, and ma petite Sadie,' Marie said. 'This is Marcel Robards, my cousin from Rouen. He comes to help with the wine harvesting. He has the bad chest so he cannot fight with the Army.'

'Monsieur Robards,' Maggie greeted the man she knew so well from Harpers as she would a stranger, taking his hand politely and smiling. She felt his strong grip and knew he appreciated her response. 'I am pleased to meet you. I hope you enjoy your stay with Marie.'

'I believe I shall,' he replied, his eyes dancing with amusement in the way she knew so well. 'My family sells wine to your country, Mademoiselle Gibbs, but I wish to learn how to make it.'

'I think it must be interesting work,' Maggie said. 'I do not know much about wine, except that I like it sweet – but I would like to learn too.'

'Then perhaps we shall talk of it later...' Marco smiled at her and turned to Sadie. 'Mademoiselle, may I welcome you to my cousin's home – perhaps you will dance with me after supper?'

Sadie looked at him for a moment and then nodded. 'Yeah, why not,' she said. 'You look harmless enough to me.'

'Sadie...' Maggie dug her in the ribs as they moved off. 'That wasn't very polite.'

'I've had enough of charming Frenchmen,' Sadie said. 'I'm not falling for that again.'

Maggie smothered a giggle. She didn't think that Sadie need worry about this particular Frenchman, but she couldn't say anything. There had to be a reason why Mr Marco was pretending to be Marie's cousin from Rouen and she wasn't going to give him away by saying something careless.

'That roast sucking pig smells good,' Sadie said. 'Shall we see if they're serving it yet? I'm hungry.'

Maggie agreed and went with her. A long table set with a white cloth was piled with fresh bread, cheese and ripe tomatoes, some fresh sliced peppers, relishes and plates full with cold chicken and ham. The pig was just being carved and they were given a slice; it was hot and nearly burned their fingers and their tongues, but the smell was so delicious that they couldn't wait to bite into it, laughing at each other as the grease ran down their chins.

'May I be of assistance?' Maggie turned as Mick O'Sullivan offered her a white linen napkin. She laughed and took it, using it and then passing it to Sadie, who needed it even more. 'That looks delicious, but I think I'll stick to the bread and cheese.'

'It's a real feast,' Maggie said as she walked with him to the table, leaving Sadie to talk to Marie. 'That cheese is delicious – I've had it before. So much nicer than we get at the hospital.'

'I'm sure it is,' he said and smiled. 'I think French cheese is always rather good; it's why we try to serve it in our restaurants.'

'Oh yes, you own some, don't you?' Maggie said, looking at him with interest. 'Mrs Harper was speaking about them once to Mrs Burrows.'

'Yes, I own shares in three,' Mick told her. 'If things go well after the war, I hope to open more.'

'I'm sure they will,' Maggie encouraged. 'Sally says she loves eating at your restaurants because the food is so good.'

'You and your friend must come and try us when you go home,' Mick replied, smiling. 'The first time will be free for you both.'

'Oh, that's lovely. We might take you up on that – if Sadie comes home. I'm not sure what she will do yet.' Her eyes went to Sadie, who was talking seriously to Marie. She guessed she was asking if she could stay with her to give birth. Suddenly, Marie gave a little shout of pleasure and flung her arms around Sadie, hugging her and kissing her on both cheeks. 'Oh, good.'

'What?' Mick asked, looking amused. 'Our hostess is pleased about something...'

'Sadie has told her she wants to have Pierre's baby here,' Maggie said in a soft voice. 'We've been keeping it secret, but Marie will tell everyone.'

Marie's pleasure was evident and she was pulling Sadie by the arm, telling all her friends and neighbours the wonderful news. Sadie looked embarrassed and yet pleased in an odd sort of way.

Marie clapped her hands suddenly and then announced in French that Sadie was carrying the child of her cousin Pierre. It went over the heads of the English soldiers and nurses, none of whom spoke French sufficiently to understand, though one or two got the gist and Maggie saw some sly smiles. Sadie's secret was out now and would probably find its way back to Matron, but at least Sadie had somewhere to come if she was dismissed.

Marie's neighbours and friends were clapping and surrounding Sadie, kissing her and hugging her. It seemed not to matter to them that she wasn't wearing a wedding ring; she was carrying the child of a man who was considered a hero and that was enough for everyone who had known him.

Mick suggested that he and Maggie should dance as the violin started a merry tune. Maggie went with him to dance under the trees. She noticed that Marco went over to speak to Sadie and that he kissed her cheek and she took his hands and held them for a moment. Maggie was curious, but she was enjoying herself dancing with Mick and it was not until he went off to fetch them a cooling drink that Sadie came up to her.

'Marie is over the moon, as you saw,' Sadie told her with a smile. 'She says I can stay forever if I choose – and Pierre's sister says that she will give me things to keep that were his, as well as money. They are all so kind...' Tears came to her eyes. 'I've been thinking, Maggie, perhaps I could stay here and keep the child – at least for a time...'

'I'm so glad,' Maggie said and squeezed her hand.

'They are all so kind – and they said it doesn't matter that we were not married,' Sadie said, looking thoughtful. 'They say Pierre loved me and he would have married me had he lived, because he was an honourable man...' Tears glistened. 'I just wish he was here, Maggie.'

'Of course, you do,' Maggie said. 'But he loved you and you have his baby to love. I don't think you could really give it up, Sadie.'

'Perhaps...' She brushed a hand over her eyes. 'I wanted to nurse, but perhaps I might find a new life here with Marie and Pierre's family.'

'I saw you talking to Marcel Robards,' Maggie said casually. 'What did he have to say to you?'

'He told me that Pierre was a brave man, that he admired him – and that if I needed anything, I was to ask him. He said that if I needed a home or money, he would help me.'

Maggie nodded and smiled, saying that it was nice of him. She wondered how the man she knew as Marco knew Pierre so well but kept her thoughts to herself. It was obvious that Sadie would be cared for by Pierre's friends and relatives and that made Maggie feel much better. It gave her hope for the future where she'd had none for Sadie and that made her smile.

'You look happy?' Mick said when he came back with their drinks.

Maggie looked at him for a moment and then smiled. 'Do you know, I am,' she said. 'I really feel happy for the first time in... months.'

Mick reached for her hand, giving her a brief squeeze. 'I'm so glad,' he said. 'And your friend – what about her?'

'Sadie has good friends now,' Maggie said. 'I don't know what she will decide to do, but she has a choice. She won't be forced back to the slums as she feared and I hope she will keep her baby.'

'Oh no, she couldn't go back to the slums,' Mick agreed instantly. 'We couldn't allow that, Maggie. Whatever else happens, I'd never let that happen to a friend of yours.'

Maggie was surprised, but then she smiled. 'You are a nice man, Captain O'Sullivan.'

'Yes, I am rather,' Mick said and his eyes twinkled at her. 'I'm very glad you know that, Miss Gibbs.'

Maggie poked him in the ribs. 'Come on, you tease,' she said. 'The night is young and I want to dance with you all night.'

37

It was another two days before Marco found Maggie as she was making her way to the canteen for a well-earned break. She smiled at him as he approached and waited for him to speak.

'Where can we speak in private?' Marco asked.

'We could go to the hut I share with Sadie – she is on duty, so we'll be quite alone.'

'And do you trust me – after the other night?'

'Of course, I do, sir,' Maggie said. 'You're a friend and I know there must be a good reason for...' She left the rest unsaid and he smiled his approval.

'Good girl,' he said. 'I always thought you a bright sensible girl and you've confirmed my opinion.' He smiled at her. 'No need for formality here, we're not at Harpers.'

Maggie smiled and nodded. 'I still think of you that way, Mr Marco.'

He nodded and said no more on the subject.

When they were alone in the hut, Maggie indicated he should sit on their only chair while she perched on her bed. 'I have some sherry if...' He shook his head. 'Perhaps you should just tell me –

what you are able to tell me, but please don't feel you need to explain.'

'I really wanted to thank you for not blowing my cover, Maggie – and to tell you that, though I cannot explain, I'm not doing anything you would think unpatriotic or wrong.'

'I knew that anyway,' Maggie replied with a smile. 'I did what any sensible person would do, sir – and I must say that I rather like your name.'

'You haven't told your friend the truth?'

'No, and I shan't. I imagine the fewer people that know, the better?'

'What a true friend you are, Maggie Gibbs,' he said. 'Thank you – and I wanted to tell you that if there is anything I can do, for you or your friend, you have only to ask.' She saw a look of sadness pass over his face. 'I knew Pierre quite well, you see – and he died helping me, so I feel I owe her whatever she asks of me...'

'I know that Pierre was a brave man. Marie told us he died while working in secret for his country. Sadie is angry with him because of it, but she knows in her heart that men have to take risks in wartime.'

'Yes, we do and so do brave women like you and Sadie. You're very close to the front line here and if things went wrong... but we shall not speak of that unless it happens.'

'We live with it every day, Marcel,' Maggie replied, giving him the name she knew he was using. She did not doubt that he was doing important secret work and since she knew and liked him, she trusted him completely. 'We see the men who have been hurt and are dying; it is an ever-present threat, but we ignore it. We have to...'

'As I said, you are brave women, all of you – and I admire you more than I can say.'

'Thank you – but I think you are in more danger, Marcel. Rest assured that I shall never betray you to anyone.'

'I knew that – but I wanted you to understand how dangerous it could be for you as well as me,' he said and she nodded, because she realised that in certain circumstances association with a spy could spell danger.

'You must go,' Maggie said. 'It wouldn't do for you to be here too long – and if anyone asks, I shall say you called with a message from Marie. Now you should go. You offered us your help – but if there is anything at all I can do to help you, you must tell me.'

He shook his head. 'Enough innocent folk are at risk now. I should not dream of involving you,' Marco replied and smiled at her. 'I shall go – but thank you and take care of yourself, Maggie Gibbs.'

'And you,' she said. 'I am glad to have seen you. I often think of Harpers' people and wonder how they are...'

'As do I, Maggie. They were good days. I hope they will come again.'

Maggie saw his grave look and felt a chill at her nape. He must be in terrible danger!

'I do hope so!'

'We may meet again at Marie's, but I shall not come here. It should be safe, but there are spies and collaborators everywhere...'

Maggie nodded and he hesitated, then leaned forward and kissed her cheek. She sat where she was and let him go. She'd always liked him and had instinctively known what he was doing, but now she felt an icy shiver at her nape. He was taking such a risk, because spies could be shot and that was surely what he was – a British spy.

Maggie shook her head, because it hardly seemed real that Mr Marco – funny, gentle Mr Marco who teased the girls and dressed

Harpers' windows so artistically – was here risking his life – for what? Maggie had no idea, but it was obviously important or he wouldn't have thanked her for not blurting out his secret.

Sighing, she got to her feet. It was time she went back to work. Maggie had been told she would be sent home soon and given two weeks' leave, but Sister Mayhew had told Matron that she wanted her back and so she would return here to this hospital and the men who needed help so desperately.

* * *

Marco glanced over his shoulder twice, but he was pretty certain he had not been followed. He was safe enough at Marie's and here at the hospital it was unlikely he would see anyone he'd known while working in the Fallen Angel. It was when he returned to Pont le-Neuve, to make contact with Jacques and some of the others, that he would be most at risk. Marie had sent a message to Pierre's home that she had a pig for sale and she hoped that might bring someone she could entrust with a message.

'It would be better if we could arrange a more secret rendezvous for you,' she'd told him.

Marie had taken to him and fussed over him as if he were one of her own. Marco had confessed his guilty regret over Pierre's death and she'd embraced him wholeheartedly.

'My cousin gave his life for France,' she'd declared. 'He believed that what you had done might bring the German advance to a halt and protect us from further invasion and he would have given his life twice over for that.' Tears stood in her eyes. 'They came through our villages and towns like a cloud of locusts, but your country drove them back to where they are now and it is British lives that protect us daily.'

'British, Canadian, French and others,' Marco had qualified

with a smile. 'Britain is a small country and we need our Allies – but fortunately we have many friends who have stood by us.'

Marie had nodded and wiped her cheeks. 'No more tears for Pierre – he has a child and that child will be brought into the world here. If the girl Pierre loved will stay here, she will become as a daughter to me, but it must be her choice – she is very sad, the poor little one.'

'Yes, of course she is – and frightened of the future I dare say.'

'We shall take care of her and the little one,' Marie had said. 'It will be a blessing to Pierre's family. When she understands this, she may learn to smile again...' Marie shook her head. 'For now, she laughs, but her eyes do not smile. She will learn in time that she is loved and then she can be happy again.'

'Perhaps she fears the shame of giving birth to a child when she is unmarried...'

'Pouff.' Marie had snapped her fingers. 'We French do not care for such things. We rejoice in new life and she will give us back a part of our beloved Pierre, so we care not if she wears a ring on her finger.'

'You are a good woman, Marie,' Marco had told her and she'd chuckled, a warm ripe chuckle that had made him grin.

'And you are a brave man, Marcel. I am proud to know you...'

The wine treading was in full swing as Marco entered the farmyard. Women of all ages, children, and youths were in the wooden vats rhythmically treading the rich black fruit into a pulp which would one day become a full-bodied red wine.

Marie was in one of the vats and she waved to him. He walked towards her and began to roll up his trousers, thinking she wanted him to join in the work, but she leaned over the side and whispered in his ear.

'Jacques sent word,' she said. 'You are to meet this evening – I will come. Lift me out and we shall have wine and bread.'

Marco helped her climb out of the vat and she wiped the red stain from her legs, pushing her feet into a pair of wooden shoes before leading the way into the kitchen. She produced a jug of the rough red wine they made themselves, before it was taken to the vinery to be mixed with other ingredients and blended to a softer finer wine, some soft white cheese and fresh bread baked that morning in her own oven.

'I was hungry,' Marco said appreciatively, enjoying the taste of the delicious food. 'It was quite a walk to the hospital.'

'You saw my little Maggie?'

'Yes, she was taking a break and we talked – she is a sensible young woman and told me I had no need to seek her out. She would not have told anyone for she understood my secret.'

Marie nodded, pleased. She'd known it all along, but he had wanted to make certain of Maggie's loyalty, as much for her own sake as his.

'So tonight, Jacques will come to the old mill – it is derelict since Paulinus died and his sons went away to foreign parts. He will wait for you there from ten to eleven and if you do not come, he will return for two nights.'

'I shall be there,' Marco said. 'I thought I should have to go to him.'

'He knows me,' Marie replied with a nod of satisfaction. 'So, you will meet and talk – and then what?'

'I'm not sure,' Marco replied. 'They want me to set up a new cell to carry on Pierre's work, men we can be certain of – but it needs willing young men.'

'I am sure there are plenty who will be ready to do whatever your Government wants, but I meant what of you, Marcel? Will you stay on – or return to England?'

'They left that up to me.' Marco frowned. 'I think I might stay – if the cell wants me. I could be a go-between and I'm ready to do more, but I won't endanger the population unnecessarily, unless everyone agrees that whatever we do is necessary for the good of France and the Allies.'

'You have a conscience, Marcel,' Marie said and frowned. 'Sometimes, you have to do things that God may weep for – but if they must be done, they must be done. We must all do what is necessary to protect those we love, Marcel.'

'I would always do that,' he agreed, 'but there are times when our actions may help the war effort and yet bring pain and grief to our friends and neighbours. Tell me, Marie, what do I do then?'

'You must speak to God in your heart and do what your conscience tells you is more important,' she told him. 'Sometimes, that will cause grief – but you have no choice.'

Marco nodded, his expression grim. He would make contact that evening with Jacques and for the next few weeks he would work to set up a group of resistance fighters. After that, he would decide whether to work with them or return to England for further orders. The future was hazy and he could not see beyond the next few weeks – he might be killed before his work was done, but he was prepared to give his life, as Pierre had been. However, he would make certain that the mother of Pierre's baby would be financially secure.

Marco was not a wealthy man, but his French grandparents had left him some jewellery and paintings, which were in his apartment at home. He would make a will and leave those to Ben Harper, his best friend. He had eight thousand pounds invested in shares and bonds and five hundred pounds in the bank. He would leave six thousand five hundred pounds to Sadie and the rest to Maggie Gibbs. He would send the will to his lawyer in England by special courier and he would leave a copy with Marie, in case the worst happened. If he survived the war, he would support Sadie and help her to bring up Pierre's child.

38

'I'm glad we decided to do this.' Sally looked at her companions. She had booked a dinner for the four of them at an expensive hotel to celebrate Beth leaving to have a child and Jenni joining them. 'I wish that Maggie could be with us as well – but my last letter from her said she was feeling much better and I feel she is with us in spirit.'

'Yes, she is,' Beth said and smiled at her across the table. 'I know we all care for her and think of her often.' She lifted her wine glass. 'To Maggie – may she be happy, find a new love and come home safely.'

'I shall drink to that,' Rachel said and touched her glass to Beth's and Sally's. 'We all have something to celebrate, don't we?' Her smile touched on Beth and Sally. 'My William is out of hospital and home at last and feeling better; Beth is having her baby – and you've had a real success at Harpers, Sally. Not only that, you've helped so many wounded men find the courage to go on living.' She smiled. 'I visited the hospital yesterday and they showed me the new library you'd set up in the day room for the men. They said it was just what they needed.'

'It was just something to help the tedium of their days. I do very little really, Rachel. I think you visit more often than I can.' She smiled at Jenni. 'And Jenni is a regular visitor too now. She has a list of consultants that she badgers, when necessary.'

'Andrew is still the best in my opinion,' Jenni said and smiled. 'However, I don't let him know that.' Her eyes twinkled with mischief. She still had times when the sadness was in her eyes, but she was recovering her old self, little by little.

'We all do what we can in our own small ways,' Sally said. 'I know I couldn't do half of what I manage if it weren't for all of you.' Her gaze moved over the faces of her closest friends. She lifted her glass. 'Shall we drink to all Harpers' heroes? Marco and Maggie and all the others out there. Whoever they are and wherever they are at this moment? We know they are doing what they have to do to keep us all safe and we love them all.'

'Yes, we do,' Beth replied, 'but Maggie most of all.'

'We'll drink to the day they all come marching home,' Rachel said. 'My William is out of the fighting now so I'm lucky. He will be tied to a desk job in future because of his leg. He's grumbling about it and I dare say his leg will ache in the wet weather, but I'm so glad he won't be fighting again.'

'Of course, you are,' Beth said, smiling at her. 'I'm glad you've got him home at last, Rachel. You had so little time together – you were married and then he was off to the war. Now at last you'll be able to begin your proper life together.'

'Yes, and I'm so excited,' Rachel said. 'It makes me feel a bit guilty, because I'm so happy and other people aren't as lucky.'

'William did his duty,' Sally told her. 'I'm not a bit ashamed to say that I'm glad Ben isn't in a fighting unit. He might regret it, but I don't, not at all.' She looked at Beth. 'You must worry so much when Jack is away, Beth...'

'Yes, I do,' Beth agreed, 'but it is what he chose to do – and he is lucky enough to get home every few months when his ship docks for a refit or just to pick up new cargo. I consider myself lucky too – it's girls like Marion, whose menfolk are in the Army and they don't see them for months on end that I feel sorry for. Sometimes, when she comes to work in the morning, she looks so sad that I feel like putting my arms around her, but of course I don't – it would just upset her.'

'I know how you feel.' Sally's eyes clouded for a moment. 'Ruth's fiancé was wounded last month and she's waiting for news of when he will be transferred back to England so that she can visit him.'

'I think we all know someone who has a lover, husband, son or brother away,' Rachel agreed. 'That is why your contributions for the wounded had such marvellous results. Have you thought what your new campaign will be?'

'Yes, I'm going to have a special day when every purchase in the store will contribute one shilling towards sending gifts to the nurses and the troops,' Sally said. 'I'm going to time it for a few weeks before Christmas and we'll have special windows and a flag day too, collecting up and down Oxford Street – and every penny of that will go to the wounded.' She smiled at her friends. 'We'll have special themes every week and lucky dips inside the store and raffle tickets and all the money we raise will go to the troops.'

'Well, it looks as if Harpers is going to be busy.' Beth gave a little sigh. 'I shall be sorry to miss it all.'

'You can pop in and see what we're up to,' Sally told her, 'and we'll be visiting you. I might give you a few small projects to do at home, if you feel like it...'

'So, I'll still be a part of it.' Beth smiled. 'Thank you, Sally. I should like that; I know I have to rest for the sake of the baby and Jack is adamant that I mustn't work after this week, but I'd like to be a part of things.'

'You'll always be a Harpers' girl,' Sally told her. 'I shan't let you slip away and be forgotten, Beth – or you, Rachel. You're both my friends and I need you.' Her smile caressed them both. She raised her wine glass again. 'To friends and Harpers' girls.'

Rachel and Beth touched their glasses to hers. Rachel and Sally sipped their wine and Beth sipped her fruit juice.

'To friends and Harpers' girls,' they said in unison. 'And to the end of the war,' Rachel added. 'May it be soon…'

* * *

Ben was sleeping in his favourite armchair when Sally got home that evening; Jenny, peaceful and sound asleep on his lap. She bent down to kiss him, feeling a surge of happiness as he woke and smiled. She was so lucky to have the man she loved and all her friends.

For a moment she thought of Maggie and her loss, but then Ben gave her Jenny to hold and the grief for her friend eased. Maggie was brave and strong and Sally was certain she would come through – just as she hoped Mick, Marco, Jack and all the other heroes out there fighting for their loved ones would.

Surely the war would end one day and they would all come home again! In the meantime, she had to keep Harpers strong and viable so they all had their jobs when they did return.

* * *

Marion smiled at her sister-in-law as she nursed her baby that evening. Sarah looked so happy these days. Dan was back at sea, but she had stopped worrying if his letters didn't arrive regularly. He'd told her he would be away for months so she wasn't to worry.

'I shan't be able to write often and I can only send letters when we reach a port so don't expect them, Sarah. Remember, no news is often good news, so just accept that I'm working and I'll write when I can.'

His sensible talking had calmed her and she'd settled in happily with her husband's family.

As for Marion, she was as content as she had ever been in her life, except for her own lack of regular letters. She continued to write to Reggie every week and to send him small parcels. Reggie had told her how welcome letters and parcels were to all the men.

It's a big moment for all of us when the post arrives. It all gets spread out on a tarpaulin on the ground and put into piles. We line up and our names are called, but some of us can't get there and then one of our mates brings us whatever comes.

They're all a little jealous of how many letters and parcels I get, Marion love. They keep telling me I'm a lucky devil – and Pete – he's a mate – asks me to read him my letters. He only gets one from his mother once a month and so I read him bits – not the private bits, but he likes to hear the news of what is going on back home. He says if I don't know how lucky I am I can ask you to write to him instead, but I do and I wouldn't change you or swap you for the world, Marion. I hope you know how much I love you – and long for the moment I can hold you in my arms...

'What are you smiling about?' Sarah asked suddenly, making Marion look up from her knitting.

'I was just thinking of something Reggie said in his last letter.' Marion sighed and tucked her knitting back in her bag. 'Do you fancy a cup of cocoa, love?'

'Yes, please, I'd love one,' Sarah said and patted her baby

gently on the back to bring up her wind. 'I think I'll... Oh...' The reason she stopped was because someone had knocked at the door.

'I'll go,' Kathy trilled and went to the door. 'It will probably be...' Her words died away as she saw the tall soldier standing there and then she laughed. 'Oh, come in, our Marion will be right pleased to see you.'

Marion turned and looked at the man standing there staring at her, gave a cry of delight and rushed to him, throwing her arms around him, and was hugged tightly to his chest.

'Reggie...' she cried on a sobbing breath. 'Oh, Reggie, why didn't you let us know?'

'I wasn't told until the last minute, so I thought I might as well surprise you all,' he said and grinned down at her. 'Did you miss me, Marion love?'

'You know I did,' she said, looking up at him with tears in her eyes. 'Oh, Reggie, it is so wonderful to have you home.'

'It's just for two weeks,' he said, 'and then I'll have a new posting – somewhere different they reckon, but I don't have to think about that now.'

'Two weeks.' Marion felt as if she was dreaming. She led him into the kitchen, never letting go of his hand. 'This is Sarah – I told you about her...'

'I'm pleased to meet you,' Sarah said. 'I'll go upstairs and let you have a little time together. Come on, Kathy. You can help me get Pamela to bed.'

Kathy nodded and followed her from the room.

Reggie took Marion into his arms and looked down at her and then he kissed her. All his love and longing were in that kiss and she clung to him, looking up at him with her own love and longing.

'I've missed you so much,' he said huskily. He suddenly dropped to one knee, looking up at her passionately. 'I want you to marry me, Marion – please say you will.'

'Yes, I will,' Marion said and hugged him as he rose and took her in his arms, holding her as if she would never let him go. 'We'll get a special licence and go away for a few days – I've got a few days' holiday left and I'm sure Mrs Burrows will say I can have it off.'

'You will?' Reggie's handsome face lit up with relief and pleasure. 'That's wonderful, Marion. I've spoken to Mum and she'll put on a little spread for us – and if anything happened, she would look out for you...'

'No, don't,' Marion said, putting her fingers to his lips softly. 'Nothing will happen, Reggie. You've come back to me this time and you will again, I know it.' She smiled up at him. 'Sarah is Dan's wife and he's my nearest relative now. She'll give her consent and we'll be married. I want it as much as you and I'm not going to waste this chance.'

'You're wonderful,' Reggie said and kissed her again. 'Mum will be over the moon. She loves you, Marion, says you're like a daughter to her already.' He kissed her fingers one by one, his eyes caressing her and then he laughed. 'Pete told me that if I was daft enough to come back without putting my ring on your finger, he was going to cut me out – I think he's half in love with you himself...'

'He doesn't stand a chance,' Marion said and looked up at him. She felt as if she were glowing with happiness. 'I'll go into work in the morning, Reggie. You make all the arrangements for Saturday at the Registry Office and then we'll have the rest of your two weeks to ourselves.'

'Yes, that will be just right,' he said. 'We'll go away for a few

days somewhere – perhaps to the seaside.' He touched her cheek.
'I'm a lucky chap...'

'I'm lucky too,' Marion said. 'I can't wait to tell them all at
Harpers. I know they will be pleased for me, especially Mrs
Burrows.'

* * *

Beth nodded and smiled as Marion poured out her exciting news
the next morning.

'I'm very happy for you, Marion,' she said, breaking all the
rules by using her given name. 'It's wonderful news that Reggie is
home and you're to marry. When I think of Maggie, I believe
you're wise to marry now and not wait – we should all take what
happiness we can in these times.'

Marion nodded, her smile dimming a little at the mention of
her friend Maggie. Maggie had waited and now she would never
marry the man she loved. Marion wouldn't do that – she would
grab her chance of happiness with both hands.

'You don't think Mrs Harper will mind my being away for a
few days?'

'She will be delighted for you, Marion. She has big plans for
later this year and I know she will be relying on you then, but you'll
be back – and Mrs Bailey will be your supervisor then, as you
know. I'm leaving this weekend to put my feet up until the birth.'

'Will you come to my wedding?' Marion asked in a breathy
voice.

'Yes please, I wouldn't miss it for the world. I'll be there – as
soon as I finish up here. I know we'll all wish you well, Marion.
You are liked and admired at Harpers and you have a future here
– so don't think of giving up just because you're married.'

'Oh, I shan't – at least, not until I have a family,' Marion said, smiling happily. 'Thank you so much for understanding, Mrs Burrows.'

'Yes – well, back to your counter now, Miss Kaye. We are about to open the department... Miss Stockbridge, to your counter please...'

Beth nodded to the two younger girls and smothered a sigh. She was going to miss her work here, but it wouldn't be the end of her being one of Harpers' girls. She would help Sally with her efforts to raise funds for the troops and keep in touch. Perhaps one day she would be able to return to the store, if only part-time, but that was for the future. In the meantime, she had a baby to look forward to and that was so exciting that it overshadowed everything else.

When she thought of her coming child, even the war seemed to fade into the background. Beth was going to rest and look after herself, because she'd longed for this and now at last it was happening. Soon she would hold her baby in her arms. She would give Jack and Fred a new life – a life that would not replace the one lost but might help to ease their pain. Once there was the sound of a child's laughter in the house, surely they could all be happy again.

Jack was still shutting a part of himself off from everyone, but perhaps when he held his son or daughter in his arms it would all come right...

'It has to,' Beth told herself. 'Jack will be fine once he sees his child, I know he will.'

* * *

Maggie read the news in her letter from Beth. Marion had been married at last and she knew how much that meant to her friend.

She felt a pang of regret that she had not been there to see her marry Reggie but then dismissed it. Maggie was needed here, as were all the nurses.

'A penny for them?'

Maggie spun round at the sound of his voice and smiled. She was learning to like the soft-spoken Irishman a lot. He visited her whenever he was in the area and without realising it, she had begun to look forward to those visits.

'One of my friends from Harpers has just married her fiancé,' she replied to his question. 'I was just thinking I must find a present to send her...'

'How about some French perfume?' Mick suggested with a smile. 'A friend of mine brought several bottles back from a visit to Paris and I bought a few from him as gifts. I've one for you, one for Sadie – and there's another going spare if it would fill the bill?'

'Mick, you're a wonder,' Maggie said and laughed. 'I'm sure she will love it.'

'Then I'll bring them on Sunday, shall I?'

'When we visit the farm together this weekend,' Maggie said and nodded. 'Yes, please. I'll look forward to that – and thank you so much.'

Sadie had now left the service and gone to live with Marie and Maggie visited her as often as she could.

'I've a pretty card or two going spare,' he said. 'This friend of mine buys them for the chaps and they send them home to their mothers, sisters and girlfriends.'

'Yes, I've seen how pretty some of them are,' Maggie agreed. He called whenever he had the chance and she was always pleased to spend a few minutes in his company. 'Nothing too sentimental but pretty would be ideal.' She tucked her arm into his as they walked to the canteen together. 'The tea doesn't get any better, Mick, but they've got some quite nice coffee in recently.'

His eyes twinkled at her. 'Now why would that be, do you think?'

'You didn't!' She poked him in the ribs and he yelled as if she'd hurt him.

'I did, just for you,' he replied. 'I told you, Maggie Gibbs, 'tis a useful fellow I am.'

'Yes, you are,' she said and held his arm. 'I'm glad you're my friend, Michael O'Sullivan.'

'And I'm truly glad to be your friend, Maggie.' His smile warmed her.

'I'm going home next week,' she told him. 'I've got two weeks' leave and then I'm coming back for at least another term of six months, perhaps more.'

'Ah, Maggie my love, 'tis music to my ears that you'll be back,' Mick replied and the smile he gave her made her spirts lift just that little bit more.

Maggie hugged Mick's arm. She supposed he must be quite a few years older than she was, but he was a kind, generous man and she liked him a lot. He had come into her life when she really needed him and Maggie knew that her heart lifted each time that he visited the hospital to see her. When she got home, she would stand by Tim's grave, lay a red rose and say her goodbyes to him, but she knew he was there in her heart and always would be. Whatever the future might bring, Tim would always be with her in spirit.

Mick was talking again, making a joke about one of his men. She knew that he was one of the first on the scene whenever there was a dangerous job to be done, Mick and his engineers, building bridges, digging tunnels and shoring them up, preparing the way for others. He made light of his work, always teasing her, telling her that the Devil himself looked after his own, in his Irish way that was so charming, making her laugh at his nonsense. Whenever he was with her, just for a few minutes, she could forget the war, forget her loss and loneliness and think of a future when she might be back at Harpers and perhaps – just perhaps – she might one day be ready to love again...

MORE FROM ROSIE CLARKE

We hope you enjoyed reading *Harpers Heroes*. If you did, please leave a review.

If you'd like to gift a copy, this book is also available as an ebook, digital audio download and audiobook CD.

Sign up to Rosie Clarke's mailing list for news, competitions and updates on future books.

http://bit.ly/RosieClarkeNewsletter

If you haven't already, explore the rest of the *Welcome to Harpers Emporium* series now!

ABOUT THE AUTHOR

Rosie Clarke is a #1 bestselling saga writer whose most recent books include *The Mulberry Lane* series. She has written over 100 novels under different pseudonyms and is a RNA Award winner. She lives in Cambridgeshire.

Visit Rosie Clarke's website: http://www.rosieclarke.co.uk

Follow Rosie on social media:

 twitter.com/AnneHerries
 bookbub.com/authors/rosie-clarke
 facebook.com/Rosie-clarke-119457351778432

ABOUT BOLDWOOD BOOKS

Boldwood Books is a fiction publishing company seeking out the best stories from around the world.

Find out more at www.boldwoodbooks.com

Sign up to the Book and Tonic newsletter for news, offers and competitions from Boldwood Books!

http://www.bit.ly/bookandtonic

We'd love to hear from you, follow us on social media:

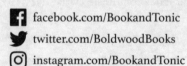

facebook.com/BookandTonic

twitter.com/BoldwoodBooks

instagram.com/BookandTonic